The Bear Gap Rebels

Book Two in the Camilla Crim Series

ISBN: 978-0-9966824-8-0

Edition: 1/2022

Cover Design by: www.ebooklaunch.com

Editing by: www.ayersedits.com

Find Emily online at www.emilyfortney.com

TO GRAMMIE FOR YOUR CREATIVE
ENCOURAGMENT

Road to LilyAye

Mirabelle's House

Rande

The Swamps

Knox's House

Bear Gap

The Bear Gap Rebels

CHAPTER ONE

I'M LOSING MY mind.

Like a parasite to its host, the voice echoing around in my head is attached so firmly that I'm utterly hopeless in removing it. Distraction works only for a moment and then I start hearing it again. I haven't told anyone, not even Tuor. I've tried everything to keep myself from going crazy, but I'm afraid it's too late . . . I'm losing my mind and I can't do anything about it.

I stand alone in the dark woods halfway between Billage, where I'm *supposed* to go, and Rande, where I *want* to go. A shiver runs its way up my back. I flex my hands in and out to fight against my body's cravings. Rain trickles through the leaves, falling in big droplets on my hair. Normally weather like this would drive me inside, but I've become like a rabid animal, unaware of and unimpeded by my surroundings.

They're all expecting me at the meeting in Billage. If I don't show up, they'll know something is wrong. I'm sure Johnny would come looking for me. He'd put his own life in danger. He could be arrested and killed and it would be my fault. I can't, I tell myself. I can't go to Rande, not now.

It's sheer pain turning my back on Rande, the one place I'm meant to be. Something in my home village calls to me. It feels wrong not to get it now. Resisting the urge to run to Rande is like refusing food after days of not eating. It's unnatural, but I do it. I push myself toward Billage, insisting to myself I'll ignore the voice until the meeting's over.

My contemplation in the woods has made me late. I jog through the trees until the street lamps come into view. I hurry nervously down a back alley, my wet feet sloshing from one dirty puddle to another. Rain gushes from the lightning-flecked sky. It's past working hours, but there's still a faint glow emanating from the window of a Warwick-owned leather shop. I stop outside the back door and pull hard on its thick wooden handle. The door doesn't yield to my tug.

I glance to my left, then to my right. No one wanders the alleys this time of night, especially not when days of rain have turned this street into a permanent mud slick. My feet feel as though they're sinking into the earth. Heavy droplets ooze from the crest of my head, around the back of my ear, and down my neck.

Knock, I tell myself, before the rain washes this row of buildings away. I raise a shaky hand, curl my fingers into a tight fist, and knock twice, very quietly. I hear nothing inside. The steady, muffled deluge of water drowns out all my other senses. The chilly air knifes me through my jacket.

The door eases open, and a tall, broad-shouldered man stares at me. He has a short trimmed mustache that curls ever so slightly at the ends. This must be Ivan. Knox described his acquaintance in Billage as *an honorable man that deserves our respect.*

Ivan's hard face and unflinching glare are certainly characteristics that Knox would be impressed by. Knox didn't say anything about Ivan's stern demeanor or that he has to be over six feet tall with a neck thicker than a maple tree.

"Leather shop's closed, ma'am," Ivan says coldly.

I clear my throat and remind myself that I'm stepping into a highly dangerous meeting that Knox didn't even want me coming to. "Pennies to pass."

Ivan watches me a moment longer before widening the door and allowing me just enough space to enter. Silence is heavy in the room aside from the light crackling of the fire. The tension is palpable. The last few months, Knox has been meeting with Ivan and other potentials, but tonight is the first time this many rebels have met in one place.

The leather shop is a square brick room with walls shared by neighbors on either side. From the outside, these conjoined buildings form a long row. Ivan closes the door behind me, running the dead bolt along its track. He stands with his back against the door and his legs spread wide in an upside-down V. The ceiling is low and I notice that Ivan's tall frame struggles to fit.

Knox stands opposite me. He leans against a thick square support beam, his long trench coat oiled dark brown from the rain. Tuor is close to Knox. His skinny frame shakes slightly. I'm not sure if it's from the chilly night or his nerves. Either way, he's putting on a brave face in front of the other rebel members.

The floor is soaked and muddy. A room full of skeptical men follows me with their eyes as I casually move from the door to stand next to Johnny. He brushes a lock of hair from his forehead and smirks at me as he scans my sopping visage. The edges of my mouth begin a half curve upward, but I stop before my lips become a full smile. Johnny's already been here for near an hour, so he's had time to dry off. The plan was for everyone to arrive separately to avoid being noticed.

When Knox told me we'd be meeting at the shop where Ivan works, I asked him why. This shop is not only surrounded on either side with neighbors, but it's Warwick owned. He explained that was actually the very reason it was chosen. The soldiers would expect us to be meeting in someone's home, but not here. We're hiding in plain sight.

Ivan speaks, his voice low and firm. "We're all here. Let's begin."

Laughter erupts from the street out front. Ivan holds up a hand, signaling all of us to be quiet. My body goes stiff. Water drips off my hair and onto the floor. The street grows quiet. Ivan gives another moment of pause before speaking.

"This is Linus and Munro." Ivan points to two men seated at a long table piled high with scraps of leather. "They work with me here." Munro is a short man with a bushy graying mustache and pink-tipped cheeks, while Linus' smooth skin and dark brown hair accentuate his youth.

Ivan points to another man wearing a pair of tan overalls. "Jol works at the canvas shop down the street. He represents four other men in his guild that support us. And these are my sons, Damion and Tommy." Ivan shifts his body to reveal two young men seated on a bench in front of the fireplace.

Men like Ivan and Jol work skilled jobs for the Warwick government. They make tents, saddles, and swords for the Warwick Militia. The pay is better than what I used to make at the farm, but I'm learning that this rebellion has nothing to do with compensation. It has to do with freedom.

"There are a few other supporters that do blacksmithing, but they stayed home to keep our numbers low tonight." Ivan turns to face me. "Gentlemen, these are Knox's people, Johnny, his nephew, Camilla, and her brother Tuor."

Linus looks directly at me and says, "You're the one that killed the governor."

Tuor stops shaking and his body tenses. I nod reluctantly. The statement does not surprise me. We discussed this before bringing me to the meeting. Explaining Portia's involvement in Governor Leo's murder was far too complicated, so I agreed to take responsibility for his death. It can't hurt our cause, having other members believing I offed the biggest Warwick supporter in our territory.

"What was it like?" Linus asks.

Tuor's eyes are on me.

"It was—" I hesitate. "He was trying to kill my brother. I just did what any of you would have done." It's quiet as everyone waits for me to expound on my story. I scan the room and decide to give their hungry gazes what they want. "He never showed us any mercy, so I didn't show any to him," I growl. "I slit his throat and watched his life slip away. I'm glad he's dead."

My last statement is not part of the lie. Governor Leo tried to have Tuor executed in exchange for a few hundred Catahli rings. I wish I had been the one to kill him. I sense Johnny next to me. He shifts uncomfortably while Linus gives me a nod of respect. It seems that I've satisfied his morbid interest.

"Our biggest challenge is numbers. I spoke with more shop workers this week. I have several that are interested but—" Ivan pauses, clasping his hands behind his back. "They're not ready yet to attend a meeting or to even know that meetings are taking place."

Tommy chimes in. "We're careful not to even say there's a group of us." Unlike his father, Tommy is slim with straight, greasy hair.

"When I recruit," Ivan continues, "I act alone. I talk as if I'm the only one who shares their concerns. So the risk of being caught is only to myself."

Munro nervously drums his fingers on the leather-strewn table. He continually looks to the front door as if someone will break through any moment.

"So how do we build our numbers? We've been at this for months. When are we going to act?" Jol asks. His voice is louder than makes anyone comfortable.

"Lower your voice," Munro scolds.

"Of course our numbers are low." Linus rises to his feet. "Ivan, you're doin' it wrong. If you told those people there was a rebellion forming, they'd be more likely to stand with us. Tell 'em we've got the girl that killed the governor!"

"Find your seat," Ivan warns, his tone still calm and steady.

Linus throws his arms up before sitting down. Ivan begins a slow walk across the room. Linus, now irritated, taps his foot furiously on the floor. The fire cracks and pops in response to Linus' temper.

"Why don't we ask Knox and his people what they think about our recruitment methods?" Ivan says. He comes to a stop only a few feet from Johnny and me.

Jol huffs. "Knox's people look like a bunch of children."

Children . . . I hate being called a child, especially by someone who doesn't know me. I don't hide my disgust. I glare icily at Jol before turning my gaze to Ivan.

"If we were found out tonight, the rebellion would be over like that." I snap my fingers and look directly at Jol. "There are too few of us to be acting loosely. What if tonight Karla discovered our location and sent a group of soldiers to flush us out? We'd be hanged at sunrise." Jol shakes his head at me. "Then who would remain to carry out the rebellion?"

"Camilla's right," Johnny says. "You haven't seen how bad it is out there. Until we have more men on our side—"

"And how are we supposed to have more numbers unless we get out there and rally the people?" Linus asks, looking as if he's ready to jump to his feet again.

"The time will come," Ivan says.

I hate to admit that Linus and Jol are right, but it's something of an impossible situation. We need a bigger group to make a stand, but how do we grow our numbers when we're constantly in fear of being caught?

"We need more people, right? What group of people has the highest population in this territory?" I ask.

It's Knox who answers me. "The farm workers."

"You people who work in Billage forget about the farm. You buy your food, but don't realize the amount of people that it takes to plant and harvest it all. If we want to win this rebellion and take back our territory, we need the support of the farm workers."

"Aren't the people that work at the farm a bunch of oafs?" Damion asks.

I give Damion a look that makes it clear that *he's* the idiot. "No, I used to work on the farm. I know what it's like. They're probably scared. And if they're not scared, then they've grown complacent. For thirteen years people have become comfortable with their lives under Warwick's thumb, but I still think they're our best chance. If we can show them the possibilities of a life outside of Warwick rule, then maybe—"

A loud banging reverberates through the workshop. It comes from the back door, inches from where I'm standing. Johnny's hand touches mine and pulls me to his side. Ivan's sons are on their feet along with Linus and Munro. A symphony of swords is drawn. I reach for my dagger.

If Karla knew where we were meeting, she wouldn't knock before entering . . . right?

Jol steps away from everyone else and darts his gaze around the room as if he suspects a traitor. Ivan, calm as usual, moves toward the door. He gives us all a warning look.

"Weapons down," he whispers. "We're working late to catch up, remember?"

Reluctantly the swords are returned to their sheaths while everyone moves about the room, taking a stance that resembles work. I pick up a scrap of leather and try to appear as if I know what to do with it. Johnny stands behind me, blocking me from the door. Ivan clears his throat before unhooking the deadbolt.

The sound of pouring rain floods into the room. I turn and peer past Ivan's broad shoulders. I see a man, soaking wet and dressed in a full Warwick Militia uniform.

CHAPTER TWO

THE SLENDER SOLDIER pushes his way into the leather shop. I sense his cocky demeanor even from across the room. He orders Ivan to close the door. With the sound of the rain muffled by the heavy door, everyone ceases their fake work, bringing the room again to a tense silence.

"We've extended our work hours tonight," Ivan says confidently, trailing behind the soldier as he inspects the room. "More gear is needed for the recruits in LilyAye. Surely you've heard of the growing militia."

Johnny shifts in an attempt to further cover me. Linus just confirmed that I'm still recognizable in this territory as the governor killer. I continue to stare past Johnny's shoulder at the intruder. As a true Warwick soldier, his physique is impeccable. His waist is thin and the top of his black leather vest is drawn tightly over his chest.

The soldier stops suddenly. The wood floor squeaks as he turns on his heels to face Johnny and me.

He lifts his sword and points its tip in my direction, then lets out an awkward, sardonic laugh. Ivan studies the soldier with a perplexing eye.

"Sir?" Ivan questions. His voice doesn't betray any fear.

"You're not working late," the soldier says flatly. Slowly I move my hand so it's poised over the handle of my dagger. "This is a rebel meeting."

I exchange a glance with Knox.

"I'm afraid you're mistaken," Ivan says coolly.

Tommy casually slips from his seat by the fire. "A *what* meeting?" he asks stupidly. He comes to stand in front of the soldier, drawing his attention away from Ivan, who's moving fluidly to the back of the soldier. "We're doing what the boss just said; workin' late."

"I don't think so," the soldier says with a smirk. His grip around the hilt of his sword tightens.

A single moment passes where no one moves, and I wonder if Ivan will keep up the facade. But then in a blink, Ivan seizes the soldier from behind. As if father and son practiced the move, Tommy ducks and secures the soldier's sword by twisting it from his hand. Ivan clasps his thick arms around the soldier's elbows and pulls him to the ground.

The curtain has fallen. Everyone produces their weapon and circles around the intruder, including me. I expect to see the soldier's lithe body wrestling against Ivan's thick frame, but instead, the stranger squints his eyes and laughs jovially.

Linus cocks his head and looks at the group in utter bemusement. Even Ivan seems unsure of what to make of the display. The soldier attempts to raise his hands in surrender.

"Whoa, whoa!" he mutters, a laugh still on his lips.

"What is this?" Linus asks.

Ivan motions with his head. "Linus, check the door."

Linus obeys, first peering out the front window, then checking that the back door is secured.

"Put him down," Knox says.

Ivan tosses the soldier onto the floor like a hunk of meat being thrown before a pack of lions. Our circle closes in on him. The soldier pauses, staring at the floor before brushing dirt from his pants and rising to stand before us. He looks around the room, locking eyes with each of us. A queer smile forms on his face.

"I mean no harm. I'm one of you," he says.

"One of us?" Tommy barks.

"How stupid do you think we are?" Linus says. His post by the door isn't keeping him from the conversation. "They've sent a spy but haven't bothered to even change his clothes."

"That doesn't make sense. If he were a spy, they wouldn't have sent him dressed like the enemy," Johnny says.

Linus snaps back, "You don't know that."

"There could be more of them. What if this is an ambush?" Tuor says.

"The man might not know what he's stumbled in to," Munro says under his breath.

I stare at the Warwick soldier, standing among a dozen men that wish to see him dead, and he doesn't seem nervous. "He knows. He knows why we're here."

Ivan raises his sword to the man. "State your business, and quickly."

Tommy shakes the soldier's own sword at his side, eager to pounce.

"Wow. I'm impressed, truly." The soldier scans the room and the litany of weapons pointing back at him. "I never expected you to be so . . . well armored."

Ivan leans in, the tip of his sword close enough that if he breathed deeply, he'd poke a hole in the soldier's neck. Straightening his vest, the intruder glares at the blade. Dark circles encompass his sharp blue eyes. His thick black lashes only add to his striking gaze.

Like the flap of a bird's wing, the soldier suddenly turns his eyes to me. I feel uneasy and it has nothing to do with the Warwick crest on his shirt. The soldier is handsome, yet haunting to look at.

"You have ten seconds to explain yourself," Ivan warns, resting his sword just below the soldier's jaw.

"My name is Reed. I thought my reason for coming here would be plain."

Reed scans the room with a hopeful expression. It's like he's waiting for an ally to reveal himself in the crowd.

"I came here because I no longer serve the Supreme Ruler. I left the militia weeks ago and have been searching for your group ever since. It hasn't been easy finding you."

Reed is taller than every other man in the room, which makes him stick out like a carrot among tomatoes. His hair, black as tar, is slicked back and covers the collar of his shirt. "I've heard the whispers for a while now that the Duffy Rebellion was alive again in Bear Gap."

Knox stands like an unmoving stone edifice. He studies Reed with solemn eyes.

"How did you find out about this meeting?" Linus growls.

A long moment passes as Reed ponders the question and then shifts to face Linus.

"I have an informant who told me meetings were taking place in Billage, small meetings. I'm eager to align myself with the right side."

"What's his name, your informant?" Knox asks.

"Her," Reed corrects. "My informant is a woman, and I don't think she'd care for me speaking her name."

Linus scoffs from across the room.

"That's rather convenient, isn't it?" Johnny says.

Tommy speaks. "I say we kill him now."

Reed laughs awkwardly as he takes a shaky step away from Tommy. For the first time since his intrusion, Reed seems unsure of himself.

Tuor scrutinizes Reed as if he were a spider he just stepped on. "He's no defector. I don't trust him."

"It took us months to trust each other. He comes in here in one night and trusts all of us?" Munro says. "Doesn't seem right."

"H—hold on. I can prove it." Reed reaches a hand into the breast of his shirt. He pulls out a rolled piece of parchment. "I can prove I'm no longer in the militia."

"What's that?" Ivan asks.

Reed holds out the parchment, which Knox snatches out of his hand. "I grew up a Warwick supporter, but when I was stationed at the Bear Gap farm, I saw how the people there were treated and I couldn't stay any longer."

"What does it say?" I ask.

Knox shifts the parchment to the nearest flame. He reads in a monotone voice, "Traitor Notice: All Warwick personnel are notified of a deserter, Reed

Thrussell. If seen, take into immediate custody and report to your superior."

"Three weeks ago I left," Reed says. "I abandoned my post when I heard there were people in this territory planning to rebel. I found that notice posted in Rande Square and stole it as evidence of my loyalty. If I'm caught, they'll kill me."

Johnny says, "He could have just written that announcement himself and be using it as a way to gain our trust."

"Does it look real?" I ask my brother.

Knox hands the notice to Tuor. "It has the Harras seal," Tuor says.

"All that means is that Karla sent him here herself. Which makes him a spy." Linus sounds exasperated.

"Why would a spy come dressed as a soldier?" I ask.

"Why would anyone walk into a rebel meeting with that uniform?" Linus retorts.

Munro takes the parchment from Linus. "This notice could have been speaking of anyone. He might not even be Reed Thrussell."

"We have to get rid of him," Damion says, his boots scraping across the wood floor as he approaches Reed.

"Quiet," Ivan says as he stretches out an arm to steady his two sons.

A tremor ripples across Reed's hand and arm. His body jolts and then suddenly stops. "I'm wearing the uniform because I only left with the clothes on my back. I take off the vest in the daytime, but in case you didn't notice, it's raining hard tonight so I wore it for protection. This is the type of weather that can chill you to a point where you never warm up again." Reed glances around the room. "Not every man that wears the black vest is evil." Reed's eyes settle on Tuor. "You used to be in the Warwick Militia too. Does your sister question your devotion?"

"That's different," I say. My voice sounds mousy.

No one speaks. Johnny shakes his head. He turns to me, his mouth half-open.

"We have to do something about him," Johnny whispers.

"But he's right," I say, keeping my voice low. "Not only with Tuor, but Lawrence too. If anyone understood the draw of Warwick loyalty, it was Lawrence, and he still managed to break away." Only to be sucked back in, I think to myself.

"Camilla." Johnny's eyebrows furrow.

Tommy rises from his seat. "How long are we going to allow this piece of scum to take up our time?"

"I agree," Ivan says. "We have to kill him. If we let him leave here tonight, we'll all be hunted down."

"Wait," I say. The men, still clinging tight to their swords, pause to stare at me. "He was part of the militia only a few weeks ago. That might be helpful to us."

"I say we kill him. Get it over with," Linus says.

"I agree. What say the rest of you?" Tommy asks.

"I don't trust him," Johnny says.

Reed's eyes fall again to me. It's as if he wants *me* to free him from this hungry pack of wolves. There's something unsettling in the way he looks at me, but then again, his execution is being spoken of freely in front of him.

A familiar urge returns to my mind. In the same way I must go to Rande, I feel the need to save Reed. His presence is a risk. Every word he says could be a lie. We could be playing right into his hand, but my gut tells me that's not the case. My gut says he's an asset to our cause.

"I have an idea," I say. The room grows quiet. "The black vests, Warwick's soldiers, they sometimes get a brand too, just like us farm workers. Right, Tuor?"

Tuor hesitates. His fingers brush the spot on his forearm where his brand resides, given to him as a child when worked on the farm. "Captains do, and other elite. Many of the soldiers that work at the farm have a brand." Tuor gains courage as he speaks. "You have to say vows before they mark you, and once you receive your brand, you're considered nothing else for the rest of your life except a Warwick soldier."

The rain outside slows, bringing an eerie calm to the room.

"The brand for the soldiers is different than my brand." I hold out the underside of my forearm to show my mutilated scar, which keeps me from ever reentering the farm. "The soldier's brand is on their bicep, a symbol of power."

I signal Reed to show everyone his brand. He rolls up the sleeve of his cotton shirt to reveal a smooth, lean arm. At the top is a brand in the shape of a large *W*.

"Mine is on thin, tender skin," I continue, comparing my brand to his. "A symbol of submission. The soldier's brand is something to be proud of. Mine is something disgusting to hide and only be brought out when absolutely necessary." I let my arms hang limply at my side. "But one thing is the same, both brands represent property of Quinten Warwick. Tell everyone what your brand means."

Reed looks at me like we're two members of the same team. He's catching my signals.

"We're told to protect it. Once we receive it, it's a part of our body, a part of our nature. If it's destroyed—"

"Like mine."

"Yes . . ." Reed looks in the direction of my hideous scar. "Like yours. It means great disgrace. A damaged brand means a soldier . . . is no longer a soldier. He's executed."

"What of all of this?" Tommy spits.

"What of it?" I snap back, challenging his anger.

"We don't need a history lesson," Linus says.

I break away from the circle and take a step closer to Reed. "If Reed is truly a deserter, then he'll have no problem destroying his brand. Even a spy wouldn't do it. It's blasphemy."

I turn to look at Johnny. He nods, but he's not pleased. He doesn't need to say it. I know what we'll have to do if Reed doesn't cut his brand. I bring up my dagger, which I've been clutching since Reed's appearance. I recall the day that Knox lent it to me and how he never asked for it back. I hold it out to Reed handle first.

"Do you agree?"

Reed eyes me curiously, considering my offer. Then his lips curl into the faintest of smiles. He lets out a breathy laugh, then takes the blade with a look of relief.

"I agree."

Reed removes his black vest, tossing it carelessly on the floor. He then takes off his white linen shirt so he stands before the group bare from the waist up. His skin is perfectly smooth, except for a ragged scar on his right shoulder. Reed notices my staring. He runs a finger over the marred divot on his shoulder.

"Sneak attack," he says and raises his eyebrows. "The first of many in my life."

I say nothing, but sense that Reed has experienced a lot of pain in his life, perhaps more than just physical. The Warwick brand is formed perfectly on his bicep, a crisp *W*. Reed raises the blade to his arm. He pauses.

"Who do you serve?" Knox asks.

He pauses a moment longer before pressing the blade into his skin. He seems to revel in the feeling as he runs my dagger down the length of his brand. Reed's arm splits open and blood erupts from the cut, fully covering what's left of the brand. No one moves, as if we're all gazing upon something magnificent.

Reed looks up, my bloody dagger gripped tightly in his hand. "I don't know who I serve, but it's not Quinten Warwick."

CHAPTER THREE

SILENCE HANGS IN the air. Reed looks at my dagger then smears the bloody blade on his pant leg. My lips are parted as he returns the weapon to my care. Munro lowers his sword. Reed has struck a cord with the rebels. Not serving Quinten Warwick is a sentiment everyone in the room can agree with.

"This doesn't mean anything," Linus says. "It could still be an act."

"For now, tie him up," Ivan instructs. He moves to the corner of the workshop and motions for Knox, Tuor, Johnny, and me to follow: "The Rande Rebels" as we've been dubbed.

"I don't like saying it, but Linus is correct," Ivan says. He looks at me, his expression strictly business. "Your test was clever but it's not foolproof."

"He seemed eager to cut his brand," I say.

Ivan shakes his head. "It's not enough."

Johnny lets out a frustrated sigh as he turns to look at Reed. Blood oozes down his arm as Linus and

Tommy tie his hands behind his back with a leather cord.

"What should we do with him?" Johnny asks.

"He might be useful to us," Tuor says. "Even if he is a spy."

"What do you mean?" Ivan asks.

"He has the brand, which means he was either at a high level in the militia or he made a serious vow to Warwick. Either way, he probably has information we can use."

Ivan lets out a grunt of agreement. "We can't leave him out of our sight. I'll keep him at my house."

Knox sets his long sword in front of him, placing both hands on its pommel. "Are you certain you want to bring him into your home?"

Ivan nods his head slowly. "I'd prefer to keep him as close to me as possible. Plus, my boys will keep an eye on him." Ivan gives Reed a sharp look. "If I suspect anything, I'll take care of him myself."

Knox nods in agreement.

"There are uncertain days ahead of us. It seems like the more that join our cause, the less friendly this territory becomes," Ivan says.

Scratching at the stubble on his chin, Knox says, "Maybe we should think about moving your people in with us."

"I think it best that I not know where you're hiding. If something happened to me, Karla wouldn't be able to torture your location out of me." Ivan takes a deep breath. "You'd be able to carry on if I were dead."

The prospect of death has become a part of my every day life. I'm learning that being a rebel member means risking everything. It would have been easier just to flee Bear Gap after Governor Leo tried to have

Tuor executed. Choosing to stand and fight is a whole other thing that I wasn't prepared for.

"It sounds like you're laying yourself down as a sacrifice," I say, unable to hide my concern.

"We're all sacrificing ourselves for the future of this territory. If you think differently, then you're fooling yourself." Ivan turns to face the rest of the room. "It's time to close this meeting. Stay vigilant as you make your way home. Munro, you'll lock up tonight."

"What are we doing with him?" Jol asks, pointing to Reed.

Ivan crosses the room and grabs Reed where he's bound at the wrists. He takes a dagger from his boot and holds it up to Reed's neck, which is half a foot higher than Ivan's. "He's coming with me." Ivan pushes Reed to the door. I run to unlock it and hold it open. The rain has settled and only a light drizzle falls from the sky. "If you have friends waiting for us, you'll be the first to die."

Ivan and Reed leave and the rest of us scatter, exiting the leather shop one by one, in the same way we arrived. Johnny squeezes my hand before we part ways. I walk casually down the alley. The rain and cool night air has left me chilled to the bone. I hug my jacket tight to my chest.

The town of Billage is quaint with neat rows of small houses. Some are occupied by supervisors or the wealthy of Bear Gap that wish to avoid the scum of Rande.

On the edge of town, I pause and look into the sky. The clouds clear to reveal a hazy white moon. A chorus of crickets sings among the trees as the final drops of rain slide off the leaves and hit the ground.

In the quiet and still of my mind, I hear the voice beckoning to me again. My feet wish to dash away from this place and run home, but not to the place I've been calling home all winter. I want to return to the shack in the swamps of Rande. It would be dangerous, utterly stupid to try and take a trip into Rande. I'd have to be a fool to do that, but logic seems to drain from my thoughts like a bucket with a hole.

I shift my body toward Rande and stare into the trees. I want it. I want it so badly I could go right now and not care what anyone back at the cabin thinks. They don't understand how much I need it anyway.

I take a step into the woods. A twig snaps under my foot. A hand reaches into the crook of my elbow and twists me around. My breath catches in my throat as I let out a shriek.

"Sh—sh—sh—sh. It's just me," Johnny says, holding a finger to my mouth.

He links his fingers through mine and pulls me into the cover of the trees. I'm zapped back to the real world after being snatched out of the middle of a dream.

"What are you doing out here?" he asks.

My mouth hangs open, dumbfounded. "Huh?"

"I watched you as I came down the road. You've just been standing here. You wanna get captured?"

I close my mouth and try to gain my composure. "I was waiting for you," I lie.

Johnny's face moves from annoyance to understanding. His lips part into a cocky grin.

"You know you shouldn't do that," he says sweetly.

I lean in toward Johnny. He brings his hands to my elbows and runs them up to my shoulders, tugging me closer to his chest.

"You won't tell Knox, will you?"

Johnny's hands stop their moving. He rolls his eyes. "Let's not talk about my uncle right now."

I chuckle. The bright moon beams through the trees. Johnny bows his head and presses his warm lips against mine. His hand stretches across my back to hold me close. I feel at home.

Johnny pulls out of our kiss and the moonlight flecks off his feathery blond hair. I take in the curvature of his pronounced jaw and the light stubble on his cheeks. From the very back of my thoughts, the voice returns. Why? Why, at a moment like this, does the voice make itself known?

"We should get back," Johnny says, glancing through the trees. I'm not sure if he's looking out for a soldier or Knox. Neither would be a welcome presence. Johnny and I haven't told the others about our . . . relationship. I haven't even told Mirabelle. Between her constant fussing and the stress of the rebellion, it seemed easier to keep it a secret.

I don't even know exactly what *it* is. One day Johnny and I were good friends, and then the next we were holding hands and stealing kisses in the snowy woods. Every day we grew closer and closer.

When the others rejected my idea to find supporters for the rebellion, Johnny supported me. When Knox resisted and called us fools, Johnny stood by my side. When it seemed easier to flee Bear Gap, Johnny stood firm. In the course of one winter, I've gone from a girl on the run to a rebel member with a . . . boyfriend?

The sound of hoof beats echo down the road. Johnny takes my hand and we run deeper into the trees. Even in the dark, I know my way through these woods by heart. I've spent most of the winter memorizing the creeks and the hills and every fallen tree. If we're attacked, I want to know my way around better than any Warwick soldier.

The faintest of lights flickers up ahead as we approach Johnny's cabin. We've made a practice of keeping the house as dark as possible at night. Only one small candle is kept in the window to help us find our way back. Still holding my hand, Johnny and I walk down the small hill where the cabin sits. We pause on the front step. Johnny leans down and kisses me once more before releasing my hand and opening the door.

Knox stands abruptly from his rocking chair in the sitting room. "I left the meeting after both of you and somehow made it back first. What held you up?"

"Is that them?" Mirabelle calls from the kitchen.

She rounds the corner with a wooden spoon in her hand and her apron tied tightly around her waist. Johnny glances at me sideways.

"I got turned around and Johnny happened to find me."

Knox looks at me with a blank expression. Does he believe my lie? It's a talent I've been able to practice lately: lying about Johnny and me, lying about the voice in my head . . .

"Well, thank goodness you're back," Mirabelle says as she returns to the kitchen. "I get so nervous thinking about you out there by yourself, wandering the streets of Billage . . ." Her voice echoes down the hall. "Soup will be done soon!"

Johnny leaves my side to sit by Knox, an attempt to distance himself from me.

"Is Tuor back?" I ask.

Slowly Knox returns to his rocking chair. He picks up an opened book that's lying on the end table and begins to read. "He's upstairs."

I pass through the sitting room and try to avoid eye contact with Knox. He doesn't look up as I climb into the loft. I swing my leg over the top of the wide ladder. Tuor sits pressed against the window, Knox's scope in his hand. The loft is the only real bedroom in the house. Johnny insisted that Mirabelle and I sleep up here so we could have some privacy.

"Tuor, all clear?" I point to the window that faces the back of Johnny's cabin. His head spins around and he looks at me with wide eyes. Relief fills his face. He spends hours sitting there keeping watch. After every meeting he makes sure we aren't followed.

"No activity so far." Tuor jumps up from his kneeling position but keeps watch out the window. "If we have to escape Bear Gap, I think it would be better to take a route to the west." Tuor crosses the room, his gaze pinned to the floor as he concentrates.

"But then we'd have to cross that gully that Johnny's always warning us about. That would be tough with the horses."

I sit at the end of Mirabelle's bed. Its old frame groans as it takes my weight.

"Yes, but there are more pine trees, which would make covering our tracks easier."

Tuor touches his hand to the side of his head and starts to claw at his hair.

"What's wrong?"

"Nothing," he mumbles.

Being away from the militia has been good for Tuor. He's usually okay if I'm around, but his demons still torment him from time to time.

"Do you ever think about Lawrence?" he asks without making eye contact.

I hesitate, not sure how Tuor wants me to answer. "I try not to."

"Why not?" Tuor comes to sit next to me on Mirabelle's bed. "He should be a part of this, a part of the rebellion."

I bow my head and stare at my hands. The cracks and calluses from working on the farm still exist.

"He did what he had to do to keep us alive. I try and focus on the work that needs to be done, not what's already happened."

It's the best answer I can come up with. Every time Lawrence comes to my mind, I feel a great amount of pity. I try to think if there was something I could have done differently the night that Captain Thatius showed up, demanding his son in exchange for our freedom.

Should we have fought? Should we have followed his caravan? Should we have made a trip to LilyAye to try and rescue him somehow? The questions are impossible to answer. All I know is that Lawrence is stuck in LilyAye with his father when he should be here fighting for the rebellion.

The unfortunate truth is that Lawrence being in LilyAye under his father's direction is probably the only thing that allows us to continue to live unseen in Johnny's cabin. Captain Thatius is the only one who knows we're hiding here. Anytime he pleases, he could deliver that information to Karla. If Lawrence were to leave, his father might just change his mind about withholding that information.

"I miss him too," I say, touching Tuor's back.

Tuor looks down at me and smiles. I rest my head on his shoulder and close my eyes. With all the danger and the bad stuff we experience everyday, I'm still thankful that I live through it with my brother by my side. I've already decided if we die fighting for this rebellion, it will be side by side. Thunder rolls through the woods and shakes the cabin. Perhaps yet another storm is brewing in Bear Gap.

Soon Tuor and I are beckoned back downstairs for a bowl of Mirabelle's soup. It's not until I take my last few bites that I realize how exhausted I am. I return to the loft to sleep. My bed is just a mat on the floor next to Mirabelle's bed. I curl up under a quilted blanket that Mirabelle made and pull the covers over my ear so my head barely shows. Tuor has finally given up his watch by the window. The storm has made it too dark to see anyway.

Mirabelle finishes her cleaning in the kitchen and soon scales the ladder into the loft. The candle downstairs is blown out and the men settle in to sleep. Johnny's cabin is small. There are no bedrooms downstairs, so they all sleep wherever they can find a spot.

Knox usually drifts off in his rocking chair. Johnny sleeps on the couch, closest to the front door. This is intentional. I've heard him say more than once that this is his house, and it's his responsibility to protect everyone inside.

Tuor sleeps in the same place every night: lying straight on his back over the threshold that leads into the kitchen. He claims it's the safest place in the house because he can keep an eye on the front door and the back door. I suspect he just likes being close to where the food is kept.

The cabin grows deathly quiet. The sounds of an owl and crickets outside fade away. Knox's heavy snoring disappears. The gentle rain on the roof has stopped. It's so odd, the sound of utter silence. It sends an eerie chill up my back.

I squeeze my eyes closed and shift deeper into my bed to try to fall asleep, but I find no rest. The thoughts begin again. I have no control over my own mind as it's flooded with images and left to wander to places I don't want it to go. Soon the thoughts are gone, replaced with voices, or rather, one singular voice.

She tells me to come home, but I don't call that place my home. Rande is not my home. This place, here with Mirabelle and Tuor, this place is my home. The voice is relentless.

Come home, she says.

Come home!

COME HOME!

CHAPTER FOUR

MY ARMS BURN as they're pulled taut behind my back. Firm hands dig into my wrists, binding me so that escape is impossible. I feel his hard body against my back. Hot breath tickles my neck. I struggle against my captor but his grip only becomes tighter. I look around at the trees as if they can save me, but it's just him and me, alone, deep in the woods.

"What are you going to do?" His mouth is so close to my ear, his gruff voice envelops all of my thoughts. "What are you going to do!"

Crying out, I shake my arms violently. I swing my body in an attempt to shake him off, but the advantage remains his.

"C'mon!" he shouts.

I push him back a few paces. He nudges me forward again. Back and forth, our feet shuffle over the forest floor like a violent dance. He taunts me, letting me feel a moment of control only to snatch it away a heartbeat later.

"What are you going to do, Camilla?"

Pain ripples up my shoulders. My heartbeat picks up its pace. My breath becomes ragged. I'm no longer in the woods. I'm at the farm, being arrested by one of Governor Leo's men. I'm exhausted and utterly spent as he ties my hands together and tosses me into the prison wagon. I stop struggling. Terror has left me frozen. I'm helpless. I'm a pitiful nothing to Warwick and his government. I'm weak.

"You're mine," my captor whispers.

I'm no one's, I think to myself. I swing my leg around his and hook my foot behind his knee. I pull tight like a serpent sucking the life out of its prey. His stance weakens. He stumbles, but he still has me. I jab with my shoulder and feel it hit his strong jaw. He moans but his grip on my hands is unchanged.

Now I'm angry. With my leg still wrapped around his, I pull again but this time allow my body to crumple with him. He loses his footing and we fall to the forest floor. I flail my legs and head until my skull connects with his face. One hand loosens on my wrist and that's all I need.

I elbow him in the stomach. He grapples for control over me, his thick hand tracing down my arm. I swing again, my elbow slamming into his ribs. I roll off his body but he still has ahold of my left wrist.

We're facing each other as he drags me toward him. I scratch at his arm, laying tracks of blood along his skin. With his free hand he reaches for me. I scream, then bring my foot up to his stomach and kick him away. He gasps for air and finally lets go of my arm. I crawl away, leaves and pine needles scratching my hands as I scramble to my feet.

I stop and turn to face him. For a moment, I watch him lying on his back. He holds a hand to his face. I inch closer. Deep, red blood pours from his nose. His eyes flicker to me.

I clear my throat. "I did what you said." My voice lacks emotion.

He doesn't respond and I wonder if I've made him mad. Did I take it too far?

Johnny sits up, leaning his head down so the blood drains onto a patch of dirt. He wipes his face, then rubs the blood onto his pant legs. His eyebrows arch upward as he gives me a rueful look. "That was perfect."

"Are you okay?

"No. I'm not." Johnny chuckles. "That's the point, isn't it?"

I hold out my hand, which Johnny takes while pinching the bridge of his nose. I pull him to his feet and remind him, "You willingly agreed to do this."

Johnny takes his free hand and hooks it around my waist to pull me close. "I knew I shouldn't have been swayed by your begging."

I laugh, shaking my head and pushing his bloody nose away from me. "I didn't *beg*. After Tuor was almost executed, I'm not taking any chances on being unprepared. If we're attacked again, I want to—"

"If?" His mood is no longer teasing.

I cross my arms over my chest. My eyes connect with his.

"You're right. It's a matter of when. *When* we're put in danger again, I want to be ready."

"You're getting stronger."

I sigh. I hope being *stronger* is enough. I've always known I was pretty strong. From years of working the fields at Governor Leo's farm, I always had more muscle than most girls my age. What I need is *skill*. I'm not going to earn my freedom by wielding a pitchfork. I need to know how to use a sword.

"I guess we're done training for the day," I say with a smirk.

Johnny rubs his sleeve under his nose, wiping away a trickle of blood.

"We'll train some more tomorrow. I want to teach you how to escape if your hands and feet are both bound."

I smile weakly. I asked Johnny to teach me how to fight, but most of what we do out here is self-defense. To fight Karla and her men, I need to know more than just how to break free from one man. I need to know how to fight, and I need to be really good. I need to be as good as a Warwick soldier. As much as I've enjoyed this time with Johnny alone in the woods, it doesn't feel like enough.

Johnny takes a step toward me. I drop my arms, aware of how close we are. His nose is starting to swell and a bruise is forming under the stubble on his chin.

"You better not have let me win," I say.

He touches his hand to mine. "Never."

Johnny looks down into my eyes. I feel exposed. Can he see the madness swirling around in my head? From the moment I woke this morning, the voice has been tormenting me. It's not normal, I tell myself. I have to tell someone that something's not right.

How do I tell Johnny I'm hearing a bizarre female voice that isn't my own? How do I explain something about myself that I don't even understand? I open my mouth to confess it all, but the words don't form. It's like someone's put a gag in my mouth. The only thing I can do is to yield to the voice. Do as she says. Maybe then she'll be satisfied and I can be at peace.

Johnny strokes his hand through my hair. He stares at me, completely oblivious to the turmoil inside.

"I need to tell you something," I blurt.

Johnny's eyebrows knit together. "What's wrong?"

"Nothing really. It's kind of dumb, foolish probably . . ."

"What?"

I pause, looking at the ground, then back at Johnny. "I left something at my father's house. When we fled, I had no time to get any of my things."

"You have everything you need here."

"I know. I know I do. It's not a necessity." I try desperately to keep my voice even and casual. "It's just . . . there's this box . . ."

"A box?"

"It's complicated, but it's something our mother left behind when we were kids and Tuor and I always played with it. It's special to us and I really want it back."

I never act coy. I barely know how, but the voice compels me to do whatever it takes to get into Rande. I pout my lips and flicker my eyelashes at Johnny.

"I was thinking you and I could go get it." I sense Johnny's hesitation. "I wouldn't ask if it didn't mean so much to me."

Johnny shifts on his feet. Again, he wipes his nose on his sleeve as the bleeding ebbs. "It's way too dangerous for any of us to walk into Rande, especially you."

"Please. I nee—" I stop myself from using the word *need*. "I really want it back. It's the only thing from our childhood that ever meant anything to me." Johnny's gaze leaves my face. "One of these days, we may have to flee to the mountains and never return to this territory. This might be my last chance to ever hold it."

"Karla's looking for *you*, Camilla. It's *your* blood she wants."

He speaks the truth. Karla wants me badly for murdering her husband even though I wasn't the one who actually killed him. As much as I may have wanted to, it was my mother who did the deed. I try hard to push the memory of that event to the back of my mind.

Johnny shakes his head. "I'm not letting you walk right into her hands."

"Let?" I spit the word. I wriggle out of Johnny's embrace. "I didn't tell you about the box to get your permission."

Johnny's taken aback by my biting words. "I didn't mean it like that."

The birds in the trees sing a tune to each other. We're bathed in the hot sun but only for a moment. Soon the clouds gather and leave Johnny and me standing in a cold, gray clearing in the woods.

"You weren't so worried about my safety when we snuck into the Justice House. That was *your* idea, remember?"

"That was different," Johnny says.

"We walked right into a den of Warwick soldiers and you didn't think twice. Now, because I want something, you're so concerned about Karla getting me. It's a simple trip. We sneak in, grab the box, and then leave. We'll be back here in a matter of hours."

Johnny sighs. He rubs his face, accidentally hitting his nose. He flinches, then says, "What if I go and get the box for you?"

"What if Malcolm's there? And besides, you don't know what the box looks like."

"Then we'll have to take Knox with us."

Everything inside of me screams, *NO!* I look at Johnny with pleading eyes. "Why can't it just be the two of us?"

"Knox is the only one that has been back to Rande since we left. Plus, if I have to take you somewhere that dangerous, I want back up."

I chuckle darkly. "Knox will never agree to that. He thinks you're a child and he *hates* me."

"I'll convince him. I'm not taking you somewhere I could so easily lose you." I fiddle with my fingers. "And he doesn't hate you."

I roll my eyes. "Maybe he doesn't hate me but he never meets my gaze. What am I to make of that?"

Johnny shakes his head. "I don't pretend to understand my uncle. My mother said that ever since he fought Quinten all those years ago, he's never been the same. Something happened that night that left him scarred."

"We're *all* scarred," I say, not buying Johnny's excuse for his uncle.

"We'll talk to him. We'll get your box. I promise."

I nod, then slip my arms around Johnny's waist. "Thank you," I say through his rumpled jacket. He holds me tight, resting his chin on my head. I glance up at the darkening sky.

"It looks like more rain," Johnny muses.

I tilt my head. Our eyes connect. I have a sinking feeling in the pit of my stomach, and it has nothing to do with another impending storm. I've lied to Johnny, again.

CHAPTER FIVE

HEAVY DROPLETS OF rain hit my forehead and slide down my face. Johnny takes my hand and we head toward home. The weeks we've spent walking back and forth from this spot in the woods have worn a narrow trail leading to Johnny's cabin. The rain picks up. We break into a run.

Not everything I've said to Johnny is a lie. It's true I want that box, but it's not for sentimental reasons. The voice is telling me to get it. No. The voice is *making* me get it. Why can't I just explain that to him? Johnny pulls me under an overhang at the back door of the cabin. He laughs, shaking water from his hair.

I part my lips, willing every fiber of my being to blurt out the truth to him. The door opens. Mirabelle stands at the threshold. A painful sigh leaves her mouth as her eyes settle on Johnny's face, particularly his nose. "What happened this time?"

We're ushered inside. The moment has passed.

"I didn't do it," Johnny says, giving me a mischievous look.

I shrug my shoulders. "He egged me on." The warmth of the cabin overtakes my senses. The smell of smoke and roasting meat is like being wrapped in a well-worn blanket. Mirabelle carries a heavy cast-iron pot from the stove and sets it on a square table in the middle of the room. Steam pours from the pot as she lifts the lid and inhales.

Mirabelle gives Johnny a sharp look as she clicks her tongue to the roof of her mouth. "Sit down," she demands as she pulls a chair out from the table. "Let me take a look."

"I'll be fine. It's just a nosebleed," Johnny says.

I look at Johnny and shake my head. He sighs, reluctantly taking a seat. I know, and he knows, that Mirabelle won't let him off that easy. She's going to patch him up whether he likes it or not.

I lean on the back of Johnny's chair as Mirabelle moves his head back and forth to get a good look at the damage. Her eyes spot the scratches on his arm and she gives us a disapproving sigh.

"It looks like you've been in a fight with a bear cub!"

Mirabelle rushes to the other side of the kitchen and pulls a white linen dishtowel from the shelf.

"No bear cub, just Camilla." He nudges me with his foot while Mirabelle's back is turned.

"I wish you two weren't out there every day play fighting."

"I want to be prepared," I say as Mirabelle crosses the room and holds the towel to Johnny's nose. He takes it in his own hand as Mirabelle inspects the cuts on his arm.

"Hold that tight to get the bleeding to stop." Mirabelle takes a step back and places her hands on her hips. She shakes her head. "There's not much I can do for it. You just have to let it heal. Maybe consider taking a break from the training . . ."

Johnny pulls the towel away, which is now spotted red. Mirabelle opens her mouth as if she's going to continue lecturing me, but she suddenly stops. I want to tell her she's acting irrationally. Our only options are to hide or fight and I'd much rather fight. I'm about to prove my point to Mirabelle but I don't. I remember that she lost her husband in a similar attempt for freedom. She's worried and scared, that's all.

Mirabelle drops her hands to her apron and lets out a long sigh. "I have some ointment upstairs that would help with those cuts on your arm."

I watch as Mirabelle turns and silently leaves the kitchen. I plop down on a chair across the table from Johnny.

"She gets upset anytime there's talk of fighting," I whisper. "How will she act when we really have to fight?"

"She'll have to face it."

It's not that Mirabelle is weak or too dumb to grasp what's going on. She just wishes we could go about it without violence. But that's impossible. The rebellion is happening even if she disapproves. That's the one thing, the *only* thing that Knox and I agree on. He wants to take back our territory more than I do.

Rain peppers the roof. I look out the window as the woods turn into a dark gray haze. The back door opens with the sound of heavy rain hitting the ground. Water pours from Knox's broad-rimmed hat. He slams the door closed and hangs his hat on a hook on the wall. Pulling off his heavy animal-skin jacket, he gives

Johnny and me a nod, which I've learned is his warmest greeting.

Without speaking, Knox crosses the room, lifts the lid to Mirabelle's pot, and gives a grunt of approval at her hot stew. He picks up a wooden bowl from a stack that Mirabelle has sitting by the washbasin and begins ladling himself some food.

Johnny looks to me then to Knox as if to warn me before he asks for Knox's help. I bite my lower lip. I'm hesitant to bring Knox into my plans to go to Rande, but if it means getting to that box, then I'm willing to do anything.

"Uncle Knox," Johnny says firmly. Knox places the lid on the pot and turns his back to us as he takes a spoonful of stew into his mouth, acting as if Johnny said nothing.

"Camilla and I need to speak with you."

"You're speaking with me now," Knox says gruffly.

Johnny groans, irritated.

Knox turns around to face us. "I want to get out of these wet clothes. Make this fast."

I look down and notice my hands are shaking. I clasp them together quickly, hoping Johnny didn't notice.

"I need to make a trip into Rande," I say. I silently scold myself for using the word *need*.

Knox stops chewing just long enough to give me a stern, "No." He shoves another large spoonful of soup into his mouth. "Where's Mirabelle?"

"You don't even know why she wants to go," Johnny says.

"The reason doesn't matter."

I glare at Knox from under furrowed brows.

He lifts a finger to point at me. "If you go into Rande and get caught by one of Karla's men, it's not just your life that's in danger. It's all of ours. They could track you back to this cabin and have all of us arrested." Knox drops the empty wooden bowl onto the table.

Johnny scoffs. "You've been back to Rande since our escape. It's okay for you to risk our lives but not Camilla? What difference does it make if you go into Rande or if we do?"

Knox has returned to Rande only once since we escaped. It was to meet with an old friend who he suspected would want a part in the rebellion. Knox's suspicious were right. The friend ended up telling Knox about Ivan, the leather shop worker in Billage.

"I know how to be careful. You don't," Knox says.

Johnny laughs sarcastically. "We're faster and stronger than you."

Surprisingly Knox keeps his cool. "I'm not the one that Karla wants."

Knox's eyes fall to me. Karla has been so consumed with finding me, her husband's murderer, that she's clueless to the uprising in her territory. Our only benefit is that Karla has mismanaged Bear Gap so much that half of her soldiers have either deserted or been put to death.

I stand from my chair, unable to hide my desperation.

"I have to go back to the shack. I have to." Knox rolls his jaw. "I know it's dangerous. That's why I need your help. You've made trips into Rande and Billage by yourself. Why can't you just take me?"

"She's asking for help," Johnny says.

I press my hands together as if I were praying. "Please, it wouldn't—"

"No," Knox says, then turns to leave.

"You do hate her, don't you?" Johnny says to Knox's back.

"Johnny . . ." I scold.

For several long moments, Knox is motionless except for the deep rise and fall of his shoulders as he draws breath.

"That's why you're acting this way." Johnny jumps from his chair. "What did she ever do to you?"

Knox slowly turns to face us. "This has nothing to do with her. *None* of us are going to Rande because it's too dangerous."

"You won't do anything to help Camilla. She's asking for help and you're turning your back."

"I've helped that girl plenty," Knox growls.

"That girl?"

The yelling agitates the voice in my head. I squint my eyes and raise a hand to my temple. It was stupid asking Knox. I knew it would be. Mirabelle enters the kitchen, a tincture of ointment in her hand. "What's all the arguing?" she asks, breathless.

Knox avoids my eyes. He claims this is about my safety but I think that's a lie.

"If anyone leaves this cabin, they won't be welcome back," Knox says before storming out the back door and diving into the rain.

Mirabelle's mouth is agape. "What is he talking about?"

"Nothing," I say, brushing past Mirabelle and leaving in similar fashion to Knox.

Johnny calls behind me. "Camilla, wait."

I grab the ladder to the loft and begin climbing. Johnny follows.

"Leave me alone."

"Why are you mad at *me*?"

I swing my leg over the top and whirl around to face Johnny. "Why would you say all of that to Knox?"

Tears threaten. Johnny looks at me, utterly dumbfounded, as he stands on the last rung of the ladder. "I was defending you."

I turn away from him to hide the growing panic on my face. I stare out the window to distract myself from crying. Knox barrels through the backyard, finding shelter in the stable. Behind me, Johnny enters the loft. His steps are slow and cautious.

"I didn't ask for that," I say

"I . . . I thought . . ."

I turn around to face Johnny, brushing a tear from my cheek. "I just want to get my box," I say, my voice back to even. Johnny's mouth hangs open as he struggles for words. "I need to go to Rande. Can't you see that?"

Johnny exhales, then nods. "We're going."

"What?"

"We'll go, you and me. Like you said. We don't need him."

I'm unable to keep from smiling. "Really?"

"What's he going to do? Scream? Yell? This is my house."

Instantly my body relaxes. I cross the room and wrap my arms around Johnny's neck. The voice is satisfied. I'll be there soon, I assure her.

"Just give me a few days, okay?"

"Why?" I ask, slipping out of our embrace.

"We'll go the next time he's hunting. He's gone for hours. It's better if he doesn't know."

"Oh . . ."

The thought of waiting a few more days leaves me nauseous. I'm not sure I can live with the voice much longer.

"Tuor will keep our secret. We'll have to convince Mirabelle that this is best," Johnny says, shaking his head.

"What if we went tonight?"

Johnny looks out the window as a crack of lightning flickers through the trees.

"The farm workers have curfews now. We'll be easier to spot at nighttime. It'd be best to go during day and just use a disguise to get around. Plus, the weather's no good. We wouldn't be able to move as fast."

I nod, agreeing to Johnny's plan. He looks at me confidently. He's done everything to try and please me. I know that. The problem is, I don't know if I can wait a few more days.

***

Nightfall comes and I find myself pacing the length of the loft. I feel like a caged animal in this place. An image flashes into my mind of my home in Rande. I'm there with Tuor and Malcolm but I'm young, still a baby. My mother appears, a genuine smile on her face. She scoops me up into her arms and rocks me tenderly. Tuor is a spirited child, flitting around the room until he finally settles at my mother's side. He tugs at her dress and begs to look at the little girl: me.

With a violent shake of my head, I toss the thought away. I look down at my hands. They're shaking.

"That never happened," I whisper to myself.

Even if it had happened, it was so long ago. Everything is different now. I walk to the window and stare into the dark forest. Then I peer down the edge of the loft.

Knox has settled in with a book. Johnny and Tuor work to clean and sharpen our small arsenal of swords. Mirabelle sews up a hole in a pair of her stockings. All of them look so . . . calm. The scene somehow irritates me more. None of them feel the misery that I'm experiencing.

"Good night." My voice sounds strange, even to me.

"Going to bed already?" Mirabelle asks.

"I'm exhausted."

The excuse is all I can muster. I burrow myself inside my bed, pulling the covers up to my neck. I force my eyes shut but sleep is the last thing on my mind. I've been awake since sunrise yet I don't feel tired. I wait until Mirabelle crawls into her bed. She moans quietly as she shifts to get comfortable. Her back is aching as usual. Soon her breathing becomes deep and steady. She's asleep.

I turn onto my back and stare at the ceiling. The storm outside has begun to wane. Knox snores loudly. He's even annoying while he sleeps. My fingers tremble as they lay impatiently on top of the blanket. Then, as if someone had just nudged me to do it, I rip the blanket off my body and quietly spring to my feet. It's time to go home.

CHAPTER SIX

I MOVE LIKE an executioner preparing for his duty, solemn and methodical. I glance at Mirabelle. She's lying on her side, unmoving aside from the steady rise and fall of her shoulder. From the hook on the wall, I grab my messenger bag and throw it across my chest. I don my fur coat, tie my hair back in a low ponytail, and pick up my boots. But I don't put them on just yet.

In my stocking feet, I cross the loft to the window. The moon is so bright, if Mirabelle woke, she'd see me instantly. Gently I pull the curtains aside and unlatch the metal hook that holds the window shut. It swings open. Bitter, damp air pours into the room.

With barely enough space for my body, I slip through the window and onto the roof that covers the sitting room below. The wood shingles creak as I gingerly place both my feet on the roof. Rainwater soaks through my socks. Unable to latch the window, I push it shut the best I can.

I creep to the edge of the roof and sit down so my feet and legs dangle off the edge. Here I pull on my boots. It's not a far jump, maybe seven feet. Jumping off the roof of Harras Manor was much higher than this, but it's not the distance that makes me nervous. It's the sound my feet will make when I land.

As if slipping into a lake of cool water, I slide off the edge of the roof and land with a *thud* onto the lawn. Slowly I straighten my crouched body. I peek inside the window, which sits above a tall stack of firewood. Through the foggy glass, I see Knox leaned back in his rocking chair, his head tilted sideways, looking as if he were dead.

I turn around to face the black woods behind Johnny's house. The distant sound of an owl hooting prickles at the hairs on my neck. In a flash, I flee from the back of the house, rounding the corner to the front lawn. I dive into the woods with no hesitation. The cold night air engulfs me. I run fast, without thinking.

I could have ridden Shae into Rande. It would be faster, but I can't risk the noise or attention she'll make. A lone rider in the middle of the night would only bring extra suspicion that I can't afford. So I go it on foot, sprinting as if I have endless energy. I have until sunrise to make it back.

The woods at night don't scare me. I've come to know them pretty well from the months of living here. My feet dip low into a valley. I splash through a shallow creek. Water seeps into my boots, making them heavy and uncomfortable, but I keep running as if I don't feel it at all. The ground is slick with mud from the storm. I slip down an embankment. My whole left side is painted with mud. I brush off what I can, and keep moving.

The land tilts upward into a steep hill. At the top, I pause only for a moment, then shuffle down the other side. I stop once more, resting my hand on a nearby tree. The grainy feel of its bark zaps me into the realness of this moment. Reality has been a distant friend. I try to think of a time before I saw the images or heard the voice, but I can't remember it. It feels like these things have been a part of my life forever.

A vision appears in my head. It feels like someone's just twisted a part of my brain. My hand flies to my forehead as I double over in pain. "Ughhh."

It's Tuor's execution. The crowd is jeering. I'm running to save Tuor, who's tied helplessly to the execution block. The executioner's sharp blade swings high. I reach to save my brother but I'm too far away. I can't get to him. A woman appears. She's the image of a hero, meant to save the day.

She vanquishes our enemies and releases my brother from his captors. The woman turns to face me and it's my mother. Her face is soft and kind. She smiles and returns Tuor to me like a gift.

"That's not what happened," I mutter.

Darkness surrounds me on all sides. My face is sweaty. I have to get that box. I have to go home and get the box like the voice wants and then this will stop. It has to stop.

A rustle in the bush causes me to turn abruptly. There's something there, but I'm not sticking around to find out what. I orient myself and then continue running. There's no time to dawdle.

In the distance I see the twinkling lights of the Rande lampposts. I stop to catch my breath. The cold air feels icy as it mixes with the sweat on my forehead. It's only a little jog to get to the swamps from here. I'll circle around to the west and avoid the town altogether.

I move slowly between the trees. My breath is heavy as I approach the river's edge. It rages from the recent rain. I walk upriver until I enter the swamps. It feels as if I'm returning to a place I've left a hundred years ago. Dilapidated shanties begin popping up to my left. Nostalgia overwhelms me. I've missed this place. As happy as I've been at Johnny's, I actually miss this place.

"You there, *stop.*"

The voice, clear and sharp, causes me to freeze. I crane my head and search for the man who just spoke. A sword is drawn from its sheath, swift and shrill. Through the branches, a soldier steps swiftly toward me. His boots sink into the soft earth, creating a squishing noise as he moves.

I turn and press my back hard against the nearest tree. It's the only thing I can do. A scuffle won't turn out well for me. It'll just draw the attention of the next closest guard. Running away will reveal my location. So I hold my breath, and hope. The soldier slices through a branch with his sword as if the trees have no right to stand between him and his duty.

The soldier steps closer to me. He creeps through the woods until I sense him standing directly on the other side of the tree that I'm hiding behind. I hold my breath and look straight ahead. It's quiet except for his heavy breath and the gentle gurgle of the swamp.

Finally I hear the soldier step away. He's not satisfied, I can tell, but he continues his march along the water. I exhale. This is my chance to go back. I could be back at Johnny's and in my bed before anyone even knows I'm gone. I could probably even get a few hours of sleep. Rande is more heavily guarded than I thought.

My body doesn't move. I can't go back. I haven't come this far to turn around without getting the thing I need. I tiptoe inland to hide between the houses. The waterline has approached so aggressively that some shacks have been abandoned. I break into a gentle run, weaving between buildings.

Torchlight catches the corner of my eye at the same time I hear someone yell, "Hey!"

I turn hard to my left. A soldier approaches, slow and lumbering. I move my hand to my jacket and place it on the handle of my dagger.

"You know the rules. You're supposed to be home by sunset," the soldier says as the moon lights his face.

His features are round and unassuming. A soldier guarding the swamps? Warwick soldiers used to never come down here. They hate the stench and the filth. He must have been the unlucky one chosen to guard this rundown neighborhood in the middle of the night.

"I . . . forgot."

"Where are you headin'?" he asks, growing suspicious now.

I tilt my head downward, avoiding the piercing light of his torch.

"Um . . ." My head sways back and forth on my neck. "I'm . . ."

He sighs. "Tell me where you're headed now or I'll have to take you in for questioning."

"Questioning?"

The word pops out of my mouth before I have time to filter it.

"Anyone out after sunset is taken to the governor."

I shift my gaze away from the portly man for a moment. In the distance, I notice a small flame bobbing back and forth. To his left I see another torch a bit closer. There are more soldiers. The swamps are littered with them.

"Okay, come 'ere," he says, taking my arm.

"Wait!"

"Nah, sorry. I gotta take you in."

"I'll tell you what I'm doing. I'm making a visit to . . ." I let my voice drop to a whisper. "Bobby Cramer's place."

The soldier pauses. He releases my wrist and gives me a quizzical look.

"I didn't want to say it. It's a bit embarrassing, but a girl will do whatever she has to, to get a few extra rings." I turn my gaze downward, feigning shyness. "I could come and see you when I'm done with him." I state my offer as if it were nothing. I swallow hard, hardly believing what I've just insinuated.

"Oh." The soldier's lips turn into an almost perfect round shape. He takes half a step away from me and adjusts his leather vest. His cheeks flush and then he turns indignant. "I don't collude with swamp swine. Tell me your name."

"Cherise Plink," I say quickly. I hold my breath, hoping that Cherise still lives here.

"Go home, Cherise. Don't let any of the others catch you."

I hesitate, then realize he's letting me go. I turn swiftly to walk away.

"Hold on," he says as I slowly turn to look at him again.

"Yeah?"

"I need to see your brand."

Instinctively I clutch at my arm. My brand is obviously still there from my seven years of laboring at Leo's farm, but it's mutilated now. It was sliced in two when I was kicked off the farm. He'll know something's amiss if he sees a brand that's been destroyed.

I hesitate and the soldier senses my concern. I clear my throat and try to lean into the darkness.

"Of course," I say with all of the confidence I can muster. I pull up the sleeve of my jacket and show my scar as if there's nothing wrong with it.

The soldier squints in my direction. I begin to pull my sleeve down, but before I can, he reaches out and grabs my forearm.

"Swamp swine," he curses. "You're coming with me."

There's no more tricking this idiot soldier. I stare into his red face and all I can think is, I have to get to my box *tonight*. Anything standing in my way must be destroyed. All these thoughts pass through my mind in a split second. With my free hand, I reach for my belt. I swing my arm up and hit the soldier in the face with the butt of my dagger.

He lets go of my wrist and staggers backward. He reaches for his sword, but before he has a chance, I drive my dagger deep into his belly. I lift my leg and kick him in the stomach. Ripping my dagger from his flesh, he falls onto the forest floor with a *thud*. All is quiet except for the sound of his gasping.

I look at my hand, smeared with his blood. My shirt is splattered red. I'm shaking. How did I . . . ? Johnny never taught me anything like that. It felt like pure instinct, like someone else's instinct. I forget about the soldier and mentally move on. I'm more focused now, alert of any torches in the distance.

My childhood house looks exactly the same, a thin cabin-like structure, built upon stilts for such seasons as we're experiencing now. Just a few more rains and these steps will be covered with water. It's all so familiar yet so strange looking. The light of a single candle flickers through the slats in the wood. Malcolm's awake? I should feel awkward coming to Malcolm's house in the middle of the night, but I don't give it a second thought. I *need* my box.

I press my hand to the knob and scan the surrounding woods one more time before opening the door. The firelight casts eerie shapes on the walls and ceiling as if it were a warning omen. Malcolm sits at the table, his back straight and tense. He looks away from the figure of a woman standing in the middle of the room; her arms draped across her chest while one hand fingers the stone around her neck.

"Mother?"

CHAPTER SEVEN

"I TOLD YOU she'd come," my mother says.

Malcolm's teeth grind together under his graying mustache. I blink, wishing the person before me were another vision, another trick of the mind. I could never conjure an image so heinous. This is not a dream. This is really her.

"Camilla, sit down."

Portia points to the open chair at the table. I try to speak but I find it difficult. I look from my mother to my father. My face begs to be told how fate has brought the three of us into the same room.

"What are you . . .?"

"Sit," my mother commands.

I remain frozen at the doorway until Portia pokes me in the shoulder with her bony finger and pushes me toward the table. I plop onto a wooden chair across from Malcolm. He glares at me as if it's my fault that she's here.

Portia commands the room as she places both hands on her hips and stares at me with shimmering green eyes. Her long cape creates a dark backdrop against her ivory skin.

"You have gotten yourself into quite a problem, haven't you? You can't even come back to Rande without nearly being captured."

She waits now, allowing me to speak.

"Me? No. *You* caused the problem. You—"

Ignoring my response, my mother clips my words and says, "You're the sister of a killer. You escaped capture, and murdered the governor. His wife is now sniffing out your blood like a hunting dog. You're trapped up there in that deplorable cabin in the middle of the woods."

"How do you know that?"

"You shouldn't have come here," Malcolm growls, his eyes locked on me as he says it.

"Malcolm," Portia croons. She takes a step toward the table and leans her body on one foot. "She had no choice. She had to come."

I scrunch my eyebrows as I look up at her tall figure.

"Don't look at me like that," she says with a hint of disgust.

"What do you mean, *I had no choice?*"

She exhales, then saunters to the corner of the shack where I used to sleep. My bed mat still lies on the floor. She bends down and picks something up off the floor. When she turns around, I see the little box resting in both her hands.

"My box!"

"You were looking for this."

"How did you know that?"

Portia drops the box onto the table as if it were a worthless piece of junk. I grab it and pull it close to my body. I look up at my mother's smiling face as satisfaction fills her swollen chest.

"How did you know I was coming to get it?"

I look to Malcolm. He's staring at the table.

"This is what I do, Camilla!" Portia spreads her arms wide. "Once I knew where you were living, your energy was so easy to lock in to. All I had to do was get you away from all those other people. It seemed you were never going to leave, though, so I had to draw you out myself."

I stare into the room at nothing in particular. It takes me several long moments to understand what she's saying. I've been a victim of her . . . powers. I feel like a puppet hanging from its strings.

"You did this? You were the voice . . ." I whisper.

Portia's lips curve into a wicked smile.

Malcolm covers his face with his hand. He knew what she was doing. I'm the only one who's an idiot.

"Camilla, you have the governor of Bear Gap hunting you down. You're never going to be able to live in this territory again. It's over. They all believe you killed the last governor. Do you think everyone is just going to forget that? Even your little rebel friends that Knox is drumming up aren't going to be keen on you for long when they realize you're just a girl who barely knows how to wield a sword."

"Shut up," I spit.

I press the bottom of my feet hard into the floor. I want to stand up in rage, but my body is held to the chair by the feeling of a thousand bricks on my shoulders and legs. I thought I had sat down of my own volition, but I realize now that she forced me to.

"You'd be dead if I hadn't saved you!" Portia yells.

"Let me out of here."

"You can continue this . . . pathetic little rebellion of yours but I'm telling you now, you will get nowhere and you'll do nothing but get you and all your friends killed. I know your new governor, Karla. She's an awful fiend."

"Like you." I grit my teeth together.

Portia gives me a mock pout. "I'm here to help you. Karla has a special place for girls like you and she is just waiting to dig in."

"This is all *your* fault."

"You have no way out." Portia enunciates every word with its own punch. "Pretty soon the sun will come up and all those hungry guards out there are going to be begging for the chance to present you to their governor like a juicy piece of mutton."

I resist the pull that holds me to my chair. Clenching my arms and hands, I make a motion to fling my body to my feet. My mother flinches slightly as I push against her incantation.

"You are strong. That doesn't come from this lump over here." Portia nods toward my father.

Malcolm's arms are held to the table like mine and I realize he's under the same spell.

"What do you want from me?"

"I want nothing but to rescue you from this predicament. I'm offering you a free pass. Leave now with me while we still have the cover of darkness. I'll get you out of this territory unscathed, and you'll be so far away from Karla she'll forget you exist."

"So my choice is between a deranged governor who hasn't even managed to sniff me out yet and . . . you? I'll take my chances with Karla."

Portia leans in, slamming her palms onto the table. Her face, inches from mine, bears an odd resemblance to my own reflection. "You want to bring down this Warwick government, right? Well, that's what I'm here to do. You really want to start a rebellion? Come with me and we'll overthrow this whole country! There's no trick here, Camilla. I'm gifting you an escape from all your problems and a chance to destroy the Supreme Ruler that commanded the execution of your brother."

Portia takes a deep breath. Slowly she returns to a standing position. I hold my lips tightly together in silent defiance. Portia runs her tongue across her lips, leaving a shimmery coat. Lifting her right hand, she stretches out her fingers and waves them gently over the table. Instantly the weight leaves my shoulders and I'm free to move. Malcolm stands. He kicks his chair in frustration and turns his back from us.

"Leave," Malcolm moans from across the room. His voice is strained and exhausted.

"I'll leave this wretched place when I wish," Portia snaps.

I come to my feet and stand toe-to-toe with my mother. She may believe that she's shocked me with her appearance tonight, but Knox warned me that Portia would show herself again. It's likely, he said, that she would come to me many times, like she did with Tuor. So I planned for this moment. I planned for what I would say to the woman who nearly cost me Tuor's life.

"I would be more content as a diseased beggar, licking the feet of Quinten Warwick, than to be daily in your presence."

I'd pondered those words and questioned if that was actually true. Quinten played an equal part in what happened to Tuor. But the difference, I reasoned, is that Quinten holds no special powers. My mother has the power to control me without touch. In the end, I'd rather deal with flesh and bones than whatever elements make up my mother's body.

The muscles in Portia's face twitch. My body is tense, on edge. I know she can kill me in an instant and perhaps now she will, but that at least would be my choice.

"You would rather cling to those people that you think love you dearly. They don't love you, Camilla. *I* am your mother. You are my blood and that will never change." Portia drifts away from me and crosses her arms over her chest. "I will not force you to come with me."

"Why not?"

"Because I want you, all of you, and that includes your free will. I want a daughter, not some . . . slave."

Something about the word *daughter* leaves me feeling strange. I've never thought of myself as anyone's daughter, not even Malcolm's. I swallow the feeling and hold my chin up high.

"Then what do you say of your spell that compelled me to come here? Where is the free will in that?"

Portia closes in again and takes a lock of my hair between her fingers. "It was for your greater good. It's true. I had to trap you, but only to show you that there's freedom available for you."

I shake my head, struggling with her twisted logic. Portia lets go of my hair. She picks up the box from the table and places it in my hands.

"I can't take full credit for bringing you here. You did have a genuine desire for the box." She takes a look around the room as if she's proud of the mess she's leaving behind. "It's time for me to leave. I'm afraid the sun's coming up and even *you* will have a tough time escaping now. When you come to your senses and decide to leave this territory for good—"

"I won't," I say through gritted teeth.

My mother's eyes lock onto mine. "If you change your mind, just ask me to come."

With the slight raise of her eyebrows, she gives me an unconvincing frown and then saunters out the door. I cross the room and lift the flap that covers the back window. The glow of a breaking sun streams through the trees. I watch as my mother walks east upriver. Her steps are quick but confident. I blink to let my eyes adjust to the new brightness. When I search through the trees for her caped figure, she's no longer there.

I turn from the window, too awestruck from what just happened to look at anything in particular. At the table, I set down the box and run my hand over the top. My mother used this happy memory between Tuor and me to trick me into her snare. I understand it now. She hoped I'd see the impossibility of getting out of the swamps without being caught, and I'd be forced to leave with her. Maybe she's still close by, waiting for me to call her name and rescue me.

Malcolm rubs the back of his neck, the stress of seeing his wife an irritation to his body. "You should be hiding in a cave." His words have bite. "What are you still doing in this territory?"

I scrunch my brows as I consider his question. What *am* I still doing in Bear Gap? "I want to save it."

"You should have left when you had a chance."

Voices chatter on the other side of the shack wall. I rush again to the window and peer across the valley. The neighbors are stirring. Soon the farm will open its gates. Like a nest of ants, they emerge from their homes and climb the hill to work. I could leave now and make a run for it. I could wait until everyone's left for the farm. Maybe there are fewer guards at that time. I could hide here until sunset but that would leave me trapped.

"They do house checks now," Malcolm says. My father's face is painted with anguish. He looks at me with a hopeless stare. "Ain't no one gets out of here without being seen . . . except your mother.

CHAPTER EIGHT

"YOU NEED TO help me," I insist.

Malcolm shakes his head. "Too many people livin' down here recognize you. They all want that reward money Karla's offering. Lina, next door, still mentions you all the time."

"She wouldn't turn me in."

"She would." Malcolm rubs at his beard. "Why do you think she keeps askin' about you?"

I swallow hard. "Please. If I'm caught, Karla will kill me."

Malcolm looks at me as if I weren't his child but instead a stranger, intruding in his home.

"I wouldn't mind a few hundred rings for myself."

I tilt my chin upward. "You'd turn me in, after I supported you my whole life?"

"I'm havin' to work at the farm myself now. It ain't easy not having you here." I stare at my father, daring him to attempt to turn me in. I reach for my dagger. The rustling of feet outside grows louder. Malcolm holds my gaze, then lets out an anguished sigh.

"Put this on," he says, tossing me a straw hat with a wide brim. "Tuck your hair inside. Maybe that hat will cover your face enough that you won't be recognized."

I touch the rough fibers of the hat with the tips of my fingers. My father slips on his boots and pulls on a jacket. I watch him stupidly.

"Put it on," he barks. "It's the best I got." I stare a moment longer as he rises to his feet and steps toward me. "I wouldn't turn you in. I wouldn't give Karla or your mother the satisfaction. Put that box in your bag and give it to me."

"I'm not giving you my box."

"You've been carrying that bag with you to work everyday since you were a kid. People will recognize it. Let me wear it and they'll just assume you left it behind."

I hold tight to the strap of my bag. I don't trust my father but what could he do with my box to hurt me? Voices echo through the cracks in the wall. The mob has started to move.

"You can take your chances with the other workers, or you can hang behind as a straggler and get noticed by a soldier. It's your choice."

Malcolm is right. This is my only chance. The more people that leave the swamps, the less my chance to get lost in the crowd of them. I shove the box into my messenger bag and hand it over. Malcolm takes my bag and throws it over his shoulder. I keep my dagger though, sticking it into my pants and flopping my shirt over top of the handle. Then I take the hat and push all of my dark curly hair inside. The hat is far too big for me, but I think it helps, because I pull the hat down as far as I can, so it sits low on my forehead.

"You go out there first," Malcolm says. "Don't walk too close to me."

I look at my father, the man I ratted out to Supervisor Benedek. Why is he helping me? I imagined Malcolm would beg for the opportunity to drag me by the collar and deliver me to the nearest Warwick soldier. His visceral hatred of this government is the only thing that keeps him on my side.

I crack open the door and look out at the bustling workers. Could my father also be pushing me into his own kind of trap? Warwick soldiers pace the swamps, watching every passerby with keen eyes. If he *is* setting me up, what other option do I have to get out of this?

The door shuts behind me as I creep along the edge of the shack. I'm hyperaware of every soldier in my line of vision. Crowds ascend the hill that leads into town. I tilt my head downward and assimilate myself with the other farm workers. I don't walk slowly. I don't walk fast. I walk the same exact speed as them. I ease my gaze to my right and see Malcolm walking not far from me. He avoids my eyes.

The soldiers stand in a formation that creates a tunnel for all the workers to walk through. They scan our bodies as we pass, cresting the hill into Rande Square.

"Where's Hensen?" one of the soldiers barks.

"How should I know?" another responds with the shrug of his shoulders.

I keep my head low to let the brim of Malcolm's straw hat cover my face. Hensen. Are they talking about the soldier I stabbed early this morning? I glance down at my jacket and am relieved to see that the blood spatter has dried to a dull brown. Breathe, I remind myself.

Bracing for the bustling sound of the town square, I'm surprised to find it oddly subdued. Where are the food and bread cart owners who beg the farm workers to buy their goods?

We pass the square and the posting tree. Reaper's Way is deathly quiet. The normal chatter of people heading to work is silenced by the overwhelming presence of Warwick soldiers. It seems no one can take a step in this town anymore without a pair of Warwick eyes on their back. We walk like mindless Warwick minions.

On my right is the Justice House. Behind me, Malcolm is keeping a steady distance. I catch the eye of a woman. I know her. I mean, I don't know her name, but I remember seeing her face at the farm when I worked there. She squints at me, the morning sun flashing off the whites of her eyes. I spin my head around quickly.

The crowd slows as we approach the entrance to the farm. My heart flip-flops at the sight of the iron gate. I want to turn around and look at Malcolm again but I can't risk seeming suspicious. What do I do now? I won't be admitted to the farm. My brand is destroyed. I need to get out of here, but I'm not leaving without my bag. I'm not leaving without the box.

Malcolm's thick hand squeezes the back of my elbow. The crowd shuffles forward a few paces. At the gate, soldiers check the credentials of each worker before allowing them to pass. On either side of me are woods. I need to escape but soldier's guard both sides of Reaper's Way.

"Here," Malcolm whispers. He hands me my bag.

A man to my left eyes me curiously. I can't help it. I turn around and the woman behind me is staring. My breathing picks up. Panicked, I twist forward.

"It *is* her," the woman says.

Malcolm leans in close to my ear. "Run."

"That's Camilla Crim!" This time she screams.

I break from the crowd, pushing sweaty bodies out of my way. A hand grazes my arm. I push myself to the left, trying to dodge the closest soldier. He grabs the back of my jacket as I scream. I fling my bag, hitting him in the side. The bag falls to the ground with a crack.

"My box," I gasp, momentarily distracted.

I look up to see Malcolm step forward. He punches the soldier hard in the mouth.

"RUN!"

I grab my bag and flee between the trees. I look back a moment later to see Malcolm helplessly lying on the ground, but I keep running. Every soldier within shouting distance is chasing me. Run, I tell myself, RUN! My father's words ring through my ears. Branches whip past my face. Behind me, heavy footsteps pursue. Malcolm's hat threatens to fly off my head and I almost let it. Instead I pull it off and hold it tight in my hand.

A soldier barks instructions. "You—north! You—round her from the south!"

I fall into a shallow creek, then claw my way up the other side. My lungs burn. I'm wishing now that I had brought Shae with me. I stumble to the ground, my body so weak and tired from the night's trip. I pull myself onto my hands and knees. Scanning the woods, I try to remember which direction is Johnny's. But I can't run back to Johnny's now. They'll just track me there and endanger everyone else.

It's quiet but only for a moment. I jump onto my feet and sprint. A horse breaks my path, galloping in front of me. I spin around, searching for an exit. Another soldier blocks my way, then another, until I'm fully surrounded my Karla's hunters.

Bound by my wrists, I'm forced out of the woods. My desperate sprint to safety didn't get me as far as I thought. Within moments I'm back among the farm workers. Malcolm stands where I left him, a look of seething anger on his face. He's restrained too. A person caught helping me won't be treated warmly by Karla. I give my father a deadpan look.

I'm pushed down Reaper's Way, a mob of gawking farm workers move aside as I'm paraded past them. I was once one of these sullen, dirty-cheeked people. Now I'm better off . . . right? My eyes flicker shut, then open, then shut again from lack of sleep. I'm too tired to struggle against my captor but manage one pathetic twist of my body, which only results in a tighter grip on my elbow.

We cross the threshold of the iron gate. The pearly white stone path that used to lead up to Harras Manor has been trampled under. It's tiny stones kicked away and strewn among the tall grass. Weeds pepper the lawn. Vines have infiltrated the delicately trimmed bushes and plants around the front of the house.

I tilt my head upward as we curve around to the back of the estate. Beneath the flapping Warwick flag that hangs from the highest pinnacle, the windows appear dim, not from lack of light, but by soot that hasn't been cleaned away. Through the dirty glass, I spot the image of a woman, a toothy smile on her face.

My captors march me past the heart of the farm. The acres and acres of rolling fields look anemic and sickly. It's still early spring, but I know this land well enough to know it should already be sprouting with white and green. How is all of Elmyra supposed to be eating from this supply?

A Warwick soldier pulls open the back door of the manor and I'm dragged through the sitting room. I recall this room as being bright with the morning sunrise, but instead it feels like a space that's been left and forgotten. In a matter of months, this stately, well-kept home has turned into a place I imagine to be infested with spirits.

We take the spiral staircase that leads to the higher floors. My mind has not forgotten the last time I was taken this way, when I was granted my meeting with Governor Leo. Only now, I have no choice in the matter, and it's Governor Karla that I'm sure is hungrily awaiting my arrival.

Light and distant moaning drifts across the stone walls. My body quivers as we pass the fourth-floor landing, where I remember Governor Leo's office was located. It feels like I'm back in the dungeons of the Justice House, that sense that I may never leave this place.

The stairwell comes to an abrupt end on the fifth and highest floor of the house. Quick, excited footsteps come hammering down the hall toward me. A barefooted woman dressed in a loose, sheer gown runs to us in movements that resemble a dance. A squeal of excitement pops from Karla's lips.

"Ah! You've found her, haven't you? Oh, I prayed as I watched from the window that it was her that had scurried into the wood. Like a little mouse fleeing a cat, that's what you looked like."

Karla playfully touches a finger to the tip of my nose. She leans in only a few inches from my face. Her cheeks are flushed red and her stringy hair falls over her bony shoulders and shrunken chest.

"Camilla Crim as you requested, Governor," the guard says.

Karla looks up and addresses the company of soldiers that surround me. "I'll forgive your trespasses for today since you've finally brought me the girl. Now stop delaying and follow me!"

The soldier who spoke a moment ago hesitates before obeying his governor. Karla skips down the hall. A hollow, tinny sound echoes over the floor and walls. We pass a room with its door hanging open. I look to my right. A young girl in a ragged cotton dress hangs on the bars of a rusty cage. I find the source of the painful cries when we pass the next room. Another girl, young and thin, lies on the ground, chains around her feet.

Weeping emanates from that same room. A crying girl sits on the cold floor, mending one of Karla's dresses. My eyebrows knit together. I turn away from the vision of the suffering girls. This place may be worse than the dungeons. It's a prison, specially reserved for young girls . . . like me.

CHAPTER NINE

AT THE END of the hall, Karla swings open the double doors to her bedroom and welcomes us in like someone might warmly invite a guest into their home. A little dog barks viciously the moment he spots us, circling about the room as if he were defending it.

A four-poster bed with a deep maroon coverlet is the centerpiece of the dark, smoky room. On the vanity sits a dagger next to a brass bowl of red powder. There's a sharp smell in the room, gardenia maybe, but it's mixed with something else I don't recognize.

"Tie her up over there," Karla instructs. She sits on the edge of her bed and watches with delight. She's jittery, her hands unable to stop moving. She seems excited and impatient like a child being tempted with a piece of candy. The dog jumps onto the bed next to her and continues his barking. His hair has been recently washed and groomed and a bow the color of Warwick maroon has been tied around his neck.

"Governor, with all due respect," the soldier begins. He carefully crosses the room and lowers his voice as he speaks. "I must insist we put her in the dungeons. It's unsafe to have her here."

"Quiet, Ralf!"

Ralf lets out an unsatisfied sigh and then signals to the other men to do as she instructed. He looks to be a good soldier, tall and fit. He wears a crisp uniform, but seems to hold back a slew of disagreements about Karla's treatment of me.

On the wall opposite Karla's bed hang two chains from the ceiling. My wrists are secured into the cuffs of the chains so that my arms hang midair next to my head. One soldier bends to the floor to pull off my boots and socks then attach another set of chains around my ankles. As he latches the iron against my skin, Karla's dog charges me but then stops short. He bares his short but sharp teeth. His bark is like a high-pitched screech that never stops.

Back and forth, the dog looks to strike at me, but then hesitates. Karla remains poised on her bed, chewing her fingernails impatiently. As the soldier moves to secure my other ankle, the dog makes his attack, striking out and biting the soldier's wrist.

The soldier yelps, leaping to his feet and grabbing his wrist as a trickle of blood oozes between his fingers. Without another thought, the soldier kicks the dog with the side of his boot, cursing its existence. Karla's face explodes with shock.

"Benny!" She scoops up her now whimpering dog. She strokes its fur before crossing the room and slapping the soldier across the face. The soldier suddenly realizes his error.

"You monster! No one touches my Benny, no one." Karla looks to Ralf. "I want him punished."

"Governor," Ralf begins.

"He should be treated as horribly as my poor Benny."

Ralf seems to search for the right words to diffuse Karla's vengeance. "A night in the stocks should cure his cruelty toward small animals."

"That won't do," Karla weeps. She turns to look out the tall, narrow window that faces the farm. "Give him to the savages in the field. Tie him up and let them beat on him like he did my Benny."

Ralf opens his mouth to protest but then stops himself. Karla's a Warwick, a cousin of Quinten's. She holds far too much power over his life. He can't say no to her.

Instead Ralf takes the bitten soldier roughly in his hands, and before removing him from Karla's room, he instructs another soldier to finish securing my chains. My ankles are bound so tight I can barely move my legs. I shake against the restraints, panic spreading to my limbs.

"She had these on her," another soldier says as he delivers my messenger bag and Malcolm's straw hat to Karla.

Incredibly despite my delirium and fear of being between these walls, I'm still very aware of the box that's tucked away in my bag. I risked torture, which I'm certain I'm about to endure, for that dumb wooden box.

"And this." The soldier pulls my dagger from his own belt and hands it to Karla. She's far less interested in my things than she is in me. She tosses my bag and the hat and my dagger onto her bed.

"Leave us," Karla says, her eyes pinned on me.

After a quiet exit, I'm left alone with Karla and her ravenous dog, who's now content to curl up on her bed. Hunger brews on Karla's face. She looks at me like she finds my appearance delicious. I rattle my chains and the sound is absorbed into the void of the castle. There's no one here to help me, no one.

Knox was right. I should have stayed at Johnny's, where it was safe. I should have been content to live in peace and safety but I had to stir things up. I had to prove to Knox that I could defend myself. I can't think about how incredibly stupid I've been. All I can think about is how terrified I am right now.

"I've waited so long for this!" Karla exclaims with a giggle.

"I didn't kill your husband." I speak quickly. It's the only thing I can think to stay and it is, after all, the truth. Karla presses her lips into a hard line. "I didn't kill him, I swear. You have the wrong person."

"Shut up!"

"I'm sorry he died. He shouldn't have died but it wasn't me who did it." I'm not sorry her husband is dead. That's a lie, but the words seem to at least throw her off balance.

Her voice is whiny like a child's. "You're ruining it!"

"It was another person, a woman. Her name is Portia."

"Stop talking," Karla growls.

"She's here in Rande. If you let me go, I can take you to her, and you can get the justice your husband deserves." The words pour from my mouth. I have no idea how I'd manage to locate my mother, but I'll worry about that later.

"Argg!" Karla slams her fists into the mattress. Benny's head pops up, his slumber disturbed.

"I didn't kill him," I shout.

"You're just a little liar. That's all."

Karla stands, steps toward me, and hits me across the face with the palm of her hand. Although she's thin, Karla's hit was worse than I expected. When she steps back, she stares at me, her cracked lips parted. Relief seems to flow over her as if doling out violence were soothing.

Karla's voice is calm now. "I finally have you all to myself."

"Please . . . I didn't kill him," I whisper. My chest heaves up and down with each terrified breath I take.

Karla takes a deep breath, then daintily leans over and kisses me on the forehead. "I must go. I have preparations to make."

She turns on her heels and scurries out the door, leaving me alone in her perfectly designed dungeon. I pull on my cuffs but the chains are bolted to the ceiling with iron rings. They rattle and shiver like a ghostly wind chime. I cry out, but all I can hear are the other unfortunate girls who've been locked up with me.

Benny wakes from his nap. The dog jumps from the bed and stands in front of me, barking incessantly like it's his job. He growls and takes a defensive stance, his long claws scratching against the floor. Every few moments he circles about the bed as if looking at me from a different spot will change my appearance. For hours Benny sings me his tune. The only variance in the melody is when he occasionally stops to gnaw at an itch on his leg.

Karla's bedroom grows incredibly hot. The fireplace blazes constantly. Normally I'd think this was a torture tactic, but Karla is so strange, I believe this might be the temperature she prefers. Every hour a girl enters to tend the fire. She's young, even younger than the others, maybe ten or eleven years old. She walks past Benny and me without even glancing in my direction. My only assumption is that it's part of her norm to see a body hanging from these chains.

Her hair is brown and straggly like Karla's. Her dress is threadbare but still better maintained than Karla's captives'. The first few times I see her, I call out, begging for a response, even if it's only a few words of encouragement. I get nothing in return. She's either well trained or simply used to ignoring requests for help.

In and out the little girl goes all day long. She brings Benny water and fresh meat scraps from the kitchen but nothing for me, not even an acknowledging glance. This inane routine continues until nightfall. It feels like weeks that I've been stuck here. The girl enters again to turn down Karla's bed. She carries a feather duster and half-heartedly dusts the dresser. The feathers lazily move across the wood, only stirring up the dust that lies there.

At Karla's vanity, the little girl picks up the gleaming dagger, dusts underneath, and then sets it down again. She crosses the middle of the room as her eyes shift in my direction. I spot her dark irises. Her little hands grasp the edge of the stuffy maroon drapes and pulls them completely over the window so that not a drop of sunlight pierces the room.

She won't help me. I know that. Pathetic pleas seem to annoy her instead of eliciting any sympathy. So I won't waste my breath, but there's still something I don't yet understand. If Karla meant to exact revenge on me for murdering her husband, then why hasn't she killed me yet?

"What will she do with me?"

The little girl turns to look at me, her hands still resting on the drapes. I follow her movements as she walks to the center of the room and stands directly in front of me.

"Whatever she likes," the girl says. Her face is placid and impartial.

We stare for a moment, then the girl starts to break away.

"Why doesn't she beat you?"

I doubt she'll indulge me with an answer, but I have nothing to lose in asking. The girl hesitates, then brings her eyes back to mine. With the feather duster still in her hand, she reaches for the cuff of her sleeve and pulls it up past her elbow. Thin, dark scars speckle her arm as if she'd been splattered with the wounds.

The maid says nothing as she lowers her sleeve. Her face is unchanged. It doesn't ask for help or even pity. Slowly she turns her body and looks to Karla's vanity. I follow her eye line and my gaze lands on the dagger.

I swallow hard, realizing the fate that lies ahead of me: death by a thousand cuts. But will I be so lucky as to find death? Or will I be forced to pick up a job like the other girls, cooking, cleaning, mending . . . ?

"Don't worry," the girl says. "She'll soon become bored with you."

I'm not sure if it's from the fire or a fever, but suddenly I feel heat rising to my face. I moan as I pull on my chains. Her empty expression only drives me crazier. My body convulses as I whip and thrash on my restraints.

"Let me out! Let me out!"

As if to add to my torture, the girl simply glares in my direction, then turns and walks out of the room. I desperately try to slip my hands from the cuffs. They're so tight, as if forged especially for small wrists. I'm soon exhausted and out of breath. A ring of blood encircles my hands where the rough iron scrapes my skin.

I pull hard on the chains. Maybe I can rip their clasps from the ceiling. I imagine that many a girl has hung here but maybe no one as strong as me. I've been training with Johnny after all. I bear my whole weight down on the chains and tug hard. I moan as if the sound escaping from my mouth could will the bolts to yield. But the screaming only stirs Benny up more.

I collapse back into my hanging position. My neck is tense and fiery with pain. My legs buckle, which only adds more strain on my wrists and arms.

Finally I scream, unconcerned about Benny's response or what Karla might do to me. I want her to walk through those doors. I want something to happen besides being left here to rot! And perhaps, I realize, that is exactly what Karla wanted.

CHAPTER TEN

IT'S DEEP INTO the night when Karla finally returns. She acts as if she's been gone a mere five minutes.

"I'm going to keep you for a long time," she says, swaying her body away from me. Benny is finally quiet. He hops onto the bed and watches his owner. Her movements are childlike. She undresses in front of me and dons a sleeping gown. Every few moments she looks over her shoulder as if to ensure she's keeping my attention. I close my eyes, too disgusted by the image of her. Karla is not pleased. She runs across the room and shakes me until I open my eyes.

"Don't do that again!" she scolds, but something in her tone tells me she hopes I will so she has a reason to punish me.

Karla's bizarre behavior continues all through the night. I'm forced to watch her as she sits at her vanity and coats her eyes in black paint and her cheeks with rouge. All the while chattering about where she purchased the rouge and how she sent a kitchen maid to the stocks today because she tried to poison her dinner.

Every time I look away or drift into unconsciousness, Karla violently wakes me. She slaps me across the face so many times that when I catch a glimpse of myself in her vanity mirror, my face is covered in bruises. It's a fun little game to her. Between striking me, she paints polish onto her toenails, feeds Benny treats, and dances around her room with an invisible partner.

With the rouge still on her cheeks, she blows out all the candles and slips into bed. Benny curls up close to his owner and I experience a moment of peace. But having time to think only sends my mind to horrid places. I've been here for one day, *one day*, and I'm on the brink of madness. Her torture comes so gently it could make an executioner queasy.

As I hang from my chains, I realize I'm not so much Karla's prisoner as I am her rag doll, a toy, a thing to flit around and play with until she's distracted with something else. There's nothing I can do but hang. My arms go numb. My body is too weak to hold me up. I slip into unconsciousness and into a world where Karla can't get me.

A cold hand smacking me across the face stirs me awake. Karla gives me an elfish grin. I feel sweaty and sick all over. My legs are so wobbly I can't stand anymore, so I'm forced to hang like a deer carcass from a meat hook. Karla rises refreshed and excited. Benny's barking has begun, and Karla is giddy.

She dresses herself in a magnificent evening gown. It's an A-line style with fluttery capped sleeves. As usual, its color is Warwick maroon, but this dress is adorned with gold stitching and an embroidered bodice. Karla completes the look with long silk gloves and then twists her hair into a messy updo that's secured with a matching gold clip. Strings of greasy hair hang around her face and neck.

"Mmmm." Karla breathes in the morning air as she pulls the curtains open. "There's to be a show this morning." I glare at her with bleary eyes. "My darling Leo never took me to the theater like I wanted." Karla undoes the hook that holds the window closed and swings its panel wide. Cool spring air rushes into the room. I gulp it in through my mouth as if it were a glass of water. Karla shivers as if the refreshing air is too harsh for her delicate skin.

She looks at me sharply. "I think you should watch this too. You'll love it." A giggle escapes Karla's lips before she rushes to the bedroom door. "Come!" she screeches down the hall. She leaves the door hanging open and rushes to the window.

A mixture of weeping and moaning sounds drift in from the hall. I can't see any of Karla's other playthings, but I imagine them bruised and malnourished and probably far thirstier than me. How long have they been trapped here? I reach for my ears to block out the sound of suffering. I just can't take one more painful thought. A Warwick soldier enters, shutting the door behind him. I feel ashamed that I can now feel some relief from the sounds of pain.

"Unchain her," Karla demands. Immediately the soldier pulls a key from his belt and begins to unlock the braces around my ankles. "Bring her to the window."

I'd have crumpled to the ground if the soldier didn't have my arms restrained the moment I was loose. It's ridiculous to think I could fight back. I can barely stand. With the soldier holding me from behind, he drags my lifeless body to the window.

"Hurry, hurry! Get her in close so she can see."

My eyes behold the rolling fields of the farm. I take in a deep breath as the air cools my sweaty brow. I can see it all: row after row of farmland, the orchards in the back, the tall stockyard fence that encompasses it all. I ponder the years I worked away in these fields and never knew what horror was taking place on the fifth floor. I wonder how close I'd come to being one of the special girls picked to tend to the governor's wife. What was it about me that Karla found so unappealing that she left me to work in the fields?

"Look! Look! There he is!" Karla pops up from her elbows, which she had resting on the windowsill, and points to a spot low in the fields, just beyond the stocks a little way. The laborers are all gathered together, the way we used to when Governor Leo would make a speech, with confused looks on their faces.

Then from the back of the house emerges Ralf holding a man by the bicep. The man is tied with his hands behind his back. Karla squeals uncontrollably. This is not just *some man*. This is the soldier that kicked Benny after the wicked dog bit him.

The soldier is led to the group of workers and forced onto his knees. I let out an achy whimper in protest. I know what's going to happen.

We watch as Ralf painfully obeys his governor, ordering the workers to strike a man who's not only one of his fellow Warwick soldiers, but likely a friend. One of the workers jumps right in, eager to have revenge on a soldier who probably barked at him in the fields or perhaps even whipped him for misbehaving. A few others join too, kicking the soldier in the stomach, then stomping on his head. Everyone is commanded to participate but some of the workers still struggle to be violent. Karla yells from the window, "You'll all be hanged if you don't do it. I swear I'll kill every one of you!"

Finally they all join in, men, women . . . children. The offending soldier is engulfed by the crowd. I feel sick. Every blow causes me to shudder while every blow fills Karla's face with elation. She quivers with excitement. The punching, the kicking, the killing of the soldier is an elixir of life to her. She gulps it down, rejuvenated.

I close my eyes. My body wilts and dies like a flower. I've worked on this farm. I know what it feels like to be constantly insulted by a Warwick soldier, to be whipped for being late or talking out. The injustices against the workers are plenteous, but even I cringe at Karla's display. It seems wrong, exchanging violence with more violence.

"Hey," she barks, snapping a finger in front of my face.

I open my eyes but struggle to see. The room spins into a foggy cloud. Benny yelps at my feet. I sink farther into the soldier's grip.

"Wake up," Karla says, but even her demands can't force my body to obey, and soon I'm enveloped in darkness.

A trickle of icy cold water down my back returns me to Karla's room. I'm again in my chains, hanging from her ceiling. Karla steps away from me, a wet rag in her hand. She grins as if she's just played a funny joke on me.

"You're not as strong as some of the others," she pouts. "A day and a half and already you're dying."

"Please—please give me water."

Taunting me, Karla slowly brings a brown cup up to my face.

"Well, I have to, don't I, if we're going to continue our fun?"

She barely tilts the cup to my mouth so that only a slow trickle touches my tongue. I suck in the cold water, but after three sips she pulls it away and watches me with fascination.

"What do you want from me?"

It's a silly question. My suffering is what she wants. I'm giving it to her this very moment. She takes a step closer, brings the cup to my lips, and allows me one more sip. Karla returns the cup to her vanity and sits on her bed so she's facing me. Benny jumps up and curls onto her lap. For a few long moments, Karla just watches me.

When she seems to have grown bored, she rises to her feet and announces that she'll be taking her noontime meal in the dining room. I can't decipher any longer if she says these things simply to hear herself speak or to tease me. It's been nearly two days since I've eaten anything. As she exits the bedroom, Benny resumes his relentless barking.

Again, I'm left alone for hours. My only reprieve from Benny's barking is the return of the young maid. This time she brings a treat for the dog. His mouth is now busy with a bone from the kitchen. I can smell the fresh meat that's been left behind and feel disgusted with myself that I wish it were me gnawing on the bone.

I fall in and out of consciousness until Karla returns and forces me to stay awake. It's then that I realize I've soiled myself. The stench that's been burning my nose is coming from me.

The curtains remain drawn. I've lost all instinct of the time of day. The only thing I know is that Karla has chosen now to pay me lots of attention.

She engages me in conversation. "Where shall I place this new vase? I spotted it in the sitting room and had to bring it here. It's so large though, I had a dreadful time calling for help to carry it up. The blue coloring reminds me of a toy I had as a little girl." Karla rubs a smudge from the vase with her thumb, then spins around to face me, a cheery smile on her face. "How does it look? Ahhh, I love it! It's still quite chilly outside. I wasn't bred for the cold weather." Karla lounges on her bed to face me. "I'll be happy when summer comes. What do you think of the wheat shortage? It seems to grow worse despite plenty of rain."

I don't answer. The wheat shortage grows worse because it appears that she's made no preparations to plant more wheat. Her madness is dizzying.

Karla twists her dirty hair between her fingers. Her face drops and her eyes turn serious. "I do wish I had my husband here with me." Like a mother guilting her child into good behavior, Karla looks at me with an expression that speaks both sadness and disappointment. I've learned to stop telling her I didn't kill Leo. Although, if his absence truly does cause her pain, I wish I had been the one to slit his throat.

"On a night like this he'd hold me and keep me warm."

Karla slinks off the bed and onto her feet. She stands in front of her vanity mirror and places a hand on her dagger. She waits, hovering over its handle until she's sure I've noticed. Then she snatches the dagger and looks closely at its gleaming blade. I close my eyes. Finally my moment has come.

CHAPTER ELEVEN

WHEN I OPEN my eyes Karla is looking directly at me. She walks toward me, her back straight and the dagger confidently at her side. She raises the blade to my face and lets the cool metal touch my cheek.

"I've had such a busy day," she says, spinning on her heels. "I think I'll just go to sleep."

Karla opens the drawer on her nightstand and gently places the dagger inside. She calls Benny to bed and envelops him in the covers. Soon it's dark and quiet. My heart thunders like a beating drum. Insanity creeps into my mind with the silent passage of time.

I'm in almost complete darkness but still the walls of Karla's bedroom seem to close in on me. The floor melts away and I'm hanging above a deep pit. The pit is infested with snakes and spiders. A link on my chain weakens and snaps.

My mother's voice is in my ear. It's the first I've heard it since seeing her at the shack. I whip my head to the right, expecting to see her dark figure. There's no one there. The pit disappears and the floor returns to my feet. Sweat pours from my scalp and bathes my eyes. I can't see it, but I know it's there. Under Karla's bed, I sense my box. All at once I realize the box is the source of my mother's voice.

***

Savage shrieks crack through my nightmare-ridden slumber. Karla's screams evolve into laughter as her face shifts from horror to delight. She's joyful as she dances around the bedroom, Benny close on her heels. I don't know what to make of this mood. It's not one I've seen before. Pure elation spills from her face as she falls to her knees in front of me. She brings both hands up under her chin and giggles. It's then that I notice the dagger in her hand.

How could I ever believe I'd be brave in the face of death? Bravery is far away and all I feel is terror. "I didn't kill him! Please, I didn't do it!"

Karla laughs, then strikes like a serpent. The knife stings my thigh, poking a hole in my trousers. Jumping to her feet, Karla licks her lips, then takes her knife and slowly runs it diagonally down my abdomen. I scream out. My voice bounces off the stone walls, growing louder and louder until I'm enveloped in the sound of my own pain.

My face is wet with tears. My body's been cut in half. I can't look down. I can't face it.

Ralf barges through the door. His face is placid yet annoyed.

Karla ignores his presence. She issues two more strikes, one on my arm and one on my knee before Ralf speaks. "This is foolish, Governor."

Karla huffs. "She's completely helpless. Look at her! Her eyes are closed like a newborn pup."

"You shouldn't be spending your time with this." Ralf speaks through gritted teeth.

Karla turns on her heels to face Ralf. Her voice goes cold. "I am your governor."

"A governor should be managing their territory. You are responsible for this farm."

"All those governor duties are boring!" Karla whines.

"If you don't get things in order, the country will starve."

I blink my eyes open. Ralf stands at the end of the bed. Karla is wet with my blood as she slaps Ralf across the face. He blinks slowly.

"Let them starve! And you too for speaking to me this way. I'll have you placed in the stocks." Karla turns from him and looks at me, her toy. "Release her from the chains."

Ralf hesitates.

"Now!" Karla screams.

Frustrated, Ralf starts by unlocking the cuffs from my ankles. When he stands to remove them from my wrists, I see splotches of red have dripped onto his hands and realize it's my blood. His eyes connect with mine. He pauses and whispers, "I'm sorry."

My head is a miry pit. I struggle to comprehend his words. Sorry? Sorry for what? Who knows how many times Ralf has watched a display like this unfold. He unhinges the final cuff from my wrist. I collapse, rolling onto my side and clutching my stomach, which feels like a warm, wet rag.

"Leave us," Karla says.

Ralf lets out an aggravated sigh. He hurries from the room, leaving the door hanging open. Karla barely notices. I peer up at my attacker. She stands over me, gripping her dagger. It's time for the final blow, I tell myself. Soon the misery will be over. I close my eyes and wait for her to end me, but instead, I feel a sting of pain on my arm. My eyes pop open. Karla has drawn a tiny cut on my bicep. She reaches out and cuts me again on my cheek.

My body jerks as I scramble backward. Like a bird pecking away at a worm, Karla's arm strikes out and cuts me again on the arm, then a little slice on my neck. I crawl backward on the rough stone floor. Her knife catches the back of my hand as I raise it to protect my face.

My back collides with the base of Karla's dresser. A glass bottle of perfume falls and shatters on the floor. I scream out, shifting on all fours and crawling to the side of the bed. A path of smeared blood trails behind me. I feel a slice across my back. I grab for her nightstand, hoping my hands will land on something to throw at her. The knife catches me on my shoulder, then the back of my thigh. My arms fall to my side, leaving bloody handprints on the nightstand and floor. I curl my legs and arms into me, clutching the hair on the side of my head. I become a motionless, bleeding lump on the floor of Karla's bedroom. Faint footsteps march down the hall.

"Governor."

The attack stops. Karla's face loses all of its pleasure. "What?" she says spinning around.

I grasp at the side of Karla's bed and pull myself up to see Ralf standing in the doorway with four other soldiers.

"This behavior must stop," he growls.

"What is this?" Karla spits. Her face turns a color that resembles Warwick maroon. "All of you shall spend a week in the stocks!"

Ralf mutters, "Shut up, you old hag."

He lunges at Karla, taking her neck in his one hand while punching her with the other. She staggers backward. Knife still in hand, Karla takes a jab at Ralf. He grabs her by the wrist but not before she manages to slice his ear.

"Stop—" Karla moans.

She tries to yell but all that comes out is gurgling. Ralf presses hard on her throat. Karla crumbles as the other soldiers close in on her. Benny goes ballistic. He jumps to the bed and barks and growls as Ralf and the other men force her onto her stomach and secure her hands behind her back.

The moment Ralf's hand leaves her neck, Karla screams out, shrill and piercing. "He hurt my Benny. No one hurts my Benny!"

Ralf kneels down and takes Karla's ragged hair in his hand. He turns her head to spit in her face.

"Cease this atrocity right now." A calm voice breaks through Karla's shrieks. "You will not harm a member of the Supreme Ruler's family."

Ralf stands, shifting his body to reveal Supervisor Benedek, the man that once made my days here at the farm miserable. He's short and scrawny compared to Ralf.

"Why not?" Ralf shouts. "She's killed too many of our men. She deserves to die."

"If you harm a Warwick"—Benedek clasps his hands clasped together under floppy sleeves—"you'll be executed."

"Who would know? The captain is here now. She's no longer our governor. We can slit her wrists and say she did it to herself."

"I'll kill you! I'll kill you!" Karla screams.

"*I* would know and I don't believe Captain Thatius would approve."

Thatius . . . I'm on the brink of passing out. Did I hear him right? That's Lawrence's father and the man who testified that my brother was a murderer.

"Pick her up," Benedek says.

Ralf roughly pulls Karla from the floor, flinging her onto her vanity chair like a rag doll. She foams at the mouth. Ralf swings his arm and hits Karla with the back of his hand so hard that her head drops and rolls on her neck as she falls into unconsciousness.

"You shouldn't have done that," Benedek says, pulling at his leather gloves.

"Do with me what you will, Supervisor, but you'll have every soldier on this farm on my side."

Supervisor Benedek adjusts his spectacles so they sit on the end of his nose. He steps farther into the room and catches a glimpse of the bloody display. Innocently I look to Benedek, hoping he'll bring me aid. He looks away, disgusted, and continues inspecting the room as if it were an intriguing piece of artwork.

"It is as bad as you said," the supervisor says.

"Let me kill her for what she's done," Ralf says, staring at Karla's limp body.

I'm not dying here, I think to myself. I need my weapon. I search the floor but only find dirty stockings, a red high-heeled shoe, and my blood speckling the tile. My head is light and dizzy. My stomach screams as I bend over. The memory of Karla shoving my bag off her bed comes back to me in a rush. I ignore the men as they argue.

My messenger bag and Malcolm's hat have slid under the bed. I pull out my bag but my dagger's not there. I run my hand along the floor and find nothing. I look across the room. Everything's blurry. The bed, the floor, the nightstand, they all appear soupy and hazy.

The nightstand. My bloody hands grapple with the nightstand drawer. Benny's incessant barking distracts. I pull open the top drawer and there lies my dagger atop a pile of other collected whips and knives. I grab it and hug my bag close to my chest, feeling the box still inside. I huddle behind the bed and pray I have enough strength to fight my way out.

"Take your men and leave," Benedek says. "We serve Warwick no matter what, and that means preserving Karla. We'll keep her locked inside. She's mad. No one can deny that." Benedek cracks the bedroom door and looks down the hall. "Get rid of them all. I don't want anyone else finding out about this stain she's brought on our reputation."

Ralf stares at Benedek, unbelieving. He turns and looks at me as if I were a dying animal.

"But first," Benedek says. "Go downstairs and greet your new governor."

Ralf and his men tentatively leave the room. Get rid of them all. I repeat the words in my mind. A panic-induced energy pulses through my body. I won't spend another moment in this room unless it's as a rotting corpse. Benedek paces impatiently next to the window. He's either forgotten I'm here or assumes I've perished. He walks to Karla and examines her face.

She's sleeping but I can tell he's still nervous in her presence.

I pull the cover off my dagger. Taking a deep breath, I stand. Carefully I skirt along the wall until Benedek notices my heavy breathing. His eyebrows are scrunched and his face looks more annoyed than confused. I stretch out my arm and see it shaking as I point my dagger at him.

"Let me go." The words are sticky in my mouth. "Or I'll kill you."

Benedek blinks at me. At the core I know him to be a coward. It's why he was wringing his hands when he thought he was alone in a room with a sleeping Karla and a dead girl. I inch toward the door.

Benedek stiffens then looks down his nose at me. "You'll bleed to death before you make it off the property."

I cross the room and retrieve my boots before slipping through the bedroom door. My body shakes with a bad fever. I look in front of and behind me, expecting to see a soldier any moment. But the hall is empty. Bloody footprints follow me. My breathing is labored.

Every noise sounds like voices echoing through a cave. I'm walking slower than I intend to be. I grab at the edge of a doorway. Inside a girl hangs from the same type of chains that I was hanging from.

"Let me out!" she screams the moment she sees me.

Her chains rattle against the wall. I stumble into the room. Other girls lie about, chained in a similar way. I approach one of the girls and stumble to the floor as I reach for her. Pulling myself up by the wall, I notice her hair is slicked with sweat. Dried blood splotches her body and the floor.

With shaky hands, I reach for the cuff around her wrist. The girl weeps in my ear and pleads for help. I fumble with the restraints but I have no way of helping her. I look over at a room full of dying girls. One hovers in the corner; she's so weak she's only been bound at her feet.

"Key?" I ask.

She cries, shaking her head. "I don't know."

I look around for an axe or a shovel. All I have is my dagger. I set my boots down and toss my bag across my chest. The strap digs into the wound on my stomach. I cringe but keep going. These girls will all die if I can't help them.

I take my dagger and try to puncture the chain. Its thick iron is not even chipped by my little blade. I pull back my arm and hit the chain again. The clanging sound mocks me. There's nothing I can do. I back away slowly, bumping into the wall behind me. My head spins. I can't help them, I realize. I feel utterly powerless.

"Please!" one of the girls yells.

I stare at them. Tears sting my eyes. I shake my head. I pick up my boots then force myself to walk out of the room. I grope down the hall. I push my emotions away. If I die with them, then there will be no one to tell Johnny and the others that Captain Thatius is in Bear Gap. So I keep moving, despite all the girls I've left behind.

The stairwell is cold and hollow. I pause at the bottom and peer into the sitting room. Expecting it to be empty, I jump back when I see it's full of Warwick soldiers. Ralf steps forward from the crowd and shakes the hand of Captain Thatius, Bear Gap's new governor. I cautiously take a step down to get a better view of the room. Ridley stands tall and stiff, clothed in his decorated Warwick uniform. My breath catches in my throat. Standing next to Captain Thatius is Lawrence.

CHAPTER TWELVE

LAWRENCE AND HIS father shake hands with the soldiers gathered in the sitting room. There is no warm smile on Lawrence's face like I remember. Dressed in a Warwick vest, he's taken the form of his father, cold, hard, emotionless . . . my eyes grow foggy as I stare.

Captain Thatius' tinny voice drifts across the room. "You are all dismissed. Return to your duties. Except for you, Ralf."

Ralf hesitates as the other soldiers exit. Captain Thatius circles the sitting room, taking a seat in a high-backed chair that faces the fields. Ralf stands at attention in front of his new governor. Lawrence is an obedient dog, moving as his father moves and never leaving his side.

Thatius speaks. "It is clear that this estate is in a deplorable condition." He surveys the room with a scrupulous eye. "Tell me what Bear Gap's greatest need is."

I slide down the wall and sit on the step, hiding myself behind a pillar. I lean my head against the cold stone wall and struggle to stay awake.

"Food is our number one concern. We don't have the hands we need to properly work the fields."

"We'll hire more workers. Recruit farther than Bear Gap. Offer them better compensation."

Ralf nods.

"Lay off the beatings until we regain their trust. There was no one guarding the gate when we arrived."

"We don't have the men. Karla pulled all of our resources into guarding the swamps. I post a man at the gate in the morning but he's often pulled away by other work."

"Fix that. Now, what of the rebellion?"

Ralf chuckles. "With respect, sir, I don't believe there is a rebellion. The governor—Karla—was obsessed with that only to get revenge for her husband." Thatius' face remains unmoving. "There are murmurs, of course, but there always exists non-Warwick supporters. Nothing to be concerned with."

"You don't find concern with the rebel that assassinated Governor Harras?"

Ralf struggles for words. "She's only a girl."

"Violence against any government agent is of great concern for me, regardless of the individual. Is it true that you have her in custody?"

"Yes, sir, but we plan to—"

"I don't want her harmed. Don't put her in the dungeons. I want her close. She will receive her punishment soon, but for now, keep her comfortable."

"Yes, sir."

I shudder, grappling for my boots. I pull them on quickly and struggle to my feet. Ralf turns toward the stairwell but it's Lawrence who hears me. He shifts his stance, and from across the room, I catch his eyes on me. I wait for him to raise a finger and point me out to his father but he doesn't. His mouth hangs open ever so slightly at the sight of me.

"One more thing," Thatius says. Ralf faces his governor. "I will rule Bear Gap as I see fit and that includes the elimination of any type of rebellion. My next priority will be to mount an attack on the remaining rebels."

"We barely have the men. Plus, we've had no luck in locating them."

Thatius looks at Ralf with an unflinching glare. "That's because you didn't know where to look."

I hug my bag closer to my chest. He plans to flush us out. The deal we struck last fall is no longer good. If I don't leave now, he'll make an attack on Johnny's cabin before they even know that Captain Thatius is back in Bear Gap.

"You may go now. Handle the situation with the girl. We'll talk again soon."

Ralf gives Captain Thatius a half bow and heads toward the stairs.

"Let me take care of her," Lawrence says flatly. I barely recognize his stilted voice.

Captain Thatius cranes his neck to look at his son. He knows that Lawrence once joined ranks with me. Why would he ever put him in charge of me now?

"I'd like to take care of Camilla," Lawrence repeats.

Thatius touches his chin. "Prove yourself, son."

My eyes widen. Slowly I step backward up the stairwell. I feel lightheaded, unsteady. Lawrence marches toward me. His walk is determined and strictly soldier-like. It's not his father I have to fear. It's him.

"Show me the fields," I hear Thatius say to Ralf.

Lawrence stands at the bottom of the stairwell. I'm frozen, too weak to move. He takes the steps, fast but controlled. He disarms my dagger and grabs my hands. I let out a whimper as he pushes me up the steps away from his father.

"Quiet," he growls in my ear.

Lawrence holds me against the wall. We watch in silence until Ralf leads Captain Thatius out of the sitting room.

"Come on," Lawrence whispers.

He pulls me down the steps by my hand. We move through the sitting room and into the front hall. It's quiet, eerily quiet. Lawrence takes me out the front door. We crouch behind the bushes that line the front of the manor. My breath comes heavy in my chest. Lawrence looks at me but he doesn't ask. He doesn't ask what happened to me or how I came to be covered in my own blood. Maybe it's because he already knows. Maybe he can't risk knowing.

I glance at the front gate, expecting to see the usual two, three, four soldiers guarding it. But it's guarded by no one. Lawrence drags me across the front lawn. I can't keep up. Karla's chains have left my ankles raw and sore. I trip and fall to my knees. The gate is only a few paces ahead. My freedom is within arm's reach.

Lawrence picks me up, pulling my arm across his neck to help me stand. Together we shuffle to the gate. Lawrence rips it open. He takes me into the shade of the woods. I want to collapse but he doesn't let me. He unhooks my arm from his neck and holds me up by my shoulders. His face is inches from mine but my eyes can't focus.

"Camilla . . . Camilla!" He speaks firmly. "I can't take you any farther. Listen. You have to get them out of the cabin. My father's coming for them. Can you hear me?"

I lazily nod my head. I touch my hand to his arm, not wanting him to let me go.

"You have to run," he says, placing my dagger back in my hand. "Get out of here!"

Lawrence's fingers loosen on my shoulders. I'm forced to stand on my own.

"Go!"

I run into the woods. My legs feel like they're tied down with bricks. Every step is agony, and I stop to catch my breath. I drop to my knees and lay all of my belongings on the forest floor. Air heaves in and out of my lungs. Leaning back on my heels, I look at my blood-stained shirt.

I button my jacket over my chest to cover my wounds from the elements. It's the best I can do. I throw my bag over my shoulder, then tuck my dagger into my jacket pocket.

I force myself to my feet. I have to keep moving. All I want to do is lie down and sleep, but I make my legs move. I stumble across a stream and drop down to the cool water. I suck in water from my cupped hands. I hear a twig snap behind me. I'm not sure if it's an animal or a soldier but I just keep moving.

Getting back to Johnny's is taking far longer than it took to get to Rande. It's like I'm walking through mud a foot thick. I pause and look to the sky. The sun has started its arch toward sunset, which means I only have a few hours of daylight.

My feet stumble on the low brush. I trip and collapse onto the forest floor. I can't stop here, I tell myself. Lying on my back, I try to scan the woods around me. The sun pierces through the trees and flashes into my eyes. My eyelids dip closed. I don't know where I am. I thought I knew these woods. I thought I knew by heart how to get to Johnny's house. I'd been practicing for months, but now everything looks the same. Nothing makes sense.

I roll onto my side. The trunk of a fat oak tree stares at me. My dagger slips from my hand. I hug my bag close to my chest and fall asleep.

CHAPTER THIRTEEN

THE DEEP HOWLING of the wind blowing through the trees nudges me awake. My body is laid out flat with my arms resting at my sides. I tremble as the pain in my stomach returns to my consciousness. My eyes flutter open. A fire blazes near my head. All around me it's dark and cold and damp. Water drips from the ceiling. Every tiny sound bounces off the walls and reverberates in my ears. I'm in a cave.

I remember being lifted off the ground, picked up, and carried through the forest, but that's all I know. I tilt my head. Through a blurry haze I see a man tending a fire. He's tall and stocky. I sit up on my elbows. The cut on my stomach burns as if someone just dropped a pile of hot coals on my skin. I whimper in pain. The room begins to rotate.

"Johnny?" I mumble.

I look down to see that I'm wrapped in a heavy animal-skin jacket. The man stands from his spot by the fire and comes to my bedside. I squint up at his towering visage. Knox kneels next to me. His face resembles the bark of an old tree, wrinkled and hard.

Without warning, he cradles the back of my neck while holding his waterskin to my mouth. I suck down the contents but my stomach can't take it. I cough violently, spewing water on the cave floor.

"Lie down. You'll bleed out," he says, standing and returning to the fire. I fall back onto my pillow. "Try not to move. I don't have what I need to stitch that cut properly."

Knox points to the middle of my body where I'm clutching my wound. I cough again and find it hard to catch my breath. From my spot on the floor, I look down the cave's corridor to its opening. It's night, but still I can see leaves and brush blowing furiously past the entrance. Lightning skips across the sky, momentarily illuminating a forest in turmoil.

"Where are we?" I croak.

"Two miles south of the cabin." Knox sets a log on the fire. "You were bleeding so badly I didn't think you'd make the trip so I brought you here."

Memories rush back into my head, horrible, frightening memories. Karla's room flickers across my mind as another bolt of lightning appears. Her stalking eyes are looking at me now. Her blade shines in the light of Knox's fire. Worst of all is the feeling that I would never leave that place. I run my fingers across my brow as if it will rub away the thoughts.

Knox watches me carefully under heavy eyelids. "Tell me what happened." His voice has an edge as if he's been waiting for me to wake so he can ask me that question.

I stare at the ceiling of the cave. I close my eyes at the thought of having to explain what happened with

Karla. Even *thinking* her name makes me tense. I don't want to have to go there. I don't want to have to think about the last few days. I don't want to explain it to anyone, especially Knox.

We sit in utter silence as the long moments drip by. The only sound between us is the wind echoing through the cave. Another bolt of lightning assaults the sky. This one is followed by a shattering crack of thunder.

"I found that box in your bag," Knox says sternly. "I know why you left."

"If you know, then why are you asking?"

Knox speaks through clenched teeth. "You left in the middle of the night and went to Rande when I told you we couldn't risk the trip."

Knox waits for me to dispute him but I can't. I press my lips together and just hope that he will leave me alone.

"I told you not to go back there. We cannot act and live the way we did before we fled. Do you understand? We are fugitives." Knox paces in front of my bed. The light of the fire strikes him from behind, leaving his face dark and shadowy. "Tell me what happened after you got the box. How did you get these cuts? Camilla, I need to know what kind of danger we're in."

When I don't answer, Knox looks away from me, irritated. He rubs at his beard, then walks away. His frustrated steps echo down the hollow cave. He turns back to me.

"Did Karla do this to you?" Knox's gruff voice reverberates through the cave. "Does she know you're in Bear Gap?" I stare at nothing. "Camilla?"

"I got caught," I say finally. "I got caught by Karla and I barely got away."

I can't meet Knox's eyes. My voice, like my body, is weak and defeated.

"Do you realize what kind of trouble you've put us in? Karla now knows you're still in this territory. This could damage all the work we've done to build the rebellion. You've jeopardized us all." Knox rubs at his chin furiously. "Do you understand what you've done?"

I know what I did was stupid. I want to scream at Knox and tell him to leave me alone but I have no power left inside of me. Karla has left me . . . empty.

"We have to get back to the cabin," I say.

"I'm not taking you back until I know our trail is cold. Karla is undoubtedly looking for you. You wouldn't get very far if we left now anyway."

"She's not the problem anymore." I've silenced Knox's berating and caught his attention. "It's the only reason I was able to escape. They . . . controlled her. She's no longer governor."

"Who then?" Knox demands.

"Captain Thatius." I hold a hand to my stomach, the aching growing worse. "He knows where the cabin is and he's mounting an attack to round up the rebels. We have to get back before his men do."

A gust of wind rushes into the cave, ripping Knox's jacket off my body and nearly blowing out the fire. Rain falls like buckets of water, splattering the cave floor.

Knox lets out an aggravated sigh. "We can't go anywhere with this storm. We're stuck here whether we like it or not." Knox spits the word. I hear him stalk away from me. I'm trapped in this slimy hole with Knox until the storm passes or one of us kills the other.

I retrieve Knox's jacket. It's too cold to lie here without it. Despite the pain, I turn onto my side and face away from Knox. He leaves me alone long enough for me to drift into a restless sleep. I wake to the sound of rain hitting the cave floor. I pull myself into a seated position and lean against the damp wall.

Reaching for my stomach, I let out a guttural moan. I inspect all the tiny scratches on my arms. They're pink and puckered and sting to the touch.

I lift my shirt and look at the wound on my stomach for the first time. Karla's knife sliced me from my left breast, across my stomach, to my right hip. My skin is split open like a bloated, rotting carcass. I touch it, sucking in air as a fresh stinging sensation strikes my middle. I drop my shirt in frustration. There's a napkin lying next to me with scraps of meat on it. The sight of food gives me a bout of nausea.

"You should eat," Knox says.

Eating is the last thing I care about. I ignore the food and stare at my lap. Confidence eludes me. I feel as weak as a dying man. Like him, I wish to lie down and cease to exist.

"What happened with Karla?" His words lack the sharpness they did before, but it doesn't make me any more eager to talk. "I've seen your wounds. Those cuts on your arm weren't meant to kill you."

My body's been poked and punctured all over. I can't keep away the dark thought that Knox is pleased by that, if only in a small way. Maybe Johnny is too. I know I've broken Mirabelle's heart by running away and Tuor . . . Tuor doesn't forgive easily even if I explain our mother's involvement.

"You should go back without me," I mumble.

I turn away from Knox as a hot tear breaks free of my eye and rolls down my nose. I squeeze my eyes closed and pray that the last few days were a dream. Dreams end. The memory of Karla feels like it will be with me forever.

"I told Mirabelle I'd find you and bring you back." Knox stares into the fire. "I keep my word."

The chill of the cave seeps through Knox's jacket, and I'm forced to seek warmth by the flames. I stagger to the fireplace, taking a seat across from Knox. He eyes me with a disgusted look. I avoid his face, keeping my eyes pinned to the flames.

Knox rips a piece of jerky from his mouth and tilts his head to look at me. "When we get back, *if* we get back, you won't be attending anymore meetings." I try to comprehend what Knox has just said. "This rebellion is delicate and I can't have you a part of it."

"What?"

"You can stay home with Mirabelle."

"Am I to kiss your feet for the rest of my life because I made a mistake?"

"I can't trust you. You bring too much risk to everything."

The aching in my stomach disappears. The throbbing in my head melts. I forget that the pain exists. Knox thinks he can ban me from the rebellion? Something inside of me severs. I rise to my feet, surprised by the steadiness I feel.

"The rebellion was *my* idea. You can't keep me from something that was my idea."

"This was my father's cause thirteen years ago, and he sacrificed everything to reject Quinten as our Supreme Ruler. You were barely alive when that happened." Knox points a fat finger at me.

I step around the fire to face Knox straight on. "You think your father's rebellion was so noble, huh? So what were you doing with your life when Mirabelle brought me to you last fall? You were huddled away under a rock. You weren't out fighting for your father's cause."

"Watch your tongue."

"The only reason you've been out in Billage meeting with supporters is because of me! It's because I asked for your help. You'd still be a useless hermit if it weren't for Mirabelle."

Knox stands. His body towers over me. "You are reckless, Camilla. You walked directly toward your enemy and didn't even blink. You are volatile and I can't have that in our group."

I burst out in laughter. "*I'm* volatile? You should look at yourself! I can tell by your expression that you want to smack me across the face right now."

A piercing crack of thunder causes the cave to shudder. Knox struggles to keep his composure. Like the raging storm outside, he won't relent.

"I would never have left my family like that. It was immature and foolish and you put us all in danger."

"I'm aware of how you see me." I almost shout the words but stop myself. "I know you think me irresponsible and stupid." I take a step toward Knox. "Do you want to know what I think of you? You're bitter and mean and so stubborn and incapable of seeing any other opinion than your own."

Knox straightens his back. His arms hang at his sides and I watch as his fists clench open and closed.

"You are no saint, Knox Duffy. What makes you so much better than me? Huh?"

"Be careful what you say." Knox's voice is deep and gravelly.

"You haven't fooled me. I know you did terrible things while in the service of Quinten Warwick." A muscle in Knox's neck twitches. "I've been gone for mere days. You left Mirabelle for years. If she still manages to speak to you after years of absence, then why can't you forgive me for one act of stupidity?"

I've trapped Knox and it feels good. He rubs at the spot in the center of his chest where my mother struck him thirteen years ago. He shifts away as if he can't bear to look at me. Rain pours in sheets as a rumble of thunder echoes against the walls.

"I screwed up, okay? I know I did. I knew it was dangerous to go to Rande. I didn't want to go. I just"— I look at my hands—"couldn't stop."

Knox turns to look at me, wrinkling his forehead in confusion.

"Then why did you go?"

I take in a deep breath and consider how to answer that question. "I had to."

There's silence between Knox and me. He studies my face. "What happened in Rande?"

This time his voice isn't angry or annoyed. It sounds foreign to me. I think I sense . . . fear.

"My mother was there. She made me go. You warned me she'd get to me and I still didn't know." I stare at the floor, my tears falling like rain. "I still didn't know what was happening."

With a note of hesitation, Knox places a comforting hand on my elbow. He says nothing. The pain in my stomach returns as my anger dissipates. I cover my face.

"I'm a fool," I mutter.

I feel a gentle tug on my elbow. I don't deny its suggestion. I collapse into Knox's chest. He holds me across my back with one arm as I sob into his shoulder. Knox smells like the damp earth.

"You're no fool," he says with a pained voice. "She can make your body not your own. I have felt it."

"I don't know how much more I can take," I admit.

Knox pulls me from our embrace. My breath cracks. I look at Knox with desperation. "Maybe . . . maybe I should give her what she wants."

"No. I won't allow you to do that. You have to be strong, Camilla, stronger than her." Knox looks different to me all of a sudden. A curtain has fallen and revealed a person I've never met.

I talk through the tears. "But if I left with her, she'd leave the rest of you alone. I could end it."

"It's not that simple. Portia wants you for something. She doesn't bring people into her life unless they serve a purpose. Whatever she's told you, it's a lie." Knox urgently shakes my body to get my attention. "Never give in to her." I stare at Knox with wide eyes. The tears stop. "Never.

CHAPTER FOURTEEN

SUNLIGHT GLIMMERS THROUGH the branches, bursting into a thousand rays as it hits the water-soaked forest. It feels like years since I've looked up into a clear sky. Birds and squirrels venture from their hiding spots. Knox and I stare into a wood that we no longer recognize.

The storm has ravaged the trees, splitting apart trunks thicker than Knox's body. Twigs and branches litter the ground. It looks like someone stuffed Bear Gap into a bottle, shook it up, and threw it on the ground.

"We make a run for it now," Knox says.

"In the daylight?"

"The storm has stopped. We'll have to risk it. We could already be too late if Thatius has sent men to the cabin." Knox hurries to our camp at the back of the cave. "Can you walk?"

"I'll manage."

Knox stamps out the fire. I pick up my bag, but Knox takes it from me and swings it over his shoulder.

He's already loaded down with his own satchel, thick coat, and long sword, but he insists I not carry anything. I button my jacket over my chest. Our short time in the cave has allowed me to regain some strength, but every move sends a sting of pain to my stomach. I don't let Knox see that it hurts that bad.

"Forget what I said about the rebel meetings," Knox says without meeting my eyes. I pause and watch him shove the remaining jerky into his satchel. "I can't keep you from anything anyway. The rebellion needs you. Don't give up on it."

I nod. I'm stubborn, but a day ago I felt low enough that I would have given up. I look around the cave one last time and actually feel a twinge of sadness to be leaving. I needed to be stuck here with Knox and know I wasn't alone when it came to my mother.

"Let's go," he says.

At the entrance to the cave, Knox glances left and right before leaving our temporary home. He keeps a few paces in front of me, his hand close to the hilt of his sword. I hobble through the graveyard of leaves and broken branches.

We move cautiously. My pace is painfully slow. Knox waits for me to hurdle over a fallen tree. His eyes are ever vigilant, scanning the freshly bathed vegetation. I clutch my stomach. Every step feels like a rip in my skin. I pause, grabbing a nearby tree for support. I double over from the pain.

"You okay?" he asks.

I nod vigorously.

"We're not far."

A horse's whinny echoes down the embankment and hits Knox and me like a punch to the face. He grabs my hand and jerks me behind the roots of a fallen tree. I moan as my body twists. I crumple to the ground. Knox cranes his neck to locate the sound. I stare at the forest floor and dig my fingernails into my pants to keep from screaming.

"It's soldiers," Knox breathes. He comes to his knees next to me and adjusts my bag on his shoulder. "We have to get back to the cabin before they do. They're headed west to avoid the rocky creek bed. We can get there faster by crossing it straight on but we'll have to run."

Before Knox asks if I can do it, I struggle to my feet and steady myself. Muffled voices drift into the ravine where we sit. I glance up the embankment. Through the trees, a line of Warwick soldiers ride their horses in the direction I know leads to the cabin. Captain Thatius has wasted no time. Like us, he waited for the storm to pass before following through with his plan.

Knox and I run east into the woods. I focus on my breathing and will myself to forget about the pain. I'll think about it when we're safe, when the five of us are back together again. I whip through the trees. Fear is my fuel. Wet leaves smack me in the face as I jump and dive through a forest that's been wrecked by the storm.

Behind me, Knox's breath is heavy. I skid to a stop on the bank of the creek. Calling it a creek isn't right. It's breached its banks. The water is thick and clouded brown with mud. A severed tree branch floats down the rushing body of water.

Without speaking, Knox takes my arm and pulls me into the water. Cold, dirty liquid fills my boots. The creek erupts around us, reaching to our waists. I stumble, but Knox drags me forward as if I were a small child. On the other side, he yanks me out and practically tosses me onto the ground.

I stand immediately and run uphill. We're close. My soaked boots feel like they've added a hundred extra pounds to my clothes. Sweat coats my brow while my body shivers from the cold water. The hill steepens. I reach from tree to tree to pull me up. Thatius' company moves through the woods twenty yards from us. Johnny, Mirabelle, and Tuor have no idea what's coming for them.

I slip on the wet leaves, but when I move my leg to stand back up, my body doesn't allow it. A slice of pain rips through my stomach all the way to my lower back. I scream out, uninhibited. It feels like I've been cut anew by Karla's blade. I touch a hand to my stomach. The wetness there is not from the river. My jacket is stained with blood.

Knox hustles up the hillside like an ox. He scoops me into his arms and carries me to the crest of the hill. We break into the clearing, Johnny's cabin a beacon. My head feels light and empty, and my arms weaken and fall limply at my side. We break through the front door as if we were the ones attacking.

Knox's voice bellows through the cabin. "Get the horses!"

Tuor stands from the couch. "Camilla?" His eyes fall to my crumpled body. I shrink into Knox's arms

Mirabelle rounds the corner from the kitchen. "Knox, what's going on?"

"They've found us. To the horses, now. Where is Johnny?"

"He's in the garden," Mirabelle says. She comes to my side. Her face is a sheen of horror but it grows blurry as the moments pass. "Where are we going?"

"The safe house." Knox pushes her down the hall and through the kitchen. Tuor is on our heels. "They're at our doorstep!"

In the backyard I see only a flash of Johnny's face before we're all in the stable. Questions are asked. What happened to Camilla? How did they find us? What is Captain Thatius doing in Bear Gap?

Most are ignored as Knox barks orders and insists everyone mount their steed. The yelling slowly turns to a quiet din. I'm raised onto a horse and held like a baby. We burst into the trees and soon the whipping branches melt into blackness.

***

I wake at dusk. I'm being jostled through a door. Johnny carries me, his arms tight around my shoulders. My eyes flicker open. Wherever we are is cozy and welcoming. A fire roars in the stone fireplace and the room is warm with candlelight. A wash basin sits close to the door along with a wooden bench that has a knitted blanket neatly folded on top of it. Most notable is the Warwick flag that hangs on the wall like a tapestry.

"I need a place to stitch her up." Johnny's voice is low.

Knox and Tuor filter past me. The door behind us is secured shut. Boots scrape across the wood floor, and whispering fills my ears.

"I have a room prepared in the cellar," Ivan says.

"We're barely out of winter," Mirabelle says. "It'll be freezing." She doesn't hide her distaste.

"It's the best I can do. I don't want any sign that I have guests."

"It'll be fine," Knox says.

Ivan opens a flap in the floor and takes us down a wooden ladder to his cellar. It feels like we're entering the pit of a nasty beast. He sets a single candle on a metal holder that hangs from the ceiling by a set of chains. The undulating flame casts moving shadows on the walls, doing nothing to improve the hospitality of the space. Bulbs of onions hang by a string from the ceiling and wooden trays of apples and pumpkins sit on the floor. The walls are stone but the floor is dirt. Ivan's sons rush around the room, rearranging crates of vegetables and carrying in what little luggage we have. Pallets made out of boxes and planks of wood line the walls. When Johnny lays me on top of one, I realize they're meant to be our beds.

"I need a basin of water and clean rags," Johnny calls behind him. "She's lost a lot of blood. It's lucky that I kept a kit in my saddle bag," he mumbles.

Johnny shuffles through a small leather bag at his side. I try to catch his eyes but he's focused on his work. His lips are drawn together tightly and he wears a stoic expression of worry. Johnny quickly unbuttons my jacket. I'm so weak that he has to raise the top half of my body in order to slip my arms out of the sleeves.

Johnny lifts my shirt, which is drenched in sticky blood. My cut looks like it has burst open. It's wider and a deeper red than it was when I last looked at it. I moan and drop my head on the wooden pallet. My body shakes furiously. Mirabelle comes to my side. She looks down at me with her hands folded.

"I'm insisting we get some more blankets down here," Mirabelle says before leaving my line of sight.

Johnny's request for water and rags is granted. He applies pressure on my still oozing stomach, then pulls a short, curved needle from his bag. Holding the needle in his mouth, Johnny produces a strand of horse hair and begins threading it through the eye of the needle. I wonder if this is how his father works: fast, methodical, and focused.

My head is light. I let my mind drift to that story Johnny told me about his parents. They live in a fishing town, Hanover, but Johnny's father used to be a doctor in Billage. For many years he was under contract with Governor Leo. He had to work on dignitaries and Warwick soldiers before caring for anyone else. Johnny hated that his father obeyed blindly.

I'm poked suddenly in the stomach. I let out a squeal and grab Johnny's arm. He ignores me. He pulls the needle up, threading the horse hair through my skin. My breath becomes ragged. Every muscle in my body tenses. I squeeze my eyes closed. Another poke strikes me where it's most tender.

Despite myself, I whimper pathetically. Mirabelle kneels at my bedside and takes my hand in hers. Again he pokes me. Again the horse hair runs right over the opening of my wound. Poke. Scrape. Poke. Scrape. Poke. Scrape. Over and over Johnny punctures me with the needle as if I were a hunk of meat being tenderized. I ask him to stop but he doesn't. Tears fall from the corners of my eyes.

Johnny snips the end of the horse hair and knots it off. He wipes the remainder of blood from my stomach and applies a cooling ointment. I hold my eyes closed, waiting for the pain to dissipate. I'm out of breath, as if I've been running. Mirabelle strokes my hair.

"It's over. It's over," she whispers into my ears.

I open my eyes cautiously, as if doing so will bring back the torture. Johnny wipes my blood from his hands. Finally his eyes meet mine and I understand why he avoided my gaze until now. He had to stitch me up and he knew it would only compound my sorrow. He places a hand on my knee and manages a half smile.

I'm bandaged up and dressed in clean, dry clothes. Mirabelle tucks me in with a stack of blankets and a pillow under my head. Tuor comes to see for himself that I'm all right. He looks at me with soft eyes. He wants to ask what Johnny and Mirabelle want to ask me too: *what happened?*

But no one asks me anything. I'm instructed to lie still and try to sleep. I don't find the last request difficult to fulfill.

It's only now that I begin to fully comprehend my status. I'm alive in a safe place and I'm back with my family. There's no good reason to worry about Karla or my mother tonight, so I won't. My eyes become heavy.

A sheet is hung down the middle of the cellar to give Mirabelle and me privacy. A man stands on the other side of the room. I squint my eyes in confusion, then remember that Reed, the Warwick soldier who intruded on our meeting, is also sleeping under Ivan's roof.

CHAPTER FIFTEEN

REED'S LOUD, OBNOXIOUS voice wakes me the next morning. My eyes pop open. Men's voices murmur through the thin sheet that divides the room. I recognize Johnny's voice first and then Tuor's and then . . . Reed's rambling breaks through. I don't trust him. If I wasn't so weak, I'd march across the room and interrogate him, but I can barely roll over.

Mirabelle stands by her bed mat. She folds her blanket and sets it neatly at the end of her bed. I peel my body from the hard pallet, doing my best to ignore the painful tugging in my stomach. It's a great feat getting into a seated position. I sit awkwardly, trying to find a comfortable spot where my stitches aren't pulling.

"How are you feeling, dear?" Mirabelle asks, rushing to my side. "Maybe you should lie back down."

"I'm fine," I groan.

Mirabelle presses her lips together. She's not fooled. I rub the tangled hair on the side of my head.

"I'm fine," I say again and this time I give her a forced smile.

I'm surprised when she suddenly stops fussing. Mirabelle sighs, taking a seat on the bed next to me. Tears form at the bottoms of her eyes as she takes my face in her hands.

"What's wrong?" I ask.

"I'm just glad you're okay." Mirabelle pulls me into a hug, forcing my head onto her shoulder. But as her hand rubs my back, sudden dread creeps up my spine. Her embrace . . . it triggers a memory. It's *Karla's* bony hand on me. It's her skeletal frame that has its arms wrapped around me. I feel the familiar panic of being trapped, chained, and touched by Karla.

I pull away. Mirabelle gives me a quizzical look but says nothing. I recoil my arms into my body, crossing them over my chest like a mummy. I haven't taken this pose in a long time. Not since I worked at the farm.

"My stomach," I say, quickly drumming up an excuse for Mirabelle.

A burst of laughter erupts from the other side of the room. I hold my aching stomach and stand, eager to distance myself from Mirabelle. I stagger to the middle of the room and unfurl the dirty sheet that divides the men from the women.

Reed leans against the cellar wall, his foot kicked up for balance and his hand furiously stroking his hair. Tuor faces him. He's engrossed in Reed's story. Johnny is not. He sits on his bed, elbows on his knees, and rolls his eyes at practically everything Reed says.

"Yeah, yeah, yeah, that was the worst. Hey, when did you do your combat training?" Reed asks, nudging Tuor on the shoulder as if they were old friends.

"Three years ago."

"Ah," Reed chuckles. "You're younger than me. I did my training seven years back. You're just a kid." Reed lets out a loud guffaw and Tuor smiles as if someone told him it's the right thing to do. "Who was your instructor?"

"Captain Gyles."

"Oh, oh, oh. I had him too! Heck of a fighter but he had terribly bad breath." Tuor laughs, which seems to fuel Reed. "Did he make your class run up suicide hill until someone vomited?"

"Yeah," Tuor sniggers. "I was the one."

Reed erupts in laughter. He doubles over and smacks his knee. It's so loud that Knox looks up from his book. My eyes dip closed, then open again. Just looking at Reed is exhausting. The raucous laughter doesn't help my pounding headache, but it is nice to see Tuor happy.

"Quiet," Knox barks.

"Eh, why don't you come share some of your war stories, Knox?" Reed says, his face turning serious. "I bet you've got lots to tell." His voice is dripping with snark.

Knox turns the page of his book. "My stories are best untold."

"We're supposed to be hiding," Johnny says. "Maybe you should shut your mouth so the neighbors don't hear us."

Reed makes a face like he might explode in anger, but then in an instant, he pulls himself back. "Sorry, everyone. I've just been stuck down here by myself. It gets lonely." Reed looks around the room as if it were property he owned. His sharp eyes fall to me.

"Camilla," he says in a singsong voice. Reed pulls away from the wall and comes to stand in the middle of the room, hands on his hips. "Look who's finally awake. I hope our storytelling didn't bother you."

"Hardly," I say sarcastically.

Johnny looks up and notices me for the first time.

"You're looking greatly improved," Reed says. He scans the length of my body.

"It's because of Johnny," I say simply.

Johnny stands and crosses the room swiftly. He pushes Reed away from me as if he were shielding me from a sword strike. "Give her some space."

The muscles in Johnny's neck twitch as he and Reed stare at each other. Knox looks up from his book, and I take a step away from Johnny.

With a smile on his lips, Reed says, "Easy . . ." His eyes move from Johnny to me. "I wouldn't want to do anything to hinder the patient's healing."

The door to the cellar opens. Johnny and Reed are temporarily distracted as Ivan descends the ladder.

"What's the news?" Knox asks, closing his book and jumping to his feet.

Ivan coolly stands before us, his legs spread wide and his thick arms hanging from his body like hunks of meat in a butcher shop.

"This is the situation we're in. It's not a good one," Ivan says. Mirabelle moves into the center of the room, easing in next to Knox. "We established this safe house some months ago when Billage was not the target of Karla's attention. Since then, the whole territory has come under scrutiny. With Captain Thatius now as governor, he's drawn his attention to all of the rebels, not just Camilla."

"What's it like out there?" Johnny asks.

"Thatius is still suffering a low soldier presence in the territory, thanks to Karla, but he's more organized than her. He's made squelching any rebel groups a priority. Direct orders from the Supreme Ruler is what I've heard."

There's a collective sigh across the room.

"So what should we do?" Mirabelle asks.

"The way I see it we have two options. We can carry on as planned with recruitment and building an army. We could use the fact that we're in the same location as an advantage. But our time here is limited. Eventually Captain Thatius will find us."

Ivan scans the room, looking each of us in the eyes. Tuor rubs his hands over his arms furiously as if he were cold, but I know it's nerves.

"What's the other option?" Johnny asks.

Ivan pauses, leaving all of us in a moment of hopeful anticipation. Maybe he has a plan or a trick that we haven't tried yet.

"We fold in," Ivan says. "I can disband the Billage members. They'll be angry, but they'll be alive."

"We'd have to leave Bear Gap," Mirabelle says.

She looks at Knox, the pain of this decision plastered on her face. If we leave, we're giving up our chance to ever walk freely again. We'd be fugitives for life. If we stay, we could die fighting for that right . . . Knox discreetly reaches over and takes Mirabelle's hand in his.

"I can arrange to get your group out of the territory. That would include you, Reed. And yes, you'd be on the run."

"No way," I say quickly.

Ivan looks directly at me. "Sometimes you need to step back in order to move forward."

Mirabelle nods in agreement.

"We have no idea what's out there," Tuor says.

My mouth hangs open in disbelief. "Are you serious?" There's unsteadiness in my voice as I wince at the pain in my stomach. "We've put so much work into this. We decided we'd stand and fight not run to the hills and hide." Something about my new lease on life has made it harder for me to hold back when I disagree. Not that I ever had a big problem with that before.

"If we run away, we'll be worse off," Johnny says. "I'd rather die in my territory than hide in some foreign land."

"Knox, what say you?" Ivan asks.

Knox's face, like usual, is a stone. He rubs at the stubble on his chin. "I don't give up anymore." He turns and looks at me. "*We* don't give up anymore."

"Hear, hear . . ." Reed says, holding up an invisible mug of ale.

"The majority rules," Ivan says. "We continue. So what's our next move?"

"We can't do anything without the support of the farm workers," I say. "They make up more than half the population of Bear Gap. We need to find a way to get to them."

"Right now you shouldn't be doing anything except getting better," Mirabelle says. She raises her eyebrows as her eyes fall to my hand clutching my stomach.

Ivan nods, taking a moment to consider what I've said. "I'll work with my boys on reaching the farm workers."

"I could help you," Reed says eagerly.

"I don't want anyone leaving this cellar." Ivan turns and places both hands on the ladder rungs. "I still have the benefit of looking like I'm Warwick loyal. All of you don't. You're useless to the rebellion until we have more support."

Without another word, Ivan disappears through the door in the cellar ceiling. I listen as he secures it closed.

"Got somewhere to be?" Johnny asks Reed, picking up their fight where they left off.

The suspicion in Johnny's voice doesn't go unnoticed. Reed's hand begins to tremble. The dark circles under his eyes are especially pronounced in the dim cellar.

"Any place away from here would be preferable," Reed says darkly. He stalks away from us.

I'm stunned at his shift in mood.

Johnny scoffs and leans in close. "Can you believe him?" He takes me by the arm and pulls me through the curtain to the girl's side. My arm tingles at his touch. "He never stops talking. He's going to get us all killed."

Johnny plops onto my bed and faces me.

"Does Ivan trust him?" I ask, meandering my way toward Johnny.

Johnny shakes his head. "Yeah, some story about how he saved Tommy's life. I think he's blinded."

I take a seat next to Johnny because I know it's what he wants me to do.

"I don't trust him either." My voice is low. I'm overly aware of how close Johnny's face is to mine. I glance into his eyes only for a moment, then turn my head away.

"He's up to something. I'm not gonna let him out of my sight."

I nod absentmindedly. I want to concentrate on what Johnny's saying, but I'm too preoccupied by our closeness. My chest builds with anxiety as Johnny eases toward me in our usual familiarity. He touches my elbow and I shudder. He brushes my arm and it feels like Karla. He leans in for a kiss. My heart tightens.

Mirabelle walks through the curtain. Johnny pulls away. I sigh in relief. Never have I been so grateful for Mirabelle's presence.

***

It's hard to know what time of the day it is in Ivan's cellar. Besides the candle in the middle of the room, the only light is the little bit of firelight that seeps through the floorboards. With Ivan and his sons away, that means it's as black as pitch down here.

Eventually Knox tells us all to stop talking so he can sleep. Mirabelle's heavy breathing used to annoy me when we slept in the loft at Johnny's. Now that we're all sleeping together in the root cellar, I can also hear Tuor mumbling and Knox's bothersome snoring. It's enough to drive me insane.

I roll from my side onto my back and stare at the dancing shadows cast onto the ceiling. I can't sleep. Something in the back of my mind is irritating me. It's like a grain of sand being rubbed slowly over an open wound. I can't determine the source of the irritation. Is it Johnny? Karla? Reed? The life of the rebellion?

I roll onto my side again. On the floor, next to my bed, is my messenger bag lying in a lump. The canvas creates an outline of the box that's still inside it. In the bustle to get to safety, I'd almost forgotten about the thing that I risked my life to retrieve. It's strange though, at Karla's, even when I was close to dying, I never considered leaving it behind. I knew if I could escape, I'd be taking it with me.

I come to my feet and grab the candle from its holder, bringing it back to my pallet bed. I bend over and take the box out of my bag and hold it in both my hands. Johnny's stitches pull at my skin. The horror I went through to get this.

The box is so plain. There's absolutely nothing special about it. I run my fingers along the curved wooden lid. A chunk has broken off at one of the bottom corners. Like a mother tending to a hurt child, I feel heartbroken. It must have cracked when I dropped it at the farm. I touch the splintered wood and graze my hand along the gaping hole, but my finger doesn't touch emptiness as I expect. It feels as though I've touched the edge of a stack of parchment. My eyebrows scrunch together as I realize there's a book hidden inside.

CHAPTER SIXTEEN

I FLING OPEN the lid but I'm surprised to find the box empty. I squint in confusion. I lift the box and hold it level with my face. I can see the stack of parchment through the crack, but when I open the lid again, it appears empty. I run my fingers along the inside, feeling the rough wood. A tiny cream-colored silk tab sticks up in one of the creases. I pull the tab and slowly lift the false bottom.

I gape at the site of a thin book sitting at the true bottom of the chest. How had I played with this thing my whole childhood but never known it held a hidden compartment? Dazed, I pull out the book and toss aside the box as if it were trash. This was the thing I needed. *This* is what drew me to Bear Gap. A feeling of satisfaction fills me.

The cover is soft, made of fabric. It looks as if it was once dark blue with a white-rose floral pattern, but it's faded severely. I run my thumb across the spine, then begin flipping through the book. Page after page is covered in thin scrawled notes.

It's a journal. Is it possible that it's been in the bottom of this box all these years? Could it have been there even before my mother acquired it? This box was hers before it was Tuor's and mine. Perhaps she never even knew it was there. How strange. There's a whisper in my ear that tells me to read. I don't resist another moment longer. I flip to the first page and begin.

#

Today I'm sixteen years old. Pa had a lovely party for me. I wore my pink dress with the big bow that sits just on my lower back. I had the greatest surprise when Mamma gave me this diary. She handed it to me in private so that Pa wouldn't know. Pa can't know. I don't feel quite right keeping a secret from him, but Mamma told me how important it is not to let him see.

I don't know why Mamma decided to talk today. It's been years since she's said a word. She's not dumb though. She can still entertain Pa's guests and make sure the servants are doing what they're supposed to. She sits so beautifully at dinner parties, like a doll. She does everything Pa tells her to do. So do I.

I'm not sure what to write in here. Maybe I'm doing it wrong . . .

I'd like to go into town more but Pa only lets me leave the farm on Sundays for church. We ride a carriage in together as a family. I like seeing children playing in the street. I wonder what it would be like to be able to run free like that. Pa says it's better for me to stay inside. I'm his special collectible, he says. If I'm left outside I could get caught in the rain and ruined.

Pa is very meticulous with me. He approves of my clothing every evening and tells my handmaiden exactly how to fix my hair. He tells our chef what to cook for me, and my tutor ensures that I follow Pa's strict curriculum. Our house is very big. It has a grand staircase in the middle. I'm not allowed to go down the steps without someone holding my hand for fear I'll fall. Pa must love me very much to take such an interest in me. Pa and I are very close. I don't like keeping this secret from him but Mamma has implored me so. She'll be punished if Pa found out about this book. She'll have to be put in the room with the nails. I hate it there. Pa has never locked me inside because he loves me dearly as I love him.

I must go now before my handmaiden returns.

Portia

#

My heart feels like it's stuck in my throat. Portia . . . as in, my mother? I flip through the pages like a mad person. *Portia, Portia, Portia* is written at the end of every entry. Soon mentions of Bear Gap and Malcolm litter the pages. This is not some random diary that's been locked in this box for decades. This is my mother's journal. This was her life. I cringe at the thought.

I slam the book closed, disgusted with myself for reading it. I hurriedly shove it back into the box as if it were a dirty or sinful thing I didn't want to be seen with. Sliding onto my back, I pull the covers just under my chin. I turn my head to look at the box sitting on the floor.

The voice returns. Through its wooden walls, the journal talks to me. I pile my arms over my ears, desperate to block the sound, but it does no good. I squeeze my eyes and try to ignore its haunting tones.

My mother's voice pecks away at my mind. I thought I'd satisfied her after seeing her in Rande, but reading the journal seems to have awakened her anew. Her presence is so much stronger now. *What do you want from me!* I scream it inside my head. You want me to learn something from these old journal entries? I scoff. It won't happen.

Finally I fall asleep. Whether it's because of sheer exhaustion or because my mother has simply allowed it, I'm not sure. A few hours after drifting to sleep, I'm awake again. I'm not in Ivan's icy cellar. I'm in Karla's hot, smoky bedroom and she's staring at me maniacally. She approaches me, dagger in hand, like a cat to its prey. My mother stands behind her and stares at me passively. She wears the frilly pink dress I imagined she wore on her sixteenth birthday.

I hang from the ceiling by a set of chains like a dead carcass. My mother watches as Karla takes her knife and pops open my stomach. Then it's not Karla anymore, it's my mother that holds the bloody knife. I scream out. Her emerald eyes are blank, devoid of feeling.

I rip off my blankets and beg for air. My face is sweaty. My stomach is tight. My stitches feel like tiny burns crisscrossed against my skin. I shake my head, telling myself none of it's real. My dreams are a chamber of horrors. Karla has dug a hole into my mind and she resides there. Like a snake, she's ready to strike whenever she pleases.

My heart beats as if an enemy was charging me this very moment. In reality all that surrounds me is a quiet, dark room. Mirabelle snores softly behind me. I rest my hand on my chest and wait for the galloping within to settle. Karla and my mother . . . I can't handle two torturers.

Knox's shuffling about announces morning. My legs are tangled in a web of blankets. Next to my bed is a puddle of wax where the candle died. It feels shameful, knowing I sat here last night and read my mother's journal. Sleep never really came to me.

Somehow I'm more tired now than I was when I went to bed.

Mirabelle wakes, rubbing her back as she stretches. She dresses and fusses over the cleanliness of the room. I have to remind her that this is a root cellar, and it won't be made clean no matter how hard she tries. She then moves on to fussing over me. Mirabelle presses the back of her hand to my forehead as I sit up in bed, my back against the wall.

"No fever. That's good," she says.

The wrinkle in the middle of her forehead tells me that she has something on her mind. Mirabelle takes a seat on the bed next to me. She folds her hands on her lap and glances at me sideways.

"Camilla, I think we should talk about what happened. It would be good for you to—"

"I can't," I say quickly. I've already relived it all last night . . .

Mirabelle looks at me surprised. I know what she's going to ask me. Undoubtedly Knox has told her what I told him in the cave about how Karla tortured me for days and how I saw my mother. Now, Mirabelle wants to hash it out.

"Camilla, it's important that—"

"I can't right now." I turn my eyes from her. "Please, I just . . . need to move on."

"But sweetie—"

"I want to feel normal. Talking about it will just remind me, and I want to forget." I meet Mirabelle's eyes. "I already talked to Knox. Doesn't that count?"

Mirabelle raises her eyebrows and lets out a chuckle. "I never thought I'd see the day when the two of you would be getting along."

"We're civil. That's all."

"I think it's a bit more than that."

"We're friends," I admit hesitantly.

"Friends . . . hm? In the same way you and Johnny are friends?" Mirabelle asks with a smirk.

I try to keep my face still. How does she know about Johnny and me? We were so careful.

"What?" I stutter, acting dumb.

Mirabelle pats my knee with her hand. "Don't look so shocked. I notice these kinds of things."

"Does Knox know?"

She shakes her head and laughs. "Not a chance. Knox is clueless when it comes to romance."

My body relaxes. It's a relief that Knox doesn't know our secret. I don't want to mess up the good thing that we have going right now. Johnny and me in a relationship would be just the thing to get him going. He'd surely say feelings and emotions would cloud our judgment. It would affect the rebellion, and right now, the rebellion is everything. I look down at my lap and frown. I don't know how much longer I'll have to keep the secret anyway. There may be no secret to keep . . .

"If you won't talk about what happened with me, then at least promise me something, Camilla."

Mirabelle's tone is suddenly serious.

I'm nervous to ask. "What kind of promise?"

"Promise me you'll never leave me like that again. It was hard enough thinking you'd been kidnapped, but it's not as bad as knowing you left on your own and didn't tell me. I know it wasn't your fault. But still . . . if you had only told me, I could have . . . even if you've made a mistake and gotten yourself into trouble just . . . just please don't leave me like that again. You can tell me anything."

"Okay."

"Promise me."

I look up at Mirabelle under heavy eyelids. "I promise."

Mirabelle takes a deep breath. She's satisfied.

"Can I come over?" A voice asks through the thin sheet. It's Johnny. Mirabelle looks at me and gives me a grin.

"What for, dear?" Mirabelle asks teasingly.

"I need to look at Camilla's stitches."

Mirabelle walks to the curtain and opens it so she's toe-to-toe with Johnny.

"Of course. I'm going to check on things over here," Mirabelle says and then slips to the other side of the room.

Johnny pulls aside the sheet. We're alone . . . again.

"Let me take a look," he says, walking toward me.

I take a deep breath. The quicker I do this, the sooner I can say I need to rest. I lift my shirt to reveal the puffy red slash on my stomach. Johnny presses the pad of his finger along the cut.

"They look good but you should be lying down to keep from moving excessively. You'll tear a stitch if you're not careful."

I pull my shirt down as if I were covering up my raw emotions. "I already feel like I'm in a cage."

Johnny runs a hand along my arm and up to my neck, inspecting all the shallow cuts Karla made with her knife. He brushes aside my hair and gently touches my ear.

"These will probably scar," Johnny says.

Karla's marks will be permanent, inside and out.

"You're still beautiful," he says with a smile.

Johnny takes his finger and traces a cut on my cheek. I avert my eyes, unable to meet Johnny's gaze. I lean away from him, blaming the move on a more comfortable position for my stomach. I stare forward, knowing what will come next. Johnny pauses, then leans in and kisses me on the cheek. From the corner of my eye, I watch as his smile drops into scowl.

"What's going on with you?"

I force myself to look at Johnny straight on. His big, light blue eyes used to bring me comfort, but now all I feel is this complicated mixture of sadness and guilt.

"Sorry. I just—"

How do I tell him I don't ever want to be held or touched again? I draw my arms in close to my chest.

I struggle for words. "I don't feel the same way I used to. Before Karla got me."

"I know. That's why I'm here." Johnny rubs my arm to comfort me.

"N—no." My mouth hangs open, begging for words. "It's too hard to be around you."

Johnny's hand falls to the bed. "You want me to leave?"

"No, I—"

"I'm trying to help you."

"I know."

"I'm trying to be here for you because I thought that's what you wanted."

"I do want it." I look away and bristle. "I don't know what I want . . ." I look back at Johnny's face. "I just know it's hard to be near you."

The words come out wrong. I struggle to find the right thing to say to keep him from being mad.

Johnny sighs. "What is it that you want, Camilla?"

"I don't know . . ."

"I've done nothing but treat you right." Johnny jumps to his feet. "I don't get you! I worry about you for four days. I have no idea where you are, only to find out you left on your own. I put all of that aside, patch you up, and treat you like nothing happened because that's what Knox told me to do and now you don't want *me*?"

Johnny's eyes settle on my face. He crosses his arms over his chest. He's angry. I've only ever seen him this angry with Knox.

"It's too much to think about. There are too many expectations. I can't . . ." I shake my head. "I can't take it."

I'm surprised by my own words. I didn't even know how I felt until I said it out loud.

"I'm sorry," I whisper. "I think I'm better off by myself."

Johnny's expression is utter disgust. He drops his arms and marches swiftly away from me.

"Johnny, I still—"

I want to explain everything to him, that he hasn't done anything wrong, that it's my own head, that I want to be with him so bad, but I just *can't* . . . I want to tell him, that despite everything, I love him deeply, but he's already disappeared behind the curtain.

CHAPTER SEVENTEEN

IT TAKES ONLY eight days to drive everyone in the cellar crazy. That's how long it's been since Ivan's come down to check on us. We hear nothing through the floorboards. Our supply of food has run low and we've begun eating raw onions and pumpkins. The confinement is torturous for Knox. He paces incessantly, rubbing at the spot on his chest. I stand with him and Tuor, staring up the ladder.

"What if Ivan's dead?" Tuor says.

"If he was dead, one of his sons would have come down," I say.

Tuor shrugs his shoulders. "Maybe they're dead too."

"We should stay down here," Mirabelle calls from her bed. "He told us not to go up. Someone could be waiting for us to emerge."

I look over at Johnny, huddled on his bed, meticulously cleaning his sword . . . again. It's also been eight dreadful days since I broke things off with Johnny. He's hardly spoken a word to me.

Being stuck in this small room is its own kind of torture for me. My nightly ritual consists of stifled crying, then restless sleep, where I'm plagued by visions of Karla. She doesn't just visit at night. I can be laughing with Tuor and something he says or does will send me into a spiral of thoughts that I can't stop.

I keep it all in my head. Everyone knows of the cuts and bruises on my body, but no one can see the wounds in my head. On occasion, I've thought of telling Mirabelle, but saying it out loud feels like turning a mythical beast into something real, something terrible that I have to face. If I keep it inside, I can pretend it doesn't exist.

"We'll wait another day," Knox says, unfolding his crossed arms. "If Ivan's not back by tomorrow, we'll have to make a plan to get out of here."

"What could have happened to him?" Mirabelle asks.

"He's dead!" Tuor says, shaking his head nervously.

Reed steps into the center of the room. "Let's keep our heads about us."

"If he's been arrested, they could be coming here to look for us," I say.

Knox chews on his bottom lip. "We'll give it another day."

Eight days . . . I sit on my pallet bed, my leg hopping up and down uncontrollably. It's been eight days since I read my mother's journal. I promised myself I'd never pick it up again. In fact, the next time I'm near a proper fire, I plan to burn it. But every day the desire to read it grows stronger.

I stand, pacing back and forth. My mother's journal seems to burn through its box home and beg for my attention. Between my tears for Johnny and my nightmares about Karla, this feels like a welcome distraction. What else am I to do in this hole?

I wait until everyone's asleep, then jump out of bed and grab the candle from its holder. Sitting on the edge of my bed, I pull the box toward me, flip open the lid, and dig out the journal. I feel a sudden release of tension when I hold it in my hand. I run my fingertips over the cover. It tingles in my hand, begging to be read.

It feels like barely ten minutes have passed, and I've read the whole of my mother's childhood entries. She grew up in Bear Gap in the days when there were wealthy men that had no affiliation to the throne. Her father owned a large farm with fields of cattle and goats.

My mother writes about her father as if she can only see the good in him, but it's obvious he had a dark side. He beat my grandmother like a stray dog, careful to never touch her where her clothes couldn't cover the bruises. But oddly, he never touched my mother. Portia's abuse was a life completely devoid of choice. Everything she ever ate, wore, or participated in was not only decided by my grandfather, but was diligently observed by him.

I recall my mother's words when she surprised me at the shack. She wanted me to make the choice to go with her or stay. I laugh softly in my bed. How desperate would I have to be to ever choose to follow in the footsteps of my mother?

I pause when a name appears suddenly in my mother's writing: Malcolm. He worked as a farmhand for my grandfather. Malcolm was smart enough then to see that my grandfather was a lunatic. One night, he killed my grandfather and stole my mother away from the only home she'd ever known. They moved to Rande, married, and my mother seemed to grow affection for him.

#

My back aches with an intensity I've never felt before. For days I've been yelping out with no inhibition every time I get one of these bolts of pain. I fear my body may rip into two parts. I never knew that birthing a baby was this much torture. I'm a fool for never assisting in a birth before.

Most girls get to watch their mother or sister go through the trial but I didn't. Mama never had another baby and Pa kept me locked up at home. I've only recently come to realize the extent of my father's containment of me.

It's harvest time. I can't believe it's been a year since we left Pa dying in that house. I adore Malcolm. He dotes on me constantly and let's me walk into town whenever I please, although I haven't done that much lately. I can hardly make it up the hill anymore with my stomach this huge. Every day my body grows bigger and it's absolutely astonishing to me that it could stretch any farther.

I was lucky to meet a neighbor that is only a twenty-minute walk from our house. Collette and Roan are a strange couple. Roan is much older than Collette but he's beautiful to look at. His hair is a silvery white color. Collette is young and timid and not overly friendly, but she's agreed to help when the baby comes. She's assisted in many births, even though she doesn't have any children of her own.

Another bolt of pain has just struck me. I'm sitting on the front steps of the house and Malcolm is now eyeing me. He knows I'm in dreadful pain but I don't think he knows how to comfort me. I find myself smiling despite the task I have ahead of me. Malcolm is gentle and kind and I'm happy to be having his baby, even though this baby was the greatest surprise I've ever experienced in my life.

I must stop writing now and go lie down. I vow I will only do this once. A second child, I fear would be more than my body or my temperament could take.

#

Malcolm, gentle and kind? I shake my head in disbelief. My mother's contentment in Rande dries up quickly. Two years pass. She's stuck at home taking care of Tuor. The house is too small. Malcolm doesn't make enough rings and she grows weary of him. *I could still be living with my father,* she writes over and over. *His servants ate better than I do.*

#

I must finally write it down. I've become completely enraptured with Roan. Never have I felt so close to any other person. He delights in everything I say. I've resisted for so long admitting this truth. It is wrong, I know, for he has a wife and I have Malcolm. But he has revealed to me that his feelings for me are strong, stronger than he ever felt for Collette. What a crime it would be to keep on living without speaking the truth. If Malcolm had found another love, I'd want to know. I'd want him to be happier with another. Roan has sworn upon death that we will be together for the rest of our lives, whatever it takes.

#

My mother takes well to infidelity. She constantly finds clever ways to leave Tuor with Malcolm and slip off to see Roan. Just as it seems that Portia will also grow bored with Roan, he tells her something that ties her to him.

#

Roan has revealed to me a secret. I have sensed for some time that he was withholding something. I had always believed there were no mysteries between the two of us, but I've grown accustomed to reading Roan's eyes.

He is the last living heir to the Catahli clan, the sacred family that mines the Catahli mineral. Supreme Ruler Bradac ravaged his family. I'd heard those stories, of course, but they'd always said that no Catahli members survived. He did survive and fled to Bear Gap for safety. At first I grew angry that my love never told me this, but his very life has depended on this secret. His wife is the only other one who carries this knowledge.

He has told me now because he plans to return to the mines and carry out his duty as a Catahli clan member. He must gain control of the mines again. He must avenge his family. He has made an oath with a man named Quinten. Quinten has vowed to assassinate the Supreme Ruler that murdered the Catahli clan and to return Roan to his home territory. In exchange, Roan must supply Quinten with all the Catahli rings he can forge in order to secure Quinten's place as ruler of Elmyra.

I would be angry with Roan, but he's begged me to come with him. He will tell his wife his true feelings for me and the two of us will live happily in Siourious. The Catahli clan was regarded like royalty, which would mean as his new wife, I'd be royalty. I didn't have to think on his offer. I told Roan I'd follow him anywhere. I want so badly a new life away from Malcolm. My true life awaits me in Siourious. I always knew Roan was too beautiful for Bear Gap and I am far too clever for the dung heap.

#

Roan and I spend every possible moment together. His plan to return to the mines will take time and we have to be patient.

Yesterday while lying in bed I asked him to tell me the secrets of the Catahli. It's bold to ask since Catahli members are vowed to silence on the mysteries of the mineral. I pled with Roan and told him that if I am to live in the mines someday, I need to understand the Catahli like he does. Finally, after much pleading, he relented.

The big secret, he says, is that the Catahli is magic. It's an energy source. The way we use it, as currency in Elmyra, is a waste. Passing it from person to person is useless. I pressed Roan to tell me more.

He is a spell caster, he finally tells me. He focuses the energy of his mind to bring certain commands to fruition. He's able to locate or summon people whose energy he can connect with.

The Catahli is bursting with energy. Anyone disciplined enough to focus their mind can draw upon its powers. With Roan being away from the mines all these years, his energy is depleted, but once he's back, he'll be drunk with energy once again.

I could not control it. I laughed at Roan. I told him such things were told as children's tales. Prove it, I insisted. He smiled at me coyly and said he didn't feel the need to prove himself, but would oblige just for me.

Roan had me sit up in bed. He sat across from me and withdrew a stone from the night table, a raw hunk of Catahli. He took a deep breath and held my shoulders. He told me not to be scared but to trust him. I chuckled, not sure what to be scared of.

He placed a warm hand lightly on my chest and closed his eyes. At first I felt nothing, then slowly my heart began to beat faster and harder. I tried to steady myself but I realized I had no control over my own body. Panic shot through me and I felt my breathing turn heavy. But like the gentle dimming of the sun at the end of the day, my heart and my breathing slowed, first to a comfortable rate, then even slower to where I felt I could fall asleep. Then Roan moved his powers from my chest and into my mind. There he showed me images he wanted me to see: his home as a child, the coast with the ocean where I have never been, and the sparkling mines in Siourious. He cast on me the smells and the sights of those places.

Roan's hand dropped from my chest and he heaved in a great breath. His shoulders hung like he was exhausted from running.

When his eyes opened, I looked into them. This time I didn't laugh. I felt tiny and awestruck and for some reason I wanted to cry. Then I opened my mouth and barely whispered the words, teach me.

#

I drop the book on my lap and scrunch up my eyebrows. Portia writes of energy, meditation, and nature. When I saw her kill a man last fall by crushing his heart, nature didn't seem to have anything to do with it. I think of the few gray-colored rings I have in my bag. I never knew there was power to be obtained from them.

A rustling noise draws my attention to the other side of the cellar. I sit up and swing my legs over the side of my bed. Quietly I walk to the curtain and pull it open just enough to see the outline of Reed creeping up the ladder and out of the cellar.

CHAPTER EIGHTEEN

I KNEW IT. I knew something wasn't right with him. I slip through the curtain and tiptoe across the room. Just as I put my hands on the bottom of the ladder, Reed disappears through the trap door. He's been sneaking out. Maybe telling an informant what the rebellion is up to. I bet Reed knows exactly where Ivan is.

I follow quietly up the ladder. Slowly I creak open the flap and slip into Ivan's kitchen. I run to the window by the door and look out into the dark street. There's no movement. I turn around to face the empty house. It feels like ages since I've been aboveground. We've been . . . forgotten.

The floorboards squeak at the other end of the house. I lift my head, my ears alert. I place a hand on the wall and let it guide my bare feet down the hallway. I pause at the opening of a small parlor. Reed stands with his back to me, his hand on the mantle, staring into a dead fireplace.

"What are you doing up here?" I ask.

Reed isn't startled. He turns and looks at me, a half smile on his face.

"I needed to think."

In daylight I could imagine this as a quaint house. Two chairs sit on either side of a small wooden table that has a chessboard a top it, but all its pieces are missing. Decorative pillow rest on both chairs and the walls are hung with homespun tapestries. A woman once lived here.

"What about you, Camilla. What are you doing up at this hour?"

I drop my hand from the wall and casually slip into the room.

"I just needed to get warm. Can't stand being trapped down there any longer."

Reed looks at me with a pensive stare. "I know you're suspicious of me."

My shoulders relax. There's relief in knowing I don't need to keep up the facade. I only wish I'd brought my dagger with me. "Where were you going? I know you didn't come up here just to think."

Reed shifts away from the fireplace and peeks out the curtain of a nearby window. "Perhaps I should tell you the story I told Ivan."

"I'm not interested in stories. I want the truth."

Reed chuckles as he turns from the window. He takes a seat in the chair by the table.

"I wish it weren't the truth." He gestures at the chair opposite him.

Hesitantly I reach forward and pull out the chair, taking a seat across the table. The black-and-white-checkered board sits perfectly in the middle.

"Do you play?"

I shake my head, keeping my lips pressed tightly together.

"I know," Reed sighs. "You're not one for small talk. I'll tell you everything. The truth. By the end of it, you'll trust me."

"Prove it."

Reed sniggers as he leans across the table. A strand of his black hair breaks from its mold and falls into his eye.

"I wasn't quite right when I was born. People called me mad. They called me deranged and twisted." I watch Reed curiously. "As a kid I acted differently than my brothers and sisters. My mother didn't think I fit in with our family. She used to leave me at home with the maid when they went on social calls. She'd lock me away in my room and try to bury my existence."

"I had a lousy mother too. What does that have to do with the rebellion?"

The twitch returns to Reed's hand. "When I was fourteen, my parents pawned me off on my uncle, who was a captain in the Warwick Militia. I barely saw my family after that. They'd finally been rid of this stain on their family. My uncle treated me like a pile of dung. He resented my presence and made sure my stay in the militia was misery." Reed chuckles derisively. "He'd make me clean out the latrine at camp or scavenge the dead bodies of our fallen men."

I knit my eyebrows together. "Why did they hate you so much?"

"Well, I guess I haven't been completely honest with you, Camilla." Reed tilts his head so his gaze is level with mine. Looking into his striking blue eyes feels like I've stepped off the edge of a cliff and fallen into a deep pit. I can't pull myself out. "When I was a young boy, I went riding with a cousin. He fell from his horse and his head struck a rock. I watched him die. I was only the age of twelve." Reed takes a deep breath. "Six months after that I was playing with my sisters, swimming in a pond. My younger sister, Esme, drowned."

I suddenly remember to breath. I blink my eyes to shake myself from his trance. "They blamed you?"

"It was a curious accident with my cousin, but when my sister died and I was also present for that, they began to blame me. Some thought I'd frozen in fear. Others thought I was too young to know what to do. But then the rumors spread. I'd killed my cousin and sister intentionally."

"How could any boy of twelve be capable of such things?"

"You understand. My family didn't. I was so distraught over what I'd seen that I became even more unstable of mind. My parents hoped the militia would straighten me out. When it seemed to only make me worse, my family finally disowned me. My horrendous uncle did away with me and had me assigned far away from him. He transferred me under a different surname so I wouldn't bring shame to our family. I was cut off completely. They didn't quite have the nerve to have me killed. But they wanted me gone."

Reed can't hide his hurt. He leans back in his chair. His shoulders slump. I curl my own arms in on myself. I know how people have treated Tuor because he was different. Treating him like a monster only makes Tuor worse. Reed's family probably created the problem themselves.

"How do you handle it?" I whisper.

"Burying the pain doesn't help. I think that's why I talk so much." Reed gives me a weak smile. My mother is my pain. I haven't told a single soul about the journal. Why do I feel compelled to tell Reed? Why would I divulge something to him that I haven't even told Tuor or Mirabelle? Maybe that's why I want to. Reed doesn't know me, so he doesn't know my past or any of the stupid things I've done. I could tell him about my mother's journal and he wouldn't judge me.

"What's troubling you, Camilla?" Reed's gaze is tender. I purse my lips.

"I never knew my mother. I grew up with just my father. It wasn't great, but it was fine. It's worse, I think, if you know someone and then they leave you." Reed nods, appearing deeply invested in every word that comes out of my mouth. "Since I never knew my mother, I never even thought about her. I just . . . didn't care. Then all of sudden last year she came back. I don't want to have anything to do with her." I say it like I'm trying to convince myself.

"Because she hurt you?"

"No, she couldn't hurt me because I didn't know her."

"Then why reject her now?"

How do I explain to Reed the details of my mother? She's somehow tangled up with the Supreme Ruler. She's heartless and manipulative. Worse yet, she's a ruthless killer.

"She's done terrible things," I say, shaking my head.

Reed gives me a confused look and shifts awkwardly in his chair.

"Then she gives me her journal."

Reed's eyes widen.

"It's this whole book about her life. She wants me to read it."

"She gave it to you?" Reed's hand jolts with the return of his tremor. His neck muscles tense.

"I don't understand why she gave it to me. Does she want me to feel bad for her?"

Reed clenches his hand in and out until the shaking stops. He takes a deep breath and says, "Stories are always different depending on who tells them. Maybe she just wants you to understand her side."

"She had a tough childhood but so did I. I've chosen a different path, one that doesn't include . . . hurting people."

Reed stares into my face but his mind is far, far away.

"I think you should give your mother a chance. Maybe she's trying to make up for past hurts."

"But why should I? She had her chance to be a good mother and she chose not to."

"It sounds like she's giving it some effort now. Isn't that worth something?"

I sigh. The sound of crickets chirping bleeds through the closed windows.

"At least listen to what she has to say. You might learn something about her you didn't know."

I give Reed a smile meant just as a courtesy. The quiet of night dissolves. The sound of footfalls and heavy breathing draws close. I'm alert. Reed jumps to his feet. The back door opens. A stampede of footsteps crosses the threshold. I leave my chair, searching for a place to hide. Reed stands and pulls a knife from his boot.

Men's voices echo through the empty house. Reed stretches out his arm to protect me. The men march down the hall and come to a stop in front of the parlor. Ivan's tall frame stands in the threshold. He's wet, covered in mud, and blood speckles his face and neck.

"We have to talk."

CHAPTER NINETEEN

REED AND I are ushered back to the cellar with Ivan and his two sons. The noise of them returning had already woken everyone downstairs. Mirabelle stands in her nightdress, looking horrified.

"What's going on?" she asks.

Knox's eyes land on Ivan. He hobbles the length of the cellar. "We've been trapped in this place like rats."

"I apologize for our absence," Ivan says. He wipes mud from his face.

We congregate in a circle around Ivan.

"What happened?" Reed asks.

"Things have deteriorated in Bear Gap. Captain Thatius has shown a strong hand. We went to the swamps to speak to the farm workers but the place was littered with soldiers. Leather workers from Billage don't have a good excuse to be in the swamps. They caught our scent. We had to cross the river to get them off our tail. We hid in the wilderness for days until we had a chance to get back here. I haven't been to work since then. They know what I am. They know I'm part of the rebellion."

Despite Ivan's exhaustion he still stands tall.

"What about the farm workers?" I ask. "Were you able to talk to anyone?"

It's Damion that speaks. "They're the ones that turned us in."

"What?" Tuor says.

"Farm workers are useless," Tommy spits.

"We got into a few houses but they turned on us once they understood why we were there," Ivan says.

"I don't understand . . ." I mumble.

"The farm workers don't trust us," Knox says.

Ivan nods. "The rebels have only made their lives harder. They want nothing to do with us."

"Without the farm workers, all we have is us and a few disgruntled tradesmen," I say.

Tommy looks at me and laughs. "Forget about the farm workers!" He scans the rest of the group. "We oughta focus on Thatius. We've got small numbers, but we could get him when he's out in town. One shot to the chest and he'd be dead."

"You'd be arrested immediately," Reed says.

"So what?" Tommy shouts. "At least it'd be over."

Ivan eyes his son.

Knox speaks. "If we killed Captain Thatius, he'd just be replaced within a fortnight with someone else."

"Knox is right," I say. "We need to control the territory and to do that we need numbers. We *need* the farm workers."

Tommy drops his arms in frustration and turns from the group. He leans against the wall in the shadows, glaring at me. "Then what do you say we do, Camilla? You've been runnin' this thing."

"Calm down," Ivan demands of his son.

A familiar note of rage builds in my chest. I wait for Johnny to defend me, but when I look over at his sullen face, I remember he no longer has a reason to stand up for me.

"We need someone the farm workers trust," Knox says.

For the first time since Ivan's return, a moment of silence settles in the room. I scrunch my eyebrows as I consider Knox's words: someone the farm workers know and trust.

"Oh no," I say out loud without realizing it. "I know someone." Everyone in the room looks at me.

"Who?" Tuor asks cautiously. It's as if he can already sense he won't like my idea.

"Malcolm."

"No," Tuor says. "Not him, Camilla."

I take Tuor by his shoulders. "Look at me," I say calmly.

Tuor rocks his head back and forth. Everyone in this room is used to Tuor losing it from time to time, everyone except Reed. I chance a look at our new member. I'm not embarrassed by Tuor but concerned that Reed might do something to make things worse.

"Look at me," I say again, my voice stern. Tuor's head comes to a stop but he keeps his arms over his ears. "You won't see him. I'll talk to him and you don't even have to be there."

"Are you sure involving your father is a good idea?" Mirabelle asks.

"Not him . . ." Tuor moans.

I release Tuor's shoulders. "Malcolm knows everyone in the swamps and he works at the farm now. He's one of them."

"Can we even trust him?" Johnny asks. It's the first he's spoken during this whole meeting. He doesn't hide his irritation with my idea.

I think back on my trip into Rande. "Yes, he wouldn't give any of us away."

Reed steps up to Tuor and places a friendly arm around his shoulder. "You hate your father, right?"

I almost pull Reed off my brother, knowing that Tuor won't take to a stranger, but Tuor just looks at him, stunned. "You don't have to like someone to get them to do something for you. If your father can get lots of people to join us, then just focus on that." Reed gives Tuor a pat on the back, then turns to face the rest of the room. "Right?"

I stare dumbfounded at Reed.

Knox speaks. "Malcolm's been delivering alcohol to people in the swamps for years. Plus, he's lived there his whole life. He could make his way from house to house without any suspicion."

"He won't do it," Tuor says, an edge still in his voice.

I rub my hands together. "He'll do it. I'll get him to. If I can just talk to him, I'll convince him."

"How would you even get to him?" Mirabelle asks. "Ivan couldn't."

Damion stands like his father, legs spread wide and his chest puffed out. "You'd need to clear the swamp of soldiers to make it work."

Tommy scoffs at the idea. Knox and I look at each other.

"A distraction?" I ask. "What would get the soldiers to leave the swamps?"

"Reed, what say you? You were one of them not too long ago," Ivan asks.

"Well . . ." Reed stretches his arms out wide as he paces the room. "If there was a fight on the farm, we'd shout for help and nearby men would come running. So I suppose if we could make them think there was danger somewhere else, they'd leave."

"What if a prisoner broke out of the dungeons?" I say, remembering my trip to the dungeons with Johnny. "That would be enough, right?"

"That's a clever idea, Camilla," Reed says. He places a finger to his mouth.

"We have horses with the Warwick brand and Reed has his uniform," I say.

"We can stage a breakout from the dungeon long enough to get you in to talk to your father," Knox says.

Mirabelle holds her arms close to her chest. "Someone's going to pretend to be a Warwick soldier?" Mirabelle lets out a worried sigh. "What if they figure out that this person is not really a soldier? Oh, I don't want to think about what they'd do."

"I'm not going back to those swamps," Tommy says.

I let out a huff of air and tilt my head in annoyance. "No. I imagine you wouldn't."

"What's that?" Tommy challenges.

I lift my head to look at Tommy straight on and say, more clearly this time, "No. I imagine you wouldn't have the guts to return to the swamps because you're scared."

Tommy's face turns a pale red. He rolls his jaw, then pushes off the wall and charges me. Mirabelle screams. My feet stay firmly planted. Ivan grabs Tommy's arm. My body tenses, ready to strike, but Tuor flies in front of me and punches Tommy in the nose. Tommy drops his head, spilling blood on the ground.

"You're dead," Tommy says as he straightens his back.

"Damion," Ivan says firmly. "Take your brother upstairs. The two of you will keep watch during this meeting."

Tommy shoots me a dirty look. I reciprocate, never letting my gaze waver. Knox comes up behind me as Damion and Tommy scale the ladder.

"You need to stop this," Knox whispers in my ear.

I look at him sideways. "Why? I'm right."

"We have to work with them. We need them."

Tuor shakes Tommy's blood from his hand.

"Are you okay?" I ask.

He nods. Once Tommy and Damion have cleared the trap door, Ivan faces us again. He stares at the floor and catches his breath.

"It was not pretty what we went through there. Camilla, your idea's not well received but we are out of options. We could keep hiding until we all rot, or we could give your father a try." Ivan locks eyes with me. "We'd be putting a lot of trust in him."

I have the first glimmer of doubt; involving Malcolm might be a bad idea. Like Ivan said, we're out of options. We're desperate. What else is there to try?

"Who's gonna pretend to be the soldier?" Mirabelle asks. "Maybe it should be Reed."

"I'm afraid that won't work. I'm a traitor. Most of the soldiers around here will recognize me. Same for Tuor. He shouldn't do it."

"I'll do it," Johnny says, stepping forward. He holds eye contact with Reed. "I've been around a dirty

Warwick soldier long enough. Playing one should be pretty easy.

CHAPTER TWENTY

I'VE NEVER SEEN Johnny as annoyed as he is now, standing in Ivan's stable wearing a Warwick uniform. He tugs uncomfortably at the vest that's too small for him. Johnny, Knox, Reed, Ivan, and I gather one final time before we make our trip into the swamps to meet with Malcolm.

"We can't afford any missteps," Knox says. "If one of us screws up, we risk the whole group. Let's go over the plan again."

Johnny rolls his eyes in contempt over his uncle's thoroughness. This is easily the fifth time we've reviewed the plan that we hastily put together.

"The four of you ride together into Rande," Knox says, pointing to Reed, Johnny, Ivan, and me. "Johnny continues to the Justice House. Camilla and Reed get into place at the top of the hill while Ivan positions himself near the posting tree. Johnny will ride from the Justice House to the swamps and call for reinforcements." Knox turns to Reed and me. "As soon as the swamps look clear, you have to move. You won't have much time. Johnny will lead the reinforcements into the woods behind the Justice House." Knox shifts his attention to Johnny. "You know what you're doing then?"

"There's a spot just west of Billage where the forest rises, then drops hard into a creek. As long as I'm over that hill before them, I can hide in the gully until they pass. Then I'll circle back to Rande."

"We are trained for situations just like this," Reed says. Johnny's eyes drift away the moment he begins speaking. "The protocol is to assemble first and make a search plan."

"Even if every single soldier sticks with protocol, that should still clear the swamps long enough to get Camilla to her father," Johnny says. He rolls his shoulders, the tight vest irritating him. "I will get the swamps clear."

"When they figure out it's a ploy," Knox says. "Ivan will signal to Camilla and Reed and you better run."

I nod in understanding.

"Then we all meet at Mirabelle's house. It was empty yesterday. Tuor and I will make sure it's clear tonight. Everybody understand?"

We saddle our horses and Knox sees us off. We slip into the night. The sun has just set. Everyone that lives in the swamps should be home, including Malcolm. The streets of Billage are sparse. Ivan leads us out of Billage and into the woods. We enter Rande from the east side, which is at the opposite end from the farm. We move slowly through the trees until the street lanterns begin flickering through the leaves.

"The posting tree should be just up ahead," I whisper.

"Maybe we should split off here," Johnny says.

"No," Ivan snaps. "We stick to the plan."

"Last time I was here there was a curfew," I say. "Any movement and we're going to get stopped. We need to stay—"

A shout rings through the forest. "Stop there!" The voice is loud and cocky. The light of a lantern weaves through the trees.

"Fall back," Ivan says under his breath.

Shae whinnies as I pull on her reins. Johnny kicks his mount to lead us back to Billage. Like a monster from the deep, another soldier appears from behind us. The moonlight glints off his drawn sword and reveals a smile of gangly teeth.

"I said, stop there," the voice calls from behind me. I turn around to see the soldier with the lantern approach. Even mounted on his horse, I can tell he's a short man. He looks young and eager to exercise some power. "Everyone off your horses," he yells, punctuating every word. "*Now.*"

"*I* found these people," Johnny says. "They were out past curfew, so I'm taking them back to the swamps."

The soldier with the teeth circles around us. The short one squints his eyes at Johnny. "What's your name, soldier?"

"Rob Spoke," Johnny says.

I can tell even through the darkness the soldier's not fooled.

"Never heard of you. Now everyone off your horses."

I swing my legs over to slip off Shae. Johnny hesitates.

"Let's go. Let's go. Move."

"They're mine," Johnny says through gritted teeth. "I will take care of them."

The short soldier nudges his horse closer to Johnny and says, "The only people authorized to be on this side of Rande are myself and Wallace over there. So either you're not Rob Spoke, or Rob Spoke is about to find himself in the stocks. Now get off your horse and get on the ground before I have Wallace run you through."

Johnny clenches his jaw and grips the reins tightly. Wallace corrals Ivan, Reed, and me with the tip of his sword.

"Join your captives," the short soldier says sarcastically. "Don't make this difficult."

Finally Johnny jumps off his horse and slowly backs away. He comes to stand next to me on my left while Reed is on my right. We prepared for something like this. The problem is, we expected to be able to pass Johnny off as a soldier. The only plan now is to fight. I casually reach for my dagger.

"Hands up," the short soldier yells. Reed raises his arms carefully. I expect him to be panicking, but when I look at his hand, it's still. Wallace takes Ivan's sword from his belt and tosses it on the ground behind him. "Hey, Wallace, hold this up to her face." Wallace takes the lantern from the soldier in charge and flashes it in my eyes. From atop his horse, the soldier lets out a joyous yelp mixed with laughter. "That's the girl!"

Wallace speaks. "What girl?"

The short soldier hops off his horse and draws his sword. He walks toward me and takes my chin in his hand. "Look, that's her! The one that killed the governor."

He flips my arm over to inspect my mutilated scar. The two men look at each and cheer at the sight of me.

"I'm gonna guess that you're no soldier," he says, turning to Johnny.

"Let's get them roped up. Everyone on your knees. Let's go!"

I fall to my knees and look over at Johnny. I want to ask him what should we do? But Johnny is so furious he won't even look me. A boot kicks me in the back and I'm forced to the ground. I feel a hand run down my side until the soldier finds my dagger. He pulls it from my belt and uses a rope to tie my hands behind my back. I still feel the dull ache of the cut on my stomach as I'm pressed to the ground.

Wallace paces back and forth with his sword drawn. "We are gonna be rich," he says, a laugh on his lips. "Taking them to Captain Thatius is going to set us up good. Rebels, I'd guess, all of you." He throws back his head and roars toward the moon.

"They thought she was gone," the short soldier says as he tightens the cord around my wrists. Satisfied with my restraints, he grabs a chunk of my hair, twists my head, and whispers in my ear, "I bet they'll untie Karla long enough so she can eat you alive."

"Don't touch her!" Johnny shouts.

"I'll touch her if I want to!" He marches toward Johnny and kicks him in the stomach. I turn my head to look away and find myself staring into Reed's blue eyes. Johnny moans as he's kicked again. Wallace laughs as he comes to stand above Reed and me.

Reed moves his arms to his side and presses the palms of his hands into the ground. In one fluid motion, he pushes himself up and grabs Wallace by the neck, pulling him to the ground. Reed buries Wallace's neck under his arm and squeezes.

"Hey!" the short soldier shouts.

He charges Reed, his sword raised to strike, but just before the tip of his blade finds its mark, Reed rips Wallace from the ground and uses him as a shield. The soldier drives his sword into the belly of his friend. All pride melts from his face. Wallace's eyes grow to the size of chicken eggs.

Johnny is on his feet. He grabs for his sword through a pile of damp leaves. Reed tosses Wallace aside, the sword still stuck in him. He takes the short soldier in his hand and slams him onto the ground. Lifting his shoulders, he slams the soldier into the ground again and again and again until the forest floor is inked with wetness.

"Give me that," Reed says as Johnny comes to his side.

Johnny unsheathes his sword and hands it to Reed. The short soldier reaches for Reed's face. Reed slaps him with the back of his hand, then takes the sword and sets the tip over the soldier's throat.

"No! Please!"

Taking a deep breath, Reed plunges the sword hard toward the ground. The soldier manages another gurgled "no" before blood erupts from his neck. Reed stares calmly at the dying man. Slowly he pulls the sword from the soldier's neck, allowing the wound to gape and bleed. Reed studies the ashen face and glossy eyes of the soldier with great interest. I can't help but notice that Reed's breathing is steady and his hand still.

CHAPTER TWENTY-ONE

JOHNNY TRIES TO untie the ropes from my wrists, but it's not until Ivan comes with my dagger that he's able to cut them off. I sit on the forest floor with my knees pointed up. Ivan hands me my dagger. Johnny touches his ribs and makes a pained look. His face is flecked with blood.

I glance over at Reed. My mind struggles to comprehend his ruthlessness. But it's war, I remind myself, and I can't question anything because he just saved all our lives. Blood appears on Reed's shirt at the base of his chest.

"You're bleeding," I tell him.

He looks at the spot and touches it with his hand. "The tip must have gotten me." He stands and looks at the two dead men at his feet.

"We should keep moving," Reed says. He helps me to my feet.

"Are you sure we should?" I ask. "Johnny's hurt and so are you. Maybe we should try another night."

"I'm inclined to agree," Ivan says. "If we ran into this much trouble just outside of town, how are we going to make it to the swamps and back?"

"It won't be long until they realize these men are missing," Reed says. "Once they find their bodies, they'll suspect rebel activity. We should do this now while we know we have two less soldiers at our backs."

I look over at Johnny, waiting for his opinion. He wipes the blood from his face. "This won't get any easier if we try another day. We do it now."

Reed drags the bodies together while Ivan cuts down some branches to cover them. In silence we mount our horses and ride into Rande. We take a quick left toward the swamps. At the top of the hill we can see the whole swamp village. It's dotted with torchlight. As we suspected, Captain Thatius has kept the area heavily guarded.

"I'm going to my spot by the posting tree," Ivan says, leaving the three of us alone.

"Johnny, can you still do this?" I ask.

Without even looking at me, Johnny kicks off his horse and heads toward the Justice House. Reed and I dismount and tie up our horses so that we're ready to run when our moment arrives.

"They're not going to completely empty the swamps of soldiers," Reed says. "You know that, right?"

"I know."

I can't get the image of him murdering those soldiers out of my mind. He did the right thing. Those soldiers were going to turn us in, but he seemed . . . unfazed. I look sideways at Reed. Through the darkness he catches me staring.

"I was so worried," he says. "There's no telling what they were going to do to you."

"Did you know them from working at the farm?"

"Oh, no." Reed shakes his head. "We must have been stationed at different places. I just saw them touching you and I lost it. I'm sorry if it scared you."

"You didn't scare me," I lie. I manage a weak smile.

Johnny's voice bursts through the night air. It's muffled but I hear him shout, " . . . breach at the Justice House . . ." and " . . . all available reinforcements requested . . ." He plays the part of a desperate Warwick soldier well. The torchlights begin to scale the hill into Rande.

"It's working," I whisper. "They're moving."

"Let's go, now."

My feet slip on the wet earth as we run down the embankment. I pause behind a thick trunk to scan the woods. There are still a few soldiers roaming the swamps.

"Follow me," I tell Reed.

I sprint down the hill until it levels off into the low land. I duck underneath the first house we come to. I know the people that live here. They have two daughters about the age of eleven, who I can hear chattering through the floorboards. A massive body of stagnant water lays before us. The smell of it brings a wash of different emotions to my mind.

I motion with my hand for Reed to follow. We move forward, running deeper into the swamp town. Firelight flickers through the wood slats of the houses as we pass. A soldier wanders a few yards away, his torch a beacon in these black woods. I pull Reed to hide underneath Lina's house.

I can see Malcolm's shack from here. Just the sight of it puts a hiccup in my chest. What if Portia is there again? What if this was another way for her to lure me to her? I suddenly feel a flush of panic. What was I thinking coming down here again?

The soldier paces away from us and I make a move for the front door of Malcolm's house. I hesitate just for a moment before pushing it open and then quickly closing it behind Reed and me. Glancing around the room, I'm relieved to see that my father is the only one here. He sits in his chair at the table as he usually does, only there's no amber bottle in his hand. I don't see any alcohol anywhere.

"I heard them rat soldiers out there shouting just now," Malcolm says. "I should have known it had something to do with you. Who's that?"

I exhale and step toward the table.

"This is Reed. We're only here for a few moments." I take a seat at the table. "I need to ask something of you."

Malcolm watches Reed as he takes long strides around the shack.

"This is about your mother, isn't it?" Malcolm asks.

"What?" I stutter, surprised he brought her up.

"You want to ask me about your mother. That's why you're here."

Reed's turns to look at Malcolm at the mention of my mother. Malcolm takes a gulp from a cup he grips in his hand.

"No." I shake my head, confused. "No, that's not it."

I'd be lying to myself if I didn't admit that my mind has been spinning with questions about my mother. I wish I could talk to someone about it, but I never thought of Malcolm as that person. I look at my father's bulbous nose and pockmarked face. He doesn't know anything about my mother anyway.

"No," I say again. "I want to talk about the farm workers, the people that live here."

Malcolm raises an eyebrow.

"Look, I need you to promise me—can you promise me that what I'm about to tell you, you'll— you'll treat it with discretion?"

Malcolm rubs his scruffy beard. "You want to know if I'll turn you in."

"Essentially yes."

"How'd you make it out?" Malcolm asks. "I assumed Karla had done you in by now. Figured she couldn't wait for a public execution and just killed you herself."

"Will you promise me secrecy?" I ask, ignoring his rambling.

Malcolm leans back in his chair. "You're still worth a lot of rings in this territory. I had a day in the stocks for punching out that soldier for you."

I swallow hard and shift away from the table. Maybe it *was* a mistake coming here. Had I misinterpreted my father the last time we spoke?

I bow my head. "Thank you for that, for saving me."

"I should turn you in, just like you did to me."

My mouth opens, surprised by his sharp words. I've not heard him talk this way in a while. Usually when he's angry, he yells and spits profanities. He hasn't forgotten about my turning him in to Benedek for illegal production.

"That was different. I did that to save Tuor," I say.

"And did it help?"

No, it didn't but I'm not admitting that to him.

"The difference is you were actually guilty, Tuor wasn't. He didn't kill anyone. He's innocent and so am I."

Malcolm chuckles. "You're far from innocent."

"What does that mean?"

"I know you didn't kill the governor," Malcolm says.

I look at Reed. He still believes I *did* kill Governor Leo. This lie is getting more complicated.

"You didn't kill that prick but you did break into the farm. And then you snatched Tuor from being executed and in the process a lot of rat soldiers died."

I look at my hands, remembering the first soldier I killed and being covered in his blood.

"I did all of that for Tuor."

"It don't matter why you did it. You broke the law, *Warwick* law."

Malcolm sets down his cup hard against the table and then leans back in his chair. He pushes his chair all the way back and props one of his feet up on the table. "You're no different than me. You're a lawbreaker, a defector—scum. The only difference is I've paid for my crimes. You haven't."

"So you expect me to turn myself in and take my punishment? I'll be executed."

Malcolm laughs. "Do you think what you did was wrong?"

"No," I say quickly. "Do you?"

Malcolm stares at me from across the table. His skin is tough and weathered. His lips are dry and cracked. He looks deep in thought, daydreaming about something from long ago.

It was a simple question, I thought. I already know the answer. He's never thought that drinking his liquor or poaching was wrong. He's never felt bad about that. But maybe it's not those sins that he's thinking on right now.

My mother left him, I remind myself. She up and left for a better life. Malcolm was forced to raise Tuor and me by himself. That still gave him no right to treat me the way he did, but between him and my mother, Malcolm was the better parent.

"I've done a lot of bad," Malcolm admits. "But now I want to do some good." Malcolm bows his head, avoiding my gaze. "For you."

I clear my throat, surprised by the first inkling of guilt I've ever seen on my father's face. I quickly recover my shocked expression. This is still Malcolm Crim. He could be playing me.

"We've started a rebellion. To take back Bear Gap from the Supreme Ruler."

I practically hold my breath, instantly regretting that I told my father. One thing I know about Malcolm; he hates our government more than he dislikes me.

"But we need more people. In order to make it work, we need the farm workers on our side. We outnumber the soldiers in this territory easily but we have to stick together."

I wait, expecting Malcolm to laugh at me.

"You're asking me to join your group?"

"I'm asking you to spread the word to those who would be on our side." Our side . . . it's a strange thing, my father and I being on the same side. "I can't talk to them. The farm workers don't trust me." Malcolm stands abruptly from the table. "You hate Warwick and so do I. Can you help me?" Carefully he places his empty cup on a shelf above the stove.

Reed stops his pacing and turns to face my father.

"I'll think on it," he says simply.

I stand too as Malcolm reaches behind his head to scratch his neck. The sound of Ivan's whistling drifts into the swamps. It reminds me that I'm on borrowed time.

"Camilla," Reed says, making sure I heard it.

"We have a meeting scheduled. Tell the farm workers to meet us at Mirabelle's old house in two days at dusk. You remember where her house is, right?"

Malcolm chuckles. "I remember."

"Is that enough time?"

"I guess we'll see," Malcolm says.

Ivan whistles again.

"Let's go," Reed says.

I look at my father, who's been beaten by life. Regularly he used to hit me across my face, yet now somehow I feel sorry for him. "Promise me you won't tell anyone I was here."

"I won't join your little rebellion," he says, ignoring my last statement. "I've caused enough trouble in this territory."

Reed grabs my arm and pulls me toward the door.

"Promise me," I say.

Just before Reed drags me from the house, Malcolm nods in agreement. Reed pulls me out the front door. Soldiers descend on the swamps. We scurry under the house to the spot where I used to hide Tuor's box.

"Search every house!" one soldier yells. His shout echoes over the swamp.

A soldier enters Lina's house and barks commands for her and her son to step outside. Another soldier passes us on our left. He stomps up the steps to my father's house and swings open the door.

"I'm not moving," I hear my father say stubbornly.

"You love hanging in those stocks, don't you," the soldier mocks.

With my father distracting the soldier, we make a break. Reed and I run toward the hill. The air is cold and prickles my skin. Reed jerks me under another shack by my arm. He holds me still as another soldier jogs past. Out into the open again, we sprint for the top of the hill. Ivan waits for us, his sword drawn. He's tense.

"We've lost our window," Ivan says through tight lips. He looks to the swamps, then behind him. "They've figured out the ruse. We're surrounded."

"We should wait for things to clear while we're under cover of the forest," Reed says.

The street fills with soldiers. The number of torches in the swamps grows with every passing moment.

"Maybe we should try to make it back to your father's," Ivan says. "Hide there until things settle."

I shake my head, looking left then right. "They're searching all the homes. We wouldn't make it."

Ivan looks again to the street. "Back the way we came is out of the question. We'll have to go around the swamps and follow upriver until things are clear."

Reed nods, scanning the dark woods. "It's not a great plan but it'll have to do."

"Follow me," Ivan says.

He jumps onto his horse and kicks off hurriedly into the woods. Reed and I mount our horses and follow a few paces behind. With barely the moonlight to guide us, we gallop downhill toward the river, avoiding the swamps.

"There could be spotters out here," Reed says. "We should go slow."

Ivan spills onto the barren bank of the River Hanover. He turns his horse around to face us. I kick Shae to go faster. Torchlight bursts suddenly from the bush that surrounds Ivan. On either side of him, a small band of soldiers emerge. I pull Shae to a skidding stop. I watch, frozen, as Ivan pushes his horse back up the hill, but he doesn't make it.

"Camilla," Reed says, grabbing my arm and pulling me to a stop. Ivan is ripped off his horse and tossed onto the ground. A soldier kicks him in the stomach and then holds him to the ground while pressing his boot into Ivan's back.

"We have to do something," I say.

Reed's grip on my arm stays firm. "There's nothing we can do."

The soldier ties Ivan's hands behind his back and pulls him to his feet. As the soldier turns around, Ivan's bloody face comes into view. It's then that I realize I have a new enemy. It's not just *some* soldier that has Ivan bound and bloody. It's Lawrence.

CHAPTER TWENTY-TWO

WE'RE TRAPPED ON all sides: the swamps behind us, the river to our right, and Rande Square to our left. I don't have time to sort out Lawrence's loyalties.

"Follow me," I say.

I push Shae forward into the woods. There could be other soldiers hiding in our path but it's better to go now while they're distracted with Ivan. Reed and I ride in silence through the woods, avoiding the streets completely. We manage to slip through the trees unnoticed by any other hidden soldiers.

It's another hour before the dark figure of Mirabelle's house comes into view. The moonlight barely illuminates the brick facade. This building has always seemed ancient to me, but as Reed and I ride closer, I can tell it's deteriorated even more over the last few months. The windows are dark and the snaking vines have taken over the front door and chimney.

A few yards out, I pull Shae to a stop. I've become far too suspicious to just walk up to any house or building. I pull my dagger from my belt. Reed looks my way, his eyes dark and solemn. We dismount and secure our horses. Reed pulls his own sword from its scabbard.

"There's an entrance to the root cellar on the side," I whisper.

Reed nods. Tall grass has taken over the lawn. I grope for the side of the house then look through a dust-coated window but there is no light within.

"There should be a door hatch around here somewhere," I say.

The door to the root cellar was once visible, but the lawn is now a tangle of thick weeds. I run my hands along the cold earth feeling for anything that's not vegetation. Reed knocks his heel on the ground in organized steps around me. A hollow thump breaks through the sound of the chirping crickets. Reed motions with his finger.

"I think I found it," he says.

I bend over and dig through the grass and weeds until I locate a rusty handle protruding. I yank on it hard. The door creaks open, the sound echoing through the trees. Reed glances around the yard before I swing the trap door the rest of the way open and step onto the cold stone steps.

It's utterly dark except for the faintest of moonlight pouring through the open door. There's no lit candle or torch to show the way. Fortunately, I know the way without any light. The tip of Reed's sword lightly scrapes the damp wall as we descend. He lets the door close so that we're in complete blackness.

The smell of mold and rotten fruit is so pungent, I cover my mouth. Behind me, Reed coughs. I grope for the door and run my hand along the splintered wood until I find the handle. I push it open and tumble into

Mirabelle's basement kitchen. Reed reaches out and grabs me by the elbow. My whole body jolts in fear at his touch. A thin line of faint light shines under the door at the top of the steps, giving the room a glow.

"This way," I whisper, using the long table to guide me to the steps.

The tip of my boot collides with the bottom step. I clumsily scale the first few steps. Reed's hand still sits in the crook of my elbow. I push open the door and creep into a dimly lit back hall. Reed follows closely as I skirt around the corner. Soft voices waft in our direction. The sound echoes against the high ceilings and big windows.

With our backs against the wall, I slowly turn my head to look at Reed. His sword is drawn and at the ready. I don't say anything and neither does he, but we exchange a thought. We must be ready for whoever is in Mirabelle's front hall. Swiftly I turn the corner and peer into the cluttered book-laden library.

Knox draws his sword as we round the corner. Tuor's eyes fall to Reed's grip on my elbow. I move into the room, shaking off his hand and returning my dagger to my belt.

"What held you up?" Knox asks, sheathing his sword.

I look to Reed and say, "We ran into some trouble."

"I knew it," Tuor says. He brings his hands to the side of his head. "What has our father done?"

"No," I say quickly. "It's not him. He'll keep things quiet."

"Ivan's been arrested," Reed says, returning his sword to its sheath.

Knox says nothing. He puts his hands on his hips and peers around the room, frustrated.

"What happened?" Tuor asks.

The image of Lawrence spinning around, Ivan in his grip, flashes across my mind. I look at Tuor, knowing that when I tell him, and I must tell him, he's going to be upset.

"It was Lawrence. They'd set up a trap for us, like they knew we were going to be there. We were funneled right into their trap. Ivan was ahead of us and we just barely got away." I look at Tuor. "Lawrence seemed to be in charge of the ambush. He's the one that arrested Ivan."

"You're wrong."

"It was him," I say gently.

"He wouldn't do that. He's on our side."

Tuor grabs at the side of his head. He turns away from me. I'm as disappointed as Tuor, but I have to admit that it wouldn't make sense for Lawrence to try to trap me. Why help me escape from Harras Manor only to arrest me again weeks later?

"How did it go with Malcolm?" Knox asks.

I nod tentatively. "Good. I mean, it went okay."

"It went well," Reed affirms.

"I think he's going to talk to some people," I say. "There's just no telling for sure if anyone will show up, but he knows where we'll be for the next couple of days."

"You don't see a problem with Father knowing that?" Tuor says. He's huddling in the corner.

"He's not going to turn us in. The only thing I know for sure about my father is that he hates Warwick soldiers more than anything else."

I look around the room anxiously. No one really knows what my father will do. He's as unpredictable as my mother.

"Johnny's not back yet?" I ask scanning the room.

"Johnny and Mirabelle have gone to bed already," Knox says.

Johnny didn't stay up to make sure I got back okay? My stomach sinks. We're not together anymore, I remind myself.

"Whatever he did out there, it worked," I say.

Knox moves to a nearby window and pulls the curtain closed. "We're going without a fire while we're here. We'll take shifts keeping watch. We all need some sleep. Go upstairs and find a bedroom. I'll keep watch tonight."

I grab my bag and reach for the stairwell's railing. My eyes are bleary as I climb the stairs one step at I time. Instinctively I walk to Mirabelle's bedroom. Mirabelle's lying like a lump under the covers.

Memories of Mirabelle's house hit me suddenly like a burst of light through an open window. This is the one place I always felt safe. I pull the door closed, drop my bag on the floor, and kick off my boots.

"Camilla?" Mirabelle calls to me, her voice laced with sleep.

"It's me."

"Glad you're safe," she mumbles.

"Go back to sleep."

I curl up under those familiar covers and fall asleep instantly.

***

It's midday when I wake. The sun is blaring through the windows. I sit up and put my feet on the floor. Mirabelle's floral carpetbag is at the end of the bed. My messenger bag has been hung on the hook by the door, and my boots have been straightened with their toes against the wall.

The hallway is empty. I lean over the railing to peer down to the library. It's also empty. The only light comes from a crack in the curtain. I feel a clench of worry. Why isn't anyone guarding the front hall? I run down the steps in my bare feet. I jump at the sound of movement. Johnny stands like a statue by a window facing the front lawn. His sword hangs from his belt but his hands are buried in his pockets.

"Everyone's downstairs," he says.

"Oh."

I take a few tentative steps into the front hall. Every surface is laden with piles of dusty books. The rug by the door has been kicked and torn. Mud cakes the floor. A window's been broken out. It's obvious where the Warwick soldiers walked as they raided this place.

"Any trouble last night?" I ask.

Johnny stands stiff from the bruised ribs. He has a red streak across his cheek.

"Nothing I couldn't handle."

I nod as he turns his face to the window. Despite all the junk in Mirabelle's house, I feel an immense emptiness. I stare at my hands. How do I form the words to make Johnny understand? I hate that he hates me.

When nothing clever comes to my mind, I say plainly, "Johnny, I'm sorry."

Slowly he turns to look at me. I wonder if he'll ignore me or pretend he doesn't know what I'm talking about.

"I thought I was going to have to watch you die last night. It scared me. I . . ." He hesitates. "I don't want to be angry with you anymore."

His honesty surprises me. After days of enduring his silence and hateful gazes, I'm now the one that feels bad.

"I'm sorry I had to push you out," I say quietly.

"Why couldn't I be a part of it? Why can't I be there to help you through it?"

I hang my head and do my best to answer honestly. "I think I'm too broken for you."

Johnny laughs, tossing his head back and forth. "What?"

"You're not broken, Camilla. Would a broken person be able to keep going after what you went through?"

"I can barely sleep at night." My voice rises in my own defense. "Mirabelle can't hug me without me drowning in panic!"

Johnny's voice turns soft. "You still wake up in the morning. You're still fighting for this rebellion. You're still here. You're not broken." He turns back to the window, peering into the distance. "I'm sorry too. I think you're right. It's best that you're by yourself for a while."

It's painful to hear those words. I don't want to be alone but I can't be with Johnny either.

"You're not broken," Johnny says again. Finally his gaze falls to me. "Nothing could break you."

I smile, a real smile. I'm forgiven. That's enough for me. "Can I ask you a favor… as a friend?"

Johnny purses his lips and tilts his head.

"I still need to practice my fighting, more than ever. Could we…" I hesitate. It's a risky request. "Could we continue our lessons?"

Johnny's face relaxes. He nods as he turns back to the window. "Report to me after breakfast. We'll get you started with a sword."

I'm more excited than I've been in a long time. I leave Johnny in the front hall. At the door to the basement kitchen I hear their voices: Tuor, Mirabelle, Knox, and Reed. I stop and listen for a moment.

My feet take the cold stone steps down to the kitchen. Mirabelle stands at the stove while everyone else is seated at the long table. Knox sits at the head and gives me a nod as I enter.

"Camilla, dear." Mirabelle wipes her hands on her apron and gives me a hug. "Have a seat and I'll get you a bowl."

"Good morning," Reed says brightly.

I sit next to Tuor, across the table from Reed. Tuor inhales a bowl of soup.

"What could you have possibly made?" I ask. "We barely have any supplies."

"Oh, just a little mushroom soup." Mirabelle places a bowl in front of me. "There are still so many mushrooms growing in the yard. I scooped some up and threw this soup together."

"It's very good," Reed says.

Mirabelle blushes. She twitters between the stove and the table. I haven't seen her this happy for months. She's back in *her* kitchen making *her* food.

"I don't want you making any more trips outside the house," Knox scolds.

Mirabelle clicks her tongue, waving away his concern.

"You don't seem to mind the fruits of that risk."

Knox pauses with a spoon full of mushroom soup in his hand.

"How did you sleep?" Reed asks me.

"I slept good, really good." I look around the table. Maybe it's because I slept in a familiar bed last night. Maybe it's because I've mended things with Johnny. Maybe it's because everyone seems content, even Knox, but when I look at everyone in the room, they feel like family. I am not alone. I could never be alone as long as I'm with them.

Despite a warm, familial breakfast and a challenging training session with Johnny, I find the desire to read my mother's journal undeniable. As soon as I'm able, I slip away to the top floor of Mirabelle's library. It's a tiny room with only a few books. My hands shaking, I hurriedly flip through my mother's journal and start reading where I last left off.

\#

For two months I have ignored the signs. It's so inconvenient. It couldn't happen at a worse time. Any day we're set to leave Bear Gap. But I must now face it. I am again pregnant. Living through the torture with Tuor was bad enough. Now I must do it again? I can't fathom the thought. I've been ringing my hands all day. I must break the news to Roan. I wouldn't be so nervous about confessing it to him except I can't be certain that he's the father.

\#

I've been a mess all day, running around this house like a mad woman. Roan was completely uninterested in knowing whether the child was his or Malcolm's. I thought he'd delight at the possibility of an heir to the Catahli mines but all he said was that he wasn't taking a pregnant woman on the journey. He won't take me. I can't go to Siourious and escape Bear Gap unless I rid myself of this parasite inside my body. My tears didn't move him. He had no sympathy for my state. I left his house and immediately consulted with the apothecary. He lives down river and is known amongst the harlots as the one to rescue them from an unwanted baby. His home was a vile place, filled with snakes and rats. It reeked of an unwashed body. But when I told him what I needed, he didn't hesitate. He handed me a bottle of thick, murky liquid and took every ring I had brought with me. He told me to drink it tonight and by the morning I would no longer be with child. I need this to work. The potion must work.

#

The potion didn't work. By some miracle I lived. I let out a long and jagged breath. There is a sick, lonely feeling that comes with realizing that from the onset of my life I wasn't wanted. I was never desired or loved by my mother. I falsely believed that she had cared for me at least a little bit during those first years of my life.

I was wrong, very wrong. I was a shackle for my mother and she couldn't wait to get away from me. Then why does she want me so badly now? Is it guilt she's feeling?

I find it hard to believe that a woman who regularly slits men's throats without a thought could feel guilt over abandoning her child so many years ago. But the person who wrote this isn't the Portia that I know now. She's selfish, that's still the same, but there's an innocence to her that somewhere along the lines was lost.

As I close the journal, I'm plagued with a far more troubling question than my mother's motives. While still married to Malcolm, Portia was deeply embroiled in an affair with Roan. So is Malcolm my father or Roan?

CHAPTER TWENTY-THREE

THE SUN SETS on our second day at Mirabelle's house. Not a single farm worker has shown up to join the rebellion. I've been distracting myself with all day fighting lessons with Johnny. The loss of romance between us has made Johnny less fearful of my wellbeing.

He challenges me like a true opponent. Without hesitation he stuck a sword in my hand. He's taught me basic swordplay along with moves that he deems, *foolish, but helpful if you're backed into a corner.*

It's been a slow realization for all of us that the farm worker plan won't work. Every day, every hour that passes, the likelihood seems less and less. Seeking help from Malcolm has failed. Looking back, I suppose it was a long shot. I'll never know if the farm workers were too scared to show up or if Malcolm never even bothered to tell anyone.

If no one shows up tonight, we'll have to regroup and come up with a new plan. With Ivan being arrested, we've lost contact with the Billage rebels. The plan was for Damion and Tommy to abandon the house and find a new place to hide, but we have no knowledge of where.

I pace the length of Mirabelle's front hall. It's my turn to keep watch. Everyone else has gone to bed. Decisions will have to be made in the morning. Malcolm or Roan…? I can't get the thought out of my head.

I run my finger across the spines of a row of books. These were Mirabelle's treasures. It must have been hard for her to leave them behind when we fled Rande. I wander back to the library and stack a few books that have fallen on the floor.

After straightening the library, I pull a cushioned chair to a nearby window where I can see out into the front lawn. I lay my head against the wall and stare into the trees bathed in moonlight. I used to wish to live in this house with Mirabelle. I'd picture myself sleeping in my own bedroom and playing outside. Mirabelle would serve all my meals in her kitchen.

Malcolm held me back. I felt I could never leave him. How stupid I was. If I could go back to when I was younger, I'd walk out on my father. If I'd done that, maybe I wouldn't still be tied up with my mother. Why do all of my thoughts always return to her? I feel attached to her now, like there's a thin cord connecting us.

I suppose I can't really call Malcolm my father that's for sure. I picture him in my head. Haven't I always resembled him; my wide hips, my square nose? I have no way of knowing what Roan looks like. Perhaps I resemble him more clearly. What about pieces of my personality? They could have easily been picked up from years of living with Malcolm.

My hand rests on the arm of the chair. I squeeze my fingers into a fist and then out again. I want to read my mother's journal right now. I want to read it badly. I test myself to see how long I can ignore it. I force myself to look out the window and be on watch like I'm supposed to be. The woods are clear.

I pop out of my seat. My bag sits on a chair across the room. I rush toward it, flip it open, and pull out the journal. The tension leaves my hands instantly. I take the book over to my spot by the window. With the faint moonlight, I open the journal and begin to read.

\#

Roan has disappeared. I searched his house today. I searched the entire territory and found no sign of him or his plain wife. He's in hiding I suppose. Is he hiding from me or Bradac? Roan is no man. A man wouldn't leave his love alone and with child. I curse his name.

\#

Months after this entry, I am born. There are hardly ten words written about my birth. The simplest task of even naming me seems difficult for my mother. The only thing I can assume is that Malcolm gave me the name Camilla. Elmyra was surprisingly a quiet place for over a year. My mother barely wrote. Then Roan and Quinten finally made their move.

\#

I haven't felt this way since Mamma's death. Every bone in my body is quivering. I've received news of Roan. He must still be alive. Word has finally spread to Rande that there is a lone surviving Catahli clan member and that he's just taken back the mines from Supreme Ruler Bradac. The rumors purport that with a small army led by a young Warwick man, Roan was able to gain control. Bradac still sits on the throne but he's weak. He's at Roan's mercy and now Roan will be more prepared than the clan was before. Surely he has used his incantation powers to place protective spells over the mines to keep Bradac's men out. I must remind myself not to think on this too much. It matters not that I believe I could help Roan with his crusade. He has chosen Collette and the mines over me.

#

I know from history that the months after Bradac lost the mines were chaos. They were a precursor to Quinten's takeover of the throne. In a few short years, Quinten would be Supreme Ruler. Money was key to Quinten's success. He needed access to the Catahli mines to secure himself as the wealthiest in Elmyra and overthrow Bradac.

In the past, the Supreme Ruler had always struck a treaty with the Catahli clan, keeping either party from gaining too much power. The Catahli people never desired to be rulers. They were peaceful and pastoral and enjoyed their work with the captivating element they were created to look after. Bradac had broken that tradition and Roan and Quinten were determined to put things back the way they were.

Roan, the last living member of the Catahli clan, actually sought out Quinten. Once Roan recovered from the slaughter of his family, vengeance took over his thoughts, and he realized he had a very valuable piece to play in the fight for rulership over Elmyra.

Roan would find a man from an elite household in Elmyra and barter with him for a safe return to the mines and future protection. Roan benefited greatly from this deal. He would essentially hold all the power. He found his puppet in the youthful, and very enterprising, Quinten Warwick. Then came the moment that I knew was close.

#

I have been without my love for over two years and although I despised him for leaving, I never lost hope. He returned today from Siourious to rescue me. His lips were filled with nothing but apologies. He had to leave abruptly, he explained. He couldn't take me while I was pregnant for my own safety.

He took my hands and pled with me to come to Siourious like we had planned. Roan needs me there. He told me I needed to have courage to leave my husband and children. Malcolm was at work so I took the children to Lina's house and then I left. I hardly packed anything. I don't need anything from my old life.

We hurried out of Rande and walked east up the river. There was a fresh coat of snow on the ground, and the water was frosted on the edges. We crested the craggy coastline. I remember absolute silence. Roan smiled at me. The two of us mounted our horses and rode north to freedom.

#

Just like that, my mother was gone. It was instantaneous, like the snapping of a tree branch during a storm. You don't know which tree holds the weak limbs. You don't know which one will suddenly give up and drop to the earth. My mother was like that. No one around her, including Malcolm, had any idea what was going through her head. She had been primed for years to leave Tuor and me.

I almost laugh out loud. I know why there are no history books written about Roan, the last living Catahli clan member. If he was fool enough to take my mother to the mines, I can only imagine what destruction she brought with her.

A voice lifts me as if from a dream. "I see you haven't given up on your mother."

Every muscle in my body jerks. The journal slips from my hand and lands with a thump on the floor.

The voice is clear and cold as it echoes through Mirabelle's front hall. I scoop up the book and bury it in my lap. Reed stares down at me with his icy blue eyes. They bore into me in a way that feels like he can see right through me. There's something both disconcerting yet warmly familiar about the way he looks at me.

I clear my throat. "I'm trying to be more open minded."

"I think that's wise." Reed moves around the couch and takes a seat next to me. "I'm sorry to interrupt you. I couldn't sleep, so I thought I'd take over your watch."

I sigh and let my feet uncurl and touch the floor. "I wanted to be here when people started coming. I wanted to be the one to greet them and assure them we were on the same side." I hug my mother's journal close to my chest. "I guess I can let that dream go."

"Don't fret," Reed says with a wave of his hand. "We'll try something else. We'll come up with a new plan."

"I don't think it will matter what we try. The farm workers just aren't interested. They're too scared or set in their ways. A rebellion doesn't work without the people."

Reed reaches out a hand and touches my back. "Don't worry. We'll figure it out."

A shiver runs up my back. I bite my lower lip to keep from reacting.

"Why don't you head to bed and let me take over?" Reed says.

I'm hesitant to agree but there's something about Reed's confidence that soothes me.

"Are you sure?"

"Absolutely. You would actually be doing me a favor." Reed winks at me. "Get some sleep. You need it."

I pause a moment, then concede. If I stayed up, I'd just keep reading and I'm trying to avoid this book. I gather my things, wish Reed goodnight, and begin scaling the steps to my bedroom. With each step I ascend, I question more and more, how did this plan fail? Did Malcolm betray me? Maybe he never spread the word. Did the farm workers hear the call but just didn't respond? Why? Are they all really that scared to step out of line and try something? I was like that once.

I step into Mirabelle's room and close the door behind me. Leaning my back against the door, I stare across the room. Mirabelle sleeps quietly in her bed. There's a flat spot next to her where I'm supposed to lie down, but sleeps not on my mind. Reed was right. We will figure it out. I'll figure it out.

I was once like those farm workers, blind and content in my sad life. So what convinced me to change my mind? It all changed when Tuor was arrested. Many of the farm workers have relatives that have been unjustly arrested and tossed into the dungeons. Maybe pointing that out will light a fire for some.

Suddenly I have an idea. I know how we can convince the farm workers to join our side. I have to tell Reed. I tiptoe across the room and hide my mother's journal inside my box, then slip back out into the hall. I lean over the railing. Moonlight beams through the tall windows bathing the front hall in a cool blue light. My enthusiastic smile falls when all I see are ripped curtains and a scuffed floor. The couch where Reed was sitting is empty. I jog down the steps, entering the front hall with a cautious eye. Turning slowly, I scan the room. He's gone.

CHAPTER TWENTY-FOUR

COULD HE HAVE stolen away to the kitchen for some food? He'd never leave his post. That's not like him. Movement catches my eye from the window across the room. I push through the rubble and peer out the dirty glass. Reed walks through the tall weeds of Mirabelle's front lawn, a small glass lantern in his hand.

He pauses, standing stiff as soldier, and adjusts the collar of his jacket. Then, as if he senses my eyes, he turns his head and looks back at the house. I duck from the window.

"Traitor," I mutter, crouched on the floor below the window. I feel as though I've been snapped from his trance. He tricked me into going to bed. I grit my teeth and feel for my dagger at my side. He's not getting away with this. I've never forgotten where he came from. Reed is still a Warwick soldier. I'll kill him before he gets to his informants.

I glance up to the balcony, wondering if I should get Tuor or Knox to come with me, but there's no time. I'll lose his trail if I wait any longer. At the front door, I quietly click open the handle and let the door swing open. I slip through and dart into the woods. The night is clear. I pull my dagger from its case and move swiftly with it at my side. I follow the pinprick of light that his lantern emits through the trees.

A half a mile through the woods, I catch up to Reed. He walks, steady and determined, along the east side of Rande, toward the river. I stop and hide behind the trunk of a tree. Reed crosses an old trail. I wait a few minutes, then cross the trail behind him. He slows his pace. I stay back, moving only when he moves. He stops at a random spot in the middle of the trees.

I crouch behind a bush. He scans the woods, then places his lantern on a nearby rock. Reed bends and grabs at something on the ground. He turns around and begins climbing into the earth. I stand and slowly walk toward the hole where he disappeared. His arm reaches up, grabs the lantern, and pulls closed a flap door.

I run to the spot. A bolder sits on the ground. I kneel next to it. An X is etched into the side. Only a few steps away is a wooden hatch covered in burlap. I touch the cloth. It's disguised with leaves and twigs. Slowly I lift the door and stare down into a black hole with an old ladder leaned against the dirt wall.

Where is he going? I look again around the dark forest. Should I keep following? My rebel instinct assumes everything is a trap. But Reed doesn't know he's being followed. For only a moment, I consider abandoning my pursuit but I have to know.

I secure my dagger to my belt and turn to place my feet on the top rung. I grab the ladder and descend into the earth, pulling the door closed after me. Every step is undetermined. I can see nothing. When I think I've reached the bottom, yet another rung of the ladder appears under my foot.

Finally I stumble onto the soggy dirt floor. The sound of my feet squishing into the cold ground goes dead against the dirt walls. I begin walking through the narrow tunnel. I have no idea where I walk but I keep moving.

The only sound is that of the squeaking rats and my dull footsteps. I feel my way through. The ceiling slopes low and I'm forced to duck. Droplets of dirty water fall and hit my arms and face. I muffle a cough into my sleeve, unable to stave off the musty smell. Finally I feel the tunnel curve and up ahead Reed's lantern becomes a beacon.

Soft light pours in as a door at the end of the tunnel is opened. I freeze between the damp walls. Reed stands at the threshold of the door. A woman faces him, petite and blonde. They exchange words. Betrayal burns in my chest. Thoughts fly through my head. Reed's been in contact with Captain Thatius, perhaps Lawrence too. He allowed Ivan to be arrested. He's kept the farm workers away. But why? Why not just turn us in? Perhaps that's what he's doing now.

Reed crosses into the room. The woman moves to close the door. I reach for my dagger and clench its handle hard. My jaw is set as I run full bore toward Reed. He turns around as my footsteps approach. His eyes twitch in confusion. I slam into his body, pushing him hard against the floor.

"What are you doing?" he shouts.

The full weight of my body lays on top of him. The lantern flies from his hand and hits the floor with a crack. I lift myself up and punch him hard across the jaw with the butt of my dagger. Blood trickles from his nose.

"I trusted you!" I shout.

Reed wraps his arms around mine and holds me in a vise. His temper flares.

"Calm down." Reed grinds his teeth in frustration.

"I should have never trusted you. You're Warwick scum like the rest of them!" I rip my arm from Reed's grasp. I raise my fist to hit him again but a hand catches my wrist. The woman stands over me. Her skinny fingers squeeze my wrist so hard the bones feel like they're being crushed. I cry out. She lets me go as I scramble away.

Reed comes to his feet. I hold my dagger in front of me. The woman marches to the door, securing it closed with an iron lock. She stands in front of me, her hands on her hips, her mouth pressed into a hard line. She scolds me with her eyes.

"I should have guessed it. Camilla Crim. Where there's trouble, you're not far behind."

"Who are *you*?"

I use the wall to slowly pull myself to my feet. I'm in a basement. It's clean and dry with crates of potatoes and carrots stacked along the walls. Huge hams hang from the ceiling. A row of shelves is neatly stocked with jars of pickles.

"You have some nerve asking who I am when you're the one who stormed into my home."

The woman standing in front of me is tiny, with a straight gray woolen skirt and tight shirt that has a collar clear up to her neck. Pinned to the lapel of her shirt is an embroidered flower. I've seen a pin like that before.

"You're Eve Lindon." I look around the room. "Is this Lindon Place?"

"Brilliant," Eve says sarcastically.

This is the woman that threw me out of Lindon Place last fall when all I was doing was trying to talk to Lawrence.

"What's going on?" I demand from Reed.

He brushes dirt from his jacket and rolls his head on his neck.

"I had hoped to show this to you at a better time but . . ." Reed sighs, wiping blood from his nose. "I know how this looks, me sneaking out in the middle of the night. Can you just—just come upstairs?"

"What's upstairs?"

Eve rolls her eyes. She's irritated, tired of my ignorance.

"Are you sure she can handle this?" Eve asks, eyeing my defensive stance.

"Camilla's smart. She'll understand. We were counting on her understanding eventually."

"*What* is upstairs?"

Eve drops her arms from her waist and turns to the stairs. "Follow me. You can put that knife away. I promise you, it's not what you think."

Reed and I exchange a look. He gestures for me to climb the stairs next, but there's no way I'm turning my back on him. I insist I go last. Eventually he obliges. I walk like a ghost, unsure of what exactly I'm seeing.

We empty into a dark, narrow hallway, then past a pantry filled with more jars of food. Eve takes us through a door into the kitchen. One of Eve's sisters bends over a basin of soapy water, washing the day's dishes. It's a big kitchen and well stocked. A line of brass pots hangs from the ceiling. Two stoves roar away as another girl stokes the fire.

I keep my dagger close, still cautious, still suspicious. Eve stops in front of the door at the end of the kitchen. She looks at me.

"Don't panic," she says sternly. "I've worked very hard to get here. If you mess this up, you won't have to worry about Captain Thatius anymore. It'll be me hunting you down."

I scrunch up my face in confusion. My mind races with what Eve and Reed could possibly be hiding behind this door. Eve raises her eyebrows, waiting for my response.

"O—okay," I say.

Eve pushes open the door. We step into the dining room, a place that I've been many times. It's set down low by a few steps. The room is old and rustic with worn wooden chairs and a cracked fireplace that smokes. The room is filled, brimming with people, but it's after-hours. Lindon Place has been closed for some time.

A man up front stands with his back to me. When he hears me enter, he turns. He's dressed in full Warwick uniform. I scan the room. Black vests speckle the room along with women, adorned with fine linens and sparkling jewelry. The room is full of soldiers, dignitaries, nobles—they're all Warwick supporters.

I stop short, gawking as they stare back. Both sides are unsure of what to make of each other. A man dressed in a linen suit stands when I enter. I recognize him as Sir Raymore. A woman seated two tables away was a judge at Tuor's trial. Some of the soldiers are foremen at the farm. In the back stands Ralf, the soldier that turned on Karla.

Sir Raymore speaks. "Why have you brought the Governor Killer?"

"Eve, I must protest," another man says. He's elderly with a trimmed white beard. "Why is she here? Her people have done nothing but cause trouble for us."

A woman sits in the chair next to him with her arms crossed. "They're just a bunch of swamp rubbish," she says under her breath.

"What did you say?" I snap.

"I've said it from the beginning," the old man says. "We can do this without the rebels and the farm peasants."

I push past Reed so I'm standing straight in front of the old man. "The people who live in the swamps are the only ones who keep this territory running."

The woman turns her head to avert my flaming gaze.

"You wouldn't have food on your table if it wasn't for them."

"She's got a mouth on her," someone else in the crowd says.

A rumble of light laughter flits through the dining room. Eve stands at the front, hands clasped in front of her, a stoic expression on her face. She's neither offended nor humored by the comments.

"Everyone shut up," she says and I'm surprised when they listen.

"What is this?" I ask, my tongue as sharp as my dagger.

Eve gives me a scolding look. "You too." She turns to address the crowd. "Our territory is in crisis. We must look past social class in order to get what we want. And what we want is to be loosed from the ties of Quinten Warwick."

Hesitant agreement ripples through the room.

"But why do we need them?" Sir Raymore says. "We have what we need."

"It's about numbers. If we stay in separate groups, we'll just end up fighting against each other. We have to unify," Reed says.

"Hold on," I say, shaking my head. "We're supposed to be working together?"

Reed steps toward me. "Camilla, your group isn't the only one I've been meeting with. Before I met you in Billage, I'd met Eve and she introduced me to these people. She's the one who told me about you and Knox."

"You were wrong to assume the farm workers were the only ones that would want change," Eve says.

The room is quiet. All eyes are on me and my dumbfounded expression. These people are supposed to be on my side? I struggle with the thought. I shake my head. How stupid could Reed be? There could easily be a spy among them. A plant, who's feigning loyalty to the rebellion. But Reed could be doing that too. Anyone could be.

Reed speaks. "These are the supporters in Bear Gap that you never thought of. Many of them are soldiers that outwardly maintain their loyalty to the throne but inwardly wish for change. Some hold leadership positions running the farm. And some are under direct command of Quinten."

"But—why didn't you tell me? Why didn't you tell me there were more?"

"You think there's risk with that little rebellion you have going on?" Eve says. "These people here have been Warwick loyal their whole lives."

"I had to know I could trust you," Reed says.

"Trust *me*?"

"You're scared of the brand, Camilla. You've been suspicious of me from the moment we met because you saw I was dressed in black."

I look around the room at the weird glances. "So they—they support us?"

"In a sense," Reed says. "It's a little bigger than your demands for a free territory."

Sir Raymore stands and speaks. "We share a goal. That is all. Wartime calls for compromises."

"Wait." I shake my head. "Wartime?"

"It's not all about Karla," Sir Raymore says. "Or even Captain Thatius. They're a symptom of a larger problem. The farm once made this territory wealthy, and now we suffer because it's no longer viable. It was all part of the Supreme Ruler's control when he took the throne."

"We mean to dethrone Quinten," Reed says. My eyes grow big. "It all begins here in Bear Gap. This territory is a large source of his power. If the rebels can occupy Bear Gap, then we have a fighting chance of cutting him off as ruler."

I find it all preposterous. Not just because I'm standing in a room full of people I'd normally regard as my enemies, but because they think they have a chance of deciding a new Supreme Ruler. A laugh spills from my lips.

"If you take out one Warwick, he'll just be replaced with another. The Warwicks are too wealthy. It'll be a hundred years before another family occupies the castle in LilyAye," I say, still chuckling.

The room falls surprisingly silent. I've just insulted their plan. I expected a harsher response. Sir Raymore's eyes avoid my gaze and he shifts uncomfortably on his feet.

A soldier in the crowd speaks up. "We don't mean to remove *all* the Warwicks."

My mouth hangs half-open in confusion.

"Tell her," Eve says as she gives Reed a scolding eye.

I look down and notice that the tick in Reed's hand has returned. He looks at me. His eyes are like fire, intense and hot. I'm too afraid to break his gaze.

"Camilla, I am not who I say I am." His tremor grows faster. "I've been lying to you."

My body turns defensive. I grip my dagger tighter. I forget that we're standing in a room full of people.

I'm almost terrified to ask. "Who are you?"

"My name is Reed, that is true, and I *am* a defector from the militia. Camilla, I need you to know, I have been completely truthful about my political views. I am a dedicated member of this rebellion."

My own hands begin to shake.

"But I am a Warwick. My name is Reed Warwick and I'm the nephew of the Supreme Ruler."

CHAPTER TWENTY-FIVE

I RAISE MY as I take two steps away from Reed. *Warwick!* All this time we've been allowing a Warwick to participate in our meetings, help on missions, *live* with us.

"We're not going to hurt you." Reed raises his hands in surrender. "I'm on your side, Camilla."

"That's impossible."

"Why? Because my last name is Warwick? I couldn't choose the family I was born into." Reed takes a tentative step toward me. "I know I'm asking for a lot, but I need you to trust me."

I shake my head furiously. "No. No. I've been hurt at the hands of these people." I use the tip of my dagger to point at the crowd. "How am I to believe we're on the same side?"

"We don't have time for this," Sir Raymore says.

"I told you," Eve says, crossing her arms over her chest. "She can't handle it."

Reed puts his hand on my back and pushes me out of the dining room. In the kitchen, I whip around to face him, my dagger still preceding me.

"I was right not to trust you," I growl.

"Remember the story I told you about my childhood? How my family shunned me? That was true."

I shake my head. I can't believe anything he says.

"That whole story is true. The only thing I didn't tell you was that the family that shunned me was the Warwick family. None of them wanted anything to do with me."

I feel my breath heavy in my chest. "Why did you come here? Why pretend to be one of us?"

"I know what you're thinking. I haven't come here as some sort of spy for my uncle. If I had, I wouldn't have told you who I was. I would have kept my true identity a secret. The only reason I didn't tell you at that first meeting was because I knew I wouldn't make it past the threshold alive if I had even uttered the name Warwick." Reed takes a deep breath. "I did come here to Bear Gap for a specific reason. I sought out your rebellion and I helped the cause because I needed to know if there were really people who wanted a different way of life. I needed to know if I had supporters."

I cringe. "Supporters? We are not your supporters."

"You are. You are, and you don't even know it." Reed eases closer and puts out both of his hands like he is offering me a gift. "Lower the dagger, please. We are not enemies."

Reed puts a cold hand on my wrist and slowly brings my arm to my side.

"I want the same thing that you do: freedom for Elmyra," Reed says. "I can bring us that freedom."

"How am I to trust you?"

"I destroyed the brand, remember? I destroyed the Warwick crest. That was real." He steps closer to me. "I hate my uncle more than you can know."

Instinctively I touch the scar on the inside of my own arm. My worried thoughts stop. I forget that I'm standing inches from a Warwick and that there's a room full of soldiers just behind us. I look down at Reed's hand on my arm. I didn't jolt. I didn't jump or panic when I felt his touch.

I want to know why. Why of all people did I not shudder when Reed touched me? I look up into Reed's piercing blue eyes. Maybe it's because I've always trusted him. I wanted to be suspicious. I wanted to find out he was a spy so I could prove Ivan wrong. If I found fault in Reed, then in an odd way, it would bring me comfort. I would have found the evil and been able to destroy it.

Reed lied, that's true, but he's never done anything to hurt us. And if I stop and think, I can see why he lied. I've always hated being known as Malcolm's daughter. There was never anything I could do about my heritage, just like there's nothing Reed can do about his.

"How? How will you bring us freedom?" I watch Reed under heavy eyebrows.

"I'm going to rule," Reed continues. "I'll undo all of the awful things that my uncle has done to our nation but I need your help."

"What about the farm?" I ask. "What about everyone who lives in poverty in Bear Gap because they're forced to labor for Quinten's failed experiment?"

Reed shakes his head. "I will get rid of all of it. There will be no national farm. I'll return the ability for citizens to farm their own land. People in Bear Gap can make and sell whatever they want."

"So, what was your plan? Get the support of the rebels and the disgruntled soldiers and then what?"

"We have to find a way to bring our groups together. Separately we're weak."

Reed straightens his back. I try to picture him as Supreme Ruler. It's an odd thought but thrilling at the same time. I could be in the presence of the man who rules Elmyra. For the first time in a long time, it feels like I have power.

"If the rebels knew which soldiers were on our side, we could move through the territory easily. We could have a headquarters and be warned if it was going to be searched." I say looking up at Reed. "We could get access to the farm."

Reed nods his head in agreement as energy seems to pass between us.

"But it'll never work. There's no way I'll get Johnny on board or Linus." I rub my forehead. "Working with those people out there . . . they'll never go for it."

"But you accepted me knowing I was soldier."

"That's different. You're one soldier. This is a whole room full of known Warwick supporters."

Reed gives me a wry look.

"Supporters of your uncle," I correct. Because Reed is a Warwick, which means that I'm technically a Warwick supporter now.

I search to clarify myself. "The people in that room have done horrible things. They've beaten and arrested people like me, farm workers."

"You're the key to making this work," Reed says.

"What do you mean?"

"You need to talk to your people, convince them that we can come together. They trust you."

I stare at Reed's face. How can I convince Knox and the others to trust the people in the dining room if I don't even trust them myself? There's no way the people in the other room feel the same way that the rebels do. It's impossible. They didn't grow up in the swamps. They haven't been forced to live one lousy ring at a time by working at the farm.

"Look, I'm sorry you had to find out like this. I knew this would be difficult. Will you help me?" Reed asks.

It would be a betrayal, joining forces with these people, right? But these men and women represent enough people that we could actually have an army. I once heard someone say to fight fire with fire. I never understood what that meant until now. I look up at Reed. I will fight one Warwick with another.

"I'm in."

A flicker of light twinkles in Reed's eye. He pauses, then stretches out a hand. I take it and we shake, sealing our agreement. I've just made a pact with the enemy.

***

Eve ushers Reed and me to the basement of Lindon Place.

"You'll need to get your people here," Eve says, stepping off the final step. She brushes a speck of dirt from her shoulder.

I chuckle. "Why would I bring a bunch of rebels here? Our wanted posters are pinned just a few steps from your front door."

"The three of us need to be close to make this work."

"So bring your people to Mirabelle's house. We have the space and it's secluded."

I look to Reed, waiting for him to agree. He nods slowly as he slicks back his hair with the palm of his hand.

"Mirabelle's house is in the middle of the woods," Eve says. "You have no way of seeing if there's an attack coming. Here, I can have all my entrances guarded. We have the protection of the soldiers. You need to remember that."

I glance around Eve's basement. Huge burlap sacks of grain sit piled in the corner. Clustered bulbs of onions hang from the low rafters. Everything's neat and orderly, not unlike Eve.

"Plus, I have a restaurant to run. I can't leave."

I hold Eve's gaze. A silent power struggle ensues. I'm already beginning to regret this deal.

Reed speaks. "It's the last place Captain Thatius would expect us to be."

"Where would we even sleep?"

Eve uncrosses her arms and marches past Reed and me to the end of the basement. "I have an attic with a door that can easily be hidden by a piece of furniture as well as a hidden bedroom. You would be safe and comfortable."

"And trapped," I add.

Eve pushes aside a stack of crates to reveal the narrow door that leads into the tunnel.

"How many secret rooms does this house have?"

Eve pulls open the door to the tunnel and gestures for us to leave. "Six."

***

It's nearly daybreak by the time Reed and I make it back to Mirabelle's house. I'm not happy about moving to Lindon Place, but I've made peace with the pact I've struck with Reed and Eve. We'd been playing this game with Captain Thatius all wrong. He can't be scared of a few disruptive rebels, but a whole territory in revolt? That can't be ignored, not even by the Supreme Ruler.

Knox is pacing the front hall when we walk in the front door. He stops and gives me a look sharp enough it could slice open my stomach again.

"Where in all of Elmyra have you been?" Knox growls.

Johnny runs down the steps, his sword at his side. His eyes fall on me. He takes the last few steps slowly.

"You're back," he says, joining us in the front hall.

"We were about to come looking for you," Knox says.

"It's my fault. We're fine," Reed says.

I take a deep breath. "But there's a lot to explain. I think we should wake the rest of the house so we can talk."

Knox's angry gaze lingers on me for a moment. Then he nods, conceding to my idea.

In the basement I light a candle and bring it to the center of the table. Knox takes a seat at the head. Mirabelle, Johnny, Reed, and Tuor take seats on either side of him. I stand. I'm either too eager or too anxious to sit down.

My explanation of the meeting at Lindon Place is met with mixed reactions.

"You're . . . a Warwick?" Mirabelle asks. She pulls her robe tighter over her chest.

"It's a lot to take in," I say. "But this is the right move for us. It's the right move for the rebellion."

Johnny clenches his jaw. "You want us to fight alongside the very men that did this to me?" Johnny points to the speckled bruises on his face.

"Not all of Quinten's soldier's support him," Reed says. "Many of them are just obeying because they have to."

Tuor begins shaking his head. "What if it's a trap?"

"Eve could just be rounding us all up in one place," Mirabelle says. "Just to offer us up to Captain Thatius."

Knox stands suddenly from the table. "We can trust her."

"How can you be sure?" Tuor asks.

"She's a daughter of Peter Lindon, an original member of the rebellion. He was captured during the Battle of Bear Gap. She has as much reason to hate Quinten Warwick as anyone else in this room."

Knox moves to the other side of the table and pours himself a cup of water, which he drinks in four gulps.

Johnny locks eyes with me. "Are you going to let yourself be deceived by a Warwick?" He stands and gestures to me from across the table. "You're playing right into his hand! He's just using you, Camilla, and he's using the rest of us."

"Look," I snap. "This is the truth. My father didn't come through. I tried to play it safe and I failed. The farm workers are not on our side. We have to move forward without them, and honestly, maybe it's better that way. We have supporters now. We have an army." I pause and look across the room. "We're doing this.

We're moving to Lindon Place and we're joining forces with Eve's people."

Knox leans against the kitchen counter. I wait for him to refute me. I wait for Mirabelle to fuss. I wait for Tuor to lose his nerve. None of that happens.

"We'll leave for Lindon Place tonight," I say.

Knox gives me a subtle nod, his most agreeable gesture.

"Do you hear that?" Reed says. His face shifts from control to fear.

"Hear what?" Tuor asks.

"Shh."

Reed points a finger to the floorboards above us. The ceiling creaks.

"Someone's upstairs," I whisper.

Knox draws his sword. Reed runs to the steps. I follow closely, pulling my dagger. At the top of the steps, we wait, listening through the door. Light footsteps move across the squeaky floor. Reed looks back at me.

I mouth the question. "Soldiers?"

Reed shrugs. He slowly turns the knob and eases the door open. Knox is behind me as we creep down the hallway. Whispered murmuring reaches my ears and it doesn't sound like soldiers.

I step out first. Two men stand in Mirabelle's front hall. One holds a hatchet; the other has a garden hoe raised above his head. Reed lets his sword fall to his side. He looks at me and smirks.

"Your father came through after all."

CHAPTER TWENTY-SIX

THE TWO MEN eye us curiously. One's older, fifties maybe, with a burly frame. The younger man scans the room. The garden hoe in his hand shakes, from nerves I think. We exchange suspicious glances.

"I recognize you," I say, keeping my voice casual.

"We recognize you too," the older man says, but his tone is not as welcoming.

They're farm workers but they don't live in the swamps. When the farm was first built, row homes were also built to accommodate the workers, but those quickly filled up. Everyone else who came to work on the farm spilled into the swamps and built homes there. These men are some of the original people living in Rande.

"I know why you're here. Let's talk," I say.

Taking a cue from Reed, I return my dagger to its case. I then raise my empty hands, a sign of goodwill. Knox isn't as compliant. He steps in line next to Reed and me but keeps his sword raised.

"You're Camilla Crim then, eh?" the older man asks. His firm grip remains on the hatchet.

"I am."

He peers at his companion. They nod to each other. "Name's Bardle. Your Pa told me about you."

Bardle steps toward me in a bold, slightly obnoxious move. He shoves his sweaty hand into mine. "I saw ya at the farm from time to time, but to be honest I never paid you any mind."

Bardle is a funny-looking man. He has scraggly hair sticking out of his head and a thick curved mustache. His skin is rough and weathered and he holds our handshake for longer than seems necessary.

"How 'bout you get your friends to put their weapons away and I'll introduce you to the rest of us," Bardle says.

"There are more of you?"

Bardle lets out a big belly laugh. It's a weird noise in comparison to the silence of suspicion. The other man holds his stance. He's far less trusting than the affable Bardle. I turn to Knox. He hesitates then secures his sword in its scabbard.

"Much appreciated," Bardle says. He steps back to the front door and waves the other farm workers into the house. Men and women alike meet us with weird stares and glances. Sixteen, I count sixteen farm workers who fill Mirabelle's library.

"When word got to us about what you were doin', my wife and I knew we had to help. She'd be here too but she had to stay back with the kids. You understand?"

"Of course," I say quickly but I don't.

"This wiry fellow here is Eddie," Bardle says. He grabs the back of the man's neck. Bardle chuckles nervously, then uses his hand to lower the garden hoe. Eddie has the face of a child with shaggy hair that's parted in the middle. His expression is anything but juvenile. He's angry, bitter.

Bardle continues. "I just can't let my babies grow up like this." He gestures to his tattered clothes. In a moment he's gone from gregarious and jolly to solemn. "I don't want my little ones workin' their life away at that farm like me." Many of the workers nod in agreement. Bardle turns back to face me. "You see, Camilla"—Bardle claps his hands together—"I represent the farm workers, at least the ones standing here and a few others who couldn't make it." He turns to face the rest of the room. "They are my family." Bardle's voice goes so low that I wonder if he'll start to cry. "Here I go again . . . let me finish with my introductions."

Bardle rests a fat hand on his chest. "We've got Lan, Carl, and Short. These three fellows here have been with me from the start. Karen and Mod." Bardle points to a chubby woman with brown frizzy hair. She stands next to a younger looking version of herself with only slightly less frizzy hair. "They're mother and daughter. Mod is an excellent cook." Bardle winks and Mod giggles.

I've seen them in the swamps before.

"Chad and Reuben are these gentleman here. They live in town close to me, been my neighbors for years. Sharon, Deb, and Cassandra are Chad's sisters." Cassandra looks barely a teen, and I wonder why her big brother let her ride along on such a dangerous trip. "We've got the Boone clan here." Bardle moves to the back of the crowd. A family of siblings with long stringy hair and grimy clothes stand close together. The one brother smirks and I notice a row of crooked teeth. "The Boone kids once spent a whole day helpin' me fix my broken roof after one of them nasty storms blew through. They're skinny! But they're strong and crafty."

"We thought the farm workers didn't want to have anything to do with us," I say.

"You have to understand, honey, we've been talking about doing somethin' like this for years."

"You have?"

"Of course. Us that used to live here before Warwick, we've always wanted to do something but it's never seemed possible."

"What makes it possible now?" Reed asks from across the room.

"Well, Governor Leo's dead now. That lunatic woman has run the territory into the ground. Even my little ten-year-old baby can see that the territory is starting to crumble."

Grunts of approval ripple across the front hall.

"We have to strike now, while the leadership is vulnerable," Eddie says. I can tell he's been waiting this whole time to make his point.

"Calm down, son," Bardle says, taking him by the back of the neck in a fatherly way.

"All we've done is talk. When are we going to do something?" Eddie says.

Bardle gives Eddie a warning eye as if they've had this conversation before. "Eddie is mighty feisty but he needs to remember that we're still well outnumbered by the Warwicks."

I bite my lower lip, realizing truly for the first time that between the farm workers, the Billage rebels, and now Eve's people, we might not be so outnumbered. I look to Reed, then Knox. Should we tell them about the others? Perhaps the time to be cautious has passed.

"Actually Eddie might be right. What if I said there were others that were willing to fight alongside us?"

For the first time in this conversation, Bardle is silent.

"Who?" Eddie asks, sensing my trepidation.

I sigh, knowing the farm workers aren't going to like our new allies. "How desperately do you want this?"

Worry melts onto Bardle's face but it's Eddie who speaks. "I'll do anything."

***

Explaining to the farm workers about Eve and the soldiers was difficult. I left out the part about Reed's true identity. It seemed more than what Bardle and his people could comprehend at this time. A tussle nearly broke out when I said that we'd be using the resources of the soldiers and that we'd all have to work together.

By the end of the meeting, I had Bardle's reticent agreement on our union with the open Warwick supporters. He sketched me a map on a piece of parchment showing which house on Reaper's Way was his. We decided, for now, the farm workers would return to their homes and work and live normally. We have to secure our plans with Eve and the others before an attack can be mounted.

We spend one more night at Mirabelle's house and use the following day to pack our things and prepare for our trip to Lindon Place. A tense mood floats about the house at the thought of venturing into town. Everyone moves with a quiet solitude, and even Mirabelle has lost some cheeriness.

"Don't be nervous, Camilla," Reed says while saddling his horse. I drop a load of bags onto the ground in Mirabelle's backyard. "I can see it on your face. There's no need to worry. Eve will protect us."

Reed's reassuring voice has a soothing quality that instantly mellows me. I nod, trying to convince myself that this plan is solid. I lift Shae's saddle onto her back and begin strapping it tight around her middle.

"We're getting there. We're making progress. This is good," he says.

I pause with my work and turn to face Reed. "I think we should keep the farm workers a secret from Eve."

Reed exhales. He can't hide his disappointment in my statement.

"Her people hate the farm workers."

"They have to learn to get along." Reed shakes his head. "We can't keep them a secret forever. We need their manpower."

"I know. But for now——"

"What good would it do?"

I avert me gaze and stare into the woods. It seems the rainy season has finally passed. The sky is clear and the sun pokes through the fresh leaves on the trees.

"What if Eve is playing us?"

Reed sighs. "She's not."

"But what if she is? If we have the farm workers on our side, and only our side, then we can use them if things end up going south with Eve's people."

Reed's gaze is hard.

"Please. It would make me feel safer if Eve didn't know."

Reed purses his lips. He leans through the space between us and places a comforting hand on my arm.

"If it makes you feel safer, then we won't tell anyone else about the farm workers until it's absolutely necessary."

CHAPTER TWENTY-SEVEN

THE SIX OF us ride through the forest at sunset, our horses loaded down with our belongings. We're somewhere on the east side of Rande not too far from the river where Knox used to live. I pull my horse to a stop. Reed dismounts and looks out across the darkening wood.

"She said to leave our horses here," he says.

"Are you sure?" Mirabelle asks.

I search through the trees to scan the mossy floor. "She'll send one of her sisters to bring them to her stables after we get there. This is the place."

"How can you tell?" Tuor asks.

I hop off Shae and point to the gray rock that has an X etched onto the side. I push aside the burlap bag adorned with dried leaves, to reveal the wooden trap door. Knox comes to my side. Peering down the trap door, he leans back on his heals and lets out a chuckle.

"Peter was smarter than I thought," he says.

"Why did he build it?" Tuor asks.

"Because he knew the rebellion would need it someday. He probably didn't know it would take this long to be in use."

"Your father never knew about this?" Mirabelle asks Knox.

"No. Peter kept this a secret. Even from us." Knox looks back at the rest of us. "I'll go down last."

"Reed and I can go first since we've already been through it," I say.

"Oh, please be careful," Mirabelle says.

I scale the ladder first, feeling that familiar tightness in my chest as I go deeper and deeper into the earth. When I hit the ground, I turn around and face an oppressive darkness. Reed touches my back when he reaches the bottom. Next comes Tuor, then Johnny, then Mirabelle. Knox is last. When he reaches the bottom, he gives me the signal to move.

We know nothing but complete blackness. In a line, we begin walking through the narrow dirt tunnel toward Lindon Place. Behind me, Mirabelle coughs. The darkness is wicked. The feeling that something could reach through the mud and strangle me, causes me to grab the crumbly wall for support. A rat scurries past my foot. My scream goes dead against the dirt walls. I stop, leaning on my knees to catch my breath.

"Are you okay?" Tuor asks.

Reed reaches his hand forward to help me stand upright.

"I'm fine."

I force my feet to keep moving. I hate feeling like I'm trapped. A thin line of light streams through the door at the end of the tunnel. Relief floods my body. I jog toward the door, knocking, the moment I get there. More silence fills the air. I knock again.

"Only once," Reed says.

Why do we have to do everything that Eve tells us to? I think to myself. Tuor is mumbling to himself behind me.

"How long is she going to make us stand here?" I ask.

The door pops open. Our eyes are assaulted by torch light. I blink to adjust to the new light and see a girl standing at the threshold. She's the spitting image of Eve; blonde, petite, and a sour look on her face. She's younger though. Her hair is in a long braid and swept over the front of her shoulder.

"How can I help you?" she asks although she doesn't sound as if she interested in helping us.

"Let us in," I say.

"I need the code."

"Are you serious? We have a delivery of bread, happy?" I push forward but the Lindon girl holds up her hand halting us.

"That is not the code," she says.

Reed rests a hand on my elbow. It's his kind way of telling me to shut up. He turns to the girl and says slowly, "We have a delivery of sourdough bread."

The girl smiles and opens the door for us. She professionally gestures us to enter the basement then shuts the door to the tunnel and bolts it locked. Two more sisters are waiting for us with swords drawn. Though small, they stand with firmness and confidence.

"Wait here," the first sister says before gracefully taking a set of steps upstairs.

I lean against a post, putting my forehead in my hands. Tuor paces the room. He's nervous but he's trying to keep it together. I guess I'm not that different from him. I'm just angry and trying to keep it together. The door at the top of the steps opens. Stiff as a soldier, Eve descends the steps.

"I guess I'll introduce you to everyone," I say.

Eve raises a hand to stop me. "No need. My name is Eve Lindon. I'm already well informed on each of you and your criminal activity within the territory."

"Criminal activity?" Mirabelle says. I chuckle at the thought of Mirabelle being involved in criminal activity.

"Why don't we start with you," Eve says staring at me. "You had your brand slashed and were kicked off the farm before becoming a well known outlaw for killing Governor Leo. Since then you've been in hiding."

I touch my hand to the inside of my arm, wondering how she knows about my brand.

"Tuor Crim is also on the run for committing murder after he mysteriously escaped the dungeons in LilyAye. And you"—Eve looks at Johnny—"Johnny Bennette, you've had your fair share of run-ins with the local infantry. You've been suspected of protests and stealing Warwick horses and a slew of other petty crimes." Without missing a beat, Eve moves to Mirabelle. "Your poor husband died during the Battle of Bear Gap and since then you've had unconfirmed ties with groups that oppose the Warwick regime. I think your presence here tonight confirms your allegiance." Mirabelle shifts on her feet and pulls the shawl around her shoulders closer to her chest. "Knox Duffy. Where should I begin? A known supporter of the rebellion that fought in the Battle of Bear Gap. Ever since, you've been very strangely a model citizen until last fall when you were suspected of involvement with the murder of the governor. I always thought you'd be beaten into submission, but I guess you still have some fight in you."

Eve holds her head high. She seems proud that she hasn't committed any of the sins that we have. I shake my head in disbelief. Tuor stares at Eve in an expression that I can only interpret as amazement.

"I have guests sleeping two stories above us on the west wing. It is imperative that not a one of you speaks until we're safe on the east wing. Now, follow me," she says.

I'm the first one up the steps. Tuor is behind me. He whispers in my ear. "She's clever."

I don't hide my disgust but I keep my mouth shut, not wanting to give Eve another reason to scold us. She leads us down a hallway then up another four steps, which empties us into a sitting rom.

The sitting room has a pianoforte, which Eve says none of us are to touch. We're taken through a hidden door on the other side of the sitting room then up two more flights of steps until we've finally arrived at the east wing.

At the top of the stairs is a window that looks down on Rande Square. There are three visible bedrooms upstairs; one for Eve, one for her mother, and then one large room for all of her sisters to share. She stops abruptly in the hall and points to a spot on the wall.

"This is the secret room," she says. "No one outside of my family knows this exists."

Eve removes a portrait from the wall, which reveals a latch just below the ceiling. She unhooks the lock. The camouflaged door hinges open to reveal a small room with a low ceiling and no windows. Eve has laid out a few blankets, some water, and a chamber pot.

"For the men," she says.

Eve gestures for them to go to their room this moment. Finally I see a flicker of suspicion from Knox.

"You want to lock us in there?" Johnny asks.

"The door locks from the outside. That's how it works."

"I told you," I say, bringing my dagger up at the ready. "She's brought us here just to hand deliver us to Captain Thatius."

Eve puts her hands on her hips. "The lock is for *your* safety."

"How are we supposed to believe that?" Knox asks.

"If you remove the lock then the door won't stay shut. Someone could see you."

"We'll take our chances. Camilla, your dagger," Knox says.

I hand it to him and he slips the blade under the latch. Using leverage he pries the nails loose that hold the latch to the wall.

"Stop that!" Eve says.

With a final yank, Knox pops it loose. The brass lock falls to the ground with a thump.

"I trust you," Knox says. "But no one is going to lock us in." He hands me my dagger.

Eve picks up the broken lock. "My father built this room."

"Your father would have done the same thing," Knox says.

"He would have at least been more tactful!" Eve turns on her heels and calls to us. "The ladies can follow me."

Eve takes Mirabelle and me into a large rectangular room where her younger sisters sleep. Eve has a total of five sisters so the room has five wooden bed frames lined up against the walls. After Eve the next oldest daughter is Marie, then Angel, then Philippa, then Dorothy, then the youngest, Detra who's only 14 years old.

"Through here is the attic," Eve says. At the end of the room she opens a half door that's only about four feet high. It also blends in with the wall. "You'll notice there's no lock on the door."

"Thank you, dear," Mirabelle says.

I'm forced to duck under the door, which leads to a narrow, spiral stair case. The attic is tiny with really only enough space for Mirabelle and me to lay out our bed mats. The roof of Lindon Place slopes steeply down either side of the room. There's only one spot in the middle where I can almost stand up straight.

Eve stands at the top of the spiral staircase with her hands folded in her lap. "Camilla, will you join me downstairs for a moment?"

CHAPTER TWENTY-EIGHT

I LOOK AT Mirabelle, who seems as confused as me by Eve's request. I'm reminded of when I was a child, and Mirabelle would shout at me from downstairs after Tuor and I would get into a tussle. I look to Eve. It feels like I'm in trouble.

"Sure," I say, dropping my bag on the ground and following Eve back downstairs.

In the kitchen, Eve places a kettle of water on the stove.

"You coddle him," she says, as she picks up a wet rag and begins wiping the counter.

I scrunch my eyebrows in confusion. It takes me a moment to understand whom she's talking about. "I don't *coddle* him. Tuor has a condition."

Eve touches the side of the kettle to test for warmth. "If a person had a splinter in their foot, is it better for them if you comfort them and leave the splinter intact, or rip it out immediately?"

"That's not—that's not the same thing."

"Coddling him only makes it worse." Eve faces me, her hands on her hips.

"You have no idea what you're speaking about."

"You need to treat him like he can function normally."

Eve won't relent. My fists squeeze into a ball. "He can't function normally."

"And he never will if you continue to say that." Eve's voice remains even.

"Who are you to tell me you know things about my brother?"

"I'm only giving you some advice," Eve says with raised eyebrows. The kettle whistles on the stove. I feel my temper rising just as the steam bursts from its spout.

"Is this why you brought me down here? To tell me how I should treat my brother?"

"Of course not." Eve produces two mugs and mixes the hot water with some tea leaves she has stored in a tin. She holds out one of the mugs for me. "Have a cup of tea with me, Camilla."

"Why would I want to do that?" I ask, feeling as if there are no social graces between the two of us.

"Because we have some things we need to talk about."

Eve directs me into the sitting room. It's quiet. Everyone else has gone to bed except for us. I sit down on a tattered red velvet couch. Eve takes a seat across from me on a wooden chair. Her back is straight as she adjusts the hem of her skirt.

"Shouldn't you be getting some sleep before breakfast?" I ask.

"I don't sleep much. I'd just be sitting here by myself if I told you to go to bed." Eve crosses her legs. "The world keeps me awake."

I hold the mug with both my hands. The tea is so hot, I can feel it burning my fingertips. "What do you want?"

"I know you don't like me very much." Her eyes settle on my face. "But more than anything, I need this rebellion to work. Little else takes priority in my life." Eve leans forward slightly, her mug in her hand. "You don't trust me and I need you to if we're going to be successful. We don't have to agree, but we have to respect each other."

Respect. That's rich coming from her.

"So you want us to get along, but only for the sake of the rebellion?"

"That's correct."

Eve is honest if nothing else. I lean back on the couch.

She continues. "I don't want anything getting in the way of our mission. Do you understand?"

"You've been a part of this rebellion for less than a fortnight!"

"Nearly my whole life actually," Eve corrects.

"I'm the one who's been exiled from my own hometown all winter. If anyone wants this rebellion to work, it's me."

"You're very focused, but you don't need this like I do, and I can't take the risk of someone who's not dedicated."

I laugh sarcastically. "You think I'm not dedicated?"

"You have distractions. Your hatred of me being one of them."

"Quinten Warwick almost had my brother executed as part of a feud he was having with my mother. That makes me more committed than you who—who has to run a restaurant in a Warwick-owned territory."

Eve takes a steady sip of her tea, then clears her throat. "You think you know, but I assure you, you don't. This rebellion has nothing to do with my business. I'd leave this place tonight if it meant a different Bear Gap for my sisters."

"So you want a better place for your family. How does that make you more dedicated than me?"

"During the first rebellion, thirteen years ago, my father was captured by Quinten along with John Duffy and many others from this territory. He was taken away and placed in a work camp somewhere around LilyAye to help build the castle that the Supreme Ruler lives in now. My mother was left alone with six children to provide for and the restaurant to keep running. She became terribly depressed and attempted to kill herself on several occasions. I was the one who found her bleeding from her wrists in her bedroom upstairs. I was a teenager when that happened."

I shift uncomfortably in my seat.

"I still don't know where my father is or if he's alive or dead."

I avert my eyes. "Why didn't you ever try to find him?"

Eve's gaze falls suddenly to the gold band on her finger. "I couldn't leave Lindon Place. Not with my mother in the state she was in and five sisters to raise. I married a man less than a year after the battle, when I was sixteen, and I told him I would only marry him if he traveled to LilyAye to find my father and bring him home."

"So he broke his promise," I guess.

"No. He kept his promise. He worshiped me. He would have done anything I asked." I note the first expression of sadness I've seen in Eve when she looks contrite. "We married and he left to find my father and bring him home." Eve looks at me. "He never returned. I went back to the last name of Lindon and continued on with running the restaurant."

"But you were so young and only married for a little while. Time has surly healed that wound." It's a cold thing to assume but Eve seems nearly devoid of emotion.

Eve laughs lightly. "How long have you known Johnny?"

"What does Johnny have to do with it?"

"You don't have to pretend with me. He followed your every move tonight, checking corners and watching your back. Now answer the question. How long have you known Johnny?"

I purse my lips. "I don't know. A few months."

"What if he disappeared tonight and you never saw him again?"

"I— It wouldn't be—"

Eve holds my eyes. She knows my real answer. A lie couldn't pass my lips if I wanted it to. Not in Eve's presence.

"So you see?" she asks. "Things weren't easy. I determined then that the road to LilyAye was too dangerous. I knew where my place was. It was here. My sisters needed me here. But they're getting quite grown now. They're ready to marry and move on with their lives. Marie is practically an old maid.

My worry for my sisters has lessened which puts my thoughts continually with my father and Alex. Year after year I feed and house the very men who took my father away from me. I can't do it any longer, Camilla. Do you understand the gravity of what we're doing? Failing would kill me, and I won't allow it."

I feel tiny next to Eve. She's horrible and rude and her intensity leaves me feeling anxious, but she's blood thirsty and I suppose that's what this rebellion needs. "Do you really think we can do it?"

"Do *you*?"

"I don't think we have a choice."

Eve's mouth turns upwards into a grin. It's a rare sight. "You're quite right. My sisters and mother have accepted that I may have to leave Lindon Place in order to make things right with our father." Eve sets her mug down on an end table. "I want you to know that I am fully committed. You and I may not like each other, but as long as you are part of the rebellion, I will not be far away."

To someone else, a phrase like that would bring comfort. To me, it leaves my stomach in knots. Wherever the rebellion is, Eve will be there too. I won't give up on the rebellion and unfortunately we need Eve, so . . . I'm staring into the eyes of my future. I feel a twinge of guilt at keeping the farm workers a secret, but the thought passes as quickly as it had come.

Eve finally releases me to go to bed. Mirabelle is already asleep when I return to the attic. I look around my new home. The only good thing about the attic is that on the wall opposite the steps is a round window. I can sit on the floor and look out at Rande Square. I can't help but stare at the street below and think about how I used to read the news on the posting tree and buy food from the cart vendors. I did all of that without fear of being seen or caught by anyone.

There is one thing starkly different about Rande Square than even from a few weeks ago. Talk of rebel activity has caused Captain Thatius to build gallows next to the posting tree. I inspect the long platform, big enough to hang several people. A pole runs the length of the platform, which would be used for securing the ropes. It's a message from the governor, a warning. It won't stop me, but I'm no fool—I know those gallows were built to hang me>

CHAPTER TWENTY-NINE

I'M NOT SURE how long I've been exiled to Eve's attic. A week, at least. Eve insists we be utterly silent during the day so that none of the diners suspect anything. As a child, I remember Mirabelle scolding me to just sit still and be respectful. I was always terrible at that command.

All I've been able to do is sleep or stare out the window and watch the people in Rande Square. I've barely seen Johnny or Tuor or had many chances to read my mother's journal. I hate being isolated and out of touch with the rebellion.

I pace in front of the window, catching glimpses of the gallows as the sun sets. Mirabelle begs me to stop walking. I resign myself to standing and staring as Rande Square becomes dark. Mirabelle drifts to sleep, her breath turning heavy. The attic glows with moonlight. Without thinking, I dig the journal from my bag, sit in front of the window, and dive between its words. It's the last comfort I have in this room.

#

The mines are so magnificent they're nearly indescribable. The Catahli grows as smooth formations on the walls and the ceiling. It glistens like gems with a very light pink hue. I learned that Catahli begins as this gorgeous pink color and then only turns gray after it has traveled many miles and been touched by many hands.

It's cool in the mines but strangely not as cold as it is aboveground. It's almost always winter in Siourious. The Catahli's color is one of its most interesting features. It can change color when exposed to certain things. When soaked in water, it turns a pale green. It can be dyed too with grapes or dandelions, which is what the wealthy do.

The most fascinating thing of all is taking the Catahli from the mines. It's not like gold or silver that can be melted down into a liquid. In extreme heat, Catahli crumbles and turns to sand. In temperate weather is when Catahli is at its strongest. Only when it's subjected to extreme cold does Catahli bend to the harvesters' will.

It's blissful in the mines with Roan. Of course Collette is here too. Roan says we need her for now but someday soon, he'll be rid of her. She's never given me a kind look. I'm under no illusion. I know she knows about Roan and me, yet she stays with him. I would never be as foolish as her to stay with a man who showed me no love.

The other day when it was just Roan and I working the mines, he took a chunk of ice and harvested a piece of Catahli. I watched the normally hard-as-stone mineral begin to yield. It morphed like a crawling slug, becoming soft with the icy touch.

"For you," he said, wrapping my fingers around the gift. It fit in the palm of my hand and was teardrop-shaped. He then leaned in and kissed my cheek.

The stone lies next to me in my bed. I'll sleep with it under my pillow tonight and see if it will grant me a wish. I'm already so happy, it's hard to believe I even have a wish. My future is vast and hopeful but I pray to the stone and ask it to give me abundant power.

For too many years, I was ruled by my father and then by Malcolm. As long as I live, I'll never let another person dictate my life.

#

I've grown impatient with Roan. I'm forced to work the mines with Collette, who despises me. I tire of looking at her smug face. I don't understand why he keeps her here. I don't understand why she stays. Roan assures me he will soon send her back to her hometown, which is only a day's journey from here. As thrilled as Roan is to have me, Collette is equally cold. Roan spends most nights in my bed. He loves me, not her. A most terrible thought crosses my mind from time to time. What if Roan tells Collette that he will someday send _me_ away?

I've thrown myself into the study of Roan's magic as a distraction. I've spent painful hours sitting and doing what he calls meditating. The mind is the key. The more I can control my mind, the more power I will discover.

My body is now constantly buzzing. I can't explain it exactly, but I feel in tune with myself and my surroundings. I'm nowhere close to being as strong as him. I have yet to manipulate a single thing around me. But I can recognize and feel the energy.

I've discovered that Siourious has a library, an ancient one. Late last night I read by candlelight a small book written by a Catahli clan member. It was thousands of years old and some of the words were so old we don't use them anymore. It talked about the Catahli and all of its mysteries. The founding members of the Catahli clan used to perform experiments on the mineral to see how it would react.

They soaked it in water and it turned a different color. They ground it up very finely into a powder and ate it with their meal. It only made them ill. Sometimes nothing happened. Like when they dug a great hole and buried the Catahli. When they dug it *up a year later, it was exactly the same. After reading the passage, I have a thought. What would happen if the Catahli was exposed to blood?*

#

Quinten Warwick entered Siourious today. We greeted him like a king, the three of us standing at attention as he rode into our little town. Proudly he led his caravan, his band of soldiers close on his heels.

I think him very consumed with himself. I caught him looking at his reflection in the pond that sits in the middle of Siourious. He surveyed the mine and all that we'd harvested with greedy approval.

It's evident that Quinten is no wise ruler, though. It's Roan who holds the power in Elmyra. He controls the money. Roan might never be able to rise to Supreme Ruler, but Quinten is nothing without Roan's mines and his ability to harvest the Catahli. The two continue to scheme and prepare to assassinate Bradac.

Perhaps this power is what has turned Roan into a liar. He promises me almost daily that Collette means nothing to him, yet after months of living in Siourious, Collette still resides in his home.

#

Collette entered my room today unexpectedly. I found myself struck with silence. What can be said to the wife of the man you're passionately in love with? Although love is an emotion I struggle to feel anymore.

Collette is pregnant, a miracle I presume since she was incapable of childbearing when I knew her in Bear Gap. The child is Roan's, conceived after our arrival in Siourious. I wanted to reach out and kill Collette and her baby. I thought she'd come to gloat but she came instead to become my ally. This is not the first time he's done this. Collette is Roan's seventh wife. The other six have either been shipped back home or disappeared all together.

I considered if Collette was simply lying to me to get me to leave Siourious, but I trust my instinct and right now I have a sick feeling brewing in the pit of my stomach. My father, who I haven't thought of in years, returns to my mind. I was an empty-headed fool when I knew him. He controlled me like a puppet and I had no idea. Malcolm too tricked me into loving him. He wanted to keep me trapped in that hole in Bear Gap. And now, Roan deceives me.

It feels as though my skin is boiling with rage. Every inch of me wants to scream out. I said that I'd never again be manipulated. Roan should make pleading prayers to his Catahli gods because I will have revenge. I'll go to my death before I kneel to Roan and work in the mines for him like some servant. He doesn't deserve the wealth of the Catahli. I don't know yet how I'll do it, but before the next full moon, I'll own the mines.

\#

Collette's belly has begun to grow. Roan has entreated me to not be angry. Although the child is his, he has no true feelings for Collette. I've been feigning our usual intimacy and pretending to be enraptured by him. He has been particularly sweet lately. He seems to take a modicum of pleasure from juggling two lovers at once.

I asked Roan a question I've been holding back for weeks. What happens when Catahli touches human blood? He scowled and looked at me like I were a demon. That's blood magic, he said, and strictly against the order of the clan. The experiment might be against the order of the clan, but the clan barely exists anymore. He told me never to speak of the blood again.

I will never speak of it again. I don't need to. From the expression on his face, I have my answer. What happens when the Catahli touches human blood? Something powerful.

Something frightening. Something that he wishes me to know nothing about.

So I stole a small crock from the kitchen. I made a cut on my wrist and let my blood drain until it filled the whole basin. It took longer than I thought, and several times I nearly collapsed onto the floor.

I dropped the piece of Catahli that Roan gave me into the crock. My blood enveloped it and hugged the Catahli close until it sank beneath its depths. I covered the bowl with a piece of cloth and hid it under my bed.

My breathing is shallow and my wrist is sore but I feel strong in spirit. Roan doesn't want me to know about the mysteries of the blood magic. He may control Elmyra but he won't control me.

#

I take in a sharp breath as I turn the page. For days my mother leaves the Catahli stone in the pot of blood without disturbing it. When she finally scoops it out, her blood is thick and she has to scrub it away from the surface of the stone. The Catahli emerges, a brilliant turquoise color.

#

Intense vibrations emit from the Catahli when I hold it to my skin. My whole body quivers. Am I the only one who can feel it? It's so strong. It seems that all of Siourious should feel its power.

Sleep is hardly necessary anymore. I sleep so little and my mind is constantly going. Channeling energy is no longer an arduous task that takes concentration. I'm able to lock onto people when I please and delve deep into their mind and body.

I've turned the Catahli into a necklace. I wear it around my neck like an amulet. I keep it close but hidden from Roan. He can't know anything about what I've done.

#

Roan is ruining the mines. His production of rings is painfully slow, too slow for what's needed. He's too loose with the secrets of the Catahli. I can run the mines better. I can make this place a sacred fortress. I can make Quinten more powerful more quickly and that's exactly what I told him when we engaged in a private meeting three days ago.

No, I'm not a clan member, but what does it matter? Roan is a reckless fool. He's a coward and that's the only reason he survived Bradac's massacre. He ran like a scared child when his beloved Catahli was being taken away.

That is the point that finally swayed our future Supreme Ruler. He thought me intelligent and probably rather beautiful as well. Quinten said he'd place me in charge of the production but I don't need his permission. Tomorrow morning, I'll deliver the news to Roan myself.

#

Roan is truly more depraved than I knew for he has tried to murder me. I confronted him with my agreement with Quinten. I revealed that I'd never settle for a man who shared his affections with another. I am not so low, not like him. When I said this, he flew into a rage.

I have become a problem. I was meant to simply be Roan's pet. When a beautiful woman shows herself smart and cunning, it's of great concern to a powerful man.

Roan wrapped his fingers around my neck and dragged me to the ground. I searched for the Catahli's power, but I admit, I found it difficult. I managed to scratch his face and push him off of me but he didn't relent. He kept his vise around my throat until I slowly lost all of my breath.

I awoke again, and there in Roan's bedroom, he struck me across the head with a mining chisel. I felt nothing. I knew nothing. I was dead, gone from the Earth.

It was half a day later that I awoke at the bottom of an embankment, deep in the woods. It was black out. My only sense *was what was buzzing around in my brain. I felt the side of my head where Roan had struck me. My hair was matted and soaked in dried blood but my skin was whole. It was as if the wound had been sewn up. There was no gash.*

My neck, where I had felt fiery pain, now felt normal. My breathing did not labor. My body was healed. Not only was it healed but I felt better, stronger. I stood from the spot where I had been left to rot. I walked through the woods as if it were alight just for me.

I threw open the door to Roan's bedroom. His eye bulged. Collette ran. I thought to tell him how much I loathed him but what good would it do? He'd be dead in only a few moments.

The amulet smoldered on my chest. This time, there was no struggle to draw on its powers. Roan raised a hand and reached inside my chest. His skinny fingers wrapped around my heart. But his grip didn't scare me and he could tell. Confusion melted onto Roan's face as he clenched down and tried to squeeze the blood from my heart.

I took my hand, and without touching him, I crushed every one of his fingers so his bones snapped. He tried with his other hand to squeeze my throat closed but I felt nothing but a faint tickle. He was so weak it was incredible that I once thought him a strong sorcerer.

Every incantation that Roan tried felt like nothing more then a pin's prick on my skin. I felt so in tune with his body, I could hear his blood course faster through his veins. I could see the air going in and out of his lungs as he breathed more heavily. Roan fell to the ground. I used his trick. I touched his heart and pumped it dry of blood. He gasped and sputtered, then died with his eyes wide open.

I now rule Siourious and the mines. I will no longer comply.

#

My breath catches in my throat. I lower the book to my lap and raise my head to gaze across the attic.

My thoughts settle on Roan, my mother's first victim. I dig deep for a modicum of sympathy for the man. I find none. What a prick, I think to myself. He deserved to die.

CHAPTER THIRTY

I NEVER REALLY understood my mother until now. Would I have acted any differently if I were in her position? Roan betrayed her in the worst way. He was supposed to love her and be the last person to hurt her. What if Johnny hurt me like that? I might rip him to shreds.

I stare through the window. The gallows taunt me as they sit against the dark backdrop of Rande Square. The longer we stay here, the more vulnerable we become. We sit in a giant hourglass. Our time of safety and planning flows by like water through a downspout. Eventually someone will hear something. Someone will grow suspicious. Someone will betray us.

The scrap of parchment that Bardle gave me slips from the open pages of the journal. I've been using it as a bookmark. Not able to read, he'd sketched a crude map of Rande with a circle around a house he says is safe. I close the book and bring the paper to my eyes. I've pondered the farm workers a lot while being relegated to Eve's attic.

A thought occurs to me as a surge of energy ripples through my body. I sit up straight and clutch the paper in my hand. An idea swirls in my mind. A plan forms slow and difficult. *No*, I mutter. It's the last place I want to go. I'd rather take on the bears that live in the wilderness beyond the river than go there, but it might just be the plan that saves this rebellion.

I won't wait until morning to tell Eve. It's too important and I might lose my nerve. I leave my mother's journal by the window and slip out of the attic. Philippa sits up in bed as I walk through the sister's bedroom. In the dark hallway, I blink rapidly to help my eyes adjust, then enter Eve's bedroom without knocking.

"Wake up," I say.

Philippa comes up behind me. "What are you doing?" she asks in a tone that resembles an accosting soldier.

"I'm not here to hurt your sister."

Eve rises, and reaches for the dagger on her nightstand. "Camilla?"

"I know how we can take this territory."

Eve pauses, studying me.

"It's okay, Philippa." She swings her legs over the bed. "I can handle Camilla."

I roll my eyes though certainly no one can see that I've done so. Philippa obeys hesitantly. Eve lights a candle on her nightstand. I close the bedroom door and wait impatiently for Eve's attention. She dons a long robe over her nightdress. Her hair is pulled into a loose ponytail that flows over her shoulder, an uncharacteristic look for someone so uptight.

"I need you to assemble a meeting."

Eve stands across the room from me with her lips pursed. "You look like you haven't been sleeping."

"I need you to assemble a meeting." This time I say it slower.

"With whom?"

"Everyone." Eve raises her eyebrows. "I want a representative from all groups to meet here at Lindon Place immediately."

"All groups?"

"Ralf and the soldiers that are on our side. My people. The Billage rebels, which means you'll have to find a reason to visit the leather shop. And then this man." I hold out the parchment for Eve. She takes it, squinting at the scribbles.

"What is this?" she asks.

"The man's name is Bardle. Get him to a meeting and I'll explain everything."

Eve shakes her head in stiff movements. "I won't do this unless I understand."

"You told me we needed to trust each other, right?"

Eve taps her left foot against the floor. "I did say that, yes."

"Then trust me."

Eve nods though her skepticism is obvious. If she's good for one thing it's getting things done. She may ponder an action before she does it, but once she decides she'll do it, there's no stopping her until it's done.

Eve starts on my request the moment the sun is up. Ralf was easy to get an invitation to. Even Bardle, who lives only a short walk from Lindon Place, agreed to attend without too much hesitation. Finding an opportunity to talk to the Billage rebels took Eve two days. Finally she was able to steal a moment with Linus as he walked home from work.

To say I'm nervous about having everyone in one place is an understatement. The nerves have more to do with the plan itself. My plan, the one I built alone, is the one I'm terrified of. I'd happily play out any other scenario but there is no other way.

Our guests enter through the back door. Al, a soldier who's frequently posted to walk Rande Square, stands guard. Tonight, he's making sure his partner doesn't see anyone entering. I wait in the basement with Knox, Johnny, and Reed. Eve has laid out a long table with parchment and pen as I requested. Tuor and Mirabelle are keeping watch upstairs.

Ralf is the first one down the steps. He nods to me but says nothing, then crosses the room to shake hands with Reed. Knox keeps a close eye on Ralf as he comes to a stop against the back wall. Dressed in full Warwick uniform, Ralf rests a hand on the hilt of his sword, which hangs from his belt. I shift on my feet, imagining what I must have looked like to Ralf on the floor of Karla's bedroom.

Next to enter the basement is Damion, accompanied by Tommy. They look around the room until their eyes settle on us. Damion comes to a stop in front of Knox and me.

"Are we gonna get my father out?" His face is a stone.

"Yes, we'll get him out," I say.

"How did it happen then?" Tommy directs the question to Knox.

I look over at Reed. "We were ambushed."

Tommy won't meet my eyes. He scoffs, then moves around the table. He doesn't believe my story.

The seven of us stand in painful silence. I can't keep my hands still. I know that, any minute, Bardle will take those steps and I don't know how he'll react at the sight of Ralf.

The door at the top of the steps opens. I jolt at the sound, but it's only Eve.

"Your man hasn't shown," Eve says, taking the last step into the basement.

I look around the room at the expectant faces, then turn back to Eve.

"How far is the house he marked on the map?" I ask.

Eve purses her lips. "Eight houses down. Maybe less."

"Could Al get me there without raising any alarm from the other soldiers?"

Tommy makes a noise of disapproval. "What do you think you're gonna do?"

"I want to talk to Bardle myself."

"If he doesn't have the guts to walk eight houses to a meeting, then we don't want him to be a part of this," Johnny says.

"Absolutely not," Eve says. "Bardle had his chance. Anyone who's not invested should be left out of this meeting. This is what you get for trying to work with farm workers."

"Farm workers?" Tommy shouts. He steps toward the table. "I've said it before. Forget about the farm workers!"

I clench my fingers into a fist, aching to punch him like Tuor did in Ivan's cellar.

"Your plan involves using the farm workers? How are they going to help us?" Ralf asks.

Despite his soldier-like demeanor, a flicker of worry crosses Ralf's face.

"I'll explain. I promise." I turn to Eve. "Can Al get me to Bardle's house without being seen?"

Eve's eyes bulge. She crosses her arms over her chest. "I'm not using Al for such a foolhardy and pointless mission."

"My plan doesn't work without the farm workers. We need them."

"Then we draft a new plan," Eve says.

My temper rises. "There is no other plan!"

"As long as you're resting your head under my roof, you will follow my rules." Eve holds my gaze. "I'm not sending you out into the streets of Rande when every soldier is looking for you. You'd risk the lives of everyone in this room."

"I'll do it," Ralf says. "I'll take you to this farm worker."

Eve's eyebrows knit together.

"Thank you," I say, nodding. I brush past Eve to head to the stairs, Ralf in tow.

Eve cuts me off, throwing her arm in my way. "I hope you know what you're doing." Her words have more bite than a poisonous snake.

I lock eyes with Eve so she knows she does not intimidate me, then I turn and face the group. "We need the farm workers. Whether you like it or not, if we want this territory, we need the farm workers on our side." I turn back to Eve. "If that means taking a risk, then I'm going to take it."

I move Eve's arm from my path. Ralf and I scale the steps. We convene at the back door of Lindon Place. I try to shake Eve from my mind. Knox appears from down the hall. He comes to my side and scratches at the back of his neck like he does when he's trying to hide his nerves.

"Stay alert," Knox says. "Bardle could be turning on us."

I take a deep breath. "They've been planning a rebellion for a decade. He's not turning on us. They've just forgotten how important it is."

"What do you think you're going to do to change his mind?" Knox asks.

I pause and consider the question. "I'm going to remind him."

Knox admonishes me again to be careful before Ralf and I exit through the back door of Lindon Place. I wear a hooded cape, which I use to cover my face. We walk through the alley, then up the side of Lindon Place to Rande Square. The gallows loom high over my head. A rickety ladder leans against the platform, the final steps of the condemned. Six nooses hang from the crossbeam, waiting to be used, enough for Tuor, Johnny, Mirabelle, Knox, Reed, and me.

Ralf takes my arm roughly in his hand and leads me down Reaper's Way. We pass a soldier who salutes Ralf but pays me no mind.

"I hope you know what you're doing," Ralf says flatly as we walk.

A line of row homes sits to our left: short, identical homes built for the farm workers. Ralf pulls me forward and marches toward a house with a red curtain covering the front window. Without knocking, he pulls open the door and tosses me inside.

"Next time you'll be in the stocks for being out past curfew," he yells as he slams the door shut.

I reach for the hood of my cape and reveal my face to a room full of farm workers. A candle flickers in the center of a square table. Bardle sits with his mouth agape. His expression shifts from horror to understanding.

"What are you doing here?" Bardle asks gruffly.

"Why didn't you come? We risked a lot to get that message to you. I've risked a lot coming here tonight."

Bardle sighs, placing his face in his hand. Eddie stands behind him, teetering back and forth on his feet. The Boone siblings fill up the rest of the room. The tension is thick.

"I told you we should have gone," Eddie says.

Bardle shakes his head. "It's complicated, Camilla."

I step into the room and stand at the head of the table. "You told me back at Mirabelle's house that you wanted change for this territory."

"I do. We all do." Bardle motions with his arm. "But there's a lot at stake. There are too many lives I can't risk."

"Nothing good ever comes without risk."

"We've got to do this, Bar," one of the Boone brothers says, his big front teeth showing as he talks.

A child's squeal breaks through the tension. A little girl in a dirty green dress tumbles into the room and calls for her daddy. She runs to Bardle. He looks at her with pain in his eyes, then scoops up the little girl and kisses her chubby cheek. A woman follows a few paces behind. She reaches out for the child but the little girl buries her face in Bardle's chest.

"Go on with your mum, now," Bardle says, handing off the girl to a woman with long straight black hair.

Bardle rubs his forehead as the little girl cries while being carried from the room. I furrow my brows. I watch Bardle. His gaze is pinned to the floor. Eddie crosses his arms over his chest.

"Sorry about that," Bardle mutters.

"I understand," I say, my voice soft. "But things will never change unless we do something. Things will never change for *her.*"

Bardle stands and turns his back to me. "Can't you just do this without us? You said yourself you already have an army. Haven't the farm workers in this territory already been through enough?"

"The plan doesn't work without the farm workers, and the only way I get the farm workers is through you."

"Can you guarantee our safety?" Bardle asks.

I pause. "No. The farm workers will be in danger, but if it works, you'll be far safer than you are now."

The room turns quiet. Eddie shoots me a furtive glance. One of the Boone sisters clears her throat and looks to her brother.

Finally it's Eddie that speaks. "What's the plan?"

I pace toward the door. "I've been plagued with nightmares ever since being trapped in Karla's bedroom." I turn to face the room. "I've been avoiding her and Thatius, secretly hoping that someone else will drag them from Bear Gap, but . . ." I drop my hands to my side. "They're the ones that are going to give us this territory back." I chuckle to myself. "They're the solution."

"What do you mean?" Bardle's voice is quiet.

"There are only three things in this territory that Quinten cares about: Karla, his cousin, Thatius, his right-hand-man, and the farm, the platform of his rulership." I step forward, placing my hands on the table. "We're going to take Karla. We're going to take

Captain Thatius, and we're going to take the farm until the Supreme Ruler becomes so hungry and desperate that he hands us Bear Gap on a platter."

CHAPTER THIRTY-ONE

IT'S A SIMPLE enough plan: occupy the farm and use Karla and Captain Thatius as bargaining chips to maintain control of the territory. That's what I told everyone when Ralf and I hurried back to Lindon Place. It's simple, but not easy. As Tommy was quick to point out, even with Ralf's soldiers, there are still a lot of them that are fiercely loyal to Quinten.

Even with some pushback from Tommy and Bardle, by the end of the evening, everyone agreed to the plan and understood their part. Damion and Tommy will assemble a meeting with the Billage rebels to get as many men as possible. Ralf will make sure his soldiers know what to do. Finally, I've made sure that Bardle and the rest of the farm workers will be on our side when the moment arises.

That moment will come in three weeks. We'll have time to solidify plans and gather weapons. Once we make our stand, that will be it. We either succeed or . . . die. Hiding in the woods isn't gonna work for the rebels anymore. We'll make ourselves known and there will be no turning back.

That was the last thing I said before I concluded our meeting in the basement of Lindon Place. Shortly after midnight, everyone left. Eve tried to usher me back to the attic but I couldn't. I simply can't be locked up after a meeting like that. I'm too nervous. My excitement is laced heavily with a dose of terror. My emotions feel like they've been plopped into a black pot that's bubbling over with a sticky liquid.

I pace the length of the sitting room hours after everyone else has gone to bed. We should have Ralf steal weapons from the armory, I think to myself. His men can assign the farm workers to strategic places in the field before the attack starts.

I'm so engrossed in my thoughts that I don't hear Johnny until he opens the door at the end of the sitting room. My body freezes at the sight of him. His expression is uncertain as he hesitates in the doorway.

"Are you okay?" he asks, clearing his throat. "I couldn't sleep and I didn't hear you come upstairs."

I consider my words before speaking. I could insist Johnny go back to bed and tell him I'm fine, but that wouldn't be the truth. It's exactly that impulse of mine that tore us apart.

I link my fingers to stop my nervous fidgeting. "I'm . . . worried, I guess." Johnny closes the door and looks at me with full interest. "I'm afraid the farm workers will get scared the day of the attack and we'll lose their help."

"You have Bardle's support now. He'll make sure—"

"Maybe three weeks is too much time to wait." I turn my back and begin pacing again. "That gives Thatius three more weeks to catch on to our plan."

"We need that time to prepare," Johnny reasons.

I spin around to face Johnny. "What if some of Ralf's soldiers are double-crossing us?" Johnny opens his mouth to speak but I cut him off. "We could be as good as dead already." I look at my hands. "This whole rebellion could be . . ."

"What?" Johnny asks.

"A joke."

Johnny says nothing. He saunters toward the middle of the room, stopping to fiddle with a doily that's been delicately laid across Eve's pianoforte. "I think you need to be reminded of some things. Remember when we started this, you didn't have any doubts."

"I was naive."

"You were clear with what you wanted, what this territory needed. What has changed?"

The lantern on the end table sputters, placing Johnny and me in a moment of darkness. "I didn't know it would be this difficult."

Johnny draws in a deep breath. He breaks from my gaze and takes a seat on the red, velvet couch.

"The last jaunt of any journey is the hardest. You're tired, injured. You've lost friends along the way, but you're so close to the end." Johnny leans forward, resting his elbows on his knees. "Don't stop now. You have everyone's support, including mine."

I remember when Johnny's encouragement was all I needed. He pulled on my arm and dragged me into the dungeons just so I could talk to Tuor. He gave me Shae and insisted I rescue Tuor when it seemed impossible. While Knox and Mirabelle doubted, it was Johnny that nodded along with everything I said. I stare across the room into Johnny's light blue eyes. How was I so foolish to push away the only person who ever truly believed in me?

I'm about to ask Johnny that very question when he says, "Camilla, I need you to do me a favor." I narrow my eyes at him. "If something happens to me or Uncle Knox, will you tell my mother?"

My instinct is to reject such an inclination. I want to tell Johnny that won't be necessary because nothing's going to happen to him, but I've grown far too cynical to believe that.

"Of course."

Johnny leans back on the couch. "I haven't spoken to my parents in some time. They don't approve of this rebellion." Johnny rubs at the back of his neck. "My *father* doesn't approve. But he still deserves to know whether his son lives or not. I trust you to do whatever it takes to get the news to them. They live in a little house in Hanover. "

"How would I be able to find it?"

"Pebble Street. It's unmarked but everyone there knows it. Plus, the road is made of a lot of pebbles."

I smirk, dropping my hands to my side. "Clever."

Johnny chuckles. I watch him from my spot in the middle of the room.

"I think my father named it. He moved there to get as far away from that farm as possible." Johnny shakes his head.

"Why are you doing this? The rebellion."

He scrunches his eyebrows in confusion.

"Your own parents don't seem to care that Quinten still holds your grandfather as a prisoner in LilyAye," I add.

"They care. They're just . . . scared. And it's not just about my grandfather. I grew up with Warwick soldiers polluting my house."

I join Johnny on the couch. "You did?"

"Governor Leo made my father treat his soldiers over other villagers. When the governor was killed, my family took it as their chance to get out of the agreement. Growing up, we always had soldiers in our home. I hated watching my father tend to their wounds and their illnesses. I knew that after my father patched them up these men would walk back to the farm and whip people like you."

Instinctively I shudder at Johnny's comment. I pull my arms together to hug myself. It's a posture I haven't taken lately, but the thought of the guard's leather whip hitting my back turns me into the old Camilla.

"All of that just so we could eat this food that was supposed to be healthier for us. And my father never stood up to any of them. He just bowed his head and did what he was supposed to do. I couldn't stand it."

"What could he have done?" I say, defending a man I've never met.

"He could have refused."

"Then he'd have been put in the stocks and you and your mother would have suffered because of it."

"It's about doing the right thing."

"After you've been hit a few hundred times, you forget about your principles," I whisper.

The scars on my back burn through my shirt. I'm flooded with that familiar feeling of being trapped. I never talk about my scars. Mirabelle's the only one who's seen them outside of the men who've given them to me. I hug my arms to my chest again and lean against the couch as if to shield my back from any further injury.

"This is why we're fighting," Johnny says. "You are only one of many who's been beaten into submission in that place."

"Sometimes I think I deserved those beatings."

Johnny shifts away from me like he's just touched something hot. "That's absurd, Camilla."

"I know. I accepted it for so long. It seems foreign to live a different way." I chuckle. "I guess I'm more like the farm workers than I knew."

Johnny takes my hand. "You didn't deserve anything that happened to you on that farm."

Shame over my scars has affected me and I didn't even know it. A solution to that shame and guilt comes to me in this moment, but it's far too scary to consider. My hands are shaking. If I do what I'm thinking, Johnny might look at me differently. He could see me as a victim. If I don't do it, my time at the farm may continue to haunt me.

I shake my head as if I'm telling myself to stop the nonsense. They're just marks on my skin, that's all. And I won't live my life in fear. I've already decided that.

"Can I show them to you?"

Johnny hesitates, unsure of what I mean.

"My scars, can I show you my scars?"

He nods his head and straightens his back. "Yeah."

I twist my body to turn away from him. Suddenly I'm riddled with nerves. For a moment I think I'll change my mind. I cross my arms and reach my hands to the bottom of my shirt. I pull it up over my head and hold the fabric close to my chest. My hair splays over my shoulders and back. He doesn't say a word or even make a sound. I want to turn and look at his face but I'm too embarrassed—too exposed. Then I feel a warm touch.

I jolt in surprise but still no words pass between us. Johnny runs his thumb down the middle of my back to the arch at the bottom, following the line of one of my many long scars. He brushes the tips of his fingers over the raised bumps. A few times I've stopped at a pool of water to inspect the scars on my back. I know how frightening they are. It looks like an angry cat has ravaged me.

Johnny pulls his hand away and I quickly bring my shirt down to cover my torso. When I face him, his mouth is spread open in a disturbed kind of awe. There's a faint rim of wetness at the bottom of his eyes.

"What's wrong?" I ask.

His eyes connect with mine. He finally closes his mouth.

"How can you ever doubt for one moment that you're doing the right thing?" Johnny's voice is low and gravelly.

I lean through the space that separates Johnny and me and place my lips on his. I pull back immediately, remembering that I'm no longer allowed to do that. Barely a moment passes before Johnny follows my lead, cupping my cheek with his other hand and kissing me hard on the lips. I close my eyes and exhale through my nose.

He tugs on my elbow. I fall into Johnny's arms and lay my head on his chest. A few tears coat my cheeks. Then I close my eyes and fall asleep, enveloped in a perfect moment until I wake to the sound of screaming.

CHAPTER THIRTY-TWO

JOHNNY'S ON HIS feet. He reaches for the blade on his belt. We both pause, unsure if the sound meant danger. The sitting room is filled with the faint glow of morning. I rub my eyes, groggy from sleep.

A second cry splits through Lindon Place. Tuor calls my name. I leap from the couch and run through the sitting room to the stairwell. Tuor stops abruptly halfway down the steps. He breathes a sigh of relief when he sees me.

"What's happened?" Johnny asks as he comes up behind me.

"It's Ivan," Tuor says.

He motions for us to come upstairs. I sprint to the window at the top of the steps just outside Eve's bedroom. Knox is there and Reed. Eve's sisters pour from their bedroom. Everyone's eyes are pinned to the window, everyone except Mirabelle.

Mirabelle paces at the end of the hall, both hands over her mouth. Her chest rises and falls in quick repetition. Another whimper escapes her lips and I understand the source of the cries.

"Camilla," she moans, reaching out a hand to pull me away from the window. Mirabelle squeezes her eyes shut against the tears. For a moment I'm immobile. Should I look?

Philippa gasps as she approaches the window. Eve's sisters chatter in hushed tones. Finally, I push through the crowd and touch the trim around the window for balance. I peer down onto Rande Square.

"Don't watch!" Mirabelle cries from the hallway.

Small clusters of farm workers huddle together like terrified kittens. An area has been cleared in front of the gallows. Across the clearing, two soldiers usher a man. His head is bowed. His shoulders are slumped, and even from this distance, I can see the markings on his face and neck. I've seen it before, a beaten man being led to the slaughter. My mind whirls back to the dungeons as I watched Tuor being led in front of the council.

Ivan is pushed up a set of steps to the platform of the gallows. He looks barely conscious as he's placed in his spot over the first trap door. A noose is tossed over the long crossbeam. It dangles so lightly that it's hard to believe it holds a threat.

The crowd below parts as another prisoner is dragged to the gallows. I gasp. It's Eddie. Unlike Ivan, Eddie fights his captors the whole way. He claws and spits and scratches like a rabid cat. Eddie yelps and curses Warwick up until he's placed next to Ivan and a gag is secured in his mouth. The executioner gracefully slings another noose over the beam.

"No," I mutter, but the horror doesn't stop there. The four Boone siblings are brought up next, two boys and two young girls.

Eve stands next to me. Her face is flat and passive.

"Philippa!" she barks. "Take your sisters to their room." Eve's sisters obey, and again, Mirabelle gives me a similar order.

"Come away from the window," Mirabelle sobs.

I consider turning my back on the six rebel members facing death, but it doesn't feel right. I spin around to find Knox.

"We have to help them," I say.

Knox solemnly shakes his head. "If we run out there, we'll be strung up with them."

"Then someone get me a bow! I'll strike them down from this window."

"You'll give away your location," Eve says.

"I can't—" My chest grows tight. I heave for air.

"I can't just watch!"

"Camilla, there's nothing to be done," Reed says calmly.

I watch Mirabelle, at the other end of the hall, bury her red face in her hands. My teeth are clenched together as I painfully turn back to peer out the window. I look just in time to see the final noose being secured around the last Boone girl's neck.

Once it seems the hangings are in order, Captain Thatius makes his appearance. He struts across the front of the gallows, Lawrence in tow. Thatius comes to a stop and slowly spins on his heels to face the crowd of farm workers. His pointed nose and sharp jaw seem to accuse the onlookers. Slowly he raises his arm, bringing the street to silence.

"These are traitors." Although he doesn't shout, Captain Thatius' placid voice echoes through Rande Square. "Traitors against myself, your governor, and our great Supreme Ruler."

In the silence, a scream of disapproval bursts from the crowd. A scuffle breaks out as a lonely protester shouts obscenities toward Thatius. Three soldiers converge on the man and quickly escort him away from the mass of people. In one swift movement, the defector is quieted.

"Rebel activity will not be tolerated in my territory," Thatius continues. "I have no intentions of being unclear. Any individual even suspected of an association with Camilla Crim or Knox Duffy or any other rebel will meet the same fate as these." Thatius turns his body and gestures at the six rebel members.

Eddie still squirms in his spot over the trap door. One of the Boone girls is crying, weeping uncontrollably while her brothers wear a brave face. The other Boone girl moves her lips but I hear no sound. Praying. The poor girl is praying in her last moments.

Thatius gives the nod. He and Lawrence step aside to make way for the main attraction. The executioner goes down the line and roughly shoves burlap sacks over the heads of each fated rebel member.

I claw at the windowsill. Please no. Please no, I mutter. No one around me moves. The executioner walks to the end of the platform, stopping behind the first Boone sister. He pauses, then in a snap, kicks the lever that opens the trap door. Her body drops like a tree in the forest. My heart is in my throat. My vision fogs on the edges as if I were in a tunnel.

In an instant the second Boone sister is loosed from her footing. The beam moans with the weight of two bodies. The executioner doesn't miss a beat. He kicks the lever on both Boone brothers, one right after the other.

Johnny turns from the window. He can't stand the sight any longer. Eve slowly raises a hand to her mouth. Eddie twitches in his spot on the platform. Surly he knows he's next. He's heard the drop of four before him. Eddie desperately grabs at the noose with his bound hands.

The executioner rests his foot on the lever.

"Don't," I beg.

He shifts his weight forward. The trapdoor flops open. Eddie sinks midair. His body convulses once, twice, then it goes still. There's a pronounced lump in my throat as I realize there's no rescue in sight.

Ivan stands alone on the gallows, aside from the man who'll take his life. I've only ever known Ivan to stand tall and proud, but right now he's hunched, barely able to stand. He seems to have no idea what's going on. I hope he doesn't.

The crowd has fallen motionless. Even the children that normally are unable to stand still seek comfort between their mother's arms. The executioner takes a firm grip on the final lever. The muscles in his arm twitch as he pulls hard. The trap door falls open. The rope snaps tight as Ivan's thick body drops. The gallows groans as it takes on the weight of Ivan's body.

Six bodies now hang limply from the gallows. They sway solemnly like the branches of a willow tree. The thick nooses encompass their necks like deadly serpents. Eve brushes a tear from her cheek before turning her back to the atrocity before us.

I turn around to see Tuor sitting on the top step, his head in his hands. Knox hobbles down the hallway and places his arm around Mirabelle. An eerie quietness fills Lindon Place. Only Reed and I remain at the window. We stare as the farm workers are finally released from the show and commanded to return to work.

"Knox, we have to go," Mirabelle cries.

"Go?" I ask, turning around to face the others.

"Six rebels were just murdered before our eyes," Mirabelle says. Her cheeks are wet with tears. "Captain Thatius called you and Knox out by name!"

"I agree. We should get out of here," Tuor says.

"If we leave now, we'll be caught immediately," Reed says.

"Maybe we should go back to Mirabelle's house," Johnny says.

I grow tired of turning my gaze between them. Back and forth, the bickering grows until Eve claps her hands together like a schoolteacher.

"I knew it was a bad idea for you to go over to Bardle's last night," Eve says, straightening her back and pulling on the bottom of her shirt.

"How did they get Eddie and the others?" Tuor asks.

"They were at Bardle's house." I admit this with some hesitation.

"They must have been caught leaving his house," Reed says.

I look around the hallway that's suddenly grown quiet. Everyone stares at me like these deaths are my fault. Perhaps they are.

"You shouldn't have gone over there and risked them," Mirabelle says, shaking her head.

"I had to." I nearly shout. "We needed their support."

"I don't think we're going to have it now," Johnny says under his breath.

"What about Al?" I say to Eve. "Isn't he supposed to keep the soldiers away from our people?"

Eve's tongue is sharp. "Al is only one man. You and Ralf decided to go over there without our say, and now we've lost the farm worker's support anyway."

"The act is done," Knox says. He speaks from behind me as he leans against the wall. "Your griping isn't gonna change the situation we're in."

"Let's just go," Mirabelle pleads. "Think about Ivan. Think about his sons."

"We can't go back to where we've been." I stare at the floor and feel myself losing all control. "Ivan's dead. He's not our concern anymore. His sons? They'd want us to avenge their father."

Reed touches my arm. "With Ivan dead, we may lose the support of the Billage rebels too."

"It's only a matter of time before Lindon Place is tied to the rebels," Eve says. "After last night, they may already know. I want all of you out of my inn now."

Eve points a bony finger in the direction of the steps. Johnny curses under his breath.

I shake my head. "You spent all that time convincing us that this was the safest place we could be. And now you're kicking us out?"

"That was before you broke the rules, Camilla." Eve takes a step toward me. "Your actions have consequences. Do you see that now?"

I press my lips into a hard line. My jaw goes tense.

"There has to be a way we can continue to work together," Knox says.

"We wouldn't have the farm workers' support if I hadn't taken that risk last night." I talk through gritted teeth.

"After today, you'll have no one's support. I told you, I needed to trust you, and you broke that trust last night. I'll continue this rebellion without you," Eve says.

I look around the hallway. Tuor avoids my gaze. Knox's expression is pained. No one refutes Eve. Worse yet, no one defends me.

"So this is all my fault?"

No one answers my question.

"Fine. We'll run away like everyone wants."

I don't give anyone a chance to beckon me back to our meeting. I storm through the sisters' bedroom and up to the attic. In blind rage, I pack my meager belongings. I ignore Mirabelle's attempt to soothe me. Soon I head for the basement.

When I pass through the upstairs hall, Knox is still talking to Eve, trying to salvage our alliance, but it's pointless. Eve has banished me and that includes Knox, Mirabelle, Tuor, and Johnny. As for Reed, I only wonder vaguely which side he'll take. My spirit is too bruised to care what he'll do.

I pace the basement of Lindon Place and consider slipping out the secret tunnel on my own. They've all thrown me to the wolves. But that would be foolish. If I do that, I may never find them again.

In my fog of anger, I almost don't hear one of Eve's sisters call my name at the top of the steps.

"There's someone here who's asking for you," she says in a soft, clear voice.

"Me?"

Maria puts a hand on her hip and instantly assumes the form of a younger Eve. "No, they're asking for that sack of flour in the corner."

It takes me a moment to catch her sarcasm, but when I do, I scrunch up my eyebrows in annoyance.

"Come," she says, beckoning me up the steps.

I leave my bag in the basement and follow Maria upstairs to the kitchen. A portly man stands in the kitchen with his back to me. When he turns around to face me, I realize it's Bardle. I stop short. His face is sullen and gray. He's the last person I expected to see. My heart thumps like a galloping horse. My mouth goes dry. It's *my* fault that Eddie is dead.

"You were right," Bardle says. His voice is deep and gravelly. It's so different from his usual cheery tone, I almost don't recognize it. "Everything you said last night was right on. I just didn't want to hear it. This ain't never gonna stop until we stand up and do something about it."

Bardle rubs at his forehead in agony. "I'm with you, Camilla. Whatever we gotta do, I'll do it and I'll get the rest of the farm workers on board too."

I open my mouth, not sure how to respond.

"But Eddie's dead," I say.

It's now Bardle's turn to give me a surprised look. "That's exactly why. Eddie deserves to be avenged. The Boone kids too." Bardle takes a step closer to me. "That's why we're gonna do it, for every farm worker that ever met their end at the hands of Warwick's national farm." Bardle makes a wide sweeping motion with his arm. "Every peasant in this territory has a friend or family member that's rotting in the dungeons or that has died from one too many cracks of the whip."

269

"Are you sure you want to do this?"

Bardle manages to give me a small smile. "Oh, darlin', don't question help when it comes to you."

I nod, feeling control returning.

"What happens next?" he asks.

I take a deep breath. "Our time is running out. We have to think about Captain Thatius'

move. He's playing a game, just like us. If he knows that Eddie and the Boone siblings are rebels, then he knows that other farm workers could be rebels. We have to act before he picks off our supporters one by one."

Bardle nods, rubbing the bushy beard on his chin. He tilts his head up and looks me in the eye. "When?"

"Tomorrow."

CHAPTER THIRTY-THREE

SUN RAYS CREST over the posting tree, lighting the dewy leaves. Reaper's Way is clear. All of the farm workers have already marched through the street on their way to the farm. Lindon Place grows quiet. The dining room empties as breakfast comes to a close. The distant sound of clattering dishes drifts through the floorboards all the way to the attic. I stand at the window and force myself to face the six dead rebels who still hang from the gallows.

With Bardle still on our side, I was able to convince Eve to let us stay at Lindon Place for one more night. It was another thing getting her back on board with my plan. It was even more complicated getting her to agree to follow through with the plan in one day instead of the three weeks that we had originally planned.

Eventually I swayed Eve by admitting that I had damaged her trust in me, but just as she was willing to align herself with the Warwick elite, she may have to skirt some of her morals in order to accomplish our shared goal.

The argument worked. Bardle relayed our plan to the farm workers. Tommy and Damion, determined to avenge their father's death, told the Billage rebels what they were to do. Eve did her part too, getting Ralf and the other soldiers on board. On the heels of a terrible tragedy, everything was finally coming together.

I dress in my knee-high boots and long trousers. Securing a belt around my waist, I attach my dagger and a sword. Both are weapons supplied by Knox. I tie a vest over my middle. One of Bardle's people made it. They claim it'll absorb a sword blow. I run my fingers over the rough, wiry fabric. Today I'll get to find out if they're right.

Mirabelle sits on her bed mat and pulls the sheath off a short blade. She tests the sharp edge against her thumb, then pushes it quickly back in the sleeve. I shake my head.

"You're disappointed in *me*?" Mirabelle says. "That's quite unusual."

"You should stay here, where it's safe."

Mirabelle comes to her feet. "I've heard it all from Knox already. *It's too dangerous. You'll be a distraction* . . . I'm not staying behind while the people I love put their life on the line. I did that once before and my husband never returned."

"Almost everyone died that day. At least you're still alive."

Mirabelle crosses the attic and takes my face in her hands. "If someone as young and precious as you is allowed to put her life on the line, then so am I. If it were up to me, you'd stay back and I'd go in your place."

I smirk at Mirabelle.

"But I know there's nothing that would keep you home."

Knox, Johnny, and Tuor are waiting for us in the dining room. Knox is livid with Mirabelle but they've argued enough. There's nothing more to be said. Reed enters. His black hair is slicked neatly back. He has shed his affable demeanor and replaced it with a hard, stoic face. It's a look more fitting to a Supreme Ruler.

"You have what you need?" Reed asks.

I pat my bag, which is slung over my shoulder. "I'm ready."

Eve hardly looks like herself with her hair pulled back and no skirt or jewelry. I look out the window facing Rande Square.

"It's time," I say, turning to face the others.

One of Eve's sisters peeks through the kitchen door. Eve raises her eyebrows in disapproval, then gives her a nod. The sister disappears into the kitchen.

"Should you talk to your family before we leave?" Mirabelle asks.

Eve gives Mirabelle a curt shake of her head. "They've already been spoken to. They know what I'm doing."

I push open the door to Lindon Place just a crack. "Is everyone ready?"

Knox pulls his long sword from his belt. The zinging sound of the metal is like a call to battle. There is nothing more to be done. We've rehearsed our plan. Our objective is clear. In my mind the deed is already complete. I ready my own sword.

I push the door so it swings wide. My eyes lock on Rande Square. Soldiers stand like vultures around the rotting dead bodies of the hanging rebel members. I give them no time to consider me. I run full bore across Rande Square, swinging my sword at the closest man.

"Stay behind me," Knox yells to Mirabelle. Johnny flanks me on the left and Tuor on my right. The soldier blocks my first strike. I slash at his hand, and his sword drops. I strike forward, gutting him with one move. Johnny is pinned to the ground. I approach from behind and rip the soldier off Johnny. I hold the man by his shoulders while Johnny scrambles to his feet and slices the soldier through his chest.

I toss away the dead body. The other soldiers are dead now too. Tuor wipes sweat from his brow. Johnny reaches out a hand and pulls Knox from the ground. I look around at what remains: just a few villagers.

"Get the horses," Knox says.

We move to the back of Lindon Place. Barely a word passes between us. At Eve's stable, we take our mounts. I give Shae a stroke on the neck before we kick off. The morning is warm and humid. We ride shoulder to shoulder down Reaper's Way. I only have seven people at my back but it feels like an army.

A soldier paces down the road toward us. He turns around and tries to make sense of us. He draws his sword and calls for help. At least fifteen soldiers answer his call. That's how many are usually stationed in front of the Justice House, a notation that Bardle made many times on his way to work.

We stop and wait. Down Reaper's Way, the soldiers ride. There's more than fifteen. I'm sure of it. Everyone draws their weapons. Tuor's eyes are pinned in front of us. Knox is stone faced. I grip Shae's reins harder. I can feel the galloping hooves through the ground.

Just before the soldiers approach us, Linus, Munro, and the other Billage rebels burst from behind the Justice House, trapping the soldiers between them and us. The Billage rebels pause in a line. Each draws a bow and quickly lays an arrow. They release and pepper the soldiers before they have a chance to understand.

Shouts ring out as the soldiers are struck from behind. A horse collapses. His rider crumples to the ground. Some soldiers turn and face the Billage rebels. Others continue to charge us. Confusion abounds in a way that I could have only hoped.

A horse-mounted soldier charges me. His sword strikes mine with an exuberant clang. Shae bucks. The soldier rides past me, then turns around to charge me again. Instead of waiting for his hit, I kick Shae and push her closer.

I'm drawn away from the crowd of chaos as we fight, back and forth. My shoulder burns with every strike. He pulls back and points the tip of his sword to my chest. I groan as I raise my sword, just barely blocking it. He presses his blade hard against mine, challenging my strength. My face contorts with the strain. He's close enough that I raise my foot and kick his side. He wobbles but keeps his mount.

Shae scuttles backward, pulling us out of sword lock. The soldier swings and nicks my bicep. I retaliate and manage to catch his exposed neck. It's not deep, but instinctively, the soldier reaches for the bleeding wound. He's distracted. I strike his other hand, knocking his sword from his grip. His eyes grow wide.

A horse gallops behind me. I turn about, expecting to see another enemy, but it's only Reed. He's breathless as he rides up next to me. I charge the soldier again. This time I'm able to kick him off his horse. He scrambles to his feet and retreats toward Rande Square.

Behind me, only rebels remain standing. He's the last soldier left. Munro comes to my side. He nocks an arrow and lets it fly. It hits the soldier squarely on his back. Munro lowers his bow and exhales.

"Are you okay?" Reed asks.

I raise a hand to my chest, feeling the thunderous beat of my heart. Karla is only a short way down the road. With every step closer, my fear of her lessens.

"I'm okay," I say with a nod. I peer across our group of fervent rebels, the original rebels. I take a moment to recall our first meeting and how far we've come since then, how much we've changed.

"Let's go take the farm!" I shout.

Jol lets out a whoop as he raises his bow into the air. Reed chuckles and slaps me on the back. I urge Shae forward. We pass the Justice House on our right. A soldier still stands guarding the door. He tips his head as we pass. He's one of our own and has been tasked with keeping the guards within the Justice House oblivious of the attack until after we've taken the farm.

The end of Reaper's Way is marked by the wide iron gate that leads into the farm. Two men guard the gate. We approach slowly. I search the woods on either side for movement. The guards draw their swords. We stop, a few yards out, and stare as if by our eyes alone we could elicit a surrender.

The soldier on the left isn't hiding his fear well. He backs up against the gate.

"We're under attack!" he yells. His partner turns and watches his panic. "We're under a—"

With the butt of his sword, the other soldier hits his partner across the head. He pulls his body from the road, then slowly opens the gate to let us pass.

CHAPTER THIRTY-FOUR

WE CROSS OVER the gate's threshold into the farm. I break into a gallop, charging toward the field. Supervisor Benedek steps from his booth and looks at us with shock. He scurries across the lawn and ducks inside the house before I can get to him. An unsuspecting guard wanders into our path. On foot, he's easily cut down.

The farm lays before us, bathed in the orange glow of the early morning sun. The fields curve and roll with miles of spring crops. The farm workers toil away as if this were just another day at work.

A cart filled with manure is pulled between rows of peas. An elderly woman uses a hoe to draw a shallow ravine as a child follows behind dropping seeds into the hole. Bardle catches my eye. Casually he moves down a row of onions, a shovel in his hand. I spot Malcolm kneeling beside a cauliflower plant. Slowly he rises to stand.

We stop at the edge of the fields. Our presence does not go unnoticed by the guards and foreman. One guard points in our direction. Another reaches for his sword. A heartbeat of time passes before I look at the small army to my back and give them the signal. Together we let out a great yell, a battle cry, a call to fight. Then at once, Bardle and the farm workers raise up their garden tools and attack.

I barrel into the fields to join the fray. No instructions are needed. Everyone knows their place. I push Shae through the low crops, up the hill toward the orchards. At the edge of the cornfields, I catch a glimpse of Foreman Mac and his protruding stomach. My heart hiccups at the sight of my old torturer.

I pause and scan the fields. Scuffles have broken out everywhere. Blood is spilled over the fresh crops. I feel a twinge of guilt as I decide to abandon my post at the farm's edge and instead make sure one particular foreman meets his death today.

Mac is running from the fight like a terrified child. I kick Shae and charge the foreman. He looks behind himself and sees me coming. I pull Shae to a stop. Mac dives between the cornstalks. With my sword at my side, I jump off of Shae and follow.

I run into the cornfield and am instantly enveloped by vegetation. The cornstalks are taller than me. The rows are tight and not easy to run through, but Mac's round figure has made him easy to track. I jog along, following the trail of broken stalks.

I stop. The din of battle is absorbed into the corn. There's barely a rustle in the leaves. I spin on my feet, searching through the green stalks for Mac. He yells. I turn just as he barrels toward me, carrying a large stick in his hand. I raise my arm but it's too late. It feels like the force of a thousand horses when he hits me across the head.

I collapse onto my back like a tree that's just had its final strike from an axe. I blink slowly. My head swims. I grapple with my hands but feel nothing. I roll onto my side and squint. Mac shuffles away through the corn.

"Coward… I'm going to kill you." My words are slurred.

I scramble to my feet, and reach for my sword but it's not there. He's taken it. I stumble after Mac and burst through the cornstalks on the other side. The screaming and clang of metal hits my aching head. My feet feel boneless. I clutch at the side of my head, barely able to keep my eyes open.

Mac runs up the field, toward the orchards, my sword in his hand. I run, charging as fast as I can. He stops to catch his breath by leaning against a toolshed. He looks behind him, then keeps running. His stubby legs crumple when he reaches the grapevines.

I reach him, lazily pulling my dagger from my belt. I cut a mark into his back. He yelps, turns around, and swings my sword at me. I jump back, but trip on a vine. Mac comes toward me, a waddle in his step. His chest heaves as he gasps for air. He points the tip of the sword to my stomach. I shuffle backward through the dirt to get away.

Someone shouts my name. Mac looks away, searching for the voice. I kick his hand, knocking my sword from his grip. Malcolm storms into view, striking Mac in the stomach with a rake. Mac collapses on his back. I crawl to Mac and find it hard to focus my gaze. The world around me is tilting and spinning. Mac moans as he twists on the ground. I hold my dagger firm to his neck.

"You were the spy," I growl. "You were Quinten's spy."

Mac gasps for air.

"You're the dirty rat that reported my every move to him," I say.

His face is a sheen of sweat. He lets out a sardonic laugh. "It only took you eight years to figure it out."

I bite my lower lip, then press the blade down hard against his throat. I moan, swiping my blade to split open his neck. Blood gurgles from the cut and pours onto my hand. I stand slowly, watching him as he begs for air. I look at my bloody blade, then at the gashing wound in Mac's neck. It's my mother's signature kill. I did it without thinking.

Hidden behind the grapevines, I fall to my knees and drop my dagger into the dirt. The farm has grown quiet.

"Camilla." My name sounds like it's being called through a tunnel.

"I'm sorry," I whisper.

I shake my head to pull myself from my trance. Malcolm stands a few yards from me leaning on the rake. His breath is heavy.

"Are you okay?" my father asks. It seems difficult for him to say the words.

"I thought you weren't going to fight with the rebels."

Malcolm shrugs. "I figured I'd end up dead either way so might as well stick it to Warwick with my last breath."

I squint at Malcolm and search him for any similarities to myself. He hates Warwick. That's the only thing we've ever been able to agree on. That single fact is all it's taken to make me friendly with people I wouldn't normally even talk to. Plus, father or not, Malcolm just saved my life. Perhaps I should give him another chance.

The sound of a galloping horse brings me to my feet. I pick my sword off the ground, ready to fight again. Reed wears a coy smile as he rounds the grapevines and comes to a stop in front of me.

"Come," he says calmly. "The farm is ours."

I move to face Harras Manor. The fields are hushed, like after a ravaging storm. The dead are strewn over the crops.

"What about Thatius?" I ask.

"There's been no movement. I think he's holed up inside." Reed points to the house with his sword. He glances at Malcolm then turns and looks at me with concern. "Camilla, your head."

"Huh?" I touch a hand to the side of my head and feel the warm blood. "We need to take the manor before reinforcements get here."

I grab my dagger and wipe Mac's blood onto my pant leg. I wince as I struggle to mount Shae. Malcolm follows on foot. The farm workers cheer as Reed and I ride down the fields. Every gallop of Shae's hooves throbs in my head. The gates to the farm are shut and barricaded. No one's getting out. Knox stands with his hands on his knees. I dismount and join him and Tuor by the stocks.

Johnny rides in from the east side of the field. He slides off his horse and hobbles toward us. There's a tear in his pants and his left thigh is wet with blood.

"Are you okay?" I ask.

Johnny waves away my concern. "I just got clipped by an arrow. I'm fine. You should be worrying about yourself."

Johnny points to my head. I touch the side of my head where Mac struck me. My hair is matted. I can feel a tiny crack in my skin. In a flash I'm reminded of the entry in my mother's journal when Roan attacked her.

"Camilla! " Tuor's face is flushed and spattered with tiny dots of blood.

Knox looks at me with disapproval.

"I'll be fine," I say, ignoring the injury. "We're not done yet." I look up at Harras Manor. The windows are dark. "Where's Mirabelle?"

"Tending to the wounded in the field," Knox says.

Ralf approaches.

"What do you think's going on in there?" I ask.

"It's hard to say."

"Are any of our soldiers inside?" Knox asks.

"No. All my men are accounted for. Any soldiers in there are not on our side."

Johnny shakes blood from his sword. "How are we going in?"

"Ralf, you take your men to the front door. Knox, you and Johnny and Linus take this back door. This is where Tuor and I will do our part."

Everyone obeys. I remove my bag from Shae and retrieve a rope. I step back and take a good look at the house. Above us is the balcony where Governor Leo used to make his speeches. I would stand in this very spot and listen to him drone on. He talked like he owned the very people who worked the farm. *I* own it now, I think to myself.

"Camilla?" Tuor asks. He stretches out a hand, waiting for me. I force my eyes to focus as I realize my head is still swimming.

I toss Tuor the roll of rope. He slings it over his shoulder and removes the sword from his belt so he's as light as possible. I take it and secure it with my weapons. Tuor approaches the brick facade.

He touches a hand to a notch and places his right foot on the windowsill. He pulls himself up, placing his left foot on a jutting brick. Again, he moves his right foot into a shallow crevice and moves his hand to pull himself up. Tuor is a spider, crawling his way up the side of the house.

He reaches the edge of the balcony and slides over its railing. Securing the rope to one of the spindles, Tuor tosses it down to me. I follow his path up the wall, using the rope for support. My shoulders burn with every pull. The sun grows hot on my neck and my head aches. At the balcony, Tuor reaches out a hand and pulls me up.

"Just like when we were kids," I say, catching my breath.

He smiles.

I return Tuor's sword and unsheathe my own. We look at each other. I nod, then step in front of the double glass doors that lead into Governor Leo's office. Together we turn the knobs and let the doors swing open. Holding my sword out in front of me, I slowly step into the room. An eerie silence envelops us.

Captain Thatius sits at the desk with his back to us. I scan the room. It's empty. Captain Thatius slowly comes to his feet. He straightens a stack of parchment, returns his quill to its inkwell, then turns to face us. His expression is complete neutrality. He raises his hands in surrender.

"You've got me," Thatius says, his voice as steady as ever. "Bear Gap is yours."

A sinking feeling grows in the pit of my stomach as I realize this was far, far too easy.

CHAPTER THIRTY-FIVE

I HAVE CAPTAIN Thatius on his knees. I'm securing a cord around his wrists as Knox comes through the door, his sword extended in front of him. He scans the room.

"It's just us," I say.

Knox relaxes slightly as he steps inside.

"Is everyone okay?" I ask.

Knox nods. "We found Karla upstairs and that other skinny twit."

"Benedek," I say.

"Yeah, him. Johnny and Linus are taking care of them. I have Tommy and Damion searching the house."

Tuor holds a sword to Thatius while I tighten the final knot on his restraints. I nudge Thatius to his feet. Reed barges into the room. His face is flushed with excitement. He walks straight toward Thatius and punches him in the nose. The blow knocks me back.

"You won't be able to lick the boots of my uncle for much longer," Reed says, sticking his face inches from Thatius'. He spits on the captain before slowly stepping away.

"Take him down the hall," I command. "I want him in a room farthest from the stairs."

Reed obliges my suggestion, taking Thatius roughly by the arm. Tuor follows as other rebels clamor down the hall to help deliver Captain Thatius to his temporary prison. Knox and I are left alone in the office. I don't feel jubilation like the others do.

"Camilla, we should talk," Knox says, closing the office door.

I shuffle through some papers on the desk. Knox lifts a towel from a basin of water that's sitting in the corner and hands it to me. I squint at him in confusion.

"For your head," he says.

Reluctantly I take the towel and hold it to my head. I'd momentarily forgotten about the wound while in the presence of Thatius. When I toss the towel on the desk, it's soaked a dark red.

"Did you encounter any soldiers on your way in?" I ask.

Knox shakes his head as I flip over another piece of parchment.

"Why wasn't he guarded?"

"There's something else," Knox says. "We found Lawrence."

I let out a painful sigh. I expected that news. Knox comes to stand on the other side of the desk so we're facing straight on.

"He was downstairs just sitting in an armchair. Like it was Sunday lunch."

"Thatius, Lawrence, Benedek, and Karla were all inside here without a single soldier to hold us off."

Knox looks up from the desk and locks eyes with me. "It's like they were bait."

"So where are all the soldiers? Where are all of Thatius' men?"

I step away from the desk, not finding any answers to my questions. I should be happy. We did it. We took the farm and captured Thatius and Karla like we planned, but something isn't right. My stomach churns with uneasiness.

I pull open the double doors and walk onto the balcony. I marvel at the view. I'll never have to question why Governor Leo loved to stand here and address the workers. It's a beautiful sight and a powerful stance. The farm workers have set up camp below. The rolling fields are dotted with bodies and splotched in blood. This is rebel land now, no longer owned by Quinten Warwick.

Knox comes to stand next to me. "You know this is where it happened."

I tilt my head and look into Knox's solemn face. "What?"

"The battle. When Quinten first invaded, it was here that we stood." The sun beats on Knox's weathered skin. His eyes are cloudy with memory. "Quinten grew this farm using the blood of the rebels that came before us."

I bow my head, remembering the stories I've heard about the Battle of Bear Gap, the *first* battle in Bear Gap. Everyone in the battle was either captured or killed, everyone except Knox.

"Why did Quinten let you live?"

It's a question that's always plagued me.

Knox's eyes turn downward. "What do you mean?"

"After the battle, you were the only one that Quinten let go free." I turn away from the fields and look at him dead on. "Why?"

"He employed me to look after your mother. You know that."

"He could have employed anyone. Why you?"

The muscles in Knox's neck tense. He takes a deep breath and says simply, "I don't know. I try not to make sense of madmen."

I search Knox's face for any hint of deceit but find none.

"Quinten had one of the farm foremen spying on me while I worked here. He kept a watch on Tuor and me for years, just waiting for the opportunity to use us to get to my mother."

Knox says nothing.

"The thing is, I can't figure out how he ever discovered that we existed in the first place."

"Portia suddenly took an interest in you," Knox says. "That's why she drew you into the swamps. She probably told Quinten herself."

I nod slowly. My mother has begun to take an unexpected interest in me. I'm not sure why, but that has only been recently.

"But Mac has been spying on me for eight years, ever since I started working at the farm. Perhaps I was even being spied on before then." Knox stares across the fields like an unmoving edifice. I turn and look at my hands. "When Portia left Bear Gap, she never gave Tuor and me another thought."

I know this, of course, from Portia's journal. Tuor and I are never mentioned again after she abandoned us. It's like we never existed.

"What do you mean?" Knox asks.

"I think Quinten knew about Tuor and me long before my mother ever told him she wanted us back." Knox slowly turns and looks at me. "Who else could have told the Supreme Ruler that we were Portia's children? Who else would have seen us as a bargaining chip to control our mother?"

Knox shrugs his shoulders. "Quinten is very powerful. When Portia's magic began to scare him, he could have easily sent a man to investigate Portia's old life. That man could have asked around town and discovered you and Tuor were her offspring. All he'd have to do is report that back to Quinten."

Knox's theory makes sense.

"We should have a talk with the captain," Knox says, suddenly changing the subject.

"If this is a trap, he's not going to tell us anything."

"We'll make him talk." Knox turns and swiftly exits the balcony.

***

Reed's knuckles are bloody. His hair is matted in sweaty chunks. Thatius sits in a chair in the middle of an unused bedroom. His face is black and puffy. Reed paces in front of Captain Thatius, flexing his fingers in and out.

The room sits at the end of the hall with windows facing both the fields and the front gate. The thick curtains are covered in dust. The cold, stone floor has only one threadbare rug, which is now speckled in blood, Thatius' blood.

Knox and I stand back. Tuor is behind Captain Thatius. Johnny, Eve, and Linus gather on the other side of the room. It's a spectacle to be seen and we're the bloodthirsty, jeering crowd. In an unexpected move, Reed strikes out and punches Thatius hard in the jaw.

Reed pauses and looks at Thatius expectantly. The captain hasn't said a word since Reed started. His face, although beaten to a pulp, still holds a stoic expression.

"We can spare your life," I say. "Whatever trick you're planning, call it off, and we'll make sure you're returned to LilyAye alive."

Thatius says nothing.

"We just want Bear Gap. Let it go and no one else has to die."

Reed allows Thatius another moment to respond before slapping the captain with the back of his hand. It seems to be all Thatius can take. His head rolls on his neck and he slips into unconsciousness.

"He's not going to talk," Eve says, moving into the center of the room. "This is pointless."

"We don't even know if this is a trap," Linus says.

"It is," Reed says, wiping sweat from his brow.

Johnny crosses the room. He walks with a noticeable limp. "Interrogating the captain is getting us nowhere."

"Camilla, what's your plan here?" Eve asks, her arms crossed over her chest. "Are we just going to sit here and do nothing?"

Plan? *This* is the plan. The plan was that once we held the farm, we were done. It was just a matter of making a deal with Quinten. A simple exchange of Karla and Captain Thatius for the release of our territory. The hard part was supposed to be over by now.

"Camilla?" Eve snaps.

I hesitate with my mouth open. "I don't know."

"What about his son?" Linus asks.

"No," I say quickly.

"No one's touching Lawrence," Tuor says, eyeing Linus.

Eve scrunches up her face in disgust. "Why not? Maybe he'll crack easier than his father."

It's Johnny that speaks. "Thatius might be able to take the torture, but what if he sees his son being beaten? That might be enough to get him to talk."

My eyes grow wide. I stare at Johnny, hardly able to believe the words he's spoken.

"Lawrence saved our lives! Now you want to repay that by torturing him?" I spit the words then grab my head in anguish.

Johnny bites his lower lip. "Lawrence has also been working alongside his father, killing rebels."

"We are not hurting Lawrence."

"Then what are we going to do with him?" Johnny asks.

"He'll stay with us," Tuor answers.

"I don't know exactly, but we're not hurting him," I say.

Johnny scoffs, shifting his weight off of his injured leg. "You know what your problem is, Camilla? You don't let anyone help you. You think you can do it all on your own and no one else's opinion matters."

"Look around us! I'm taking help from all of these people."

"You've been bullheaded with this rebellion from day one!"

"I think you should calm down, son," Linus says.

I squint my eyes in confusion. Where is Johnny coming from? Knox crosses the room and takes Johnny by the shoulders, gently pushing him away from me.

"All you've done is keep secrets from me and make decisions by yourself," Johnny says. "Lawrence might be the only way we can get ourselves out of this trap, and you don't get to be the only person who decides how we handle him." Johnny pushes against Knox. He addresses the room. "What does everyone else think we should do?"

"We should do with Lawrence whatever is necessary," Eve chimes in.

"If he knows things, we should at least talk to him," Reed says. The backs of his hands have begun to bruise.

"Fine, *I'll* talk to Lawrence," I say.

Johnny chuckles. "There you go again. Why do *you* get to talk to him?"

"I think we should discuss this at another time," Knox says.

Johnny holds my gaze, then steps back in surrender.

"What has gotten into you?" I ask, my voice softer than before.

Shouting wafts through the open windows of the bedroom. I tilt my head and look around the room. The shouting comes again, loud and desperate. I run to the window that faces the front of the house. Knox follows, close on my heels. Standing in clean formation outside the iron gate is an army of Warwick soldiers. These aren't Ralf's defecting soldiers, though. These are men who are still loyal to Quinten and still loyal to Captain Thatius.

Knox eases in behind me and peers out the window. "We found our missing soldiers."

CHAPTER THIRTY-SIX

MY BLOOD HEATS up as a gnawing pulse quickens in my neck. The sight of an army on our doorstep sobers everyone in the room.

"We should gather our fighters together," Linus says. "Get ready for an attack."

"But they're not doing anything," I say, staring at the unmoving mass of soldiers.

"They're not here to attack," Knox says. "Not yet."

"They want to make a deal." Reed's words are icy.

I turn from the window and head for the door.

"Where are you going?" Johnny calls.

I spin around to face him. "I'm going to do my best to find out what their next move is. I'm going to talk to Lawrence. And you can't stop me."

I storm from the room and march down the hallway. Shaking my head, I try to understand what's made Johnny so angry. It was only two nights ago that we kissed in Eve's sitting room. What's changed since then?

I descend the spiral staircase to the second floor of Harras Manor. At the landing, I pause and glance up to the highest story of the house. I've been told they have Karla locked up there in her bedroom. I grip the railing hard. I feel dizzy all of sudden. I narrowly escaped this place a month ago and now I'm doing everything I can to defend it.

A sick feeling grows in my stomach at being this close to Karla and her prison. I turn away from the upper floor and leave the stairwell. Upstairs is a dirty, nasty thing that I plan to avoid for as long as possible.

I push open the door to the room where Lawrence is being held and let it click shut behind me. Lawrence sits in a chair in the middle of what looks like a storage room. His hands are tied behind his back. Barrels of maps and parchments line the wall. It's dimly lit. There are no candles and the curtains have been drawn over the windows.

Lawrence watches me enter, his silken black hair falling into his eyes. He wears a scowl. He's tense, frustrated. I soften my gaze. Something about my argument with Johnny has left me feeling sympathetic toward Lawrence.

"I've been asking for you! You don't know what you've gotten yourself into," Lawrence says.

"What do you mean?"

"Th—this rebellion," Lawrence stutters angrily. "What were you thinking?"

I stay close to the wall, keeping my distance from Lawrence. "I thought you'd be proud of us for continuing the work."

Lawrence throws his head back. "I didn't sacrifice myself to my father so that you could go and get yourself back into danger."

I scrunch up my eyebrows. "What was the point of doing it then?"

"So you could live!"

I lean against the wall and fold my arms across my chest. "You never really wanted a change then? You went back to your old ways, the ways of your father."

"I saved your life twice and both times you ran right back into trouble. I can't save you this time."

I pause and consider Lawrence. He's a dichotomy. On one hand he seems desperate to protect me and the rebels, but on the other hand, he continues to stand on the side of his father, the man that's been tasked with squashing the rebellion.

"Then whose side are you on?"

Lawrence lets out a long sigh. "I'm on the side where everyone I love lives."

"I was there when you arrested Ivan. I'm sure some of these rebels would love to see you dead for your part in the hangings." I push off from the wall and step toward Lawrence. "They want to torture *you*. I'm not going to be able to hold them off for much longer."

"I had to show loyalty to my father. You understand that, right?"

"You can't blame your father for your actions. You can't blame anyone for the things you do. At some point, you have to choose a side."

Lawrence drops his head.

I let my arms fall to my side, resigned that Lawrence will forever try to serve two masters. I cross the room and place my hand on the doorknob.

"Camilla," Lawrence calls.

I turn around.

"If you don't accept their demands, they're going to start killing the prisoners." Lawrence's lips make a hard line. "The ones in the Justice House."

My heart sinks. The prisoners in the Justice House are the loved ones of the very farm workers that helped take the farm today, Bardle's people.

"Your father knew our plan, didn't he?"

Lawrence nods slowly.

"How?"

"Someone hasn't been loyal to you."

I click open the door to the sound of someone running up the stairwell. Hollow, thumping footsteps march down the hall. I step out and see Ralf running in my direction.

"Camilla, the soldiers want to talk to you."

"Me?"

"They asked for you specifically."

"Where did they come from?" I demand.

I close the door to the storage room and walk with Ralf toward the stairwell.

"We think they were hiding in the Justice House."

"I thought you said you had enough of your men in the Justice House to keep control?"

"We did. We did," Ralf says.

"You were supposed to protect the prisoners until we made a deal with Quinten."

"Captain Thatius ordered all of his guards at the last minute to assemble at the Justice House. There was no time to get word to us." Ralf wipes sweat from his brow. "Camilla, they knew we were coming to the farm."

I pause at the stairwell. "I know."

"He's trapped us here on purpose."

I start down the spiral stairwell as Ralf follows behind.

"But why would he stay here if he knew we were coming?"

Ralf's heavy footfalls echo through the stair tower. "He knew we wouldn't kill him because we need him alive to barter."

At the bottom of the steps, I walk into the sitting room and peer out the large windows to the back lawn. The farm workers have set up camp outside. Bardle hurries about, giving instruction to his people. I wring my hands together at the thought of Lawrence's words. I can admit now, finally, that the farm workers have more at stake in this rebellion than I do.

"Do you think the barter will still work?" Ralf asks.

"I don't know," I sigh. "I want to wait to talk to the soldiers."

"Why?"

I take a deep breath. "We need to gain control of the situation. Tell them I'm being treated for an injury, and I'll be over to talk after I've rested. Can you hold them off for a few hours?"

Ralf hesitates. "I know the man in charge. I'll speak with him."

I nod and Ralf exits out the back door. My excuse isn't a lie. In the hours after the battle, my head has begun to throb and burn. I walk down a hallway that breaks off from the sitting room. It leads to the kitchen. Two long tables sit in the middle of the stone-walled room. They're stacked high with pots and butcher knives. The glass cabinet in the corner is filled with fine china and wine glasses.

Mirabelle has turned the room into a triage space to treat those who were injured during the battle.

People lie shoulder to shoulder in a line like a set of toy soldiers. I walk cautiously to the threshold. Mirabelle kneels on the floor next to a young woman who's holding a hand to her bloody stomach.

Mirabelle stands and wipes sweat from her brow. Her white apron is smeared with blood. She sees me standing in the doorway. I expect her to call my name or pull me into a hug, but she only gives me an exhausted, half-hearted smile. Mirabelle picks up a piece of linen from a basket on the floor and hands it to me.

"Put this on your head. I don't know how you're still walking around with a cut that bad." My head stings when I put the linen there. It throbs like a pulsing heartbeat. "You should have come to me sooner."

"I . . . couldn't." My voice is almost a whisper. "I had things to do."

Moaning wafts through the room. It sounds like a haunted forest. It's almost more than I can handle. Having to look into the faces of the people who were injured . . . it feels like it's my fault.

"There's not much more that can be done." Mirabelle speaks candidly as she moves to one of the long tables. There she has a pile of sheets I assume she stole from the upstairs bedrooms. Using a kitchen knife, Mirabelle cuts the fabric into strips.

"This is all I can do," she says. "There's no medicine in this whole house."

"Are you sure?"

"I've searched every room. They've taken the food too. There's not a loaf of bread or bottle of wine anywhere." Mirabelle tosses the knife on the table in frustration.

"We have the farm. We'll pick new stuff."

Mirabelle shakes her head but says nothing. Finally she pulls out a stool and orders me to sit. Her usual tenderness is gone. She uses water to clean away the dried blood from my face and scalp. Hurriedly she stitches up my head. I claw at my pant legs as she threads the needle across my temple.

"I have to help the others," she says after quickly tying off my last stitch.

Mirabelle brushes past me as she moves between her patients. I force myself to stare at every injured person. Maybe the reality of it all will help me negotiate with Thatius' soldiers.

I leave the makeshift hospital and force myself to visit Bardle at the farm worker's camp. It doesn't look like a place that's been built after a battle. There are women and children. Meals are being prepared over the fire, scant meals from the little bit of crops that are available in the fields.

"You've worked the farm," Bardle says. "You understand. It's spring. There isn't much to harvest yet. Normally we'd still be eating our winter reserves."

"I know."

"Isn't there any food storage inside?" he asks.

I shake my head.

Bardle's cheerful cheeks are flushed red. He rubs at the back of his neck and pulls me a few paces away from the camp. "Those soldiers at the gate are making my people nervous. How long are we going to be stuck in here?"

I purse my lips and quickly debate what information I should share with Bardle.

"It could be a while," I admit.

"Hon, listen. We've got injured folks here and people are gonna start getting hungry quick. Some of our families are still outside these walls. People are starting to get worried."

"We still have Captain Thatius and Karla. We'll make a deal, I promise." I glance around the barren farm. "For now, keep your people calm."

***

It's past midday. The sun has begun to sink toward the horizon. After a meeting with Knox and Reed, I finally concede to Ralf's urging to go speak to the soldiers. We round the corner of the Harras Manor and head for the gate. Ralf and his men have barricaded the gate with wagons and tools from the farm.

A man stands waiting for me. He's dressed in a pristine Warwick vest. He's tall and broad shouldered and watches me with pity as I approach. Clemson is his name, Ralf tells me.

"Ralf," Clemson muses. "I always wondered how you ranked so high when your loyalties were neutral at best."

"I have loyalties. They're just not with Quinten Warwick."

Clemson takes a breath as he looks me over. He stretches out a hand. "Camilla, I presume."

I look at him with a passive face and decide to keep my hands to myself.

Clemson lets out an awkward chuckle when he realizes I'm rejecting his handshake. "That's fine. But you needn't be cold. This is simply a business transaction. We can be civil."

"Don't be coy," Ralf says.

"This isn't a business transaction. People have died. People have died for freedom," I say.

"You're in a bit of a situation," Clemson says. "You weren't expecting the governor to outsmart you."

"Back off our gate or the governor is dead," I say.

Clemson's face is unchanged. "We're willing to compromise. Return the farm to us and we'll let your people go home, unharmed."

"We're not giving up the farm."

Clemson looks over my head. "You'll never make it as a leader if you don't learn to negotiate."

"A negotiation implies that both parties compromise," I say firmly.

Clemson laughs at my snarky comment. "Then what's your offer?"

"We keep the farm. We keep the whole territory and Captain Thatius and Karla are returned safely into the hands of the Supreme Ruler."

"Interesting," Clemson muses. He continues to gaze across the field, not bothering to look me in the eyes. "No deal."

"Then they die. And I can promise you, Karla will be the first to go."

Clemson exhales and tilts his head down to finally look me in the face. "No, I don't think she will. See, if you kill Karla and the captain, then you've got nothing left to bargain with. The problem with your plan, Camilla, is that you think you have more power than you actually do." Clemson eases a hand onto the hilt of his sword. "In two days' time, I will have a fresh set of men in Bear Gap ready to take control of this farm. You have no such reinforcements. You've dealt all your cards. I can see all your moves."

Clemson draws breath. "You have one more move you can make to get out of this alive. It's going to be the Supreme Ruler's move. Along with my fresh soldiers, the Supreme Ruler will be making an appearance in Bear Gap, and he's going to make you a simple offer. Give up the farm quietly or it will be forcibly taken from you."

I stand with my arms crossed and my face set.

"Now I know how you rebels are. You enjoy putting up a fight, but I'd advise you to take the easier path on this one."

"And what about Karla and Captain Thatius? What if they die during the fight? Your men have no way of guaranteeing their safe extraction. How does the Supreme Ruler feel about that?"

Clemson shrugs his shoulder. "Unfortunate casualties." Clemson sighs as if he's grown bored with this conversation. "I'll give you some time to think on this conversation, but don't wait too long. By the time the Supreme Ruler arrives, he will be expecting your answer."

I take a shaky breath and bury my quivering hand beneath the folds of my arm. I can't let Clemson see my nerves. Quinten is coming *here*. Of course he is. We've just commandeered his national farm. My plan, it seems, has a flaw. Perhaps the lives of Karla and Captain Thatius weren't as important as I thought.

CHAPTER THIRTY-SEVEN

RALF AND I leave Clemson standing by the gate. He'll be ushered back to his side of the fence and we'll return to our silent standoff. A clock is ticking down the quiet though. I have a decision to make. *We* have a decision to make.

If I surrender, the farm workers will likely live and go back to their old lives. Quinten will need them to continue working the farm. I will certainly be imprisoned and probably executed for my part in the rebellion. I'd imagine Knox and Tuor and the others will meet a similar fate. But at least I'd be sparing the lives of the farm workers. That is assuming that Quinten keep his side of the deal.

I don't stop walking until I hear Bardle call my name. I'm stopped short at the farm worker's camp as he grabs my arm.

"What's going on with those soldiers?" Bardle asks.

Behind him, an expectant crowd of farm workers eavesdrops on our conversation. I'm tempted to brush him off, but he deserves to know.

"If we don't give them our hostages, then they're going to attack."

Bardle looks at me with a blank expression.

"You should prepare your people," I say.

I leave Bardle at the farm worker's camp and slip back inside Harras Manor. In the sitting room, I drop the facade and let my anxious mood show. I bite hard on my fingernail.

"Clemson is bluffing," Ralf says. "He wants you to think they don't care about Karla's and Thatius' lives so you'll give them up and take the deal."

"Yeah, maybe. Either way, we lose. If we give them up voluntarily, we'd be ending the whole rebellion. If we put up a fight against Quinten's army, we'll lose. We were supposed to have these two days to release the prisoners and secure the territory."

"I'm going to set up a watch schedule for the night. Tomorrow we should prepare ourselves to fight."

As sunset approaches, we build up our defenses, setting up a perimeter around the farm. A dedicated watch team is placed on Captain Thatius and Karla. Clemson could be bluffing about the value of their lives. Either way, I don't want anything to happen to them.

Some people are instructed to sleep so that they're fresh for tomorrow. I'm one of those people, but with a decision like this on my mind, sleep is just a fantasy. Harras Manor is too noisy a place.

There's the occasional shout from Ralf's men outside, communicating to each other across the fields. There's pacing in the hallways from people keeping watch. The drone of voices and moaning from the sickroom downstairs churns my stomach.

Then there's Karla, who haunts me from her bedroom upstairs. She's grown a habit of randomly bursting into shouts and screeches for no reason in particular. Tonight she's gone on for hours, howling and crying.

I toss and turn, trying to find a way to drown her out, but it's impossible. Just before sunrise, I give up on getting any quality sleep. I sit up in bed. I've taken up residence in one of the bedrooms down the hall from where Thatius is being kept.

Karla is driving me mad. Maybe this is all part of Thatius' plan. Karla will act so crazy that we'll be begging Quinten to take her back. I shake my head. No, no, that can't be it.

I touch my stomach. A thin cut remains where she sliced me. Still, the pain is present in my mind. I remind myself that it's *her* that's held in captivity this time, not me. Another of Karla's screeches echoes down the stairwell and across the hall. I toss off my covers and jump out of bed.

I tiptoe up the stairwell tower and stand at the end of the hall on the fifth floor. The floor stretches out before me like an endless road. I'm outside my body and watching myself stagger down this very hall, leaving bloody footprints in my wake. In my vision, I follow the sounds of the girls crying in Karla's makeshift dungeon.

When I round the corner to the first room, there are no girls. The room is dark and empty. I suppose Benedek's order to "get rid of them all" was completed. I scurry to the next room. There are no girls here either, but Benny jumps off a chair and comes charging at me. I hurriedly shut the door, trapping Karla's wretched dog inside.

Karla yelps again, her voice clear and loud. Only the wooden door to her bedroom muffles the sound. I reach for the knob and find my hand shaking. I pull it open quickly. A flush of horror washes over me as my eyes settle on Karla, strung up by the very chains she put me in.

Tommy and Damion are there, keeping watch over the demon. Karla looks at me and falls silent. Suddenly she doesn't seem so scary. She appears small and pathetic, weak. My shoulders relax. I take a deep, calming breath.

"Do you need something?" Tommy asks. I've grown used to his perpetual attitude toward me.

My body seems to float out of Karla's trance and I feel like myself again. I look to Tommy, who's leaning against Karla's dresser.

"Don't give her any water to drink," I say before closing the door and leaving Karla's den. Her howling persists but now I'm able to sleep.

***

Knox keeps watch in the sitting room. He peers out the tall glass windows onto a dew-laden farm. The sun has just begun to rise. Voices from the kitchen grow louder as I reach the ground floor. Knox turns when he hears me enter. He rubs at his forehead in agony. I look down the hallway toward the kitchen and give Knox a questioning look.

"Things have gotten worse with the injured," he says.

"What do you mean?" I ask, moving into the room.

"See for yourself."

Knox leads me into the sickroom. It's a cavern of moaning, delirious people. I stumble inside. The foul stench of vomit and blood hangs like a warm cloud. I cover my mouth as I walk through rows and rows of injured rebels, farm workers, and soldiers until I find Mirabelle.

Her hair's a frazzled mess. She's not running around like I'd expect her to be. Instead, she's kneeling and gently caressing the sweaty brow of a young man. She sucks in air as she raises her head to look at me. Her face is painted with grief.

"There's nothing I can do for him," she whispers.

Not being able to help a person in need is torture for Mirabelle. She dips a crumpled-up rag into a bowl of murky, tepid water and wipes sweaty beads from the man's forehead. It's then that I realize the sick man is Johnny.

"What happened?" I breathe. I fall to my knees beside Mirabelle. "He seemed fine yesterday."

Johnny is barely recognizable. His face has a white, pasty quality. The left leg of his pants has been torn away and a crude bandage placed over the wound he got from a stray arrow. The linen is sticky with congealed blood. Purple spindly veins creep outward from the wound.

"Many of the other's have it too. I think they put something on their arrows," Mirabelle says.

My mouth hangs open. "Poison?"

"I think so. I have no idea how to treat it, and even if I did, I doubt we have what we need here."

Johnny's eyes flutter open. He twists and turns on the floor as if he were having a bad nightmare.

"That's the fever." Mirabelle sighs.

Knox stands next to us. His brows are furrowed as he stares down at his nephew. Just yesterday Johnny and I argued. Now he looks like he's dying. Perhaps he is dying . . .

I stand suddenly. Knox places a tender hand on my back. I turn and look into his stone-like face. Everything has fallen to pieces, yet Knox has stayed constant. He's become someone I can depend on. If this rebellion has to go down fighting, I'm glad to know Knox will be by my side.

A blistering scream echoes through the kitchen, but it's not the cry of one of Mirabelle's patients. Knox runs down the row of injured people, and I follow close on his heels. We run through the sitting room and burst through the back doors into the farm worker's camp.

The farm workers are buzzing around like a nest of wasps. A woman is on her knees, clutching her face in horror. I turn and look toward the gate, following the woman's gaze. Swung over the stockyard fence hangs the dead body of a man. A rope is tethered around his neck and secured to the top of a post like an ornament.

"It's him! It's him!" The woman screams. "That's my husband!"

"No," I mutter. We were supposed to have until tomorrow to make a decision. I shake my head. Clemson is pushing me, trying to get me to crack.

Panic races through the crowd of farm workers like a forest fire. A mother pulls her son from the sight and covers his eyes. Another woman runs to comfort the one whose husband is hanging on the fence. Bardle stumbles into the fray and tries to make sense of the screams and shouts.

"What's going on?" Bardle demands.

"That's my husband," the woman cries, pointing toward the fence.

Bardle makes a feeble attempt to comfort the woman. "I know this is hard," he mumbles, kneeling next to her.

Knox stares at me for a moment, then grips my elbow.

"Did you know about this?" He speaks close to my ear.

I draw a shaky breath. "I—Lawrence told me but I thought we had another day."

There's a rustling noise coming from the spot on the wall where the man hangs. Another body is slung over and hung on display. Gasps ripple throughout the farm workers.

"That's Daniel," a man shouts. "That—that's my brother!"

Murmuring morphs into clamoring as more farm workers stand and look upon the fence.

"Everyone stay calm," Bardle instructs, moving throughout the camp.

"Make it stop," a woman yells.

"We have to do something." Knox pulls me away from the farm worker's camp. "They're going to turn on us."

"What is there to do? Clemson wants Captain Thatius and Karla. They're all we have."

Knox bites on his lower lip as he watches anarchy breed throughout the crowd of farm workers. Yet again, a noise draws our attention to the spot on the fence. A third body is tossed over. This time it's a woman. The tumult grows louder.

Bardle tries desperately to calm the farm workers to no avail. He catches my eye and marches toward Knox and me.

"Make the deal," he says. There's pain in his voice.

I shake my head. "I can't. If I do, this is all over."

"I know," Bardle says. "I want out. I want this over. Make the deal and let us go home."

Bardle can barely get out his plea before we're swarmed by the mob of farm workers. Knox and I are cornered against the back of the Harras Manor. Knox takes my hand and pulls me inside, barricading the door behind us.

"What do we do?" I ask in a panic. "We can't give in to those soldiers. That's exactly what Thatius wants."

The farm workers pound on the glass window panes. Knox paces in front of me.

"If we don't, they're just going to keep killing prisoners," he says.

I rub the side of my head where Mac split it open. A burst of dizziness overtakes me. I squat to the floor, holding my forehead in my hand. Knox rushes to my side. He puts both hands on my shoulders.

"I'm okay. I'm okay," I insist. I look up at Knox. The farm workers call for our blood. "Thatius knew the farm workers would turn on us. He put the enemy in our own ranks. We failed."

"Trying is never a failure," Knox says firmly.

Glass shatters. An oil lantern flies through the room. Knox shoves me out of the way. I hit my back on the bottom of the stairs. The lantern falls at Knox's feet and explodes into a column of fire. He screams, crumpling to the ground. His whole body is engulfed in the flames.

Farm workers barge through the broken window. The mob runs toward me. I roll onto my hands and knees and crawl toward Knox. He writhes on the floor, the flames consuming his body. Farm workers storm the stairs. I reach out my hands to help Knox, but in a jolt of horror, I realize I'll burn if I touch him.

"No," I cry. "No!"

I run to the couch and grab a bearskin blanket. I throw it onto Knox, smothering the fire. When I pull the blanket away, he's motionless. My mouth is agape. My lungs feel tight. The farm workers blow past us and march up the steps.

"Knox," I mutter.

I hear a tussle upstairs. They'll have to get past Tuor and Eve to get to Thatius. They can have him, I think to myself. I don't want this rebellion anymore. I scream for Mirabelle as loudly as I can. Knox's chest looks like a chunk of his flesh was scooped away. The fire melted a wound from his waist to his neck and up the side of his head.

Mirabelle runs from the kitchen. Her eyes fall to Knox's still body. Mirabelle collapses next to him. The sound of furniture being tossed and turned over wafts down the stairwell as shouts echo from upstairs.

"We have to get him out of here," I say.

I run to Knox's feet and motion for Mirabelle to take his shoulders. We drag him across the hard floor to the kitchen. A path of smeared blood follows us. I push Knox over the threshold and slam the kitchen door closed behind us.

Mirabelle holds her hands over her mouth.

"Mirabelle, tell me what to do," I shout.

She can't pull her eyes away from him.

"Mirabelle!" I snap.

She kneels next to Knox, looking at him as if he were a broken teacup. "We need to get his shirt off and I need linens."

I scramble to the table and pull all the bed sheets into my arms. Mirabelle gingerly peels away what remains of Knox's jacket and shirt revealing his raw, bloody flesh.

"Water. Get me water," she says.

I run between the two tables. Pots and dishes clatter to the ground as I search for water. I find a basin sitting next to a patient. There's only a shallow pooling of dirty water, but I pick it up and bring it to Mirabelle. She lifts the basin and pours its contents on Knox's wounds.

Taking a strip of linen, Mirabelle dabs the skin around the burn, soaking up blood and dirt. Then she takes a bandage and lays it across Knox's chest. Mirabelle takes a long look at Knox, then leans back on her heels, covering her eyes. Tears streak Mirabelle's face.

"What's next?" I demand. "Tell me what to do."

Mirabelle's body shakes as she sobs into her hands.

"Mirabelle," I scold.

Slowly she pulls her hands away to reveal her glossy eyes. "There is nothing else to do. There's not a single thing I can do."

My eyes drop to Knox's lifeless body. His chest rises and falls with shallow breaths. Tears sting my eyes. I can't take one more horror. I need Knox. I need his help. I need his counsel. I can't do this on my own.

"Will he live?" I whisper.

Mirabelle takes in a long shaky breath. "No."

CHAPTER THIRTY-EIGHT

I SIT ON the kitchen floor with my back leaned against the wall. Arms folded across my chest, I stare listlessly at Knox's ravaged body. Aside from the slight rise of his chest, he looks to be already dead. Mirabelle is on her knees placing a rolled up sheet under Knox's head. She wipes dirt from his face with a damp rag and then covers him with a blanket.

At this very moment, Quinten is riding to Bear Gap, expecting me to agree to his terms, and I don't even have Knox to help me. He and Johnny are both dying and all Mirabelle and I can do is watch. Above us the scuffle continues. Shouts bellow through the thin walls of Harras Manor. Doors are opened, then slammed shut. Heavy footfalls pound the floor. The farm workers raid the rooms where Thatius and Karla are being held. A part of me hopes they succeed so this can all be over.

"You've got to stop them," Mirabelle croaks. She brushes a tear away.

I give her a questioning look.

"If the farm workers get Captain Thatius and Karla, the rebellion is dead."

"I know." I stare at the floor.

"You can't let that happen." Mirabelle shakes her head. "We've worked too hard for this. Knox . . ." Mirabelle's voice falters. "Knox would want us to finish. His death has to mean something."

"But you didn't even want this rebellion."

"I didn't want the last rebellion either, but sometimes things come to you and you can't help it. You just have to accept it." Mirabelle strokes Knox's face. She looks up at me with glistening eyes. "I wanted freedom as much as you did. I just didn't want to give anything up for it." Mirabelle's gaze falls to Knox's body. "I didn't want to give anyone up."

A crash of glass and wood reverberates through the walls, followed by a piercing yelp.

"Go," Mirabelle whispers. "If we are all to die, let us at least save the rebellion. Do it for Knox," she pleads.

Knox's motionless body reminds me of a warrior that's fought his whole life and has finally, after decades of hard work, laid down to rest. He pioneered the old rebellion, lost his father, spent half of his life tracking my wicked mother, and still somehow I convinced him to start the rebellion all over again. He saved my life after I escaped Karla. The least I can do is avenge him now.

I exit the kitchen, pulling its heavy door closed behind me. The windows of the sitting room look like they've been blown out by a great wind. A small fire burns one of the armchairs from where the lantern was thrown. The sound of clashing iron rumbles down the stairs.

I peer through the glass doors at the farm worker camp. Women huddle together in clusters, weeping into each other's shoulders. Bardle is hunched over a fire with his face in his hands.

The shouting splits into my aching head. I take caution as I jog out the back door and look across the lawn. I run toward the gate and try to avoid the three bodies hanging over the stockyard fence. I call for Ralf as I approach. My voice is cracked and dry. The morning sun grows hot on my forehead.

"What in all of Elmyra is going on in there?" Ralf asks, pacing before me.

I rest my hands on my knees to catch my breath.

"The farm workers want to give over Thatius and Karla to make the killings stop."

Ralf reaches the sword on his belt. "We can't let that happen."

"Gather your archers and come with me."

Ralf nods. He yells for his men and I take them to stand in a line in front of the farm worker's camp.

"We can't let these men through with our hostages," Ralf says, marching down his row of archers.

I pull Ralf aside and say, "I don't want it to come to this. I don't want anyone to have to die."

"I understand. But if they don't surrender—" Ralf raises his eyebrows. He doesn't need to finish his statement. Like a true soldier, Ralf will do whatever is necessary to complete the mission.

"Here they come," Ralf says, pointing to the back door.

Through the broken glass, the mob of farm workers carries a screaming Karla.

"Raise your bows," Ralf commands.

Behind me, Ralf's men set their arrows. The farm workers carry blood-soaked knives and shovels. Their mouths foam like rabid animals. Just like a wild animal, it's impossible to know what they'll do next.

"Give us Karla," I say.

"We're not giving back anyone!" one of the farm workers shouts. "We're comin' back for the captain too."

"You don't understand what you're doing."

A farm worker steps forward, shaking his crude weapon. "They're killing our family!"

Karla bucks against her restraints.

"If you surrender Karla and Captain Thatius, not only will we have lost all of our leverage, but they will kill your loved ones regardless. And we'll all be dead too."

Karla chomps her teeth together like a snapping turtle. She bites the forearm of her captor, drawing blood. The man holding her curses and throws her into the dust. She claws to get away, but the farm workers start kicking her.

I reach for my dagger. "Stop this!"

Karla's ravaged by the blows. She's no use to us dead either. I look to Ralf. His face is set.

"Ready," he calls to his archers.

One of the farm workers rips Karla from the ground. He holds her like a shield in front of himself. "You'd kill your own people?"

"Release Karla," I say with a low voice.

"Don't do this," Bardle yells, running from the farm worker's camp. "They only want to save their families."

I raise my chin and turn back to the riotous group of men. "Release Karla or they will shoot."

"You're defending the life of a Warwick!" the one holding Karla says.

"Yes," I say, thinking of Reed.

"We're not giving her up."

The mob of farm workers agrees with a unison of shouts. They grip Karla and start pushing her toward the yard. I look to Bardle for help, but even he can't talk sense into them.

Before I can think of another argument, Ralf turns to his archers and gives them the signal. The snap of bows is followed by a symphony of thumps as the arrows strike the farm workers. Screams erupt from the camp behind me.

The only man left standing is the one holding Karla. He looks at me, shaking, wondering if they'll shoot him too. Ralf instructs his men to set another arrow.

"Let her go," I say, my voice practically a whisper.

The man pauses. He looks around at the writhing bodies on the ground, then throws Karla away from him. With trembling arms, he raises his hands in surrender. Ralf signals for the archers to lower their bows. One of Ralf's men grabs Karla and forces her onto her stomach.

"Get her back upstairs," I say. My hands shake as I return my dagger to its holder. Bardle runs to the men on the ground, men that are his friends.

"It didn't have to be like this…" Bardle croaks. He stares unbelieving at the bleeding farm rebels.

Forcing my gaze towards Ralf, I steel myself and say, "The ones that are still alive, make sure they're taken inside." He nods and continues about his work as if he didn't just order the execution of men that were meant to be on his side. I sidestep Karla and walk back into the Harras Manor in a daze. I take the stairwell to the fourth floor and stagger down the hall toward the room where Thatius is being held.

The hallway is a minefield of dead bodies. I glance at their faces. Some are farm workers. One of them is Linus, and then I see Munro. I cover my mouth with my hand to choke back a cry. It's clear they put up a fight to protect our plan, to protect the rebellion.

The door to the bedroom is closed. Chunks of wood are missing where it was struck with iron. I draw my dagger and reach for the knob but it won't turn. It's locked.

"Tuor?" I call with a shaky voice.

I hear movement within. I step back, my dagger raised and ready. The door creaks open. Tuor falls into me with a tight hug. When he pulls away, I see his eye is bruised and there's blood on the sleeve of his shirt.

"You're okay," I breathe.

Tuor rubs sweat from his forehead. "We barricaded ourselves."

I step over the threshold and find the room in utter disarray. The frame of the bed is cracked. The curtains are torn and blood splatters the walls. The only ones left standing are Tuor, Reed, Eve, and Captain Thatius, still tied as a prisoner to his chair.

"We still have him," Reed says. "It's going to be okay."

I fall against the wall, leaning hard, too emotionally tired to even stand. I stare at nothing in particular.

"What's wrong?" Reed asks, bunching up his eyebrows.

"Knox is hurt badly and Johnny's not doing good either." I shake my head. "The rebellion will by okay, that's true."

I look up and face Reed, Tuor, and Eve. "But they won't be here to see it."

Tuor sighs and musses up his hair.

"If Johnny dies . . ." I can barely say the words. "I'll have to find a way to tell his parents." I remember the conversation we had in Eve's sitting room. I didn't want to hear it, but the least I can do is follow through on my promise.

"I am sorry," Eve says stiffly. "It's difficult to watch a loved one pass."

I nod, grateful for her modicum of humanity. It's then I remember that Johnny's father is a doctor. Why wait to travel to Hanover and break the news of Johnny or Knox's death if Johnny's father could help them? I push off the wall and disappear from the room without another word.

In the kitchen, I force Mirabelle to stand and give me her attention. "What about Johnny's father?"

Mirabelle raises her head, a handkerchief held to her mouth.

"He was a doctor. What if we got Knox and Johnny to him? Do you think he could help?"

Mirabelle lets her hand fall to her lap. Her cheeks are shimmery with tears.

"He's a skilled physician," Mirabelle admits.

She hesitates, then nods. I feel alive again at the prospect of saving them.

"Do you think there's a chance Knox could live?"

Mirabelle shrugs. "Perhaps. If Marc lets us through the door."

Quickly I turn on my heels and head for the door.

"Where are you going?" Mirabelle asks in surprise.

"We're taking them to Hanover."

"How? We're trapped here."

I pause at the threshold. "I don't know yet, but I'm going to figure it out."

Mirabelle slowly shakes her head. "This is the end for them, Camilla. You tried your best."

"They might still die, but If I do nothing else, I'll get Knox and Johnny home."

CHAPTER THIRTY-NINE

I SIT ON the hot roof of the Harras Manor and contemplate an impossible escape plan. I use my hand to block the noontime sun from my eyes as I peer across Bear Gap. Beyond the stockyard fence that encompasses the farm is a smattering of deep green trees. Clemson's men are still congregated at the gate, but now that I can see everything, I spot movement along the outside of the fence. Certainly he has men posted along the perimeter.

Reed hates my idea. When we're so close to victory, why I would want to leave? All morning he tried to convince me to wait until after the deal with Quinten was settled. He doesn't understand—Knox and Johnny don't have that long. They need help now, and I need to get out of the farm before Quinten shows up with more soldiers. It's why I've decided we'll be leaving for Hanover tonight.

I squint and focus on the landscape. The fastest way to Johnny's parents would be south, straight through the farm gate, and toward the swamps. Then we could walk downriver to Hanover. The problem is, I have to find a way to get Knox's deadweight over the wall first.

I pull my knees up to my chest and rest my arms on top. Maybe I could ask Clemson for a truce, a temporary treaty just to let me get them to a doctor. That's preposterous, I think to myself. They've trapped us in here with no food or medicine. Why would he let us seek out a doctor?

An old saying pops into my head: "Perspective is the map to any decision." So I stand and slowly walk to the north side of the farm. The clay tiles shift under my weight. I'm reminded of last fall when I traipsed across this very roof with Lawrence. I shake my head, urging myself to stay focused.

With my hands on my hips, I stare into the thick woods along the north side of the fence. It's the opposite direction of Hanover, but perhaps there's an answer here. Clemson is guarding the outside perimeter of the fence, but the farm is huge. His force is still scarce. They can't guard every spot.

It's then that I see it, and I know my plan. A dense thorn forest takes over a large section of the fence. The spiked branches are so intrusive they've begun to grow over the top of the wall. No soldier would bother to guard there because you'd have to be mad to traverse a thorn forest. It's the perfect spot for us to make our escape.

***

Reed argues with me the whole walk from Harras Manor to the spot on the fence where the thorn forest grows. The cold night air breezes through the tail of my shirt. The sky is a deep blue and laden with smoke from the farm worker camp. The fields are a dark canvas only slightly illuminated by the half moon.

Tuor and Mirabelle carry Knox's body on a stretcher. This afternoon, Johnny's fever finally broke and he's able to walk by himself. Reed uses this as a reason to convince me to stay.

"This isn't a good time for you leave," he says as we walk side by side. His sword clangs against his boot.

"I have to do this."

Reed sighs. "I need you *here*. What if my uncle doesn't entertain a negotiation and we end up fighting?"

"Then it will benefit you to have someone outside these walls who can help."

We come to a stop in the middle of the fence where the thorn branches are creeping over the top.

"You're insufferable," Reed growls. "Has anyone ever told you that?"

I raise my eyebrows. "Many times."

Mirabelle and Tuor set Knox on the ground and Johnny leans against the fence to catch his breath.

"You can make this negotiation without me. You should be Supreme Ruler, not your uncle and not me. I'm too weak to be a leader of anything, but you, you have . . . guts." I look up into Reed's blue eyes. "The only destiny that remains for me is getting my friends to Hanover."

Reed concedes by giving me a contrite look. He sticks out his hand to shake mine. Without saying it, we both know this may be the last time we see each other.

I stare at the magnitude of the fence. It's twice my height and made of thick logs placed vertically next to each other. It would be impossible to get Knox over the fence, so Reed and Tuor hack away at the crevice between two poles.

Reed lets out a low grunt as he knocks one of the logs loose. He uses the axe to dig around the base and break it free of the hole it sits in. The log groans as it releases from the wall. Reed and Tuor carefully lower it to the ground. Thorny branches detach from the log and spring into the opening. Brittle twigs snap off and float to the ground. I look on, wondering if this was a good idea.

Hurriedly I give Tuor a hug. He'll be staying behind as well at my insistence. I need as many people as possible holding things together here. Besides, saving Knox's life is my mission.

"Good luck," Reed whispers.

Johnny staggers into the opening first, machete in hand. Fighting against a two-day fever, he lazily hacks away two large branches. Mirabelle and I pick up Knox's stretcher and approach the opening.

Knox's dead weight is more than I expected. We tilt the makeshift bed to fit through the narrow hole. Immediately I'm poked down my arm and chest. I let the thorns scrape my face and jacket, keeping my hands on Knox's bed and my focus forward.

Reed and Tuor push the log back up over the opening, leaving us in a darkened wood exploding with sharp edges. Johnny slashes the iron machete through crumbling gray branches. The sound is akin to crunching dried bones.

The thorn forest is thick like a tangled ball of wire. The trees are short with long sad-looking branches that hang low enough to scrape the earth. It's a tree that will spread wild if it's not destroyed. It kills low brush and vegetation, just leaving a bare dirt forest floor.

We wrangle Knox through the scant path that Johnny's made for us. With every step I'm snagged and pulled backward by a briar, making the trek slow and painful. The real horror of these trees is the long needles that protrude from every vine and branch. Mirabelle's face contorts in agony as she's scraped across the forearm. Even with thick pants, it feels like tiny swords cutting my legs. No one speaks. We suppress our cries, knowing that there could be a guard within earshot.

Johnny stumbles, clutching at his leg. I want to push him to just keep moving, but he shouldn't be walking at all. He stands straight and hacks a huge branch from its trunk. The prickly branch falls with a thud. With the hideous thing gone from our view, I can finally see green up ahead.

Johnny falls to his knees as we take our final steps out of the thorn forest. We set Knox on the ground. I feel the tension in my hands and wrists from carrying Knox's body. Johnny's face is speckled with drops of blood. I kneel in front of him and wipe his face with the sleeve of my shirt. Even through the darkness, Johnny's face looks sallow. Blood is seeping through the bandage on his thigh. He struggles to open his eyes.

"Drink," I whisper, handing Johnny the waterskin.

He manages a sip, then hands it back to me.

"I can do this," he says, answering a question I never asked. I know he can do it. Johnny is willful and strong but this isn't a test of his will. I don't know if his body will allow him to make the rest of the trip.

I give my weary companions the signal that means we have to keep moving. Mirabelle and I pick up Knox. Johnny stays at our side. It's quiet at first. There's no chatter from the soldiers' camp or crackling of fire from inside the wall. I could imagine in this moment that there's no battle being waged for Bear Gap. There are no opposing sides. There's only the solitude of the woods.

A rustle to our left catches my attention. We stop. It's a soldier, pacing with his long sword along the fence. He's far enough away that I pull us deeper into the woods. Firelight catches my line of vision. Straight ahead is a soldier atop a horse, carrying a torch.

We turn around, back toward the fence. I urge Mirabelle to pick up the pace. We jog, fast enough to get through, but slow enough not to be heard. Then I spot another soldier pacing the fence. They have them stationed every twenty yards or so, which means their coverage is better than I thought.

A shout echoes from behind me. I twist my body to see. We've been spotted. I stop and think. We can't go back. That's not an option. We're laden down with Knox. The longer we linger in these woods, the better chance we'll cross paths with another soldier.

"Run," I say, quiet but urgent.

We move through the woods like a wagon with a broken wheel. Johnny's limp is painfully pronounced. I watch the fence, keeping distance. Finally, we round the corner of the farm where Harras Manor sits. Straight ahead, through the woods, is the river but only a half mile to our left is the gate where the soldiers have their camp.

Johnny's breath is heavy, labored. Another shout erupts to my right. I keep pushing. We weave through the trees and skip over the brush. They're behind us, not far, but we scurry through the woods like mice. I'm hoping we're too small and insignificant for them to see.

Another soldier stands against the fence to my left, but he doesn't see us and he doesn't get the signal fast enough. I turn us away from the farm and run deeper into the woods. The shouts from behind us fade. We'll make it, I think to myself. If it's the last thing I do, I'll get us there.

Torchlight blasts into our faces. The tall trees illuminate around us all at once as if the gods had just turned on the sun. I stop so abruptly that Mirabelle bumps the back of me with Knox's stretcher. The soldier's mouth curves into an ironic smirk. He draws his sword.

The soldier swipes at Johnny. He blocks with his machete.

I drop the stretcher, letting Knox fall to the forest floor and pull up my own sword. I run at the soldier. We fight in darkness as his torch falls to the ground and is snuffed out by the dirt.

Johnny makes a strike, but it's returned quickly. He's knocked on his back, barely able to block. The soldier stands over Johnny as the two are locked, sword on sword. I come from behind, raising my sword high. The soldier hears me. He turns his head and lets out a cry for help, but his voice is cut off as I bring the sword down across his back.

I don't hesitate. I don't stop. I don't ponder.

Mirabelle's on her knees next to Knox. I can't distinguish between Johnny's painful moans and the sounds of the dying soldier. I help Johnny from the ground and pick up Knox's stretcher. I continue in a jog, forcing Johnny and Mirabelle to keep stride with me.

I hear the river before I see it. It's a welcome sign. It means we're close. I allow us a moment's pause at the riverbank. It's still flowing ferociously from the winter melt and weeks of rain. Johnny clutches at his leg but I give him no time to think on it.

We run parallel downriver until we reach the town of Hanover. It's a fishing village just west of Rande. Johnny tells me to continue along the river until we reach the first of three bridges that connect the banks in Hanover.

Mirabelle points out the first bridge. An early dawn light has begun to illuminate this small town. Hanover is cut in half by the river. Both banks are covered in shanties. We pause and watch men fish from the bridge on the river's edge. Nets and traps are tossed in and brought back out. An elderly woman sits on a stool repairing nets.

Johnny's face is covered in sweat. His fever has returned. I finally allow him a moment to sit down and rest. He props himself against a tree and lets his eyes dip closed.

"You're almost home. I'm going to get you there."

Johnny places a hand on top of mine. I expect him to thank me or perhaps apologize for the last time we argued but instead he breathes a word of warning. "They're not going to like you."

CHAPTER FORTY

THE SMELL OF rotting fish hits my nose like a kick to the stomach. Fish heads and carcasses litter the riverbanks. We're met with stares as we cross the first bridge at daybreak. Although Hanover is a part of Bear Gap territory, this little town seems unaffected by the events at the farm.

Johnny leads us down an avenue called Pebble Way. River rocks line the edges of the street. At the end of it, sits a stone house, set back in a grove of trees. I wonder vaguely how long it's been since Johnny last saw his parents. Probably not since he met me.

"This is it," Johnny says. He hesitates, staring at the meager cottage in front of us.

The house is quaint but dark. No firelight flickers within. Johnny hobbles to the front door. He runs his fingers through his sweaty hair, perhaps trying to make himself look slightly better. He knocks, heavy and solemn.

My ears are primed to hear any sound from within, but the only noise is that of light footsteps across the floor. The door opens and a man in a white linen nightgown stands at the threshold. He's wearing spectacles and holds a hand to his chest in surprise.

I can imagine what we look like, showing up on this man's front step just after dawn. We're dirty with mud and sweat. There's still dried blood under my fingernails.

"What is this?" the man gasps.

"Father, I need your help."

"Your son is injured," I say firmly. "Please let us in."

"Marc," Mirabelle says, her voice quiet. "It's Knox too."

It seems those are the only words she can manage to get out of her mouth. Marc's forehead creases in a mixture of concern and disapproval. He looks at his son and ever so slightly shakes his head back and forth.

After several long moments of shocked silence, Marc reaches out a hand and touches Johnny's forehead. He pulls his hand back quickly and makes an unhappy face. Then Marc pushes past me and scrutinizes Knox. He pulls off Mirabelle's crude bandages and recoils from the smell.

"How long has he been in this state?" Marc asks.

I rub an ache in my forehead. "I've sort of lost track of time. A day, I suppose."

With the swift turn of his head, Marc asks, "What sort of trouble have you gotten yourselves into?"

I want to answer his questions sarcastically, but I know that won't do anything to help Johnny and Knox. So I keep my lips closed.

"Uncle Knox could die," Johnny says.

"It looks that way," Marc says in a tone that lacks emotion.

When I look into Marc's eyes, I don't see any semblance of Johnny. In fact, they look nothing alike. Marc is thin with a long head and a straight back. His expression is that of an intelligent man and I hope that gives Knox a fighting chance.

Marc sighs. "Follow me."

Johnny's father widens the door and flicks his hand to let us in. A woman appears as we enter the house. Her mouth hangs open. She's dusky looking with wide hips and long straight brown hair that's streaked with gray.

Mirabelle and I carry Knox through a small sitting area that leads into a kitchen. As we pass, Johnny's mother touches a hand to her mouth. She calls for Johnny and takes him in her arms. At the back of the house, Marc directs us to his exam room.

There's a long, thin table in the middle of the room where we place Knox's body. Everyone files into the room, gathering around Knox. Johnny's mother and Mirabelle embrace but no words are exchanged.

The wall behind Marc has four long shelves that are lined with jars and tinctures filled with different-colored liquids. Marc quickly lights the candles in the room. He rinses his hand in a basin of water and puts on a crisp white apron before pulling up the sleeves of his nightgown.

He removes the bandages from Knox's chest, dumping the blood-soaked linen in a nearby bowl. Soon Knox's entire chest is exposed. His skin is a dark red. The cavernous wound is filled with pus. The burn has festered and is covered in thick, sticky blood. Johnny's father pauses and places his hands behind his back as he stares at Knox.

Johnny leans against the wall, unable to stand on his own. He looks at his uncle with a lifeless expression.

"Marc?" Mirabelle begs.

He contemplates Knox for several more moments, then lifts his head to meet our gaze. "These wounds are infected," he says matter-of-factly. "The burn has destroyed his skin and I can guarantee you he's in excruciating pain."

The man speaks of Knox as if he's completely detached from him and not a member of his family. Then Marc turns to Johnny, whose eyes are cemented to Knox's body.

"Rebekah," Marc says, addressing his wife. "Take our son out of this room. Start him on a treatment of oil of oregano and get his wound properly cleaned."

Johnny pauses, then limps out of the room without any further prodding. I've never seen Johnny comply so quickly. Rebekah follows swiftly behind her son.

"Is there anything we can do?" I ask in a small voice.

Marc lets out a puff of air. "Clean towels from the cedar chest, and quickly."

It's Mirabelle that leaves the room in search of the cedar chest. Knox's chest rises in painful breaths. I move in close, next to Marc.

"Please let me help. He was trying to protect me when he got hurt. I have to help."

"Always trying to be the hero," Marc mutters. He picks up a pair of tweezers and begins picking debris from Knox's wounds. "I don't want to know anything about what you were doing."

Mirabelle returns with the towels. "Take one of those and soak up the blood so I can have better visibility."

I grab a towel and institute myself as Marc's aid whether he likes it or not. It takes him hours to tweeze the wound clean. The work is meticulous, but I do exactly as he says without question. Several times, Mirabelle flushes the wounds with a concoction of warm water and some tinctures she pulls off Marc's shelf.

Knox's entire chest is washed down and he's given proper dressings with clean towels soaked in tea tree oil. The bandage is kept loose over the burn. Marc explains that there's not much more to be done except to let it heal.

He finishes by using a dropper to give Knox a dose of oil of oregano, which is meant to help with his infection. Normally the dose would be given with a mixture of water but Knox can't swallow.

It's sunset by the time we're finished. Marc takes a step away from his brother-in-law and looks at his body as if it were a shattered vase. We all know what this is. This is just a ritual we must do to say we tried our best to help Knox. Maybe it will make him more comfortable. That's the best that I can hope.

"I've done all I can do," Marc says, tossing a bloody rag on the exam table. His eyes light on Mirabelle and me. "I know what this is about. I know what all of you were doing. I've heard the rumors of what's happening at the farm. I don't appreciate you making a mess of things, and then bringing that mess to *my* home."

Mirabelle tries to hold Marc's gaze. "Knox chose to—"

"I know what Knox has chosen. I will treat him because he is family, but that is the only reason. I want nothing to do with the Bear Gap rebels." Marc's voice drops. "You have put me and my family in great danger. Get your things and get out of here. I want you gone."

CHAPTER FORTY-ONE

JOHNNY'S FATHER BRUSHES past us, leaving Mirabelle and me alone with Knox. Mirabelle puts her hands on Knox's body, bows her head, and struggles to hold back tears. The silence in the room doesn't sound like silence. It sounds like screaming. That's what I want to do—scream as loudly as I can.

Mirabelle's hand falls to the pocket of Knox's pants. She pauses, then reaches in and pulls out a book, small enough to fit in the palm of her hand. Her mouth hangs open as she flips open the delicate pages. Out falls a dried flower that looks to have been pressed in the book for ages. Mirabelle carefully picks up the flower, its petals a light blue, and puts it back between the pages.

"He kept it," she whispers.

I want to ask Mirabelle why Knox carries a book with him wherever he goes. I want to ask her what it means, and why she recognizes it, but I'm not sure she could explain it. I've conceded that there are mysteries between Knox and Mirabelle that I'll never know. So I don't ask. Instead I watch as Mirabelle runs her fingers along the spine of the book.

She turns suddenly and pulls me into a hug. I feel her weeping on my shoulder. I know these tears are not because we've been kicked out of this house, or because many people have died. These are tears of lost love.

Love. I couldn't recognize the love between Knox and Mirabelle until recently, until I felt this painful yet wonderful feeling for Johnny. Mirabelle releases me from our hug and returns her gaze to Knox.

What if it was Johnny lying on this table? What things would I wish I could say to him? Knowing Johnny has been a wave of emotions: highest highs and deepest lows. How is it possible to care for someone so deeply, and at the same time feel so much tumult?

I amble into the empty sitting room, leaving Mirabelle to say her goodbyes to Knox. I look around at Johnny's parents' home. It's warm and cozy. A narrow set of steps follows along the wall to the upstairs bedrooms. Despite Marc's unkindness toward us, I can imagine that Johnny still had a more stable upbringing than me.

I stare at the steps. What if Johnny falls to his father's will and leaves the rebellion? What if, like Knox, Johnny succumbs to his injuries? What if he's decided he doesn't want anything to do with me and simply keeps away? That would be the worst scenario I could imagine.

Quickly, I jog up the steps. I glance right, then left down the hallway. To the left are an open door and a bed with rumpled sheets. I go right and follow the murmuring of men's voices. The door to the next bedroom is cracked open. I peek inside but only see an elderly woman sleeping in a four-poster bed. I scrunch up my eyebrows. She's Johnny's grandmother perhaps.

I step onto the threshold of the third bedroom and find Johnny propped up on a short bed. Marc kneels over his son's wounded leg. Rebekah stands by Johnny's head, a tincture of oregano oil in her hand.

I hesitate, fiddling with my fingernails. Johnny eyes me sympathetically. Marc turns and gives me a scowl. "I don't need your assistance anymore. You've done enough damage here."

"I didn't come here for that," I say.

"Father, Camilla's the one that got me here and Mirabelle tended to me. You should be thanking them."

"We'll leave. Don't worry. I just want to talk to Johnny before we go."

"Leave?" Johnny says, practically shouting. He gives his father a disgusted look. "You told them to leave?"

"Yes, we're taking on enough risk housing you and your uncle."

Marc pokes at Johnny's wound with a pair of tweezers. He has a fresh bandage and already his complexion has improved from a day of lying down. Johnny pulls his leg away from his father's care and sits up on the edge of the bed.

"My leg is fine. Leave me be."

Marc stands slowly. He presses down the front of his shirt with both hands. "Your leg wouldn't be fine if it weren't for your mother and me. People like her are trouble," Marc says.

"I'm sick of this," Johnny says, shaking his head. He staggers to his feet. Rebekah reaches out a hand to steady her son. "You're so scared. It's sickening."

"It's wisdom," Marc corrects. "It comes from years of learning. You'd do well to listen to me for once."

Johnny laughs sardonically. "Wisdom..." he mutters.

"Both of you stop," Rebekah says through gritted teeth.

"You need to let them stay," Johnny says, swaying on his feet. He stumbles towards the dresser near the door where I stand. "You can't send them out into the night with no food and no sleep. Not after everything they've been through to get me here."

"Johnny's right," Rebekah pleads with her husband.

Marc draws breath. "Fine." He scans the room and lets his eyes rest on me. He looks upon me like I'm a piece of garbage. "One night, just to recuperate, and then you will leave."

I nod, trying to feel grateful. Johnny gives an unsatisfied sigh but he seems to give up the fight. Marc and Rebekah retire to their bedroom, leaving Johnny and me alone. The room is plain with nothing on the walls or anything decorative at all.

I close the door behind me. "You should be off your leg," I say.

Johnny takes a deep breath, then hobbles back to the bed. "I know. He just gets me so angry."

I saunter toward the bed until finally dropping to take a seat next to Johnny. Immediately he places his hand on top of mine.

"Thank you for getting us here," Johnny says. He looks at me with soft eyes. My spirit momentarily soars. "What do you think is happening back at the farm?"

"I don't know. I haven't thought about it," I say. Johnny tilts his head in surprise. "All I've cared about for the last two days is getting you and Knox here."

Johnny looks away, staring at his lap. "I'll have to stay here for now. With Uncle Knox the way he is, I—I at least need to stay until things are . . . finished."

"I understand." I shake my head, searching for the right words.

"I'm sorry," Johnny says before I have a chance to say anything.

"For what?"

"The other day, when I yelled at you about doing everything your way."

"It's true though," I concede.

Johnny laughs. "Yeah, it is, but I was angry because"—he looks me in the eyes—"I know about the journal."

My stomach drops. "How do you—"

"Reed told me, accidentally. He assumed you'd already told me. It just made me so angry, Camilla." He takes his hand off mine. "Why do you keep the most important things from me?"

His words cut me deep. They cut me deep because they're true. I've kept so many secrets from Johnny. I could try to blame my mother, but the truth is the decision to keep secrets from him was mine, and mine alone.

"I don't know why I do that," I say softly. I let my head drop and pull my hands into my lap. "I think—I think, maybe, I'm not ready for this type of relationship." I find the courage to raise my gaze to Johnny's eyes. "You want someone who's more devoted."

Johnny doesn't deny that. He nods slowly.

"I—" My voice cracks. "I do love you, Johnny."

Johnny's body goes still. "I know. I love you too. I think I fell in love with you when I saw you light that Warwick flag on fire."

I chuckle, welcoming the lightness to the conversation.

"Carry on the rebellion, Camilla, until I get back."

"I will."

Johnny and I embrace. As we pull away, I wonder what's appropriate after such an exchange. It's so different from the last time we parted ways. No yelling or arguing. We seem more in sync in departure than we ever were when we were together. So I lean in and kiss Johnny one last time.

I've learned to assume every time could be the last time. Johnny may never make it back to the farm. *I* may never make it back to the farm. A million things could happen before I see Johnny again and I don't want to regret a thing.

I insist that Johnny lay down and continue to rest. I leave him alone in his room with his leg comfortably propped up. The house is quiet as I exit into the hallway. The wood floor creaks as I slowly move across it. I try to be quiet but as I step in front of the grandmother's bedroom, the floor lets out a great groan.

"Who's there?" comes a frantic, raspy voice. I freeze in the hallway. "Come here. Don't loiter. It's rude."

CHAPTER FORTY-TWO

FORCED TO OBEY the voice, I swing around to stand in the doorway of Johnny's grandmother's bedroom. The elderly woman lies flat on her back, buried under a pile of quilts, with a sleeping cap on her head. An oil lamp burns on her nightstand, the only light in the room.

"Have you brought me my breakfast?" she asks with a tone of displeasure. "I haven't eaten in a day and a half!"

"Breakfast? It's evening."

"It certainly is not. We just let the cows out to pasture. Mother's in the kitchen fixing breakfast as we speak. I can smell it!"

I turn and look behind me as if I might see a woman making breakfast, but there's no one there and there's definitely no smell of food in the hallway.

"I think you're confused," I say slowly. Johnny's grandmother squirms under her covers, trying to pull herself into a seated position. "Let me help you." I cross the room and reach my arm around her back but she swats me away.

"I don't need you to lift me up! Just let me grab your arms."

Her bony fingers grip hard onto my forearms. She pulls herself up with a surprising amount of strength for a woman of her age. She exhales in exhaustion as she tries to adjust the pillows around her back.

"Hand me that one," she instructs while pointing at a small cross-stitched pillow at her feet. I grab it and help her shove it behind her back for support.

Her face sags with wrinkles and light brown spots show where she stood in the sun too long. She looks down at her gaunt hands and then up at me. It's like she's seeing me for the first time.

"Who are you?"

"My name's Camilla."

Unsure of what to do, I stretch my hand out to shake with hers. Something about my gesture initiates a mood change.

"Nice to meet you, Camilla. I'm Devon Duffy. It's lovely to have you." Devon takes my hand and daintily pats the top of it. "Please, take a seat."

She points to a chair that's set against the wall. I pick it up and bring it next to the bed so I'm facing her.

"We have had a terrible winter," Devon says, shaking her head. "How is your family holding up?"

"We're good." I speak hesitantly.

"We've had an awful time getting the draft right on the stove. Every time John puts in another log for me, the whole house fills with smoke."

I match Devon's dramatic expression. "You don't say?" I smile at her.

"I wouldn't lie about that! And then Becky has been terribly ill. It's in her lungs and the cough just won't go away."

"How old is Becky now?" I ask, realizing it's of Rebekah, Johnny's mother, that she speaks.

Devon pauses before answering. "She just turned thirteen. Can you believe my little girl is thirteen?"

I shake my head. "I can't."

Johnny's grandmother doesn't think me a random visitor. She acts like we're childhood friends. She has no idea that her little Becky is a grown woman with a grown son. She doesn't know that her son, Knox, is lying downstairs almost dead, and she has no clue who I really am.

"How is your son doing?" I ask cautiously.

Devon's face falls. She pauses as if she's transporting to another decade. "Knoxy was almost killed tonight because of me."

Her voice turns solemn. I scrunch up my eyebrows. Am I wrong about her level of confusion?

"What do you mean?" I ask.

"I saw his knee. It looks—" Devon's voice croaks. "It just looks terrible. Do you think he'll be able to walk again?"

Her eyes flicker up at me as moisture settles on her bottom lids. I think of Knox's persistent limp that he's had since the day I met him.

"His knee is fine. It's Knox's chest that was hurt."

"I shouldn't have gone out looking for him." Tears stream down Devon's cheeks. "I couldn't stand the thought of my John lying on that field all alone." She vigorously shakes her head. "I never wanted Knoxy to come out looking for me. I didn't want him to get hurt."

"I know." I touch my hand to hers.

I realize now that Devon isn't crazy. She's just stuck on another day, another time, when Knox hurt his knee. We've traveled through time, I think, to a different memory. She seems shaken up by the event. I look into her glassy eyes and I see terror. I'm not sure I should, but I decide to indulge Devon's story.

"How did Knox get hurt?" I ask.

"They shouldn't have challenged that Warwick boy," Devon growls.

"What?"

"I knew it was a bad idea but I still supported John. And he took Knoxy along with him. He was too impressionable and too sensitive over what happened with Belle. It made him do stupid things."

"Belle? Do you mean Mirabelle?"

Devon raises her head to look me in the eye. "Ohhhh, he loves Belle so much. He loves her too much. That girl will ruin his life. *She's* the reason he went out there to fight today."

Fighting? I think to myself.

"Knox was fighting *Quinten* Warwick?" I ask.

"He claims to be the Supreme Ruler but John won't call him that."

I lean back in my chair and stare across the room. Johnny's grandmother is stuck on a day from thirteen years ago. She thinks it's the day the Battle in Bear Gap took place, when Quinten defended his throne and squashed the rebellion. In many ways, Knox has been stuck on that day too.

"What happened?" I ask urging her on.

"Knoxy came back all bloody and bruised and told me that John was dead. My John, my beautiful John was dead. Becky is trying to make me go to bed but I can't sleep. She's trying to drug me with a tonic that her wretched husband taught her how to make. But a few herbs aren't going to help me sleep on a night like this. I need John. I need *my* John."

"But John wasn't dead, was he?" I ask.

Johnny's grandfather wasn't killed during the Battle of Bear Gap. He was captured and taken to LilyAye, and to this day, they don't know if he's alive or dead. I wonder what Devon, from thirteen years ago, thought had happened to her husband.

"I had to find out," she cries. "I went out there to find him."

Devon's eyes shift downward and she seems to forget that I'm in the room. It's like she's there, she's actually in Bear Gap as the mother of an unruly son and a husband who's sacrificing it all for his territory. Her voice drops to an ominous, monotone level.

"The grass was soaked in blood. I felt it leaking through my shoes. Every body I passed, I paused and looked at their face. I searched for John everywhere. I searched for my John but I couldn't find him."

A tear falls down her wrinkled and splotchy face.

"I just wanted to see him one last time and hold him in my arms."

"But you didn't find him."

"No." Her face tightens and turns into an angry scowl. "I found that bratty boy and his witch instead."

I cock my head sharply to the right. I hesitate before I ask, "Witch?"

"The boy yelled at me and grabbed me by the arm. He shook me." Devon takes her upper arm in the opposite hand as if she can feel the memory of the grasp this very moment. "Knoxy shot the boy," she says triumphantly. "He shot him good in the shoulder with an arrow. Then that witch was furious. She ran after us."

"Devon, what makes you think there was a witch there?"

Devon's eyes leave the quilted blanket on her legs and connect with mine.

"She put out her hand," Devon says slowly. She stretches her bony, fragile arm toward me and tilts up her hand so the flat palm is facing me. "And she squeezed Knoxy's heart like this."

My body turns cold. She doesn't need to say anymore. I know what she's describing. I've seen it for myself. My mother was there. She was there the night of the battle, but she wasn't fighting on Bear Gap's side. She was fighting for Quinten. My gaze falls back to Devon. She saw my mother that night.

"What did she look like?" I whisper. "The witch?"

"She had this necklace that I couldn't stop staring at. Oh . . . " Devon puts both her hands on her cheeks and shakes her head. "We can't tell anyone what happened. No one would believe what we saw." Her gaze grows intense around me. "You can't tell anyone what I told you. They won't believe us."

My eyes drift away from her worried face as I picture Devon and Knox returning from the battlefield and not being able to tell anyone about the nightmare they'd witnessed.

"We can't tell them," she mutters.

"We won't. We won't tell anybody."

I touch Devon's frail arm to comfort her.

"I have to go," I say, standing from my chair. I turn from Devon awkwardly.

"I hope my Knoxy will be okay," she says softly.

"He'll be just fine," I say with a smile.

I look back at Devon's distant gaze once more before slipping out the door and closing it behind me. I pause for a moment in the hallway. Every time I saw Knox rubbing his chest I knew it was because of my mother. He told me that, or at least I figured it out.

I knew that she had once damaged his heart, but I thought it happened over the years that he followed her and reported back to Quinten. He never told me she was there during the Battle of Bear Gap. He also didn't tell me that his mother was there and that she nearly died. He left that detail out.

I step forward and touch my hands to the staircase banister. Everywhere I go, my mother finds a way to be there too. I take the stairs and find Mirabelle still in the exam room with Knox. She's sitting in a chair with her head lying on the table next to his chest. Mirabelle's asleep. A single candle burns in the small room. It does nothing to boost the mood of being around a dying man. I circle the table, finding it difficult to look at Knox. It's my fault that he's hurt. The lantern was aimed at *me*. Knox pushed me out of the way and took the blow. I look at him quizzically. Why did he do that?

Finally I find a chair, and determine to stay by Mirabelle's side through the night. I lean my chair against the wall and search for a comfortable position for my head. It'll be an uncomfortable night's sleep, but I need to try to rest at least a little.

A shriek wakes me hours later. I stand, wiping sleep from my eyes. Mirabelle's crouched over Knox like a scavenging bird. She holds a hand to her mouth. When she looks up, her cheeks are streaked with tears. She lets her hand drop to the table and parts her lips.

"He's awake."

CHAPTER FORTY-THREE

SUNLIGHT ILLUMINATES KNOX'S shaking body. His eyes, wide and aware, turn to look at me wildly. I stand with my mouth agape. He stretches out his arm and grasps my wrist, squeezing it tightly. I jolt.

"I'm sorry," he croaks. "I'm sorry."

"What?" I can barely speak.

"Get Marc!" Mirabelle yells.

I take a step backward, horrified by the sight. Knox pulls me closer to him.

"I'm sorry," he moans.

"Hurry!" Mirabelle shouts.

Knox's head rolls away from me, and his eyes blink shut like he were a candle that's just been blown out. I feel his grip loosen on my hand. I run from the room and fly up the steps. At the end of the hall, I storm into Johnny's parents' bedroom.

"Knox is awake," I announce.

Rebekah sits up in bed.

"He's awake!" I yell.

Rebekah rouses her husband from sleep. I step out of the room and allow them to pass me. Marc throws on a robe and they both run down the steps and into the exam room. Marc is able to bring Knox back to consciousness by having him inhale smelling salts.

Rebekah mixes an elixir at the work table. She moves about the room without needing much instruction from her husband. They've done this before.

"His heartbeat is irregular," Marc says as he holds a finger to Knox's throat.

"His heartbeat has been that way for a long time," Rebekah says.

"That doesn't make it good."

Knox's wild eyes dart around the room with a look of terrified confusion.

"What can I do?" I ask, expecting Marc to banish me from his exam room.

"Prop him up so we can give him the medicine."

Mirabelle begs for divine intervention. "Please, please, please . . ." She takes Knox's hand in hers. His body seems to relax with her touch.

I run to the end of Knox's bed. I lift him up as best I can, and an uncomfortable moan escapes his mouth. The deadweight of his head and shoulders strains my neck.

"Take this drink, Knox," Rebekah says. Her voice is sweet but shaky.

She holds the cup of dark liquid to Knox's lips and tips it toward him. He takes the tiniest of sips and then coughs the drink from his mouth.

"He needs to drink it," Marc says firmly.

Rebekah tries again but the liquid just dribbles down his chin and neck.

"It's his throat," Marc says. "He can't swallow properly. Get me a clean rag."

Rebekah leaves the cup on the table and fetches a neatly folded white rag from a drawer in Marc's work bench. Knox's head grows heavy in my arms. Sweat seeps through his hair and onto my skin.

"Lay him back," Marc instructs me.

I set Knox's head down gently as Rebekah dips a corner of the rag in the cup, soaking it with her tonic.

"Chew on this," she says placing the wet rag on his tongue.

He bites down hard, chomping the rag between his teeth. Rebekah coaxes it out of his mouth, soaks it again, then returns it to his mouth. I hear Rebekah breathe a small sigh of relief. The rag seems to be working. I watch for an hour as Rebekah slowly gives Knox the tonic. He goes from fevered shaking to restlessness.

Soon, we're all banished from the exam room, even Mirabelle. Marc insists he needs quiet and calm to work. Mirabelle, Johnny, and I sit outside the exam room like a group of solemn funeral attenders.

The miracle of Knox waking is short lived. By midday Knox has a raging fever. Marc tells us that he's contracted a secondary infection. It came on quickly. Marc has made it clear that he doesn't have much time left.

In my exhaustion, I look over at Johnny. He sits with his elbows on his knees. Occasionally he'll put his head in his hands. I want to sidle up next to him and rest my head on his shoulders, but I decide not to.

The door to the exam room opens. I sit up, ready and alert. Johnny looks at his father with a deadpan face. Rebekah exits the exam room with her husband

and quickly disappears upstairs, wiping tears from her cheeks.

Marc walks toward me. I scrunch my eyebrows in confusion as he approaches. I straighten my back, feeling the burn of his gaze on me.

"Knox wants to talk to you," Marc says, rubbing his hands together as if to warm them.

"Me?" I ask.

Mirabelle looks my way.

"I can't go in there." The thought of looking into Knox's dying eyes causes my whole body to go stiff.

"He wants to talk to Camilla?" Mirabelle croaks.

"He keeps asking for her," Marc says.

I look to Mirabelle for advice. Her face contorts in worry.

"You have to go," she says finally. She brushes a tear away with a handkerchief.

Why? Why would I be Knox's dying wish? Mirabelle gives me a reassuring nod. I stand from the couch. I catch the attention of Johnny as I walk past. He's likely asking himself the same questions. What could Knox want to say to me in his last moments?

I move past the kitchen and place my hand on the exam-room door. It almost feels insulting being the one to be with Knox instead of someone in his family. I push open the door. Knox coughs harshly as I enter.

"Camilla?" Knox's voice is strained and scratchy like dried tree bark.

"I'm here."

I take a tentative step toward his bed. His head is propped up with pillows, and he's encased in so many blankets I imagine he must be growing warm, yet his body is quivering beneath the quilts.

"It's my penance that I would be in my right mind when it's finally time for me to die," he says.

Knox's face is awash of any color. Sweat settles on his forehead, creating a wet, sickly sheen. I open my mouth to speak but I'm at a loss for words.

"I don't need you to say anything, Camilla. I just need you to listen, that's all."

"Why do you want to see me?"

"I've made so many mistakes in my life. It's taken me this long to come to terms with them."

I move around the corner of the table so I'm face to face with Knox. I recognize his expression. It's the same one he had when he first saw me last fall. Pain and guilt are painted across the very soul of Knox Duffy.

"I've settled my debt with everyone I can . . . except for you." Knox bursts into a coughing fit. I hand him a rag to cover his mouth. "As hard as it is, I will do it, before I die."

I shift my body slightly to face Knox straight on. His body has shrunk and he's become almost skinny. It's difficult to look upon him, but I realize I'll never have the chance to look into his eyes again so I force myself to stare.

"What debt do you have to settle with me?" There's trepidation in my voice. I'm terrified to hear the answer.

"It's my fault that Tuor was arrested last fall."

CHAPTER FORTY-FOUR

MY FACE COLLAPSES into utter confusion. I chuckle nervously.

"What? What do you mean?"

"It is *all* my fault. Everything that's happened to you and Tuor is my fault."

"How could it be your fault? Tuor was arrested because Quinten commanded he be arrested." I lean in closer to Knox's bed. The fever, I think, has left him delusional. "I know the story. Quinten used Tuor to get to my mother. He was bait."

Knox gasps for air. He shifts in his bed, his face contorting with every move. "Remember when I told you about the Battle in Bear Gap? I fought Quinten and I meant to kill him."

"Yeah."

"I thought he had killed my father. Camilla, he destroyed my life. So I acted foolishly. I attacked him and barely left with my life. I promised him my humble servitude if he would let me live."

"I remember," I say.

Knox shakes his head, his neck straining with every twist. He brings a hand up to touch the cut on his neck.

"I didn't tell you everything about that encounter."

Knox no longer sounds like a man confused by fever. His voice is controlled yet he turns his eyes from me. My heart beats faster.

Knox continues to speak, his voice harsh and gravelly. "It took more than a promise of servitude for me to stay alive that night. I told Quinten that I knew your mother, that I knew her well and that . . . I knew her children."

"I don't understand. You told Quinten that you knew Tuor and me?"

Knox attempts to clear his throat, hacking phlegm into a rag. He can't look me in the eye. He grits his teeth in agony.

"I led Quinten to believe that your mother cared for you and your brother greatly, and that the two of you could be used as bargaining chips to control Portia."

"What are you saying? *You* gave him the idea?"

"The only reason Quinten knows who you and Tuor are is because I showed him."

Throbbing swells in my head. I touch the wound that Mac left there. Slowly, I shake my head in disbelief. My stomach sinks as the feeling of betrayal rises in my chest. I stagger backward, away from Knox's sick bed.

"You sold us out to the Supreme Ruler?" My words drip with malice.

Knox doesn't hide his sin. "Yes, in exchange for my life."

"*You're* the reason Quinten came after Tuor." I point my shaking finger at Knox's emaciated body.

"Quinten's been following the two of you since you were kids. He was just waiting for his moment to use you."

My body quivers. Tears threaten, hot, angry tears. My breath quakes as I look unflinchingly at Knox. I told him all about my mother and what she'd done to me. I admitted so much to Knox in the cave. I'd grown to depend on him. I actually trusted him. He watched me question over and over again, *why Tuor?*

"I asked you. At the farm, I asked you about this and you pretended you didn't know."

"I couldn't tell you the truth then." Knox holds his throat while he speaks. "We had to focus on the battle."

"But you've had thirteen years to tell me!" I'm shouting now. My voice is unsteady. "I thought my mother was terrible for what she's done—but *you?* You fed two innocent children to the wolves!"

"I know," Knox says softly.

"So that's why you've been helping me. Last year when Mirabelle begged for your help, you only helped because you felt guilty. It's why you came looking for me when I left to sneak into Rande. It's why you saved me from the farm workers. It's not because you care about me. It's because you're riddled with guilt!"

Knox finally looks at my face, but it's me who struggles now to meet his eyes. "It started that way, yes."

"*You're* the reason for all of this?" I ask desperately, hoping for a different answer.

"I'm sorry, Camilla."

A few tears finally give way, falling down my hot cheeks. The crippled man lying in front of me is the real reason my brother almost died last year. It's his fault that we were taken through so much heartache.

Knox speaks. "I know what I did. I can't hide it any longer."

I stare at the lump of a dying man in front of me. He can barely hold up his head. I could wrap my hands around his neck and strangle him so easily. I clench my hand in and out, imagining myself doing that very thing. I take a step closer to the exam table. I place my hands on the surface, and think about ending Knox's life right now.

"I've grown to care for you a great deal." His voice is barely audible, as if he had just enough strength to say the truth and then give up the ghost. "It's true, I sometimes acted out of guilt." Knox reaches out his hand to touch me. "But I think of you as a daughter."

Daughter? *Daughter?* How insulting that word has become. The only people who've ever called me daughter have let me down. I take a deep breath in through my nose and wipe the tears from my cheeks. My lips are set in a tight line. I stare at Knox under heavy eyelids.

"I'm not your daughter," I growl. "I'm not your friend. I'm not even a fellow rebel member. You are nothing to me, Knox Duffy. I knew I hated you. From the first time I saw you, I hated you." I lean in close to Knox's scarred, red face. He already wears the scent of death. "Think on that while you're taking your last breath."

I watch Knox just long enough to make sure he heard me. His eyes dip closed. I step away from the table and slowly turn on my heels. I exit the exam room in a daze. Mirabelle stands suddenly as I enter the sitting room. I tilt my head to look at her, my mouth hanging open.

"What happened?" she asks.

Johnny sits up straight. "Is Uncle Knox—is he gone?"

I exhale. "No," I say flatly. I move into the center of the room, studying the floor as I walk.

"What did he want?" Mirabelle asks. I sense caution in her voice, like she doesn't really want me to answer.

I stop and turn to face Mirabelle. "You knew, didn't you?"

"What are you talking about, dear?"

I examine the expression on her face. Her skin is covered with splotchy red spots, the result of hours of crying. Her hands are still dirty from the trip to Hanover. She's worn and frazzled, and like always, she appears innocent.

"You knew about the deal that Knox made with Quinten Warwick," I say.

My words hang in the air for several long moments. Mirabelle bites her lower lip, hesitating. Her face melts into an expression of horror.

"What deal?" Johnny asks, rising to his feet.

I take a step toward Mirabelle and say, "The deal where he bargained the lives of Tuor and me to save his own skin. You knew about it, didn't you?"

"I—" Mirabelle stutters, her mouth agape.

When Mirabelle still doesn't answer, my anger percolates.

"Tell me you didn't know!" I shout, tears bursting from my eyes. "Please tell me you had no idea, please."

Mirabelle brushes away a tear with the handkerchief in her hand.

"I knew," she says in a small voice.

"All these years, you lied?"

"I couldn't tell you the truth," she says, stepping toward me. "It was so long ago when all of that happened. You were just a kid. Knox and I were very foolish back then. We did things we shouldn't have. I just thought it was best if we moved on and didn't tell anyone."

"You knew what he had done and you never told me? You let me wonder why Tuor was arrested. You let me believe that my brother murdered someone!"

"I didn't think of it like that." Mirabelle wrings her hands together. She eases in close to me. "Please don't hold this against Knox. He made one mistake, years ago. It isn't right to hold it against him forever."

"Right? It's not right?" I spit. "You're defending the man who has ruined my life! Were you ever going to tell me? Were you ever going to tell me I was on the Supreme Ruler's list?"

Mirabelle hesitates. "I hoped I would never have to . . ."

"What about last fall? Did you understand what was happening when Tuor was arrested?"

Mirabelle's face falls. "We knew—we knew it was Quinten playing his hand."

I turn from Mirabelle, stepping away from her, wanting to keep distance. Johnny stands as a spectator. He looks as shocked as me.

"What was your plan, exactly?" I ask, turning to face Mirabelle. "How were you planning to keep this information from me?"

Mirabelle sniffles as she holds her hands together in front of her. "Knox and I decided long ago that we would do everything we could to protect you and Tuor.

I couldn't do much when Tuor left for LilyAye, but I stayed by your side at the farm and checked in on you and Malcolm. I hoped that Quinten would just forget about you someday." Mirabelle shakes her head, brushing away another tear. "Knox and I parted ways and he broke his end of the deal. I was so angry with him." She looks up at me with tear-soaked cheeks. "That's why I insisted on getting Knox's help when Tuor got arrested and I knew what was going on."

I scoff in utter amazement. "So you and Knox only stuck around me to cover up his betrayal?"

"What? No!" Mirabelle says. She steps to me and takes my hand in hers. "That's not it at all. We love you."

I look down at Mirabelle's tender touch and find it repulsive. It's a lie. She and Knox together have done their best to deceive me for most of my life.

"I don't think you do," I say solemnly. I rip my hand from her grasp. "I'm leaving. I don't ever want to see you or Knox again."

"Camilla," Mirabelle breathes.

I give Johnny a sympathetic look. I hope he understands. My messenger bag is laying in a lump by the front door, where I dropped it when we arrived yesterday. I sling it over my shoulder and reach for the knob.

"Camilla." Mirabelle follows me to the door. I slam it shut in her face. "Camilla!"

I walk down the street to the sound of Mirabelle screaming my name.

CHAPTER FORTY-FIVE

WHAT IS IT about running through the woods at night that makes me feel like I've done something terrible? Thieves and murderers flee in the dark. All unsavory behaviors take place after the sun has hidden behind the treetops. It's as if the light is too ashamed to look upon such sins.

I must be a rotten thing, because all I've done since the start of this rebellion is run by the cover of night. I'm tired of it. The darkness has left me confused. My intuition is blurry and out of focus. That's the thing about daylight—it makes everything clear.

I've never felt clearer about things than I do right now, sitting on a warm rock in the middle of the woods. The sun sparkles through the leaves, casting intricate shapes on the ground. I'm somewhere north of Hanover. I'm not exactly sure where I am but I'm okay with that. I'm alone and it's quiet.

I don't know what waits for me in Rande. I've determined to leave behind Knox and Mirabelle. I can continue on the rebellion without them. I'm just not sure there will be a rebellion to return to. Reed may not have been able to broker a deal with his uncle. He could have surrendered or held his ground, eliciting an attack.

A small fire burns in front of me. I stare into its blazing tendrils as if the light will burn away all the darkness I've seen. My mother's journal rests atop my fingers. Her voice has become so regular in my mind that I forget she's there. She's become a part of me.

In the flurry of battle and trying to save Knox, I could almost imagine that I didn't hear Portia whispering in my ears, but she's never truly been gone. I call to her now, in my head. I know she can hear me. I ask her to come, and soon she appears before me.

My mother is tall, slender, beautiful, but beautiful like the poisonous butterfly that on occasion appears in Bear Gap. The brilliant colors lure you in, but the moment the butterfly lands on your finger it emits its poison.

Portia looks at me now. Her emerald eyes glow like a serpent.

"You don't look surprised to see me?" my mother says. She tilts her head in delight. "Perhaps you're growing fond of our encounters."

I shake the journal in my hand. "I figured it out," I say with a smirk. "This journal ties me to you. As long as I have it in my possession, you can enter my mind."

A grin spreads across Portia's lips. "Technically I can enter your mind without it. The journal just makes it a little easier."

"Why do you want me?"

"Because I like you."

"The real reason. What is it you want from me?"

Portia chuckles as she steps around the perimeter of the fire. She raises her eyebrows and looks at me knowingly.

"Fine, I can't fool you, daughter of mine. I do need something from you but it is with the purest intentions."

"I don't think you've ever had a pure intention in your life." I hold up her journal. "From what I read in here, everything you've done was for yourself."

Portia purses her lips and crosses her arms over her chest.

She draws breath and says, "I'm afraid there's a storm coming."

I squint my eyes and peer into the clear sky. "A storm?"

"Not an actual storm. A *Warwick* storm. Before, I offered you the chance to be by my side, and now I'm telling you, I need you. I need you to help me prepare for what's coming."

"I'll take my chances," I say sardonically.

"Have I ever lied to you, Camilla? I know I haven't been the greatest mother, but I've never lied to you." Portia kneels next to the fire so she's eye level with me. She moves her thin hand over the fire, letting the warmth tickle her skin. "Didn't I tell you Knox and those other people would let you down? They don't love you. Admittedly I don't think I could say that I love you either, but at least with me, you get the truth."

The betrayal by Knox has been painful in a way that's left me feeling foolish and bruised. It was Knox who warned me never to give in to my mother. *Never, never!* he implored. I put all my trust in Knox and found him to be as deceitful as Portia, maybe more so. My mother has never tried to hide who she was.

In the end, I'm glad I learned the truth about Knox and what he did. Now I can rid my life of him. But I'm left questioning my own judgment. Have I had it wrong all along? Have I joined ranks with the wrong side? Knox is against Quinten Warwick, but so is Portia.

Portia raises her eyebrows expectantly. Her teeth show in a jubilant smile. She's reading my thoughts, I realize in a flurry. The sliver of openness I felt for my mother closes like the slamming of a door. I scoff and give her a scowl.

Her mouth curves downward. "Oh, don't be angry about that!"

"I'm not angry at you. I'm angry at myself for thinking there was anything good in you."

"We don't need to be good people to beat Quinten Warwick."

I look down at the book in my hand, the journal, my mother's journal. I feel its vibrations emanating through my fingers. There's magic within its pages. It holds a power that I don't fully understand, but I know it connects me with my mother. It's allowed her to chisel into my brain and make a home there.

I raise my eyes to look at her squarely. I won't allow it anymore. She won't control me anymore. With the flick of my wrist, I toss the journal into the fire. Portia lunges forward to rescue the book.

"No!" she screeches, reaching into the flames.

I leap from my seat and push her away. To my surprise, my mother falls to the ground like a frail old woman. She's awestruck, and for the first time, I see her face painted with worry. I look down at her with a mixture of confusion and disgust.

Portia takes a shallow breath, then scrambles to her feet. She's barely able to meet my eyes. She flexes her fingers in and out and shakes her arms. Quickly she touches the turquoise stone on her neck, as if to ensure that it's still there.

"What's wrong with you?" I ask, but she doesn't answer.

My mother gives me a look of hurt and betrayal. She then turns and disappears into the woods without another word. I look back into the fire and watch as the flames lap around the edges of the journal. The fire erupts in a sudden burst, as if it were hungry for the book. The floral pattern turns black. The parchment melts as it's devoured. The voice in my head fizzles.

**

I stamp out the fire, kicking up the ashes that were once my mother's journal. I roll my head on my neck. It feels glorious to be loosed from such a vise. Whatever lies ahead of me in Rande, I can deal with. If things have fallen apart, I will find Tuor and we'll finally leave Bear Gap like he's wanted to do.

I pull out my dagger, keeping it at my side. I walk east through the woods. As I approach Rande, raucous shouting drifts through the trees. My body is tense and on guard. Soldiers could be descending on this place in hordes.

Reaper's Way stretches out in front of me. To my left is the gate to the farm. Only a few men mingle there. An odd mood has taken over Rande. The dirt road is filled with people, running, bellowing . . . cheering?

A soldier barrels toward me. A queasy panic overtakes me. I turn to duck back into the trees, but before I find cover, a hand grabs my arm. The soldier spins me around. His face is flushed and exuberant.

"We did it!" he announces.

I hesitate with my dagger. He's one of Ralf's men, a soldier that's no longer loyal to his Supreme Ruler. He laughs at my dumbfounded look.

"We did it," he says again, chuckling. "We're free."

CHAPTER FORTY-SIX

I AWAKE IN a bedroom on the fourth floor of the Harras Manor, except it's no longer called that. No one by the name of Harras lives or rules here any longer. Instead it's been dubbed the Bear Gap House.

Many people live here now, including Ralf, who's assumed the role of governor, although not a soul will call him that. Ralf himself has openly cursed anyone who dares utter that word followed by his name. He won't be associated with such a foul title.

A lot has changed at the national farm in two weeks. First and most importantly, it won't be a national farm for much longer. As per the terms of Quinten's treaty with the people of Bear Gap, any citizen who works on the farm, supplying food to LilyAye and other surrounding territories, will be compensated handsomely until new farms can be built.

None of that would have been possible without the agreement Reed struck with his uncle. I nearly fainted when Reed showed it to me upon my return to the farm. Bear Gap was declared its own territory, separate from Supreme Ruler intervention. The farm will no longer be enforced and the Justice House could be done with as we pleased. Which meant many prisoners were released that same day.

Of course terms of the treaty stated the safe return of Captain Thatius and Karla. It seemed unjust to hand over these people after the harm they'd caused, but they were always a means to an end, simple playing pieces in our big game. The game that we had won.

Ralf, Reed, and I have not relaxed a moment in the weeks since the treaty was made. Quinten still has a large army, even though many other defectors fled to Bear Gap for the simple reason of finding safety in our jurisdiction. No one fully trusts Quinten, especially his own nephew, so preparations have been made to fortify Bear Gap should an attack ever happen.

I dress for the day and stare out my bedroom window, which faces the farm. It's a different place than when I worked here. The stockyard fence remains, but it's for our safety only. No one is beaten or whipped inside its walls.

Although I feel safe here, I still dress as if I'm heading into battle. My boots are tightly secured. My hair is often pulled back, and I still carry my dagger wherever I go. I'm more vigilant than ever. We have something now, something to protect. We have a free territory and it wasn't easy to come by. I'll kill anyone who tries to take it away.

In the hallway I pass Malcolm. He nods to me. He's also been living here since we fought. It's strange being on the same side as him. There's no alcohol at The Bear Gap house which means he's gone two weeks without a drink. I don't think too much about whether Malcolm is really my father or not. I've learned that it doesn't matter whom you share your blood with. It's who chooses to love you day after day.

I enter the office a few doors down from my bedroom. The desk is there, the one that both Thatius and Governor Leo once sat behind. Instead, Reed is there, poring over some documents.

"Any word from our spies?" I ask.

"Everything still seems to be quiet." His head tilts to look me in the face. "Quinten's made no move against us that we can tell."

Reed looks sharp with his clean, pressed shirt and his dark hair slicked back. His image is a far cry from the ragged fighter that he was a few weeks ago. On his face are a few lingering cuts from when we raided this place.

The door to the office opens. It's Penelope, one of the surviving farm workers. She works in the kitchen downstairs.

"I'm sorry to interrupt," Penelope says, her short brown hair falling into her eyes. Penelope looks at me. "She's here again, askin' for you."

Reed looks at me with a piercing gaze, wondering what I'll say.

"Tell her if she's hungry to help herself to our food reserves but I don't care to talk to her."

Penelope hesitates. "Are you sure?"

"Penelope," I say with a stern voice. "I'm sure."

Penelope disappears behind the door. Reed says nothing. He looks back at his papers.

"What do I have to say to her?" I ask, defending myself.

Reed shakes his head. "I agree with you. I think it's wise to distance yourself from Mirabelle. She's not to be trusted."

Even after Mirabelle's betrayal, those words are still hard to hear, *she's not to be trusted*. She lied about something major, something that I asked her and Knox about directly. It still hurts. A week ago she started coming by the farm, looking for me. When she learned that I was living here, she started coming by everyday, asking to speak to me.

I suspect that what prompted her first visit was the death of Knox. Frankly I'm surprised he lived as long as he did.

"What did you want to speak to me about?" I ask, remembering the reason I came to the office in the first place.

Reed sets his papers on the table, drawing his attention to me. "I want to make you an offer. I first came to Bear Gap to discover if I had supporters. Many people here don't know I bear the name Warwick and I don't want them to. There's too much heartache associated with that name." Reed sits back in his chair. "Bear Gap was always a starting point for me. This is a pivotal territory and we've taken control of it. The people control it." Reed corrects himself. "I want the title of Supreme Ruler, not so that I can oppress like my uncle does, but so that I can do to all of Elmyra what we've done here."

"It might take a lifetime to do that."

"It didn't take a lifetime for my uncle to take the throne."

"That's true." I stare into Reed's blue eyes. "But he had help that we don't." My mother. My mother was helping him, but Reed doesn't know that.

"Camilla, do you want to stay in Bear Gap for the rest of your life?"

I'm taken aback by the question.

"Where else would I go?"

"There doesn't seem to be anything left for you here. You've broken ties with Mirabelle and Knox. Although you're on good terms with your father, his presence wouldn't keep you here. Plus there's no romance left between you and Johnny."

I blush at Reed's frankness.

"It's my home."

Reed looks around the newly christened Bear Gap House. "*This* is your home?"

"No, but Tuor's here."

"I want Tuor to come along too," Reed says.

I lean forward. "Come along where?"

"Our spies haven't just been scouting for an attack," Reed says, picking back up his pieces of parchment. "I've been having them spy on Quinten. He's weak, Camilla. Losing Bear Gap was a big blow. We need to move on the opportunity while we have the upper hand."

"What do you need me for?"

"I want you to come to LilyAye with me. I have supporters there that are waiting for my return. They can keep us safe. You've done so well in restoring this territory. I want you to help me do that in LilyAye too."

I hesitate, not sure what to say. "But what about Bear Gap? Don't you think we should stay here and make sure things continue to improve?"

"Ralf is doing a fine job of that. He can handle it." Reed pushes off the desk and comes to his feet. He saunters toward the glass doors that open onto the balcony. "Quinten is not going to hold to this treaty. Do you understand that, Camilla?"

"I—I hadn't thought about it. I'm just trying to get by, one day at a time."

"He *can't* keep the treaty. He's barely a ruler without Bear Gap."

I follow behind Reed as he opens the doors and steps onto the balcony. I eye him intently as he approaches the marble railing and places his hands on the edge. He turns back to make sure I'm there.

"My uncle will eventually attack us. Once he builds up his army, gets some more money, whatever it is he's planning, eventually he will try to take back Bear Gap. If you think we can just have this territory to ourselves, then I'm afraid you're sorely mistaken."

"So . . ." I ease up next to Reed. The farm stretches out before us. It's colored a light green. Weeks of hard work have begun to make the farm plenteous again. "If I came to LilyAye with you, what exactly would I be doing?"

I'm nervous.

"I want you to help me assassinate my uncle." Reed says it matter-of-factly.

I knew Reed wanted to be Supreme Ruler eventually, but I thought that was a plan for down the road, and I didn't know that assassination was part of his plan. We *just* finished our work in Bear Gap, and by Reed's own words, we still have a lot to do here.

"I don't know," I say, slowly shaking my head. A warm breeze floats past Reed and me. Early morning sun lights his fair skin. "I've barely taken a breath. I'm not sure I'm ready for—"

"Camilla, we've started something here. Don't think for one moment that we're done. We've just begun. We can't stop now."

I purse my lips. I look down upon the fields. Workers walk the narrow dirt paths to begin their work. What is keeping me in Bear Gap? Reed's words ring in my ears. What's keeping me here? Nothing. There is nothing here for me.

"I've never left this territory before," I say.

Reed smirks. "Then you're in for a surprise."

I laugh, looking as far as I can across the territory. Miles in this direction sits LilyAye. It's the epicenter of the Warwick family. It's a mystical city to me. What I know of it only comes from stories.

"Are you with me?" he asks, drawing my attention back to the balcony.

I turn and face Reed Warwick. His crystal blue eyes beckon me. I consider what will become of Elmyra in another thirteen years if the rebels just accept this treaty and leave Quinten alone. He has to be dethroned. He has to be cut off. He has to be killed.

I place my hand in Reed's and shake it firmly. "I'm with you."

EPILOGUE

LILYAYE, THE FOLLOWING night.

Quinten Warwick sits poised at his desk, dressed in his nightclothes. The room is dark and hollow. The state of Elmyra has not allowed the Supreme Ruler to sleep well these past few months. If he were to admit the truth to himself, his stress has little to do with the rebellion that's broken out in Bear Gap. It has more to do with Portia, who seems to taunt him day and night.

His plans to capture and kill Portia have done nothing but anger her further. Quinten rubs at the ache in his temples. The tall oak door to his office slowly opens. Although done gently, the noise grates on Quinten's nerves.

"What is it?" he barks.

The intruder closes the door behind him and moves through the shadows of the vast room. Only when he stops directly in front of Quinten's desk does the singular oil lantern in the room illuminate the figure of Captain Ridley Thatius.

"My liege," he says, greeting his Supreme Ruler.

Although Thatius speaks formally, he cannot hide the torment he's recently experienced. One eye is still bruised shut with a deep purple color surrounding it. His right arm hangs in a sling and he walks cautiously due to his bruised ribs.

Quinten raises his head and gives Thatius a disdainful look. The captain is here at his request, but the meeting will not bode well for one of Quinten's most loyal subjects. Quinten tosses his quill pen on the surface of the desk. Ink splotches the document he'd been working on, but he doesn't seem to care. Quinten stands abruptly. He moves around his wide desk and pauses only to glare at Thatius.

"My thanks," Thatius says after many long moments of silence. "You rescued me from a most grave situation."

"You cost me my most profitable territory."

"Yes, my liege."

"Not only did you have no success in quelling that pesky rebellion when it was nothing but a few zealots, but you let them capture you!"

Quinten slams his fist onto his desk. Thatius jolts. A small hourglass shudders from the impact.

"You were once so valuable to me, Ridley, but now you've caused me nothing but trouble. You proved yourself incapable of being a governor. You could not bring order to Bear Gap and now I've lost a quarter of my kingdom."

"Things in Bear Gap did not go the way I had hoped," Thatius admits. "I will do all I can to prove my servitude and win back your adoration."

"I would have to be a fool to put you in charge of anything!" Quinten says. He chuckles as he moves back around the desk.

"My liege, I—"

"Ah, shut up! Just shut up."

Quinten wipes sweat from his forehead. He lets out an aggravated sigh and plops back into his desk chair.

"What will you do with me?" Thatius asks timidly.

"I think a demotion seems in order." Quinten quips. "Perhaps something that involves no thinking at all."

Thatius pauses, his chin held high, then nods curtly.

"Go home, Ridley," Quinten says with the wave of his hand. "Leave my sight."

***

Thatius turns on his heels. His footsteps echo through the large bedroom. Just as he's about to pass through the door, Quinten calls to him. "Be thankful Karla was there too or I'd have let the rebels gut you just for the fun of it."

Thatius says nothing. No glimmer of annoyance flashes across his face. Quietly, he opens the heavy door and slowly closes it behind him, careful not make any excess noise.

The captain moves through the dark hallways of the LilyAye castle. His squire waits for him with his horse at the ready. The moonlight illuminates the quiet streets of the capital city.

The flickering street lamps guide him through a course of cobblestone streets. His horse comes to a stop in front of a tall Catahli-built house. It's magnificent with a smooth, shiny facade. Ridley takes the steps that lead up to his front door as a servant guides his horse to the stables in the back of the house.

Inside the front hall is a clear, blue pond inlaid into the Catahli floor. Silvery fish swirl in and out of the green vegetation that grows there. A female servant dressed in a long white dress stands, waiting to remove Ridley's jacket and belt. He holds up his hand signaling to her that her services aren't needed.

"I won't be staying long," he says.

Ridley's footsteps echo on the hard floor. The only light in the house comes from a few sparsely lit, tall candlesticks. Past the dining room, he pauses at the doorway that leads into the parlor. Two chairs draped in brilliant black bear skin are a stark contrast to the pearly white Catahli floor.

Lawrence looks up from a book in his lap as his father waits for his presence to be noticed. Taking a deep breath, Lawrence gives his father a stiff nod and forces himself to say the words that are required of him.

"Good evening, Father."

The polite exchange gives no hint that father and son were recently engaged in a dangerous hostage situation.

"I'm quite glad to see us home again," Thatius says.

Lawrence looks at his father from under heavy eyelids.

"What a joy." Lawrence's tone drips with sarcasm but that doesn't matter to Ridley. It's the words that he cares about.

Ridley has his son in the position he wants him. Lawrence doesn't have to be happy; Ridley thinks to himself, he just has to obey. Disappearing from the shadowed hallway, Ridley takes the Catahli-formed steps to the second floor.

At the end of the long narrow hallway, Ridley turns a crystal doorknob, opening the door to a sweet-smelling bedroom. In the middle of the room is a grand bed, large enough to sleep ten grown men. A pink silken blanket covers the shiny wood-framed bed. Tucked into the far right side of the bed is Ridley's wife.

Her handmaiden has loosely braided her black hair. Ridley crosses the room in a wide gait. She sleeps peacefully as cool air flows in from the open window. The sound of the city is a comfort to Ridley after months of only hearing crickets at nighttime. He leans down and kisses his wife's cheek before leaving his elegant home.

Ridley rides again into the streets of LilyAye. He leads his horse down the wide main street of the town. To his left and right are Catahli-built homes similar to his, but with their own unique style. One house has a flowing purple cloth draped across its front balcony. Another has flowers growing in pockets that have been carved directly into the walls of the house. These are the homes of the LilyAye elite, the rich, the important.

The beautiful main street of LilyAye quickly transforms into the slums. Ridley stops and tethers his horse before going on foot down a dingy, muddy alley. Stray dogs wander the street in the same way that wary women do. Even at this late hour, children are heard playing in the puddles. A baby's piercing scream leaks from a nearby open window.

Ridley stops in front of a wood hut with a straw roof. A fat lady stands in the doorway. She steps aside at the sight of Ridley and lets him pass without question. A dark-skinned woman sits at a table with a baby in her lap. She blinks at Ridley but says nothing. Ridley steps over a broken clay pot. He moves to the back of the hut, where a wooden ladder leads to an upstairs loft.

At the top of the ladder, the loft is blocked off by a sheet that hangs floor to ceiling to create privacy for its resident on the other side. Ridley pushes the blanket aside.

A candle burns on a short side table. There's a low straw bed in the middle of the room and on top sits a woman, her back turned to Ridley. Long chestnut-colored hair drapes down her narrow back.

Ridley takes a knee to the floor and bows low. She stands, her confident steps landing in front of Ridley. She takes a thin finger and tilts Ridley's chin upward, signaling for him to stand. Portia's sparkling green eyes meet his as Ridley rises.

"So good to see you, Ridley. I'm pleased to see you've been released from the rebels. How frightening."

"It was an ordeal. Not every part of our plan will play out as we hope."

Portia nods solemnly. "That is true. Yet, you don't give up. It's what I love about you." Portia moves her body like a snake, pacing in front of Ridley. "No need to keep me in suspense. What's the news?"

Thatius smiles broadly, something he so rarely does. "This part of our plan goes accordingly. She has agreed to travel to LilyAye."

"Don't tease me," Portia coos.

"She has practically made a vow that she'll come."

The tension dissipates. Ridley can't help but smirk at delivering the news to his master. Portia is pleased. She places a hand on Ridley's shoulder.

"You've played your part well. Relax for a bit. The real work will start again soon."

"I'm ever grateful," Thatius says, once again bowing.

Portia crosses her arms over her chest and brings a hand to her mouth, biting down on her fingernail. She bares her teeth, revealing a maleficent yet satisfied smile.

THE END

Pronunciation Guide

CHARACTERS
Camilla: Kuh-mil-uh
Tuor: Toor (like tour)
Bradac: Bra-dak

PLACES
Elmyra: Ehl-meye-ruh
LilyAye: Lilee-eye
Billage: Bill-ehj (like village)
Rande: Randee (like Randy)
Siourious: Sur-ee-ohs

OTHER
Catahli: Kuh-tah-lee

Want to know what happens next?

Camilla's story does not end here. Her story continues in the thrilling sequel, *The Dark Ruler*. Flip the page to read a preview of book three in the Camilla Crim series.

***

Visit www.emilyfortney.com to explore the entire Camilla Crim series and grab a **FREE** eBook by signing up for Emily's email newsletter.

***

If you enjoyed this book, please leave a 5-star review on Goodreads or the online retailer where you purchased it. Also, pass this book on to a friend. Good books are meant to be shared.

Sneak peak of

The Dark Ruler

CHAPTER ONE

HEAT RISES FROM the sunbaked clay roof tiles and warms the backs of my legs. I sit atop the Bear Gap House, leaning on the palms of my hands, and stare out across the farm. Villagers dot the fields as they crouch to harvest the last of the onions and cabbage. The sun hangs like a great fireball, resting on the treetops. I love these long days, but sadly, the summer is waning fast.

Bear Gap is a different territory than it was three months ago. The villagers are here by choice. Soldiers and whips are nothing more than a part of our history. A wooden stockyard fence still encompasses the property. Its pointed tips are reminiscent of a time when they were meant to keep us corralled inside. Now, that very wall is our main defense against the man who had it built: Quinten Warwick.

Finding order after the Warwick government was disbanded in Bear Gap was difficult. The national farm, which resided in our territory, had to be restructured. No one was forced into slave labor anymore, but we still had to eat. The whole country needed to eat. Part of our agreement with Quinten is that we'd keep the farm running, but the crown would pay us for the fruits and vegetables we produced. Once a month we have a tense meeting with some Warwick soldiers at the territory border where we make the exchange of goods.

Laughter draws my attention to the ground just below me. I lean forward, peeking over the edge of the roof, and catch a glimpse of Tuor's narrow face. He stands in the spot where once he languished in the stocks. The stocks are still there, but they're no longer used to satisfy a Warwick whim.

Tuor leans against the wooden contraption. Another boisterous laugh escapes his lips. He runs a hand nervously through his messy hair. I squint to see who he's talking to. A petite woman walks into my line of view. Eve . . . I sigh audibly and lean back on my hands.

What is she doing with my brother? I've seen her hanging around a lot over the summer. Although she's technically on our side, a rebel, our personalities don't blend well. I endured her company during the Bear Gap occupation but don't care to socialize with her anymore. I shake my head to put Eve out of my mind. I'm happy at the Bear Gap House, and I won't let this slight annoyance get in the way of that.

The murmuring voices of the villagers drifting in from the fields are evidence of a peaceful territory. Sure, The Supreme Ruler could come back here at any time and try to claim what's his, but he hasn't yet. We've spent the last three months building our defenses and putting spies on the road leading in and out of Bear Gap.

It's been quiet, and I like it like that. I run my fingertips along the mutilated Warwick brand on the inside of my arm. It's a relic of my past life when I was just a cog in Quinten's wheel. I look at it often and remind myself that I'll never go back.

Maybe that's why I've been spending so much time on the roof. Something about being at the highest peak puts me at ease. Being able to see the treetops and feel the wind gives me clarity. I lift my face to the darkening sky. Closing my eyes, I breathe in the fresh air. Maybe this is Tuor's and my opportunity to finally be safe and *free*.

My name catches on the light breeze. I open my eyes just slightly, suspicious if what I heard was real. The voice comes again. It's far off and muffled, but there's no doubt someone is calling for me. Hoping to not be found, I stretch out my legs and lay flat with my hands on my stomach. I just want to enjoy one of the last days of summer.

"Camilla." The voice is soft and timid.

I groan, letting my eyelids slowly open. Penelope stands on the ladder at the edge of the roof. Her face twists into a cringe.

"Hey . . . I'm sorry to disturb your . . . alone time, but he really wants to see you," she says.

I prop myself up on my elbows. One of the young farm workers from the Warwick regime, Penelope stuck around the Bear Gap House after the rebels took over, mostly because she didn't have anywhere else to go.

"He says it's important," Penelope adds, gnawing on her lower lip.

I gaze at the reddening skyline. "He always says it's important."

"Sorry . . . I could tell him I couldn't find you."

"No, it's okay. I can't ignore the chief forever," I say with a grin.

Penelope's cheeks blush as she lets out a chuckle.

"I'll be down in a minute," I say.

"Okay. See you at dinner!" Penelope says cheerfully before starting her descent down the ladder.

It's true that I've been avoiding Reed. I know what he's going to say, and I'm not ready to hear it. We were supposed to leave for our mission three months ago. I've continually come up with an excuse to wait just a few more weeks, but I can't ignore him forever. He's a Warwick. It's in their nature to be demanding.

Setting my foot on the first ladder rung, I lower myself down the side of the Bear Gap House. My view of the farm and the fields slowly shrinks as I scale the side of the five-story building. I stop just a few feet down and reach out to grab a nearby window that leads to the fourth-story stairwell.

I stretch my leg across the space from the ladder into the open window, then make a quick jump to pull the rest of my body through. I tumble into the spiral stairwell and brush dirt from my loose cotton shirt. One of Ralf's soldiers walks past me while heading downstairs. He gives me a curious look.

"Good evening," he says with a nod.

I plaster an awkward smile on my face. There's no point in taking the ladder all the way to the ground just to climb these stairs again, I reason with myself. Down the hall, footsteps click across the hard floor.

"There you are." Reed stands at the threshold of his office. "Come," he beckons before disappearing through the door. I reluctantly follow.

When the rebels gained control, Reed took over the governor's old office. Even though Ralf is technically in charge of the territory he had no interest in calling this room his. He muttered something about the ghosts of them who used to occupy it. Reed however, seemed eager to take the best room in the manor.

A thick mahogany desk sits in the center of the room. Reed stands behind it, poring over stacks of parchment. Behind him is a set of glass double doors leading out onto the balcony that overlooks the fields.

"I've been trying to meet with you for days," Reed says, taking a seat in the high-backed leather chair.

"This is a big place. I guess we just didn't cross paths."

I move into the room, resting a hand on the back of one of the chairs facing Reed's desk. He glances at me from under heavy eyelids. His crystal-blue eyes and dark circles still make me uncomfortable, no matter how long I've known him.

"Sit. I received word from one of our spies in LilyAye. Quinten is planning to travel soon. As you know, he hasn't left his castle since the rebels took over Bear Gap. This is a big deal, Camilla. He'll be vulnerable. This is our chance."

My chest tightens. I ease into the chair. *Our chance.*

"We've known since the day we took over this territory that my uncle would be back," Reed says. "Even with the deal we made, the whole country is still suffering with Bear Gap's now limited resources."

"So you think he's planning an attack on Bear Gap?" I ask, a lump forming in my throat.

"I know he is." Reed locks his gaze with mine. "This is our opportunity to not only save Bear Gap, but to secure my position as the new Supreme Ruler."

"Do you think now is the right time?"

"It's the perfect opportunity. He'll be out of the protection of his castle and the walls of LilyAye. We'll get him on the road and stop him before he can make it here. This won't be like the last attempt."

A few weeks after the rebel take over Reed and I and a small company saddled up and headed to LilyAye, thinking we'd be able to cut down Quinten easily. We barely made it to the territory border before we were met with hostility and had to retreat.

Reed continues. "With me being the rightful heir to the Warwick fortune, once he's dead, I'll claim the throne." Reed studies a map on his desk. I nod, unsure of how to respond. "Quinten's planning this attack in a month, maybe six weeks, at least that's what our spy has heard. It will take several days, perhaps weeks for us to get to LilyAye. If we leave tomorrow, that should give us enough time to take the LilyAye Road, barring any incidents. Then we'll connect with the rebels in LilyAye and shore up our plan before Quinten ever mounts a horse. I've already spoken with Ralf and informed him that you and I will be leaving our posts."

"You told him *what?* I haven't agreed to this."

Reed tilts his head, confused.

"What about Ralf? Can he carry on here without us?" I ask.

"It's not going to be easy for him running Bear Gap in our absence, but killing my uncle is more important," Reed says matter-of-factly. "You should be a part of this mission, Camilla."

Turning his attention back to his desk, Reed says, "I'd like you to get your horse readied in the morning. Pack light. Everything you'll need can be provided in LilyAye."

I stare across the desk at Reed, my lips parted in hesitation.

"I don't think I want to come to LilyAye with you." The words tumble from my mouth.

Reed's face contorts into an angry scowl as he clenches his jaw. "You don't wish to see my uncle dead anymore?"

"No, I do. I want him dead more than anything. I just don't want to be the one to do it."

The more I speak, the more confident I feel about my decision. The wrinkles on Reed's forehead deepen.

"Explain yourself," Reed demands.

"I like the way things are right now. The territory is thriving. Things are peaceful, and I get to see my brother every day. I've never lived like this before, without fear or desperation. I don't want it to end."

"The reason you're living such a good life is because of what I—what *we* did to take this territory from Quinten. We have to make sure we don't ever have to deal with him again."

"I know." I look down at my hands. "I know all of that. I think someone should travel to LilyAye and assassinate him. It's just, why does it have to be me?"

Reed's expression softens. "It has to be you."

"Why?"

"You're . . ." Reed searches for words. "You're the passion behind this rebellion. You built it from the ground up, and you and I outwitted the Supreme Ruler together. We must do it again."

I lean back in my chair and slowly shake my head. "I think I'm done with that life. All I wanted was my brother. Now I have him. Why can't you and Ralf finish the job? I'll stay here and run Bear Gap."

Reed leans across his desk and locks eyes with me.

"At the beginning of the summer, after we took over Bear Gap, you agreed to go to LilyAye with me. We made a deal. We shook hands."

I let my gaze wander around the room. The paintings, the furniture, nothing has changed since I sat in this very room with Governor Leo and argued for my brother's life.

"I'm aware," I say.

Reed stares at me intently.

"Just give me a little time to think about it."

"What is there to think about?" Reed lets out a slightly hysterical laugh. "This is the opportunity we've been waiting for!"

I stand abruptly. The chair screeches against the floor. "My life has been dictated for me since the day I was born." I point to my chest. "After everything I've done for this territory, I get to choose my life now."

"Fine," Reed says, his voice back to his normal tone. "Take the evening to think about it, but I need an answer. We leave tomorrow." He points his quill pen at me. "And Camilla, remember that if you don't come with me to take care of Quinten, who knows how much longer you'll be able to live your life here in peace?"

Purchase *The Dark Ruler* to read what happens next.

EMILY FORTNEY is the author of the Camilla Crim series. Currently living in Pennsylvania with her husband, Emily is passionate about dark chocolate, Earl Grey tea, and her cat.

Emily absolutely LOVES hearing from her readers! Connect with her over at www.emilyfortney.com